Before Perys could do anything to prevent it, the motor-cycle fell over. Fortunately, there was a high bank alongside and Annie toppled back on this.

Despite his best efforts to ensure that neither Annie nor the motor-cycle suffered harm, Perys found himself lying on the bank beside her.

'Are you all right, Annie?' he asked anxiously, as he sat up.

Much to his relief, she began giggling.

Looking down at her, Perys had an overwhelming urge to kiss her – and immediately substituted action for thought.

He took her by surprise, but she neither responded, nor resisted.

Nonplussed by her failure to react, Perys pulled back.

Still without moving, Annie looked up at him and she was no longer giggling. 'Why did you do that?'

'I . . . I'm sorry, Annie.'

'Why did you do it? Why did you kiss me?' She repeated her question, ignoring his apology.

'Because I wanted to. I think I've wanted to for a very long time.'

She studied his expression for some moments before saying, 'If you really mean that, then you've no need to be sorry about it. I'm not.'

The Lost Years

E. V. Thompson

A *Time Warner* Paperback

First published in Great Britain in 2002 by Time Warner Books
This edition published by Time Warner Paperbacks in 2003

Copyright © 2002 E. V. Thompson

The moral right of the author has been asserted.

A CIP catalogue record for this book
is available from the British Library.

ISBN 0 7515 3149 9

Typeset by Palimpsest Book Production Limited,
Polmont, Stirlingshire
Printed and bound in Great Britain by
Clays Ltd, St Ives plc

Time Warner Paperbacks
An imprint of
Time Warner Books UK
Brettenham House
Lancaster Place
London WC2E 7EN

www.TimeWarnerBooks.co.uk

Author's Note

The Tremayne family owned Heligan for more than 400 eventful years and it would be impossible to write a credible historical novel around this great Cornish house without making use of their surname.

Nevertheless, although many of the background facts of my story are a matter of history, and the young men of the family served their country with outstanding gallantry in the First World War, all the main characters depicted herein are fictitious and any resemblance to real persons, living or dead, is purely coincidental.

'There are some men to whom things just seem to happen. I believe Tremayne is one of these.'

The Lieutenant Colonel did not add what was in his mind, that such men either became heroes or were soon killed in action.

Prologue

In the study of the great house of Heligan, Perys Sampson Tremayne pushed back his chair and rose to his feet. After clutching the edge of the desk for a moment to steady himself, he limped across the room to the window, his slippered feet silent on a carpet that had been rendered threadbare in places by more than two hundred years of wear.

A number of heavy ledgers lay open on the desk. Among them were smaller notebooks, their cardboard covers bound in red, marbled paper. These were the labour books for the Tremayne estate for the years 1914 to 1918.

Entered in the notebooks were the names of men who had been employed in and around the extensive grounds of the Cornish manor house during the four years of the war. Against each name was listed details of their daily tasks and the money they were paid at the end of a working week. In most cases the sum amounted to little more than a pound.

On the first page of the book for 1914 were the names of almost two dozen men. By the last day of war the number had dwindled to eight.

The names had changed, too. Of the remaining eight, only three had been employed at Heligan at the commencement of 'the war to end all wars'.

The reason for the disappearance of those whose surnames had been familiar around the great house for generations was summed up initially in three words written against their names on various dates.

The words said, simply, '*Left to enlist*'. Their stark finality hid more sorrow than Perys cared to think about.

Although not an immediate member of the family who had occupied Heligan for centuries, Perys *was* a Tremayne. He had stayed at the house before and during the war. Many of the named men were known to him.

This, and curiosity, was why he had been looking through the labour books, seeking names of those it was hoped might soon return to work at Heligan; to resume a way of life far removed from the horrors experienced on the bloody battlefields.

There were so pitifully few left alive that Perys had suddenly felt the need to put aside the books. Yet now the view from the window served only to remind him of the world that so many of the Heligan men would never see again. Many who had helped shape the gardens, woods and fields now lay mouldering far from this small corner of Cornwall.

'*Killed in action, May, 1915*'; '*Lost at sea, July, 1917*'; '*Died of wounds, November, 1918*'. A few strokes of a pen were all that had been needed to write off the lives and achievements of men who had known the view he was seeing now – and who had loved it, as he did.

Some of the deaths he took more personally than others. Those of men, mostly older than he, who had shown kindness to him when he first came to Heligan in the year the war began. There were others with whom he had served, and a few who had offered him comfort and solace when it was believed he might never walk again as a result of his wounded leg.

Such thoughts were running through Perys's mind as he looked out of the window, his gaze travelling over gardens that struggled to maintain the glory they had known in those pre-war days.

In the near distance was the busy little fishing village of Mevagissey. It nestled within a comforting cradle of steep cliffs, at the far end of the valley that sloped down from the house. Here, enterprising fishermen had built houses as closely knit as the fisher-families themselves.

Perys wondered what deep sorrows were hidden within the walls of those houses – and in so many others scattered about the rolling countryside on either side of the village. Even the genuine sympathy of a caring community would not have been able to assuage the anguish of families tragically bereaved by war.

His glance shifted beyond the village, to where the sea sparkled with a silver sheen in the early winter sunshine. It was a gentle sea today, dotted with the boats of working fishermen. No longer was there a need to keep a look-out for the sleek, grey menace of a surfacing submarine, intent upon adding a defence-less fishing boat to the list of its 'kills'.

Perys tried to shake free of such thoughts, reminding himself that they should now be consigned to history. Europe was once more at peace. It was time to forget the past and go in search of the future.

It would not be easy.

Turning away from the window, he glanced at the open labour books and limped to the desk to close them.

His glance fell upon one of the names, and he paused as it provoked other memories. Memories of someone whose name would not be found in this book – or in any of the others.

Although inextricably woven into the pattern of the great house and its lands, the incidents he recalled were so far removed from the Heligan of 1918 that they might have taken place a million miles away . . .

1

The train which brought Perys Tremayne from London to the Cornish town of St Austell in the summer of 1914 was painted in the gleaming chocolate and cream livery of the Great Western Railway. A brass plate curving around a wheel arch of the polished green locomotive proudly proclaimed that this was the *City of Truro*.

Almost nineteen years of age, Perys stepped down from the carriage dragging a large leather suitcase after him. He glanced uncertainly along the long platform. The Tremayne family had large landholdings in Cornwall, but it was his first visit to the area.

'Can I take your suitcase, sir?' A uniformed porter put the question to him.

'Yes . . . no!' Perys contradicted himself and hurriedly explained, 'I'm expecting to be met by someone from Heligan.'

'Ah! You'll be the young Master Tremayne. Martin

Bray, the Heligan coachman, is waiting for you farther along the platform. He and I were talking before the train came in. He said I was to look out for you.'

As he was talking, the porter relieved Perys of the heavy suitcase. Picking it up with difficulty, he began walking in a lop-sided fashion along the platform towards a liveried coachman who was hurrying to meet them.

When porter and coachman met, the suitcase changed hands once again. As the porter pocketed the coin Perys handed him and touched his cap, the coachman said, 'I'm Martin, one of Mister Tremayne's coachmen. I trust you've had a pleasant journey, Master Perys?'

'It was quite enjoyable,' Perys replied, 'but I didn't expect to have a *carriage* here to meet me!'

'Ah well, you chose a good day to arrive. As you might know, you have an aunt and her two daughters staying at Heligan at the moment. They've had dresses altered for a ball and I was told to pick them up while I was in Saint Austell. They're in the luggage box of the carriage. I'd have collected them in the pony cart – and you with 'em – but it's looking as though it's going to rain. Your aunt didn't want to risk getting the dresses spoiled, so I was told to bring the light carriage.'

Perys had been unaware that other members of the Tremayne family were staying at Heligan House, and might have been offended by the presumption that dresses were more important than he, but the thought never occurred to him.

In the eyes of the Tremaynes they *would* have assumed more importance. Perys belonged to a branch

6

of the family only just close enough to the squires of Heligan to be acknowledged as possessing a right to the ancient family name. What was even worse, his mother had committed the unforgivable sin of loving another cousin rather too much.

The family had frowned upon their increasing affection for each other, and they planned an elopement. Unfortunately, fate was to play a decisive role on behalf of the family. The cousin Perys's mother intended marrying died in a tragic shooting accident. Eight months later, Perys was born into a life that would always be coloured by the disgrace his mother had brought upon the family.

When Perys was eight years of age his mother died of lung fever, but the shame did not die with her. It was transferred to her son.

His grandparents became his guardians, but they were in the habit of spending a great deal of the year travelling in Europe. They had no wish to assume responsibility for their illegitimate grandson. He was sent away to boarding school, first to a small establishment in Sussex, run by a clergyman, then to a minor public school in Oxfordshire.

Perys quite enjoyed the clergyman's school. He was quick to learn and the cleric's wife was kind-hearted and motherly. The public school was far less pleasant. Somehow, details of his birth were discovered and the other boys referred to him as 'the bastard'.

As a result of the bullying he received, Perys learned to fight – and fight well. He became a skilful and determined boxer and, in due course, the bullying and name-calling ceased. Unfortunately, by this time he had earned a reputation as 'unruly' and was classified as 'unable to relate to his fellow pupils'. It meant he was punished far more often than any other boy in the school.

Only in his final year, when there was no one remaining who would dare take him on, did things improve and he was left to enjoy his studies.

It was then Perys showed that, despite all the problems he had suffered, his schooling had not been wasted. Albeit grudgingly, the headmaster conceded that Perys had finally 'settled down and showed considerable promise as a scholar'. He recommended to Perys's grandparents that he should be allowed to go on to university in order to develop the promise he was belatedly exhibiting.

Perys's grandfather had other ideas. He and his ailing wife intended to take up permanent residence in Italy. Perys had become almost a stranger to them. They had no wish for his company between university terms. Furthermore, they were determined to waste no more money on his education. It was time for him to make his own way in the world.

It was decided he should join the army.

Because Hugh Tremayne of Heligan, a distant relative of Perys, had close associations with the Duke of Cornwall Light Infantry, Cornwall seemed a good place from which Perys should embark upon a military career. They acted upon their decision right away.

'You've come to Cornwall to join the army, I believe, Master Perys?'

The coachman put the question as Perys helped him to lift the heavy suitcase onto a rack above the luggage box at the rear of the coach. There was room for it inside the compartment, but the coachman would not risk crushing the carefully boxed ball-gowns.

'I think that's what's been planned for me,' Perys agreed.

'You should do well, Master Perys. You belong to a family with a proud military tradition. My grand-father was very fond of telling how he watched the brave charge of the Light Brigade at Balaklava in the Crimean War. Arthur Tremayne, uncle of the present squire, was leading his men in the charge that day. Grandpa always thought it the most wonderful thing he'd ever seen. Said it made him proud to be British. He was even more proud to be able to say he was a near neighbour of Captain Arthur.'

Perys had studied details of the battle and was aware of the Tremayne involvement. A misunderstood order had been responsible for an ill-conceived charge in which more than six hundred cavalrymen rode to almost certain death for no good reason. Almost three hundred of the men became casualties, together with as many good horses. The charge had been an act of crass stupidity.

He said nothing of his thoughts to the coachman.

'. . . I had an uncle who fought in the Boer War with the Cornwall regiment too, sir.' Suddenly less enthu-siastic, Martin added, 'He was killed at Paardeberg. My aunt never got over losing him.'

Perys murmured a few suitably sympathetic words and Martin returned his thoughts to the present. 'We'd best be on our way, sir. There's a nasty storm in the offing.'

Checking the luggage was secured, the coachman

saw Perys safely seated inside the carriage. A few moments later the two-horse vehicle trundled up the steep slope from the station yard, heading for Heligan House, some six miles distant.

2

Rain was already falling by the time the carriage reached the outskirts of the town of St Austell. Suddenly, the coachman brought the vehicle to an abrupt halt.

Climbing to the ground, he opened the carriage door and said, 'We've just passed my sister Annie, Master Perys. She's on her way back from market to my father's farm. It's at Tregassick, just up beside Heligan. I think this rain will become very heavy before long. Would you mind if I allowed her to ride with me on the outside of the carriage? It would get her home a lot quicker than if she walked.'

'By all means let her ride with us,' Perys said, 'but not on the outside of the carriage. She'd be soaked by the time she arrived. She can come in here with me.'

For a moment it seemed Martin might put up an argument against Perys's suggestion, but it was raining harder now and he wanted to don the waterproof coat kept in the box beneath the coachman's seat. Besides, as Annie would be dropped off before they reached Heligan, he was unlikely to be in trouble from those at the great house.

'Annie, young Master Tremayne says you can ride in the coach with him. Quickly now, get in before the inside gets wet. It's tipping with rain already . . . No, not with the basket. I'll tie that on the back.'

Moments later, a young woman scrambled inside the carriage. She had been sheltering beneath a tree so was not too wet, but the carriage had come along just in time. As the door closed behind her, rain began beating a noisy tattoo on the roof of the vehicle.

The girl was hatless, but a shake of her head was sufficient to bring a semblance of order to her windswept hair.

Looking at Perys with a directness that belied the servility of her words, she said, 'It's very kind of you to allow me to ride in your carriage. Thank you, sir.'

At that moment Martin whipped the horses into motion and Perys moved quickly to catch Annie as she was flung from her seat by the sudden and violent movement.

He caught her in a full embrace and when she recovered and sat back in her seat she was decidedly flustered. 'I'm sorry . . . that took me by surprise.'

'I'm not complaining,' Perys said, astonishing himself with his boldness. 'It's a good job I was here to catch you.'

'Yes . . . thank you.' Reaching inside a patch pocket sewn on the front of her dress, she pulled out a small bag. 'I bought some sweets in town. Would you like one?'

He took a boiled sweet from her and for a while

12

they sat facing each other, enjoying the sharp taste and saying nothing.

It was Annie who broke the silence. 'Martin called you Master Tremayne, but I don't think I've seen you before. I thought I'd met everyone from the big house, our farm being so close.'

'Then you'll know more about the Tremaynes than I do. I'm a distant relative. So distant I've never before been to Heligan and have met none of the family who live there. To tell you the truth, I'm more than a little nervous about the whole business.'

'Then why are you going there now . . . sir?'

It was an impertinent question and for a few moments Annie held her breath, in anticipation of a sharp response, but Perys did not seem to have taken offence.

'I suppose it's because I don't have anywhere else to go . . .'

She thought he sounded almost apologetic, but he had not finished talking.

'. . . Both my parents died many years ago. My grandparents became my guardians, but they've spent much of their lives abroad. Now my grandmother isn't too well and they are going to live abroad permanently. My grandfather has decided I should join the army. Hugh Tremayne is my great-uncle, albeit twice removed – or something similar – and it seems he has some influence with the regiment base here in Cornwall. He has agreed to arrange an interview for me. If I am accepted I will become an officer in the Duke of Cornwall's Light Infantry.'

Perys stated the facts without any display of enthusiasm and Annie felt a moment's sympathy for her

13

travelling companion. At the same time she wondered why his grandparents had apparently not wanted him to spend at least *some* time abroad with them.

She did not voice the question, but was aware there must be a great deal this young man had not told her. On the other hand, there was no reason why he should have told her anything . . . but he was speaking again.

'Do you mind not calling me "sir", Annie? My name is Perys.'

She was uncertain how to reply to this request, so she said, 'It's a very unusual name.'

'It's an old Tremayne name,' Perys explained. 'I believe the first recorded member of the family, some hundreds of years ago, was named Perys.'

The carriage had reached an exposed expanse of road now, and rain, driven by a strong wind, rattled the glass in the doors.

'Your brother will be getting very wet,' commented Perys, sympathetically.

'He's wearing a stout waterproof coat,' declared Annie. 'He's better off than he'd be if he was at work on the farm.'

'Is your father the owner of the farm?' Perys queried.

'No, he's a tenant farmer. The farm belongs to one of the Tremaynes, although it's administered by the Heligan Estate. Almost all the land around Heligan belongs to one or other of the Tremaynes. They sometimes think they own the people, too.'

It was an unguarded remark; Annie had momentarily forgotten to whom she was talking. With some dismay, she attempted to make amends.

'Mind you, Squire Tremayne never bothers us,

although he takes an interest in whatever Pa is doing on the farm.'

Her initial comment had not passed unnoticed. To her embarrassment, Perys pursued the matter. 'Then who in the family *does* bother you?'

'No one. I'm sorry, I spoke out of turn.'

'Look, Annie, I know no one in the family here in Cornwall. To be perfectly honest with you, I would be grateful for anything you are able to tell me about Heligan and the people who live there. I don't even know how many Tremaynes are there at the moment – but I am sure you do.'

Once again Annie's sympathy went out to Perys. If all he said was true, then, despite his family connections, he was virtually alone in the world. Yet she decided to be cautious in what she said to him.

'Well, although the house is owned by the squire, Hugh Tremayne, he spends a lot of time abroad and he's not at the house right now . . .'

She went on to describe those members of the family who were currently staying at the house. It seemed there was one of Hugh Tremayne's nephews, a couple of years older than Perys, and another relative with her two daughters, for whom Martin had collected the dresses.

Perys formed the opinion that Annie did not particularly like the nephew. He tried to question her about him in more detail, but apart from saying his name was Edward she would not be drawn further.

He would have pressed the matter, but there was a sudden shout from Martin. Heaving on the reins, he applied the brakes of the carriage at the same time, with such force that the coach slewed across the

15

narrow country road. This time it was Perys's turn to be thrown from his seat, to Annie's side of the vehicle.

'What the . . . ?' As the carriage came to a standstill, Perys regained his balance and looked out of one of the windows.

He was startled to see a thoroughly soaked and bedraggled young boy standing in the roadway, his clothes plastered with mud. He was gesticulating wildly to Martin and shouting, the words lost amidst the din of wind and rain.

Beyond him, on the far side of a very sharp bend, the road appeared to be blocked by a landslide that had undoubtedly been caused by the exceptionally heavy rain.

'What is it?' Annie asked Perys. 'What's the matter?'

'The road's blocked. There's a boy out there. He seems very excited about something. Stay where you are, I'll try to find out what's happening.'

The door opened suddenly and a very wet Martin leaned inside the carriage. 'There's been a landslip, Master Perys. Young Wesley Dunn and his father, Henry, were on their way from Mevagissey to Saint Austell with a handcart loaded with fish to put on the London train. The landslip caught them and it's carried the cart and Henry off the road and down the slope towards the river. He's down there somewhere, buried with cart and fish beneath tons of earth.'

Behind him, the tearful boy called, 'Please! Do something. Pa's down there . . .'

When Perys jumped to the ground from the carriage he was able to see more clearly the trail of devastation left by the landslide. It had swept from the wooded ground rising high above one side of the

16

road, and down a steep incline on the other, carrying trees, rocks and earth with it. Dangerously close to the river at the bottom of the slope the wheel of a cart protruded at an angle from a great heap of mud and debris.

'Let's get down there,' Perys said to Martin. Without waiting for a reply he began scrambling and sliding down the landslide into the field.

It was impossible to maintain a footing on the rain-sodden earth, and Perys came dangerously close to careering on, into the river. He stopped himself only by grabbing at the exposed portion of the wheel. Of Henry Dunn there was no sign.

'Help me dig away the earth around the cart,' Perys said, when Martin joined him, somewhat more cautiously, 'but be careful, there are some large boulders here and the whole lot seems very unstable.'

He and Martin began digging away with their bare hands, joined a few moments later by Annie and the boy.

Perys suggested Annie should return to the carriage, but she declared she had no intention of sitting doing nothing while they dug for the missing fisherman. He did not argue with her.

Soon the rescue party was joined by a couple of men who had been walking on the road. The rain had eased considerably now, but everyone involved was soaked through and plastered in sticky, cloying earth.

Suddenly, Annie shouted to the others. Digging at the front of the cart she had uncovered an arm – and it moved!

The handcart had landed on one of the large rocks when it came to rest, trapping the upper part of the man's body in the space between cart and ground, his legs pinned down by earth and smaller rocks.

Within fifteen minutes of her discovery they were pulling the fisherman clear. He appeared to have a badly broken leg and was in great pain – but he was alive. His young son, Wesley, was weeping, relief mixed with anguish. He had been convinced his father must have died in the landslide.

'What do we do with him now?'

The question was put by Martin when the rescue party reached the carriage with their burden.

'We take him to the nearest hospital,' Perys said. 'Is there one in Saint Austell?'

The coachman nodded.

'Then what are we waiting for? Turn the carriage around and we'll be on our way.'

3

The carriage carrying Perys Tremayne to Heligan arrived at the great house more than three hours later than expected – and Edward Tremayne was furious!

A petulant young man of perhaps twenty-three years of age, he made no attempt to welcome Perys. Instead, he directed a tirade of near-hysterical invective at the unfortunate coachman.

'Where the devil have you been? I was due at Caerhays more than two hours ago to partner Sir Philip Carminow at bridge. They'll not be able to play without me. You'll have ruined the whole evening for everyone. I've a damned good mind to dismiss you on the spot.'

'That's hardly fair!' Perys stepped down from the carriage and confronted the second cousin he had never met before today. 'It's not Martin's fault we are so late, there was an emergency . . .'

He did not feel it necessary to add that the carriage

had taken Annie as far as the lane leading to her farm en route to Heligan. On the way she had tried to remove some of the mud from Perys's coat, but without any discernible success.

'No one is asking *you* for an explanation,' Edward retorted angrily. Looking Perys up and down with increasing distaste, he added, 'Good God, man, look at you! Has Martin allowed you inside the carriage in that state? It will need to be thoroughly cleaned before anyone can ride in it. Dammit! That's the final straw! Martin . . . you *are* dismissed. Don't dare to show your face at Heligan again.'

'Now just a minute!' Perys stepped forward and again spoke heatedly in defence of the unfortunate coachman. 'You can't dismiss him out of hand like that. You haven't even asked him to explain *why* he's late.'

Edward seemed to swell with indignant anger. 'Don't you tell me what I can or cannot do. I'll not take orders from a bastard.'

Perys paled. It was a term that had not been applied to him for so long he had forgotten how much it hurt. Recovering quickly, he said, 'I'll not stand by and see a man dismissed for stopping to save another man's life – especially by someone throwing a tantrum simply because he's late for a card game.'

'How *dare* you speak to me in such a way!' Edward's face was contorted with rage now. 'Great-Uncle Hugh will hear of this – not that he'll be surprised to learn you've taken the part of a servant. It's in the breeding. The family has always wondered whether your father was one of the servants rather than your mother's cousin . . .'

20

Perys had heard enough. Taking a couple of rapid paces forward he swung a punch that connected with Edward's nose and sent him staggering backwards until he tripped and fell to the ground among some shrubbery, demolishing a fuchsia bush in the process.

'What on earth is going on here?'

The shocked question came from a tall, distinguished woman. She had emerged from the house too late to see Perys strike his cousin, but had witnessed Edward's disappearance into the shrubbery.

Clawing his way out of the bushes, Edward cried out plaintively, 'He hit me. The b— Cousin Perys struck me.' Dabbing at his nose, his hand came away bloody. 'I'm bleeding, Aunt Maude. I think my nose is broken.'

Turning to Perys, Maude Tremayne looked sternly at him, taking in his wet and muddy state. 'If you are Perys, it would seem you are already living up to your reputation, young man. I think you have some explaining to do.'

'I can tell you *exactly* what happened, Mother.'

A younger and much prettier version of the older woman appeared in the doorway of the house, glaring at the bleeding Edward.

'What do you know of this, Morwenna?' her mother demanded.

'I had my bedroom window open and heard everything. Edward was furious because Martin was late bringing the carriage back from Saint Austell. When Cousin Perys tried to explain that they were late because Martin had helped to save someone's life, Edward called him a horrible name then told Martin he was dismissed. When Cousin Perys protested,

21

Edward said some awful things about Perys's mother. Things no gentleman could possibly accept – and no lady should overhear. Cousin Perys hit Edward, and if he has a broken nose as a result, it is no more than he deserves. Had he said such things about you I would have had no hesitation in taking a riding crop to him.'

Edward had been taken aback by the unexpected intervention of Morwenna and he now stood his ground uncertainly.

'I think you had better go inside and have someone staunch that bleeding, Edward.' Maude Tremayne made it sound like a suggestion, but the look accompanying her words left him in no doubt it was a command.

He obeyed without question.

Ignoring Perys for the moment, Maude said to the coachman, 'Were you able to collect our dresses, Martin?'

'Yes, ma'am, they are safe in the luggage box of the carriage. Shall I fetch them for you?'

'Not in the state you are in! We will not risk them becoming soiled. I will have one of the house servants bring them inside. In the meantime I suggest you go off and get yourself cleaned up.'

Instead of hurrying away, Martin remained, looking at her uncertainly. Maude asked, sharply, 'Is there something else?'

'Yes, ma'am, Master Edward said I was dismissed.'

'Master Edward has no authority over Heligan servants. I shall ask Master Perys to tell me what occurred to make you late returning with the carriage. If you were indeed delayed because you helped to save a

22

life there will be no question of dismissal. However, you will say nothing to the other servants about what has just happened, do you understand?'

'Yes, ma'am, and thank you. Thank you too, Master Perys.'

As Martin hurried away, Maude looked critically at Perys. 'You need to clean up too, but first I would like you to tell me all that happened on your journey from Saint Austell. It would appear you have had a most unfortunate introduction to Heligan.'

4

Later that evening Perys came downstairs to dinner. He had bathed and was wearing clothes from his suit-case, hurriedly ironed for him by a young housemaid.

When the maid had returned the clothes to him it was made clear that despite Maude Tremayne's warning to Martin, the house servants were well aware of what had occurred outside the house. It was a lesson to him in the close relationships that existed among the servants.

After hanging up his clothes, the maid, who had told Perys her name was Polly, looked at him rather shyly before saying, 'It was very kind of you to take Martin's part when Master Edward wanted to dismiss him, sir.'

Surprised and a little concerned that she should know about the incident, it was a moment before he recovered sufficiently to say, 'I could hardly allow him to be dismissed when much of what he did was on my instructions, Polly. Besides, I consider his conduct warrants a reward, not punishment.'

'He *has* been rewarded, sir. Mistress Maude sent for him and told him that the master would be proud of the way he had behaved, then gave him five guineas.'

Maude Tremayne rose in Perys's estimation. 'Good! He thoroughly deserved it.' Looking at the girl who was a pretty young thing, he asked, 'Is Martin a special friend of yours?'

The girl blushed. 'We've known each other since we were small, sir. When I lost my parents it was Martin who got me a live-in post at Heligan. We're going to marry as soon as we've saved enough money.'

'I'm happy for both of you, Polly,' Perys said. 'I've no doubt Martin will make you a very good husband.'

'I think so too, sir . . . and thank you again.'

Perys was left with the thought that if he had made an enemy of Edward Tremayne, he had gained friends among the servants.

Passing the open door of the lounge as he sought the dining-room, he discovered that not all the Tremayne family were as ill-disposed towards him as Edward.

'Perys! Come in here and join us.'

Morwenna called to him from the lounge. In response, Perys entered the room cautiously. Morwenna had said, 'Join *us*.' It was possible Edward was in the room with her.

He need not have been concerned. The only other person in the room was a girl of about sixteen who so resembled Morwenna and her mother that it came as no surprise when she was introduced to him as Arabella, Morwenna's younger sister.

The young girl greeted Perys warmly, saying

25

forthrightly, 'So *you* are second cousin Perys! I expected the person who gave Edward a bloody nose to be much bigger.'

'Arabella! We will not talk about that,' warned Morwenna.

'Why not? It was you who said somebody should have done it years ago. Edward is thoroughly obnoxious, as we all know.'

'It might be as well if we make talk of Edward taboo during dinner. I am quite certain we can find many far more pleasant subjects to discuss.' Maude had quietly entered the room through the door behind Perys. She was in time to hear Arabella's assessment of her absent cousin.

Standing to one side in order that Maude might pass into the room, Perys asked hesitantly, 'Will Edward be dining with us?'

'No.' Giving him an enigmatic look, Maude added, 'He feels he needs to rest. He insisted that we call a doctor from Mevagissey. You will no doubt be relieved to know that, although he has bled profusely, nothing is broken. What is more, Edward has decided to return to his family home in Devon first thing tomorrow morning. He will remain there until it is time for him to return to his studies at Cambridge.'

Arabella clapped her hands in delight and Maude gave her a look of mock disapproval. It was evident to Perys that Edward was not the most popular member of the Tremayne family.

'Shall we make our way to the dining-room?' Maude suggested. 'Perys must be absolutely famished after such an eventful day . . .'

* * *

26

Perys had very little to say during dinner. In truth, he had spent little time in the company of women and felt particularly shy in the presence of these unfamiliar relatives. Nevertheless, he answered all the questions that were put to him, and from the chatter of Maude and her two daughters was able to piece together something of their lives.

Maude was a widow, her husband having been killed in the Boer War, fourteen years before, when Morwenna was six and Arabella two. She had brought up her daughters at their family home in London, helped by other members of the large and wealthy Tremayne family.

The subject of Perys's own mother and grandparents was studiously avoided. However, he was questioned about his schooling and the career he proposed following in the army.

Unused to confiding in others, Perys replied hesitantly, 'I haven't discussed it with anyone yet and I first have to be accepted in the Duke of Cornwall Light Infantry. But what I would really like to do, eventually, is join the Royal Flying Corps as a pilot.'

There was a squeak of excitement from Arabella, while the others looked more doubtful.

'Is that not rather dangerous?' asked Maude.

'They do seem to have a great many flying accidents,' admitted Perys. 'It's a very new skill, but it must be exciting to be able to fly. What's more, I believe it will one day prove its worth to the army – and to the navy. We had a French boy at school whose brother was a pilot. I think the French army takes flying far more seriously than we do.'

'You know, of course, that two of your distant

cousins are flyers? John, and Rupert, whose mother married a Pilkington.'

'Yes, I was hoping I might meet one of them while I am in Cornwall.'

'I am sure it would have proved extremely useful to you. John is a naval flyer and rather reticent about what he does, but Rupert is always ready to talk about aeroplanes and such things to anyone with even the remotest interest in flying. Unfortunately, John is in France at the moment and not expected back for a month or two. I have no idea where Rupert might be.'

Perys was disappointed. Far keener to become a flyer than to pursue a career in the regular army, he had been hoping one of the two cousins might be able to help him.

'When are you attending your interview for the infantry?' Morwenna asked.

'It's not certain,' Perys replied. 'Great-Uncle Hugh was going to leave a letter for me, telling me what I should do, together with an introduction to the recruiting officer of the regiment at Bodmin. I was hoping to find it in my room . . .'

'Ah! That will be the rather bulky envelope that was left for me, with instructions that I should hand it to you on your arrival at Heligan,' said Maude. 'I had quite forgotten it until now. What a good thing you reminded me. You shall have it after dinner.'

'I hope Perys doesn't have to go right away,' Arabella said. 'I wanted him to escort Morwenna and I to some of the places of interest around here. Edward never would.'

'I am quite sure Perys has many of his own things to do,' said Maude.

'I doubt whether an interview can be arranged very quickly,' Perys said. 'And as I have never before been to Cornwall I would welcome an opportunity to see something of the area. I'd be delighted if Arabella and Morwenna might be allowed to accompany me.'

Arabella clapped her hands in delight, then looked at her mother uncertainly as she remembered Perys's unfortunate background.

'That is a very kind offer, Perys,' said Maude. 'It *would* be nice if the girls were able to see something of the countryside while we are in Cornwall. I will probably come too on occasions, if I may. That is, of course, if the rumours of an impending war prove unfounded.'

5

Perys spent the day after his arrival exploring the extensive gardens of Heligan House and generally familiarising himself with his surroundings. He did not have company because Maude and her two daughters were spending the day some eighteen miles away at Lanhydrock House, home of Lord Clifden and his family, prior to attending a ball at the house that evening.

Their absence suited Perys. The girls and their mother had been kind to him, but he was not yet a fully accepted member of the family. Both they and he needed to adjust to his presence in the household.

However, Maude was not spurning him. She had taken the family off half-an-hour earlier than planned in order to personally deliver a letter written by Hugh Tremayne. Addressed to the recruiting officer at the Duke of Cornwall Light Infantry barracks, it recommended Perys for a commission in the county regiment.

She was doing this as a special favour to Perys as she was acquainted with the officer in question. Major Peter Stokes had served in the Boer War with her late husband, and she believed her interest might further the cause of her young relative. She was aware that he would need all the help he could get because the officer was also a close friend of Edward's father.

Arabella had wanted her new-found cousin to accompany them to Lanhydrock, but he had saved Maude any possible embarrassment by pleading tiredness after his journey to Cornwall and the events of the previous day. Besides, as he pointed out to the disappointed young girl, he had not been invited. The unexpected arrival of an additional male guest, when they were expecting only a mother and two daughters, might prove inconvenient to their hosts.

In truth, he was happy to spend the day in his own way, free of all pressures, although he was to learn little about the workings of the estate. The talk of everyone he met – servants, gardeners, labourers and stable hands – was of war.

The previous day, the newspaper Perys had purchased on the railway station in London had been full of similar dire predictions of an imminent war in Europe.

Austria-Hungary had already declared war on Serbia, as a direct consequence of the assassination of Archduke Franz Ferdinand, heir to the Austro-Hungarian throne. The Archduke had been killed by a Balkan student while on an official visit to Sarajevo, capital of Bosnia. The student was believed to be a member of a secret society which enjoyed support from Serbia.

There were few people in Great Britain who understood the confused politics of the Balkans. Yet because of a whole series of pacts which existed between the various European countries, it was feared many other nations would be drawn into the conflict, however remote they might be from the turbulence which had long been a feature of Balkan countries.

But war seemed far off to Perys as he strolled around the grounds of Heligan House, enjoying the warmth of a beautiful English summer day.

Particularly impressed with the horses in the Heligan stables, he picked out a pretty dappled mare that the groom promised would be ready for him to ride the following morning.

Perys had breakfast alone before taking his ride. The two Tremayne girls and their mother were not expected home from Lanhydrock until that evening. Although there was a thick bank of cloud far out over the sea, it was a warm morning and Perys was looking forward to seeing the countryside from the back of a horse.

The mare was an easy ride and Perys chose a route that took him along the cliffs, where he enjoyed the breeze coming off the sea.

He had not been riding for long, however, when the breeze began to strengthen alarmingly. The clouds he had seen gathering in a dense, dark mass on the horizon now began rushing in towards the land.

Turning his horse, Perys rode back the way he had come. Skirting Mevagissey, he headed in a direction that he hoped would return him to Heligan House. He had just turned in to a lonely valley that followed the course of a small, fast-running stream when, suddenly, the mare went lame in one of its front legs.

Dismounting immediately, Perys checked the hoof in case a stone was lodged there. He found nothing. The mishap put him in a quandary. Not certain of his exact location in relation to Heligan, he did not want to lead the lame animal any farther than was absolutely necessary.

Higher up the valley, not too far away, he spotted the thatched roof of a farmhouse. He decided to make for it and ask directions from the farmer.

His arrival in the farmyard caused alarm to a number of geese who noisily announced his presence as they fled in ungainly alarm. The sound brought a pleasant, dark-haired woman to the door of the house. Wearing a floral apron, she was wiping flour-powdered hands on a clean, white cloth.

The appearance of a stranger with a horse was an unusual occurrence in this small farmstead, hidden as it was from the view of those passing along the nearest road. Harriet Bray's expression revealed her surprise, but she greeted him civilly enough.

'Good morning, sir. Is there something I can do for you?'

'I wonder whether your husband is around the farm?' Perys replied. 'My horse has gone lame and I am a stranger here. Perhaps I might leave the horse with you and get directions to take me back to Heligan. Once there I'm quite sure one of the grooms will come out to take a look.' Belatedly, he added, 'I am Perys Tremayne.'

Harriet's expression changed to one of pleasure. 'I'm delighted to meet you, sir! Our Martin told us how you spoke up for him and wouldn't let Master Edward dismiss him.'

Perys realised he had stumbled upon the farm of the parents of Martin and Annie. Uncomfortably, he wondered what else Martin might have told his mother, but she was talking once more.

'Of course you can leave the horse here, Master Perys. My husband will be very sorry to have missed you, but it's market day in Saint Austell. He's taken our latest litter of pigs to sell there. Thirteen, and not a runt among 'em. But where are my manners? There's a heavy shower on its way, won't you come inside the house for a drink until it passes over? Annie will settle the horse in one of the stalls before the rain reaches us.' Raising her voice, Harriet called, 'Annie! Annie! We have a visitor. Show yourself, girl.'

Annie had been milking one of the farm's four cows when the geese gave warning of the arrival of Perys and his lame horse. A quick glance from the milking parlour was sufficient to discover the identity of the visitor. Annie had spent the few minutes since then trying to tidy her dress and her hair.

The latter had been hanging loose, but after frantically using her fingers as a makeshift comb, she drew it back and tied it with a length of tape, hastily cut from her apron ties. The apron itself was then discarded and left hanging from a nail in the milking parlour. Emerging from the building, Annie acted out her surprise at seeing Perys.

She might have fooled him – but not her mother.

Harriet viewed her daughter with a degree of concern. She had never before known Annie try to impress any young man. She was not happy that the first should be a member of the squire's family. But she consoled herself with the knowledge that Perys was

34

not likely to be at Heligan for very long. If what Martin had told her in strict confidence was true, he was also unlikely to become a regular visitor to the great house.

Perys knew nothing of her thoughts. Tethering the horse, he smiled at the girl. 'Hello, Annie. I'm glad to see that the soaking you received on the day of my arrival has had no lasting effect on you.'

'Likewise, sir,' Annie replied, dropping Perys the briefest of curtsies. 'But if you hadn't made it to Tregassick you'd have been in for another soaking today.'

As she spoke, one or two raindrops fell, ahead of what would undoubtedly be another deluge.

A momentary frown crossed Perys's face. 'I do wish you would stop calling me "sir", Annie. It makes me feel terribly old. My name is Perys.'

Deciding it was time she gave her daughter and this young man something else to think about, Harriet said, 'If we don't move, we're all likely to get a soaking. Come into the house while Annie settles the horse, Master Perys. We have milk, or tea . . . there might even be a drop of cider if you would prefer.'

'Milk will be fine, Mrs Bray, thank you.'

He followed the farmer's wife inside the house while Annie unhitched the horse and quickly led it away.

The furniture inside the farmhouse was plain. Much of it looked as though it might have been made by an amateur carpenter. Nevertheless, it was serviceable and the house itself was spotlessly clean.

When Harriet opened the door to the little-used front room, Perys said quickly, 'Might we use the kitchen instead, Mrs Bray? I am sure I will feel far more comfortable there.'

35

Doubtfully, the farmer's wife said, 'It's a bit of a mess right now. I've been cooking . . .'

Smiling at her, Perys said, 'I know, I can smell baking – I've no doubt it's quite delicious.'

'Oh, my dear soul! I left some scones in the oven . . .'

There was no suggestion of going into the best room now, and Perys followed the hurrying Harriet to the kitchen.

Opening the door of the oven situated at the side of the fire, she pulled out a tray of scones. It was followed by a second, and a third. To her relief, they were cooked to perfection.

When Annie came into the kitchen, only just ahead of the rain that was now beating against the window panes, Perys was sitting at the table, a glass of milk in front of him and a half-eaten buttered scone in his hand.

She looked questioningly at her mother, and Harriet said, apologetically, 'Master Perys insisted on coming in here.'

'It was the wonderful cooking smells,' Perys explained. 'And the taste is even better! They really are delicious. I hope you're going to teach Polly up at the house how to cook these, Mrs Bray, or Martin will never leave home.'

Pleased that Perys was displaying an interest in Martin, Harriet said, 'The girl can cook well enough. She'll make him a good wife.'

'It hasn't taken you very long to learn what's going on at Heligan,' said Annie, ignoring the frown her mother gave her for being overly familiar.

'Polly very kindly ironed some of my clothes ready

36

for dinner on my first night,' Perys explained. 'She thanked me for speaking up for Martin and explained that they were to be married. I am also grateful to you for telling me who was staying at Heligan, Annie. It helped a great deal.'

'I'm sure you managed to sort things out well enough by yourself,' she said.

Harriet drew in her breath sharply at what she considered to be her daughter's impertinence, but Perys was more concerned with how much Annie knew about him. At the same time he felt the truth would matter far less to her than it did to members of the Tremayne family.

'Would you like another scone . . . or some more milk, perhaps?' Harriet was determined to steer the conversation towards safer ground.

'Yes please to both offers, Mrs Bray. I don't think I've ever tasted scones like these before.'

Throwing her daughter what was intended to be a warning glance, Harriet put two more scones on Perys's plate and moved the butter dish towards him. 'I think the rain will move on directly,' she said. 'I don't know what's got into the weather these days, with such squalls sweeping in out of nowhere. At this time of year we should be having haymaking weather.'

'Have you heard that Henry Dunn came home from hospital last night?' Annie asked Perys. When he looked momentarily blank, she explained, 'Henry was the man we dug out of the landslip on the Pentewan Road. He's got a broken leg, and a couple of ribs are injured too, but he's going to be all right.'

'That's good news,' declared Perys. 'I'd like to call on him some time.'

'Why don't we go now?' Annie suggested. 'The rain seems to have almost stopped.'

She sounded a little too eager and Harriet said, firmly, 'You have work to do about the farm, my girl. Cows don't milk themselves – and your pa said you were to bring the sheep from the bottom field in closer to the house.'

'I have things to do, too,' Perys said, reluctantly. 'I must get back to Heligan and tell them about the mare. She ought to have someone look at her as soon as possible.'

Annie was disappointed but Harriet's relief was short-lived.

'Could we make it some time this evening?' Perys asked. 'Morwenna and Arabella are bringing friends to Heligan from Lanhydrock tonight. I really would like an excuse to be out of the house while they are there.'

It would have been churlish and embarrassing for Harriet to refuse permission for Annie to accompany Perys, and she said, 'I think that would be all right. Perhaps Martin could go, too.'

'Then that's settled,' said Annie. 'Come to the farm whenever you're ready . . . Perys.'

Her mother's expression showed such disapproval that Annie decided it was not the moment to tell her that Martin had informed her he would be required at Heligan that evening. He was to take Morwenna's and Arabella's friends home when they were ready to leave.

6

Mevagissey was a pretty little fishing village, with houses and fish-cellars crowded together and streets so narrow that for most of their length only the smallest of wagons were able to pass each other.

There was an inner and an outer harbour and both were crowded with boats. These were mainly fishing vessels; only half-a-dozen had steam engines. The remainder were sailing vessels, their owners reliant upon the vagaries of the wind to earn a living.

A smell of fish pervaded the whole village and was especially strong in the harbour area. Many boats had come in on a rising tide and their cargoes were being unloaded in large quantities by men in heavy boots and faded, baggy jerseys.

The fishermen Perys and Annie met with along the way regarded him with suspicion and her with only the briefest of nods.

After receiving a scowl from a bearded fisherman

with a stubby pipe held firmly between his teeth, Perys commented to Annie, 'The men here don't seem particularly friendly.'

She smiled. 'They're all right, but they're fish and we're farm. Although Ma came from here originally, we all tend to keep to our own. Besides, you're a stranger – and a well-dressed stranger at that. For all they know you might be an official of some sort. Most officials who find their way here have a nasty habit of costing folk money. Don't worry, by the time we leave Henry Dunn's house, word will have gone around who you are. They already know what you did for him. You'll find you'll be treated very differently then.'

She took the basket that he had carried to the village from Tregassick Farm. Inside were a dozen eggs, a large piece of farmhouse butter and a number of the scones baked by Annie's mother.

Henry Dunn's house was one of many that clung to the side of a cliff overlooking the inner harbour. When they entered the house they found the injured fisherman seated in a wooden armchair, a plaster-of-Paris cast on his outstretched leg.

He greeted them breathlessly, explaining that damage to his ribs had put painful pressure upon one of his lungs. Nevertheless, he thanked both Perys and Annie for the part they had played in his rescue, adding, 'What more can I say? I owe my life to you both. If you hadn't found me and pulled me out from under all that mud and taken me to the hospital I certainly wouldn't be here now—'

A fit of coughing caused him to break off. After

fighting for breath for a few moments, he unexpectedly began weeping.

Perys was embarrassed by the emotion shown by the fisherman, although he knew it was caused by the low state of his health. He was relieved when the man's wife motioned for them to follow her into the kitchen. Here she thanked Annie for the food she had brought for them.

'Things are going to be hard with us for a while, until Henry's on his feet again. Our Wesley's gone out with the boats today, but he'll get no more than a boy's wages, and my cleaning job up at the vicarage is for only a couple of hours each morning. Still, I'm thankful that Henry's alive – and at least I haven't got our Eliza at home to be fed.'

Annie displayed a lack of interest that Perys found unsettling.

'She's up by Liskeard with my sister,' continued the fisherman's wife, seemingly unaware of Annie's indifference. 'The one who's married to a railway porter. She's expecting her first any day now. Eliza's gone up there to be with her. She doesn't even know her father's been involved in an accident. I'll need to send her a postcard, I suppose, although I'd rather not. As soon as she knows, she'll be home like a shot, and there's nothing she can do here.'

Annie asked nothing about the Dunns' absent daughter and Perys realised she disapproved of her for some reason.

'Well, I hope Henry's up and about soon,' said Annie. 'I'll call in on you again, probably when Ma does some more baking.'

'It was very kind of you to come to see Henry

today,' said the injured man's wife, 'and especially kind of you, sir. We're all thankful for what you did. If you hadn't come along and had the Heligan carriage take Henry into hospital, he wouldn't be with us today. The doctor said as much.'

'I'd like to call in on him again too, if I may,' Perys said. 'I hope that next time I'm here he'll be a whole lot better.'

As Perys and Annie made their way back through Mevagissey, it seemed to the astounded Perys that they were walking through a different village. There were smiles for them where before there had been scowls, and many of the fishermen touched their caps to him in a gesture of respect.

When he mentioned the remarkable change of attitude to Annie, she smiled. 'I told you what it would be like once they realised who you were. You'll never be fully accepted here because they're fishermen and you're not, but you've helped one of them. As a result they'll never do you a bad turn and you'll not need to ask twice for their help if ever you have need of it. You needn't worry too much about Henry Dunn, either. He's a fisherman – and Mevagissey fishermen take care of their own.'

'Could I expect Eliza Dunn to offer me help if I were to need it?' Perys asked, unexpectedly.

'What do you know of Eliza?' Annie asked, sharply.

'Nothing at all,' he replied, 'but I was watching you when Mrs Dunn was talking about her. I formed the impression that you don't like her very much. I was curious, that's all.'

'I don't have anything to do with Eliza Dunn,' Annie said, suddenly tight-lipped. 'I prefer it that way.

If you want to know anything about Eliza you'll need to ask Martin – but don't mention her name when Polly's around. Mind you, I've no doubt your cousin Edward could tell you as much about her as anyone else, if you cared to ask him.'

Perys could not visualise a situation arising when he would question Edward Tremayne about Eliza. He decided he would drop the subject.

All too soon, it seemed, they came within sight of Tregassick Farm. He could see a couple of children running in and out of one of the farm buildings and Annie explained that they probably belonged to the wife of another farmer who was paying them a visit.

'That doesn't mean you can't come in,' she added quickly when she saw him hesitate. 'Pa is anxious to meet you.'

'I'll make it some other time, if you don't mind,' Perys said, reluctantly. He felt it would cause a certain amount of embarrassment if the farmer were to receive an unexpected visit from a relative of his landlord when others were visiting the farm.

'Just as you wish,' Annie shrugged, successfully hiding her disappointment. 'We'll no doubt meet up again before you leave Heligan.'

'I sincerely hope so, Annie . . .' He paused for a moment before saying, 'Do you think your parents would mind if I called in at the farm occasionally?'

Annie wanted to say it would pose no problem, but common sense told her that regular visits would be frowned upon – by both families.

'There's nothing to prevent you dropping by occasionally,' she said, eventually, 'but what would Squire Tremayne say about you becoming friendly with us?

After all, you're one of his family and Martin is a servant at Heligan.'

'I doubt very much whether Great-Uncle Hugh will return to Heligan before I join the army,' Perys said. 'Besides, I'm not so close to him that he would care very much who I choose for my friends. And there's no one else to whom it would matter.'

Even as he was saying the words, Perys wondered what Maude Tremayne and her daughters would think if he became unduly friendly with the daughter of the Bray family of Tregassick Farm, the sister of Heligan's young coachman.

7

'Did you enjoy the ball at Lanhydrock?'

Perys put the question to Maude and her daughters at breakfast next morning.

'No!' Arabella spoke with considerable feeling. 'All anyone could talk about was this stupid old war they think is about to happen.'

Perys glanced at Maude, but a slight movement of her head suggested she had no wish to talk about the matter in front of the girls.

'Where were you last evening, Perys? I wanted to introduce you to my friend. I had told her all about you and she was looking forward to meeting you.' Arabella was inclined to pout when something disappointed her. She was pouting now.

It was also apparent to Perys that although Arabella had voiced the question, Morwenna was equally interested.

'I went to Mevagissey, to visit Henry Dunn, the

man Martin and I helped to rescue from the landslide,' he replied, easily. 'When I had to leave the horse at Tregassick Farm they told me Mr Dunn had been released from hospital. He's actually in rather a bad way. He has a broken leg and ribs and there seems to be some pressure on one of his lungs. I will probably visit him again to see if he is improving.'

'The poor man,' Maude said, vaguely sympathetic.

'I hope he was duly grateful to you,' Morwenna said. 'It sounds as though he is lucky to be alive.'

'He was embarrassingly grateful,' Perys replied. 'In fact he broke down while he was speaking. I feel he should still be in hospital, but I suppose that would cost money and he's not a wealthy man.'

'I am surprised you were able to find his house,' Morwenna commented. 'Mevagissey is such a *warren* of houses.'

The remark was made in apparent innocence, but Perys had an uncomfortable feeling that there was more to it than that.

'It certainly wasn't the easiest house to find,' he agreed, hoping Morwenna would not probe further.

His hopes were dashed immediately, but her questioning did not take the direction he feared.

'Does the fisherman have a daughter named Eliza?' she asked.

Perys was aware from Maude's expression of disapproval that once again there was more to Morwenna's question than was apparent.

'I think Mrs Dunn did mention a daughter named Eliza. She's at Liskeard, taking care of a relative who is expecting a baby. Why, do you know her?'

Morwenna and her mother exchanged glances, and

it was Maude who replied, 'The girl was found in the grounds of Heligan and brought to me. It seems she is greatly smitten with Martin, the coachman, and was hoping to waylay him. I warned her to stay away from Heligan and sent her home.'

'But . . . isn't Martin engaged to Polly?'

'He is, and after speaking to him I am quite satisfied he has given her no encouragement whatsoever.'

'You are far too gullible, Mother,' declared Morwenna. 'Eliza was not here looking for Martin. She has ideas *well* above her station in life.'

'Morwenna! I will not have you repeating servants' gossip in front of Arabella.'

'What gossip, Mother?' asked Arabella. 'Do you mean that linking her with Edward? I saw him speaking to a girl once, in the garden. She was not one of the servants and they seemed very friendly. It was probably Eliza Dunn, and I know all about her reputation . . .'

'That is quite enough, Arabella – you too, Morwenna.' Maude spoke in a tone that brooked no argument. 'I forbid you to mention the subject again.'

Perys had listened to the conversation with increasing interest. If the gossip were true, so many things fell into place. If Edward was having an affair with Eliza Dunn and her name had been linked with Martin, it went a long way towards explaining why he had been so unreasonably angry with the coachman on the day of Perys's arrival. It would also explain Annie's hint that Edward could tell him all he needed to know about Eliza.

'Now, what plans do we all have for the day?' Maude was determined to change the subject.

'We've been at Heligan for more than two weeks and I still haven't been to Mevagissey,' complained Arabella. 'Will you take me there, Perys? *Please?*'

Perys glanced at Maude, who, in turn, looked questioningly at Morwenna. The older of the two daughters shrugged. 'I am quite happy to go there with Perys and Arabella, but I don't want to remain there for too long. The smell of fish becomes quite overwhelming after a while.'

Apparently satisfied, Maude said to Perys, 'Would you mind accompanying the girls to the village if you are doing nothing else, Perys? I know Arabella has been dying to have a look around. I would not have been happy for her to go with Edward. I feel you are rather more responsible.'

Having been paid such an unexpected compliment, Perys felt he could not refuse. 'I'll be delighted to escort both girls to the village. Shall we say, in an hour's time?'

'Can't we go right away?' asked a delighted Arabella.

'I want to go to the stables first, to check on the horse I took out yesterday,' Perys replied.

'We won't need a horse today,' said Morwenna. 'It's only a short walk.'

'I know,' Perys agreed, 'but the mare went lame when I was riding her. I'm concerned about her.'

This was quite true, but Perys was also hoping he might meet with Martin at the stables. He wondered whether Annie might have said anything to him about *their* visit to Mevagissey.

'You should be grateful that Perys has agreed to take you,' Maude said.

'I am,' Arabella declared, '*very* grateful. Thank you, Perys. I *am* glad you have come to stay at Heligan. You are so much nicer than Edward.'

Morwenna looked mildly amused, but Maude did not. She had realised from the day of Perys's arrival at Heligan that Arabella was smitten with him. It was no more than a schoolgirl's infatuation, of course, but Maude felt it was time Arabella put such preoccupations behind her. She was approaching an age when she should be looking forward to meeting prospective husbands. Perys did not come into such a category.

However, if world events were moving in the direction predicted by most of the men who had attended the Lanhydrock ball, it was doubtful whether she needed to be too concerned about Arabella's infatuation with Perys. Most of those in contact with the government in London were of the opinion that orders had already gone out to the service chiefs to prepare for war. It was firmly believed that any conflict was unlikely to last longer than a few months. Nevertheless, the army and navy would need to be brought up to strength very quickly – and Perys was destined for the army.

Maude had no wish to see him exposed to the dangers of battle, but she was aware he would need to undertake army training, possibly followed by flying instruction, all of which would take time. By then, she told herself, the worst of the fighting might be over. In any case, she and her two daughters were unlikely to meet up with Perys in the future.

8

When he visited the stables, Perys was disappointed to learn that Martin had gone to St Austell on an errand for Maude. However, he was delighted to learn that the dappled mare was now hardly limping at all. He set off for Mevagissey with the girls feeling much relieved. The day had started well.

By the time it was over world events would have taken a course that would touch the lives of every man, woman and child on the Heligan estates, with repercussions that extended far, far beyond the Cornish borders.

But a drama of a much more local nature swiftly unfolded as Perys, Morwenna and Arabella neared Mevagissey. As they walked together, a rocket, fired into the air from the harbour area, rose into the sky, emitting a loud and shrill noise that startled the three walkers.

'I wonder if that's a signal to launch the lifeboat?'

Perys cried. 'If it is, something must be happening off the coast. Let's hurry and find out what's going on.'

His surmise was correct. By the time the trio reached the harbour the lifeboat had already been launched. They were in time to see it clear the outer harbour and begin battling against a choppy sea. While most of the lifeboatmen continued pulling lustily on the oars, others raised the sails in order to take advantage of the stiff breeze.

Many of the villagers had turned out to follow the progress of the lifeboat, and they lined the wall of the outer harbour. Perys and the two girls were able to find a place among them.

It was unnecessary for the three new arrivals to ask why the lifeboat had been launched. Not far offshore a large sailing barque was wallowing in the swell with sails flapping. Flames, fanned by the wind, jumped ever higher from one of the holds.

The crew evacuating the stricken vessel seemed to be in a state of panic. Watched by the onlookers onshore, one of the ship's boats dropped in a lop-sided manner from its davits, pitching the occupants into the sea. It remained dangling vertically from a single davit, dipping into the sea with each roll of the stricken ship.

Due to the conditions there were no fishing boats in the immediate vicinity. Those that were at sea were working in the more sheltered waters of nearby St Austell Bay, out of sight of the drama taking place off Mevagissey.

A couple of seamen still remained on deck, but boats from the burning vessel were putting as much distance between themselves and the stricken ship as possible, the crews hauling on their oars with considerable urgency.

'What is happening?' queried Arabella. 'Why aren't they trying to save the rest of the men on board?'

Those about them seemed as mystified as Arabella, but her questions were answered in an horrific manner only minutes later.

A loud explosion rent the air, the sound bouncing back from the cliffs around the small fishing village. At the same time, timbers from the barque were flung high into the air, pursued by hungry flames. As debris rained down it was apparent the ship's boats had not succeeded in putting sufficient distance between themselves and the ship.

They disappeared inside a swirling cloud of smoke, and some of the Mevagissey women and children screamed.

In a distressed voice, Arabella cried, 'What's happened? Why did it explode like that?'

'The ship was obviously carrying explosives,' Perys replied grimly. 'The crew must have known. That's why they were trying so desperately to get away.'

The water around the explosion had settled now and the smoke was drifting away, borne out into the bay by the wind. Those onshore caught only a fleeting glimpse of the fore section of the ship as it slid beneath the surface of the water. All that remained was a vast area covered with debris.

Yet, by some quirk of fate, one of the ship's boats was still afloat.

Men who had been watching from the shore now ran to the harbour, hauling on ropes to bring moored vessels of varying sizes to the quayside. At the same time a cry went up for any man who could handle an oar to man the boats.

'Morwenna . . . you and Arabella stay right here. I'm going to help.'

Without waiting for a response from the two young women, Perys ran to where three men were hauling in a boat that could have accommodated a crew of six. When it bumped against the stone harbourside the men jumped into it and Perys went with them.

Looking critically at Perys and the manner of his dress, one of the men asked, 'Do you know anything about crewing a boat?'

'I did some rowing at school.'

This was an understatement. He had been stroke oarsman in the most successful eights the school had ever known.

'This isn't a school outing on some inland river—'

'Shut up!' This from the oldest of the three men. 'He'll do.'

As they were pushing the boat off from the harbour wall another two men jumped on board, providing a full crew.

Speed in reaching the scene of the foundered ship was essential and the six men bent their backs to the task of propelling themselves through the water as fast as was humanly possible.

Despite his prowess in the school eights, Perys had difficulty keeping up with the others. Even so, they quickly overhauled a couple of smaller boats which had put out before them, and were soon among the floating wreckage of ship and cargo. It was there they plucked their first survivor from the sea.

The man had suffered an injury to his left arm.

Clinging to a large piece of timber, he was close to exhaustion, but he possessed enough strength to scream when his injured arm was banged against the side as he was hauled inside the boat.

Suddenly, something attracted Perys's attention in the water. He stopped rowing, causing the oars on his side of the boat to foul each other.

'What the hell do you think you're doing?' demanded the fisherman who had queried Perys's ability to man an oar.

'I saw something in the water . . . over there.' He pointed to a confused tangle of sail and rigging from the stricken vessel.

'It's just wreckage,' said another of the crewmen, then, 'Look! There's someone in the water, up ahead.'

The fishermen took up their oars again, but amidst the tangle of rigging close to the boat, Perys was certain he had seen a man's head momentarily rise clear of the water before disappearing once more beneath the surface.

Further argument with the others would only waste precious time. Kicking off his shoes, Perys stood up and dived into the water.

It was cold enough to take his breath away, and as he came to the surface he was aware of the angry shouts of the men he had just abandoned so dramatically.

Reaching the spot where he had seen the head, Perys dived beneath the wreckage. He touched something that moved, but was forced to the surface before he could be certain. Drawing in a deep breath, he dived again. This time he found the body of a man, but when he tried to take it with him to the surface, he realised it was entangled in rigging.

He struggled to free the man, but did not succeed until he had almost exhausted all the air he had taken in and it felt as though his lungs would burst. Then, with the inert body in his arms, he kicked out for the surface.

When he emerged with his burden, the men in the boat put up a shout of encouragement. A few minutes later the seaman was taken from him, then Perys was hauled into the boat to the congratulations of the crew.

Perys feared his rescue attempt had been in vain, but, laid face down over one of the thwarts, the rescued man had his back pummelled by one of the crew and he suddenly coughed. Water gushed from his mouth and his whole body twitched . . . He was alive.

Soon afterwards, Perys and his fellow crewmen rescued another two men, while the Mevagissey lifeboat rescued others, by which time a number of fishing boats had arrived, drawn to the scene by the sound of the explosion.

In addition to the partly drowned man, one of the other crewmen was badly injured. The oldest man in the Mevagissey boat, who had assumed command, said, 'There are enough boats out here to carry on the search now, we'll get these men back to shore.'

The lifeboat coxwain had been of the same opinion; he was already taking his boat back to the harbour. The boat in which Perys was a crewman followed behind.

The seamen sat huddled quietly together as the boat headed back towards the harbour, the more seriously injured man rocking backwards and forwards, as though by so doing he might lessen his pain.

The men spoke sufficient English to give their nationality as Russian, but they were unable to tell their rescuers anything else.

When the boat bumped against a flight of stone steps built into the wall of Mevagissey's outer harbour, a number of young boys eagerly secured it while older men helped the survivors ashore.

The injured men were taken to the lifeboat station, which had been turned into a temporary first aid post. There, Perys, his clothes dripping water, was surprised to find Morwenna capably assisting the local doctor. With her was a pale-faced Arabella.

9

Miraculously, only three members of the unfortunate barque's crew died in the explosion which wrecked their ship, but many were injured. Morwenna and the local doctor were kept busy until help arrived from the St Austell Hospital, summoned to Mevagissey by a telephone appeal from the local coastguard.

Despite being urged to go home and change out of his wet clothes, Perys remained until Morwenna was ready to return to Heligan. She left Mevagissey with the warm thanks of the doctor ringing in her ears for the important part she had played in the dramatic rescue of the Russian seamen.

As they made their way back to Heligan House, Perys said, wryly, 'That was rather more excitement than we expected to find when we set out this morning.'

'It was indeed!' Morwenna agreed. 'Did I hear one of the fishermen say that if you ever decided to take up fishing he would be happy to have you in his crew?'

'Yes,' Perys said. Holding out his hands, he added, sheepishly, 'but he hadn't seen these.' He extended his fingers to reveal a mess of bloody blisters and torn skin.

'Perys!' Arabella was horrified. 'They are *awful*! You must be in agonies of pain – as well as uncomfortably wet.'

'You should have showed your hands to me when we were in the village,' Morwenna chided. 'I could have treated them there.'

'I would have felt foolish,' Perys confessed. 'There were far more serious injuries for you to deal with – and I thought you dealt with them magnificently. Where did you learn such skills?'

'Morwenna has spent two years working as a nurse in a hospital in London,' Arabella answered proudly for her sister. 'I'll be going there when we return home. It's become a family tradition, following in the footsteps of Great-Aunt Florence.'

'Great-Aunt Florence?' Perys wondered whether the name should mean something to him.

'Florence Nightingale,' Morwenna explained. 'She is related to us on Mother's side of the family. She was responsible for making nursing a respectable profession during the Crimean War. Unfortunately, in so doing she managed to upset a great many senior army officers, so when you join the army it might not be a good idea to boast of the family connection. But we need to get you to Heligan and out of those wet clothes. Before we do that let's see how many handkerchiefs we can muster between us to clean up your hands and bind them up until we reach home and I am able to deal with them properly . . .'

They managed to find three handkerchiefs between them and Morwenna used the smallest to wash his hands clean before binding the other two around them to protect the painful broken blisters.

As she worked, Perys said, 'Florence Nightingale would have been proud of the work you have done today.'

'I think she would have felt the same about many of the Mevagissey women,' Morwenna said. Giving Perys a look he could not interpret, she added, 'Eliza Dunn among them.'

Not particularly interested, Perys asked, 'Oh? When did she return to the village?'

'Late last night. It seems she came back from Liskeard as soon as word reached her of her father's accident. She asked me to thank you for the part you played in rescuing him – and for going to visit him yesterday. You and Annie Bray.'

Aware of the implied disapproval, Perys said, 'Yes, Annie took a basket of food to him from her mother.'

'I believe Annie is a very pretty girl,' said Morwenna, seemingly disinclined to drop the matter.

'I suppose she is.' Perys felt angry with himself for feeling there was a need to justify visiting Henry Dunn in company with Annie, but he was aware that if he explained the circumstances of his first meeting with her it might cause unnecessary trouble for Martin.

He was saved from further explanations by the sight of one of the Heligan gardeners hurrying along the path towards the village.

When the man reached them, he spoke breathlessly to Perys, seemingly oblivious of the other's wet condition. 'I'm on my way to Mevagissey to speak to the coastguard. Have you heard the news?'

Thinking the gardener was talking about the foundering of the ship in the bay, Perys replied, 'About the wreck of the Russian ship? Yes, we've all been involved in the rescue of the crew.'

'No, not that,' said the excited gardener, 'something far more serious. Mrs Tremayne has just had a telephone call from someone in London. Germany has invaded Belgium. Our government has given them until midnight tonight to withdraw their troops.'

'What if they refuse?' Morwenna asked, anxiously.

'Then we'll go to war with them,' said the gardener. 'No doubt they *will* do as they're told, but there's many folk who hope they don't. It's about time we taught 'em a lesson they won't forget in a hurry.'

'What will the coastguard be able to do about it?' Perys asked, uncertain what the import of the gardener's news was likely to be.

'The Tremayne boat is in the harbour right now. Mrs Tremayne thinks that if there is likely to be any trouble the boat will be safer in Tregiskey Cove.'

A boat-house belonging to Heligan House was situated in Tregiskey Cove, just around the coast from the fishing village. Perys doubted whether such a move was really necessary. The small fishing harbour of Mevagissey was hardly likely to be the target of an attack in the event of a war between Great Britain and Germany. But the Heligan employee seemed to regard his errand as being of great importance and Perys kept his thoughts to himself.

'You'd better be on your way – although I doubt whether you'll find anyone interested in moving the Tremayne boat right now,' he said. 'When we left Mevagissey all the able-bodied men were at sea, salvaging what they could from the Russian ship.'

When the gardener had gone, Morwenna asked, 'What does it all mean, Perys? I mean, what the gardener was saying? What will *actually* happen if the Germans refuse to leave Belgium by midnight?'

'I suppose we will go to war,' Perys replied. 'Though I doubt very much if it will come to that. The Germans have threatened war on more than one occasion. They will back down when they realise our government means what it says. Mind you, if there *is* a war I should be able to get into the army far more quickly than I expected – then into the Royal Flying Corps. They will want all the men they can get.' Echoing the earlier thoughts of Maude, he added, 'The trouble is, all the excitement will probably be over before I even start my training . . .'

'. . . It would be downright foolish to underestimate the Germans and their army. They laid their plans for a war very carefully many years ago. We *will* beat them eventually, of course, but it will be a bitter struggle while it lasts. This is a sad day for all the countries involved.'

In the sitting-room at Heligan, Maude was holding forth. Now in dry clothes, Perys was acutely aware of his heavily bandaged hands. Such an inconvenience could hardly have come at a more inopportune time. Nevertheless, he would not allow it to interfere with his plans.

'I will ride to Bodmin tomorrow,' he said. 'If the Germans fail to respond to the deadline the army will need every man they can get. I might be able to join before the year is over.'

'Why is everyone so anxious to go off to war . . . to fight?' Arabella was visibly upset. The knowledge that her father had been killed in the Boer War had coloured the whole of her young life and she found the thought of Perys going away to war distressing.

Embarrassed by Arabella's concern for him, Perys excused himself from the company of the three women by saying he was going to the stables to ensure there would be a horse available to him in the morning.

When he had gone, Maude said to her daughters, 'Hopefully war might yet be averted. News of what is happening came from your cousin Rupert, fresh from the War Office in London. Senior officers there believe that when the Germans realise Britain is serious in its intentions, they will seek peace. Even if they do not, our generals are convinced that any fighting will be over by Christmas. I personally think our military men unduly optimistic, but who am I to argue with their views? Now, let us put all talk of war to one side. Tell me more of your adventures in Mevagissey. Everyone in the house heard the commotion, and the servants told me a ship had exploded at sea. I also learned you were both of great assistance to the doctor in treating the injured. But I was not aware Perys was so closely involved too! You must tell me everything about it . . .'

10

Germany did *not* comply with the ultimatum given by the British government. As a result, at 11.05p.m., British time, on Tuesday 4 August, 1914, a declaration of war was handed to the German Ambassador in London.

News of this was obtained by Maude Tremayne in a telephone call to London early the following morning. Perys set out for Bodmin immediately.

The visit to the army barracks left him feeling utterly frustrated and bewildered. His first problem was that nobody knew the whereabouts of Major Stokes, the recruiting officer. The only certainty was that he was *not* at Bodmin.

The barracks themselves were the scene of chaotic activity. Harassed officers to whom Perys managed to speak seemed to assume that every man not already in uniform was a reservist, answering the army's call for mobilisation. They showed little interest in a young man making enquiries about a future career as an officer.

Perys was eventually fortunate enough to find a captain who appeared to be working in an administrative capacity in the office of the commanding officer. Although he too was busy, he listened sympathetically to Perys and, searching through a filing cabinet, pulled out a thin file.

Reading through it he frowned, then looked at Perys uncertainly. 'You are Perys Sampson Tremayne?'

'That's right,' Perys said, delighted that he seemed to be getting somewhere at last.

Closing the file and returning it to the cabinet, the officer said, 'I am sorry, old chap, but it seems that Major Stokes feels unable to recommend you for a commission.'

Perys was flabbergasted. His education, plus the recommendation of his uncle – not to mention the present emergency – should have been more than enough to have him accepted.

'But why? Does he give a reason?'

The captain shook his head. 'He doesn't have to, really. But don't be too downhearted about it. How old are you?'

'Almost nineteen.' Perys found it difficult to accept that his application had been turned down for no apparent reason.

'If you are really keen to join the army I suggest you enlist. If you are officer material you will soon be noticed and a commission should follow. Besides, it will give time for those to heal.' He indicated Perys's bandaged hands. 'What have you done to them, anything serious?'

'No.' Perys did not elaborate. 'But . . . my application. My great-uncle wrote a letter of recommendation to Major Stokes. I was given a virtual guarantee of a commission.'

'I'm sorry, young man. I've told you what is on your file – and that is more than I should have said. You can come in to see the major on his return, if you wish, but he is not a man prone to changing his mind. Now, if you will excuse me, I have a great deal of work to do . . .'

After stammering his thanks to the captain, Perys left the office and made his way to where he had tethered the Heligan horse. He was thoroughly dismayed. His whole future had been built about a service career. He could think of no reason why his application should have been turned down. It was, of course, possible it had something to do with his dubious parentage. Yet given the recommendation of Hugh Tremayne and the education he had received, it was highly unlikely to be the sole reason. Many great soldiers had been born in similar circumstances.

There had to be some other reason. Perhaps there had been a misunderstanding. He needed to discuss it with Maude. She knew Major Stokes and might be able to provide some answers.

Approaching Heligan, Perys was forced to a halt at a set of hurdles placed across the lane between two open field gates on either side. A few minutes later a flock of sheep was driven between them, from one field to the other. The shepherdess was Annie.

Apologising for keeping him waiting, she closed the gate of the field that now contained the sheep. Perys dismounted and helped her to move the hurdles into the field from which the sheep had come.

Pointing to his bandaged hands, Annie asked, sympathetically, 'Did you hurt those yesterday?'

'Yes. I feel a bit foolish about it, really, getting blisters just through rowing a boat.'

'From what I've heard there was rather more to it than just rowing a boat. Folk in Mevagissey say the man you rescued was the ship's captain. They are full of praise for you – and for Miss Morwenna, too. One or two have said they'd rather be treated by her than by the doctor.'

'I believe she has had a very thorough training as a nurse,' Perys explained.

'Such skills will be needed if this war goes on for very long,' Annie commented. After a moment's hesitation, she added, 'Do you think it will mean you'll be going away sooner than you expected?'

A pained expression crossed Perys's face. 'I don't know. I've just come from the army barracks at Bodmin and nothing seems to be very certain.' Not wishing to tell her exactly what had happened there, he added, 'All the senior officers are away on some war business or another. Those who are left are so busy coping with mobilisation that they have no time to deal with anything else.'

'Martin upset Ma this morning by saying that if it looks as though the war is going to last for a while he'll join the army. He believes most of the men at Heligan will do the same.'

It was an eventuality that had not occurred to Perys. He wondered how Heligan would cope if many of the workforce employed in the house and on the estate left to join the army or the navy.

'Do you have time to come to the farm for a drink?' Annie asked.

Although he was pleased that Annie had made the suggestion, Perys shook his head. 'I would love to, Annie, but I had better get back to Heligan and find out what everyone intends doing. This war will change a great many things.'

'I am sure it will,' Annie agreed, seriously. 'Are you likely to stay on at Heligan if you don't join the army right away?'

'Probably. The truth is that right now I have nowhere else to go. My grandparents have already shut up their house – although they might decide to return to England if it looks as though Italy will come into the war on the side of the Germans.'

Annie felt deep sympathy for Perys. Although he was a member of the family that owned most of the countryside in this part of Cornwall, he had no roots, no permanent home, and, seemingly, no one who really cared what happened to him.

'If you *do* stay at Heligan for a while you are always welcome to call on us at Tregassick.'

'Thank you, Annie, I appreciate the offer. I shall certainly pay you a visit if I stay – and will let you know if I am to leave.'

'I hope that won't be for a while . . .' Aware that she was being what her mother would refer to as 'far too forward', Annie turned to go.

Suddenly, she stopped and turned back to him. 'Perys . . . will you speak to Martin and try to persuade him to stay on at Heligan, for a while, at least, and not to rush into joining the army?'

'I'll try, Annie, but I can't guarantee how successful

I'm likely to be. You see, I understand exactly how he feels.'

When Perys repeated to Maude what he had been told by the captain at the army barracks in Bodmin, she listened in thoughtful silence.

'. . . It baffles me, Aunt Maude. Great-Uncle Hugh recommended me – and you personally delivered the letter and my application to the commanding officer's office, together with my references. Even my headmaster felt I was well suited for an army career.'

'I don't think it has anything at all to do with your qualifications for a service career, Perys. I believe it is your cousin Edward's way of taking revenge for the bloody nose you gave him. It is perfectly true that my husband served with Major Stokes in the Boer War, but so too did Edward's father. The two remain firm friends.'

'I had hoped that once Edward calmed down he might have accepted that he went too far,' Perys said, ruefully. 'It seems I was wrong.'

'None of this is your fault,' Arabella protested. 'There was nothing else you could have done after he said what he did. He is lucky you didn't do far more to him. I know *I* will never speak to him again for as long as I live.'

'The problem is that it leaves me with a very uncertain future,' Perys said to Maude. 'I have an allowance from my grandfather, but it's by no means generous and is conditional upon my joining the army as soon as possible after completing my education. Perhaps I should do what the captain at Bodmin suggested. Enlist as a recruit and hope to gain a commission.'

'That is not a good idea at all,' Maude said, firmly. 'As the widow of an army officer I have had considerable experience of service life. Whatever the captain may have told you, obtaining a commission from the ranks is the exception rather than the rule – even in wartime. The best thing you could do is to have a chat with your cousin Rupert Pilkington. He is in the Royal Flying Corps – I believe I may have mentioned him to you before. When I spoke to him on the telephone he said he hoped to come to Cornwall very soon, flying an aeroplane, I believe, to seek possible sites for an airfield. You have said your true ambition is to become a flyer. Rupert might be of some help to you.'

The news greatly excited Perys. If Rupert *did* come to Cornwall he could indeed be a great help. There might also be an opportunity to have a close look at an aeroplane! Yet he was puzzled.

'Why would the RFC want an airfield in Cornwall? We're an awfully long way from France.'

'That is quite true, but an aeroplane, or an airship, could fly out over the sea and report on any German naval ships that might be making their way along the English Channel.'

The idea made sense to Perys. It also meant the Royal Flying Corps was likely to undertake a great many more tasks in wartime than anyone had ever envisaged when the corps was formed.

'When will Rupert be here?' Perys asked, eagerly.

'He was not terribly sure, but expected it to be some time in the next few days.' Maude smiled at Perys's eagerness. 'Be patient, Perys. I agree with the DCLI captain on one thing. Your hands need to heal before you can do anything more about a service career.'

11

Events in Europe moved with a frightening speed. During the first few weeks of the war many battles were fought by the armies of Britain, Belgium and France – and many were lost.

The British army, which included a battalion of the Duke of Cornwall Light Infantry, had been blooded early in the fighting. Now, together with the armies of its allies, it was in full retreat.

The infant Royal Flying Corps was being used to support the army and was operating under war conditions for the first time in its short history. It had scored its first victories and also suffered its first casualties. As an instrument of warfare it had given the world a glimpse of its enormous potential, but at the same time exposed immediate shortcomings.

Not least among the latter was the dismissive attitude of senior army commanders to the current role of the Royal Flying Corps – and the even greater role it might play in the future. It was an attitude that pervaded the army from the commander-in-chief down. Most senior officers had been drilled in battle tactics of the late nineteenth century and found it difficult to accept new concepts. A commander of the British Expeditionary Force in France scornfully dismissed the suggestion that aircraft be used to obtain information about the enemy, pompously declaring that the only way for a commander to get information was 'by the use of cavalry'.

Despite this, now the war had begun, reconnaissance in support of those involved in 'the real business of fighting a war' was the only role envisaged for the Royal Flying Corps.

This was not the view of the pilots themselves. Reconnaissance duties *were* undertaken, and performed skilfully and effectively, but the pilots also succeeded in bringing down German aircraft by a number of often bizarre means. The Flying Corps also experimented with bombing techniques which included the use of weighted darts and the occasional hand grenade.

News of such activities reached those at Heligan from various sources, but not from pilot Rupert Pilkington. By the time Rupert's 'few days' had become three weeks, Perys had almost given up hope that his relative would be able to fulfil his intention of visiting Cornwall.

He was still undecided about his own future. Maude's implacable opposition to the suggestion that he should enlist in the army after he had passed his nineteenth birthday meant that he had not seriously considered the matter since mentioning it to her.

Maude had, however, announced her intention of

71

returning to London with her two daughters in the very near future. Morwenna was a trained nurse and casualties from the front in France would soon be filling the hospitals of the capital. Her skills would be urgently needed.

It was intended that Arabella too should follow in the footsteps of her famous ancestor. She was eager to commence her training, but Perys was of the opinion that the younger of the two Tremayne girls would never achieve the calm efficiency of her sister.

Once Maude was gone from Heligan, Perys knew he would need to reach an early decision about his own plans. He could not remain at Heligan for very much longer unless he was able to earn money to support himself. There was also the increasing pressure of watching local young men going off to war. Perys felt he too should be playing a part in the increasingly fierce conflict raging in Europe.

Heligan had already lost a number of its work force. Three reservists had left in the first week of the war. The same number had since enlisted, joining many men from Mevagissey and other surrounding villages.

Because of the sudden dearth of workers, Perys spent a week helping to gather in the wheat on Heligan Home Farm. He followed it by helping out the Brays on Tregassick Farm.

He was working in one of the Tregassick fields, wielding a pitchfork and loading sheaves of corn on to a farmcart, when he heard a sound that was alien to the Cornish countryside. It was the steady drone of a petrol engine.

At first, Perys thought it must be a motor-car. This in itself was unusual enough to attract attention, but as the sound grew louder it became apparent this was no motor vehicle.

Suddenly, Annie cried excitedly, 'Look. Up there in the sky.'

Following the direction of her pointed finger, Perys saw something approaching, high above the ground. It was an aeroplane!

Throwing down his pitchfork, he cried, 'It's Rupert! I'd given up all hope that he would really come.'

He had no need to explain in any more detail. He had already told Annie of Rupert's intention to fly to Cornwall and visit Heligan.

'I must go, Annie. I'm sorry . . .'

'How do you know where he's going to come down?' she asked.

'There's only one field flat and clear enough for him to land in. It's just the other side of Heligan. I want to be there to meet him.'

Wasting no more time in conversation, Perys sprinted off. There was a deep, wooded valley between him and the field in question, but a track climbed the hill on the far side of the valley, skirting the field.

The run would test his fitness to the limit, but he was determined to be the first to greet Rupert when the aeroplane landed.

It was a close thing. Had the pilot not made two passes over the field to ensure there were no hidden hazards, Perys would not have achieved his aim. As it was, although his chest was heaving alarmingly as he fought to regain his breath, he reached the field in time to see the aeroplane float to the ground, its engine coughing noisily.

It bounced twice before coming to a halt, then

turned slowly and trundled across the grass towards the nearest point to Heligan, which happened to be the gate where Perys was standing.

Stopping short of the gate, the aeroplane's engine noise increased momentarily before ceasing altogether. The propeller cut through the air in silence for a moment or two, then came to a spasmodic halt.

The aeroplane had two open cockpits, but only the rear one was occupied. The pilot unfastened a safety belt and pushed his goggles up to his forehead before extricating himself and climbing stiffly from the aeroplane to the ground.

As he did so, one of the Heligan gamekeepers appeared behind Perys, a double-barrelled shotgun carried in the crook of his arm. He looked uncertainly from Perys to the airman and Perys realised the gamekeeper was uncertain whether or not the pilot of the aeroplane was friend or enemy.

The pilot removed his flying helmet and ran fingers through his overlong blond hair before speaking to Perys. 'You there, will you keep a watch on my aeroplane for an hour or so and make certain no one touches anything? I am paying a call on Heligan.'

Perys was dressed in clothes that were appropriate for gathering in the harvest. He realised Rupert had mistaken him for a farmworker.

Turning to the wary gamekeeper, he said, 'It's all right, Frank. It's Rupert Pilkington, a relative.' Then, returning his attention to the flyer, he said, 'I think Frank will be a much better guard than I. What's more, he's armed.' Smiling at Rupert, he added, 'I'm Perys Tremayne. Would you like me to show you the way to the house?'

'I'm terribly sorry, I thought you were one of the farmworkers.' Extending a hand, he said, 'Please forgive me, I am Rupert.'

Taking his hand and shaking it warmly, Perys said, 'It was an understandable mistake. I was helping to gather in the harvest at Tregassick Farm. So many men have gone off to war there's a shortage of labour in the farms about Heligan at the moment . . . but before we go up to the house, would you mind if I had a look over your aeroplane?'

'Of course not. Aunt Maude has told me you're keen to join the Royal Flying Corps. Have you had anything to do with aeroplanes?'

Reaching out to touch the taut canvas of one of the plane's wings, Perys shook his head. 'Nothing at all, although I have discussed them at some length with a friend at school. He's French and his brother is a French army pilot.'

Rupert nodded approval. 'The French have some fine aeroplanes – and damned good pilots to fly them. Come across to the cockpit and I'll show you the controls and explain what they do.'

Perys learned that the aircraft was a BE2c; 'BE' being the initials of Bleriot Experimental. He was deeply interested and asked a great many questions. His inspection came to an end with the arrival of Morwenna and Arabella to greet their cousin.

Arabella looked at the fragile aeroplane in disbelief. 'Rupert, you actually put your trust in this flimsy thing to take you up into the sky?'

Rupert smiled. 'Of course. What's more, I have actually taken it to France and fought against a German pilot while I was flying it. Mind you, we were both using revolvers and neither of us was a terribly good shot.'

Arabella shuddered. 'I would rather not think about such things, especially if Perys is going to be a pilot.'

Such a positive declaration of concern for Perys startled Rupert. He looked enquiringly at Perys, who was embarrassed by Arabella's remark.

'If Perys becomes a pilot I have no doubt he will be a good one,' Rupert said. 'And for much of his time a good pilot has more control of his own destiny than the most efficient infantry officer.'

'In that case I'll try to be a *very* good pilot,' Perys said, meaningfully.

'That's the spirit!' Rupert said, jovially. His glance rested upon Morwenna who had not yet joined in the conversation. Speaking to her now, he said, 'You have grown up considerably since we last met, Morwenna.'

Perys was surprised to see her blush as she replied, 'That is hardly surprising, Rupert. I was only fourteen then.'

'Is it really so long ago? It is terribly remiss of me not to have called on you and your mother before this. Never mind, I am here now.'

'You have been far too busy doing exciting things to think of relatives,' Morwenna replied.

There was something in their manner that made Perys think that Morwenna had probably once looked upon Rupert in the same way as Arabella now regarded him.

He wondered whether Maude had viewed the situation with the misgivings he was aware she had about him. Sadly, he thought the answer would undoubtedly be that she had not.

12

Although Rupert had made a joking reference to the part he had played in the war so far, he had in fact been involved in the forcing down of a German aeroplane and the destruction of another. He also felt very strongly that he should be in France with his squadron right now. Instead, he had been sent back to England to attend a meeting at the War Office to discuss the future role of the Royal Flying Corps. When the meeting had ended, one of the senior officers remembered he had still not carried out the proposed survey of possible airfield sites in Cornwall and decided he should fulfil the task right away.

Perys had taken an instant liking to Rupert and it seemed the flyer liked him too. Much of their conversation during the all-too-brief visit of the airman to Heligan concerned flying and the activities of the Royal Flying Corps.

When Rupert said it was time for him to leave,

Perys looked so crestfallen that after a few moments' thought, Rupert said to him, 'Just how serious are you about joining the RFC, Perys?'

'I have never been more serious about anything,' Perys replied, emphatically. 'I had no real doubts before, but after talking to you, nothing will stop me from becoming a pilot.'

'In that case,' Rupert said, 'how would you like to come with me to check out a couple of airfield sites I have in mind in the west of Cornwall?'

Perys could hardly believe what he was hearing. 'You mean . . . *fly* there with you?'

'I am certainly not going to use any other means of transport,' Rupert declared, amused by Perys's excited disbelief. 'Do you have any warm clothing?'

'I have one or two things in my room.'

'Then go and put them *all* on,' Rupert said. 'You'll be sitting immediately behind the propeller and it can be very cold once we are in the air. Hurry up now, I need to be off pretty quickly if I am to return you and get myself back to the Central Flying School in Wiltshire before dark.'

When Perys had hurried from the room, closely followed by the two girls, Rupert was left alone with Maude and he commented, 'He seems a likeable lad – and very keen to join the RFC.'

'He *is* a likeable boy,' Maude replied, 'and one of whom I feel the Tremayne family could be proud. It is a great pity there was such a scandal over his birth.'

'When I spoke to you by telephone you told me he had been refused a commission in the county regiment. Were the circumstances of his birth the reason?'

Maude shook her head. 'No, I believe the refusal

was a direct result of Perys giving Cousin Edward a well-deserved bloody nose. Edward's father is a close friend of the commanding officer of the regimental barracks here in Cornwall.'

'Perys did that to Edward? Good for him! I have been tempted to do the same on many occasions. If that is the only reason he was refused a commission, I think he would do well in the RFC. We have need of young men who are spirited, courageous and determined.'

'You will find Perys possesses all those qualities,' Maude declared. 'I intend writing to his grandfather to say he is being less than generous to a young man who I firmly believe will one day bring great credit to the family.'

Rupert was impressed by Maude's praise of Perys and he said, 'You have a reputation in the family as being the most level-headed of the Tremayne women, Maude. If that is your opinion of Perys I have no doubt he will be a credit not only to his family, but to his country too. We will see how he enjoys his flight with me, then decide how best we might help him.'

Now he knew he was actually going to fly in the aeroplane, Perys looked at the BE2c more critically when he and the others arrived at the field where it was parked.

It appeared more frail and smaller than it had before.

'Having second thoughts about going up?'

About to climb into the cockpit, Rupert paused and grinned at Perys.

Perys shook his head, and lied, 'No, but I *am* excited about it.'

'I was terrified when I went up for my first lesson,' Rupert confessed. 'So much so that I almost changed my mind about transferring to the RFC. But once in the air it was like nothing I had ever known. You'll find it the same. Now, stand by to swing the propeller, and don't forget what I told you. Swing and get your hands – and yourself – out of the way immediately. It probably won't do anything unexpected, but however long it takes, jump back every time. Once I have the engine started get into the cockpit as quickly as you can.'

It took a few swings for Perys to get used to the resistance of the engine to his efforts. At the seventh attempt the engine started as he jumped back, only to die again immediately. However, after the next swing the engine picked up in a series of noisy explosions and quickly gathered speed. Fighting against the slipstream, Perys scrambled over the wing and dropped awkwardly into the forward of the two cockpits. Once there he fastened the safety belt and pulled over his eyes the goggles Rupert had produced for him.

The noise from the engine increased and suddenly the aeroplane began moving. From the cockpit, Perys returned the waves of Maude and the two girls who had come to witness the beginning of his great adventure.

The field had appeared perfectly flat to Perys when he looked at it a few days before, but the BE2c seemed to be finding a multitude of grass clumps. He thought, wryly, that the aeroplane felt as though it was waddling in the manner of a duck on dry land.

Then the aeroplane turned. The engine noise rose to a crescendo, the whole machine began to shake, and moments later it began to move forward at a rapidly increasing speed.

Suddenly there were no more bumps beneath the wheels. In spite of this, Perys did not realise they had left the ground until he saw some trees to one side of the BE2c and realised the aeroplane was *above* them.

A tap came upon his shoulder and Perys turned to see Rupert grinning at him and holding up a thumb in a signal that all was well.

Perys grinned back at the pilot and nodded emphatically.

He had been apprehensive about this, his first flight, concerned that he might not enjoy the experience. Might even be frightened. However, now he was actually in the sky, in an aeroplane, he was filled with an overwhelming sense of exhilaration. It was the most exciting thing he had ever done. Perhaps ever *would* do.

They were still gaining height but already he could see the Cornish coastline stretching ahead and the small fishing villages and hamlets dotted along its irregular length. It was like looking at a large-scale map, etched in coloured relief.

Another tap on the shoulder and with a snake-like movement of his hand, Rupert indicated that he intended following the coast to the westward, flying a little distance offshore.

Perys nodded acknowledgement of the information and before long they had reached the Lizard, the promontory stretching into the English Channel, its tip being the most southerly point of mainland Britain.

Rupert might easily have flown across the neck of the small peninsula. Instead, he chose to turn south, following the coast, seeking out a potential airfield.

The BE2c had passed the tip of the Lizard and was over the sea, performing a slow, wide turn before heading westward once more, when Perys chanced to glance out of the seaward side of his cockpit. On the far horizon he could just make out smoke from a ship's funnel. Purely as a matter of interest, he turned and attracted Rupert's attention, pointing out to sea in an exaggerated fashion, fully expecting Rupert to do no more than acknowledge the fact that he too had seen the ship.

Much to the surprise of Perys, Rupert levelled the aircraft in order to obtain a steadier view of the distant vessel. After a few minutes he banked the aeroplane in the opposite direction and began heading out farther into the Channel.

Perys looked back at Rupert in surprise, but instead of trying to make impossible conversation, Rupert reached forward and handed him a pair of binoculars, making signs that he was to use them to examine the ship he had spotted.

As they drew nearer, Perys became increasingly impressed by the size of the vessel, which was taking shape as a large warship. He never doubted that it was a *British* warship, although he was unable to make out details of the ensign flying at the stern of the ship.

Suddenly, smoke belched forth from the muzzle of the ship's guns and shortly afterwards soft puffballs of smoke began bursting in the vicinity of the BE2c, although none were particularly close.

Horrified, Perys realised they had stumbled across a German warship. He expected Rupert to turn about immediately and head back for land. Instead, after rummaging about in his cockpit, the pilot reached across the distance between them and, tapping Perys's head to gain his attention, handed him a pencil and writing pad. Making signs that Perys was to draw the German ship, Rupert then banked and flew closer, in order that Perys might be able to sketch it in more detail.

Three times Rupert flew the BE2c back and forth the length of the warship, in order that Perys should miss no detail of the vessel and its armament.

By this time the shell bursts had moved closer to the aeroplane as the aim of the German gunners improved. When one burst so close that Perys felt quite certain shrapnel from it must have hit them, Rupert signalled it was time to go. He turned the BE2c in a breathtaking manoeuvre that would have jettisoned his passenger had he not been strapped in, and headed back towards the coast of Cornwall, out of range of the guns that had wasted so many shells trying to blast them from the sky.

13

Soon the BE2c was once more flying over the land mass of the Lizard peninsula. They were much lower now and the German warship had long since disappeared out of sight beyond the horizon.

Rupert was evidently seeking a suitable landing ground. As Perys hurriedly put the finishing touches to his sketch of the warship, calling on his memory, the aeroplane banked and began a steep descent.

Looking over the edge of the cockpit, Perys could see what appeared to be a mansion house set in spacious grounds. Leading to the house from the road was a long, straight driveway flanked by trees which were set well back.

As the aeroplane flew lower, the space between the trees did not seem as great as Perys had first believed and he thought that Rupert would make a preliminary pass over them to see if it was safe to land, but Rupert was wasting no time. Throttling back the engine, he lined the aeroplane up with the driveway and went straight in.

It was a perfect landing, but Perys thought Rupert might have overestimated the length of the drive. When the plane came to a halt and the engine was cut, they were within hailing distance of the front entrance of the impressive house.

It seemed the owner of the house thought they were far *too* close. He had been in a nearby orangery when the sound of the aircraft's engine disturbed his contemplation of the fruits of his tropical plants. He began hobbling towards the plane as the two flyers climbed to the ground, his stick waving menacingly in their direction every few steps.

'Oh Lord!' groaned Rupert. 'It's Admiral Sir Roger Trispen. I have no time to give him explanations. Deal with him for me, Perys. I need to go inside and make an urgent telephone call to the navy at Plymouth.'

Without waiting to discover whether Perys was in agreement with his request, Rupert hurried to the door of the house where a butler stood, clearly perplexed by the mode of transport used by these unexpected visitors.

A few words from Rupert were sufficient to convince the butler he had come to the house on a matter of the greatest importance. It was left to Perys to deal with the irate owner of the house.

Breathlessly reaching the aeroplane, the retired admiral waved his stick angrily at Perys. 'What the devil do you mean by bringing this infernal machine down in my garden, eh? You've frightened the lives out of the sheep on the home farm, had the chickens hanging themselves on the wire netting and my dogs have taken off so fast they're probably halfway to Truro by now!'

'I'm sorry, sir,' Perys apologised warily, watching the raised walking stick with considerable apprehension. 'It is an emergency.'

'Emergency . . . ? *Emergency?* If there's an emergency it's the one *you've* created! I'll need to send a groom out to look for my dogs. *That's* an emergency. Who are you, anyway? And what are you doing wasting your time down here with a flying machine when there's a war going on in France, eh?'

'I'm Perys Tremayne, sir. The aeroplane is being piloted by my cousin, Rupert – Rupert Pilkington. He's inside making a telephone call.'

'Using my telephone? We'll soon see about that . . .'

As the admiral turned to make his way to the house, Perys hurriedly explained, 'He's telephoning the navy at Plymouth, sir. To tell them of the German warship we sighted off the Lizard.'

Perys's words stopped the old man in his tracks. Turning back to Perys he snapped, 'You've seen a German ship? A warship? What sort of vessel was it?'

'I don't know, sir – but Rupert had me sketch it from the air. I have the sketch in the aeroplane . . .'

Relieved that the admiral's anger seemed to have left him for a moment, Perys hurried to the aeroplane and took the drawing from the cockpit. When he handed the sketch to the irate man, it was studied in silence for some minutes. Then, no longer angry, Sir Roger demanded, 'You've seen this ship off the Lizard? In which direction was she heading?'

'East, sir, and there's no doubt about it being

German. It was firing at us as we flew close enough to make the drawing.'

'You're damned lucky they didn't bring you down. You've just seen the *Dortmund*. It's a fast, heavy cruiser, one of Germany's most powerful warships. I don't know who your cousin is speaking to, but I'll get on to the flag officer in Plymouth right away. Immediate action needs to be taken and they'll take a sight more notice of an admiral than some RFC officer.'

Once inside the house, Admiral Sir Roger Trispen quickly displayed the qualities that had earned him elevation to senior naval rank. The duty officer to whom Rupert had been talking had been inclined to cast doubt on the veracity of the Royal Flying Corps officer's report. However, when Sir Roger took over the telephone the naval officer swiftly put him through to the flag officer, a fellow admiral.

Ten minutes later, Sir Roger replaced the telephone earpiece on the instrument and turned to his visitors with an air of great satisfaction. 'Well, gentlemen, it seems that even an ageing, retired admiral is still capable of serving his country, although if the *Dortmund* is intercepted – as it must be – a great many sailors' lives will be saved and the country will have you to thank. The British navy is blockading the North Sea to prevent German warships leaving their dock-yards. It won't be expecting an attack from such a powerful ship coming from seaward. No doubt the *Dortmund*'s captain was hoping to slip through the Dover Straits during the night and catch us napping. Thanks to you two, the tables will have been well and truly turned. Can I offer you both a drink to celebrate your success?'

Rupert declined the invitation on behalf of both of them, explaining that he needed to return to Heligan and make arrangements for his aircraft to be guarded overnight by a couple of the Heligan workers. He had given up all thoughts of returning to the Central Flying School at Upavon that evening. It would be foolish to risk losing his way in the darkness. Besides, the School also instructed pilots in the skills required for night flying. The unexpected arrival of another aeroplane could pose a serious danger to a novice pilot.

The return of the BE2c to Heligan created even more excitement than its earlier arrival. Word had spread via the Heligan servants that Rupert and Perys would be returning, and a number of the occupants of surrounding farms and houses had gathered to witness their arrival.

Among their number, Perys caught sight of Annie. He waved to her before climbing stiffly from the aeroplane, proud that she had been present to see him return from the flight.

Annie gave a brief, self-conscious acknowledgement of his greeting, pleased to have been singled out by Perys.

'That's a very pretty young woman,' commented Rupert, who had witnessed the exchange.

'Her father has a farm just over there . . .' Perys waved a hand in the vague direction of Tregassick. 'Her brother is a coachman at Heligan.'

Maude and her two daughters arrived on the scene at that moment and Perys was relieved when Rupert did not pursue the subject of his relationship with

Annie in front of them. However, he was embarrassed that Annie witnessed the overeffusive and proprietary welcome given to him by the younger of the two sisters.

He looked for her, to gauge her reaction, but failed to see her. She appeared to have left.

A number of the Heligan house workers were among the spectators and before Perys and Rupert left the field accompanied by Maude, Morwenna and Arabella, Rupert arranged for four of the men to take turns guarding the aeroplane overnight, with orders to allow no one anywhere near it.

Talk over dinner that evening was dominated by the events of the day. Rupert was generous with praise for what he referred to as 'Perys's cool courage' when the BE2c had been subjected to the considerable firepower of the German cruiser. He made it clear it was the sketch made by Perys that had enabled Admiral Sir Roger Trispen to identify the warship immediately and so pass valuable information on to the authorities.

'Weren't you frightened at all?' Arabella asked Perys, gazing at him wide-eyed.

'To be perfectly honest I was far too busy making certain my sketch of the ship was accurate,' Perys said. 'Besides, Rupert kept changing the aeroplane's height and distance from the ship. The Germans just couldn't get the range right.'

Arabella's expression of hero worship for her young relative concerned Maude, but there was more praise to come from Rupert.

'You showed more courage than a great many observers I have known, Perys. I shall be including that fact in my report of the incident. From what I have seen of you I am convinced you will make a first-class pilot. When the time comes for you to apply to join the Royal Flying Corps I will be happy to provide you with a reference saying exactly that.'

14

After dinner Perys decided to check that the aeroplane was safe and being properly guarded. Arabella created such a fuss about accompanying him that Maude agreed – on condition that a reluctant Morwenna went with them.

Seated on the lawn outside the great house, overlooking the well-kept and colourful gardens, Rupert was enjoying a drink with Maude. From somewhere far away a cow was complaining about something, otherwise all was warm and peaceful.

After taking a sip from his glass, Rupert placed it on the table in front of him and said, 'This seems a world away from the tragic mayhem in France. I feel quite guilty that I should be enjoying myself in such a fashion while so many good men are out there fighting for their lives.'

'You haven't exactly been divorced from the war,' Maude pointed out. 'In fact, I would say that what you have achieved today has made a very valuable contribution.'

'Perys is the one who should be given the credit for that,' Rupert pointed out. 'It was he who first saw the smoke from the *Dortmund* and who produced an excellent sketch while we were under fire. He behaved exceptionally well. If he was not so keen to become a pilot I would persuade him to join the Royal Flying Corps as an observer – and have him posted to my squadron. Many pilots owe their lives to a good observer.'

Maude sighed. 'It seems tragic that young men like Perys should be thrown into war so soon after leaving school. Life has so much more to offer them.'

'I agree with you,' Rupert said, seriously, 'but the war will claim the lives of a great many young men like Perys before it is won. However, if enough of them possess a similar courage, the war will be brought to a speedy conclusion. He has a cool head in an emergency.'

'He will not be found lacking in courage, either.' Maude proceeded to tell Rupert of the part played by Perys in the rescue of the Russian seamen off Mevagissey.

'I am more convinced than ever that he will do well in the Royal Flying Corps,' Rupert commented. 'There are some people who go through life without anything happening to disturb their routine. Others seem to trip over adventure wherever they are and whatever they do. Perys is one of the latter. It is hardly surprising the two girls are so fond of him.'

Aware that there was more to Rupert's last remark than met the eye, Maude admitted, 'Arabella has a young girl's crush on him, but it will pass. As for Morwenna . . . she likes Perys, certainly – as we *all* like him – but there is no more to it than that. To be truthful, we all feel terribly sorry for him. Life has been quite unfair to Perys, and his grandfather's behaviour has been nothing short of scandalous. There would appear to have been no affection at all in the life of poor Perys. I find it incredibly sad.'

It was Rupert's turn to remain silent for some minutes before saying, 'Perhaps it is time someone showed Perys the regard in which we all hold him.'

Maude looked at him enquiringly. 'What are you suggesting?'

'Well, as I see it, the thing he wants more than anything in the world right now is to become a pilot with the Royal Flying Corps. He *should* have no difficulty in achieving such an ambition, but there is a way his acceptance can be virtually guaranteed . . .'

'How?'

'By ensuring he is in possession of a flying licence before he applies to join. Brooklands is where many pilots have qualified in the past. It is in the process of being taken over by our people, but there are still a number of instructors and examiners there. I know one particularly well. He is acknowledged as the best flying instructor in the country. I would be more than happy to arrange for Perys to take a flying course with him. With a pilot's licence a commission in the Royal Flying Corps is assured. Cousin Edward's father may have influence here in Cornwall, but it does not extend to the RFC. Besides, we are finding that those who march to the beat of their own drum make the best pilots.'

'This flying course . . . is it expensive?'

'Seventy-five pounds. But I will be happy to foot the bill and make the necessary arrangements for accommodation for Perys while he's under instruction at Brooklands.'

'How long will it take?'

'If he's lucky enough to have a spell of good weather he could easily pick up his licence in no more than a week or so.'

'As speedily as that?' Maude was incredulous. 'In that case, I will be happy to accommodate him at my home in Knightsbridge, although that might pose problems for him in reaching Brooklands each day.'

'I think I can solve that problem,' Rupert declared. 'I own a Sunbeam motor-cycle that my father bought me when I first began flying. It has hardly had any use because I have developed a taste for driving his motor-car. Perys can have the use of it.' He hesitated before adding, 'Although I have said that Perys should be able to complete his flying course in little more than a week, if the weather is *not* fine it might take a great deal longer. Is that likely to pose you any problems in view of Arabella's infatuation with him?'

'It might – if Arabella had nothing else to think about. But I intend taking the girls back to London in a couple of days' time. Casualties from our army in France are arriving at hospitals in the city. There will be work for Morwenna – and for me too. I have arranged for Arabella to commence her nursing training immediately upon our return. She will be far too busy to think of anything else for quite some time.'

Rupert smiled. 'I can see you have everything in hand, Aunt Maude. Now, I think it is time I prepared myself for the morning. I wish to make an early start. We will tell Perys of our plans for him over breakfast and see if he approves.'

The proposals put to Perys the next morning rendered him almost speechless. Unused to such thoughtfulness and generosity, he could only stammer out his thanks. Suddenly, all he wanted in life had become possible.

'When will I be able to begin my lessons?' he asked. 'And what shall I do until then?'

'You will remain at Heligan,' Maude said, with her usual authority. 'I will send a telegram to your great-uncle Hugh explaining what is happening and follow it up with a lengthy letter. He has no plans to return here in the near future so he is certain to agree.'

'Then it would seem that all is settled,' declared Rupert. 'I will have the motor-cycle sent here right away, Perys. It should give you plenty of time to practise on it. Then you can either ride it to London, or take it on the train with you, whichever you prefer.'

'You are all being so kind, I just don't know how to thank you.' Perys felt foolishly close to tears.

'I should be thanking *you*,' declared Rupert. 'So too should their Lordships at the Admiralty. They were unaware that a German heavy cruiser like the *Dortmund* was on the loose. They thought they had it bottled up in one of the North Sea ports with the rest of the German navy. It could have proved very embarrassing and not a little costly had you not spotted it. When I reach the Central Flying School I will find out what happened as a result of your keen-sightedness and accurate drawing and let you know.' Leaning back in his chair, he glanced around the table, his gaze resting on Morwenna for slightly longer than on the others. 'Now, regrettably, I must be on my way. It has been a most enjoyable and exciting visit to Cornwall, but I have much to do. I hope you young people are coming to see me off?'

The reply was instant and unanimous. A few minutes later the four were making their way to where the aeroplane had been left overnight.

The sleepy guards had performed their duties well and were rewarded by Rupert with a guinea each. The sum represented almost a full week's wages for the men and was gratefully received.

Twenty minutes later, Perys, Morwenna and Arabella were waving farewell as Rupert taxied his aeroplane downwind before turning and with throttle wide open accelerating across the field. The BE2c climbed into the sky, gaining height before banking and heading eastwards towards the plains of Wiltshire.

Perys watched with mixed feelings as the aeroplane grew smaller until it was no more than a distant dot in the sky. He had a very real sense of loss. He had liked Rupert very much and, flying in the BE2c, he had felt a sense of exhilaration that was like nothing he had ever experienced before. Only one thing could have made it completely perfect: to be in control of the aeroplane. To be the pilot.

'It won't be very long before it is you soaring away into the sky, flying your own aeroplane . . .' Morwenna's words broke into his thoughts.

'Do you think you will *really* enjoy being a pilot?' Arabella asked. 'It looks terribly dangerous.'

Not wishing to reveal the true depth of his feeling for flying, Perys replied merely, 'I want to fly very much.'

'Arabella is right though, Perys, it *is* dangerous.'

Perys wondered whether Morwenna was thinking of him, or of the pilot of the aeroplane that had just disappeared in the sky. Rupert had kissed both sisters, but his embrace for Morwenna had showed considerably more warmth than that given to her sister.

Perys felt that a marriage between the two would meet with unanimous approval in the family. Yet again the thought reminded him of the fact that *he* was not fully accepted as a respectable Tremayne.

The feeling remained with him even after Arabella said, 'It's going to be fun having you stay with us in London, Perys. I do hope it takes far longer than you expect to gain your pilot's licence.'

15

Maude and her two daughters left Heligan in mid-September. Morwenna was pleased to be returning to London because she knew she would be doing something to help the war effort by caring for the soldiers who had been wounded in the desperate fighting taking place in France and Belgium.

Things were going seriously wrong for the Allies. A friend had telephoned Maude to say that casualties from the battle-front were swamping the London hospitals. Medical staff were finding it hard to cope with the unexpectedly high numbers and every available doctor and nurse was being called in to help. Morwenna would be kept busy.

Arabella was thrilled that she too would be following in the family tradition. However, she was tearful at the imminent parting from Perys.

'You must come to London soon,' she said to him after successfully getting him on his own for a few moments at St Austell station on the day of their departure. 'Please don't forget me, Perys. I shall be thinking of you every moment of the day, and for much of the night, too.'

'I shall never forget any of you, Arabella. You, Morwenna and your mother have all been very kind to me.'

'That is *not* what I meant, Perys, as you must know very well,' Arabella said, petulantly. 'You are particularly special to me.'

Perys was saved from further embarrassment by the return of Maude and Morwenna, accompanied by the station master.

'The train is on time and will be here in a few minutes, Perys,' Maude said, choosing not to observe the tears that had welled up in Arabella's eyes. 'We all look forward to having you to stay with us in London very soon. In the meantime, you have a new toy to play with at Heligan. The station master has informed me that the motor-cycle Rupert promised to send you arrived on the overnight train from London. You can collect it when we have gone and either ride it back to Heligan or have it secured to the carriage and learn to ride it at your leisure.'

'I think I had better allow Martin to take it on the carriage and learn to ride it at Heligan,' Perys replied. 'I have never ridden a motor-cycle before. I would hate to have an accident on my first day. It is very kind of Rupert to loan it to me.' Changing the subject, he said, 'You have been very kind to me too, Aunt Maude. You, Morwenna and Arabella. I can't remember spending a happier few weeks. I shall miss you all.'

'We are going to miss you too,' Maude said. Stepping forward, she embraced him warmly and kissed him on the cheek. 'I wish we had all met many years ago. Never mind, you will soon be joining us in London and will be made very welcome there.'

At that moment the train came into view along the track, a shrill blast from the locomotive's whistle giving a warning of its approach.

It hissed to a noisy halt and for a few minutes all was bustle as Maude and the two girls were settled in their carriage, two station porters helping with their luggage. Then, with another shrill message from the whistle, the train jerked into motion.

Arabella waved from the open window of the compartment until she passed from Perys's view. He was feeling very alone on the station when he was joined by Martin.

'The station master just showed me the motor-bike that's arrived for you, Master Perys. It's a beauty! I've had it roped on to the back of the coach. I suggest we call in at the garage and buy some petrol before we go back to Heligan.'

The motor-cycle was a two-geared Sunbeam and appeared to be new. Perys thought that once again Rupert had provided him with the means to enjoy a new and exciting experience.

There was a bag strapped to the machine's pillion. When Perys removed and opened it he discovered it contained instructions for driving and maintaining the motor-cycle. Keeping the bag with him, he decided he would read the instructions on the journey to Heligan.

*   *   *

Perys took his first ride on the motor-cycle immediately after lunch. At first he had some difficulty starting the machine, but once he grasped the purpose of the ignition lever the rest was comparatively simple.

He had ridden pedal-cycles at school, so balancing on the two-wheeled machine posed no particular problem. He made a noisy exit along the Heligan House driveway, pursued by the applause of the house servants and gardeners who had gathered to watch his maiden ride on a machine that was still very much a novelty in the Cornish countryside.

By the time he had negotiated the long driveway to the road he was confident he would be able to maintain his balance on the machine. Half-an-hour later, after putting the motor-cycle through its paces along narrow lanes, he had mastered everything except changing gear from low to high and, even more difficult perhaps, from high to low.

However, by the time he approached the lane that led to Tregassick Farm he felt sufficiently confident of his riding skills to want to show them off to Annie. Turning off the road, he headed for the farm.

The sound of the Sunbeam's engine sent geese and chickens fleeing in noisy complaint from the farmyard, and had calves and heifers crashing heavily against the wooden barriers of their pens.

Walter Bray was repairing a manger in the milking parlour when Perys made his unintentionally dramatic entrance. The farmer came into the yard, hammer in hand, as a sheepish Perys switched off the motor-cycle's engine.

'I'm sorry, Mr Bray, I seem to have caused some consternation among your livestock.'

A soft-spoken, mild-mannered man, Walter Bray said, 'That's a good word for it, Master Perys. I suspect 'tisn't only the livestock you've mazed.' Walter had seen Annie show herself briefly at the farmhouse door to witness the arrival of Perys. She had quickly disappeared inside. 'Still, there's no harm done. They'll settle down again in a minute or two.'

'I came to show Annie – and you, of course – the motor-bike. Isn't it a beauty?'

'I suppose it is if you like that sort of thing. I'd rather be sitting on something that has a leg on each corner myself. But then I'm a bit old now to want to change my ways. Go on inside the house. Our Annie is in there doing the housework for her ma, who's down in the village washing and cleaning for a sick aunt of hers. Annie will no doubt appreciate this machine of yours more than me. She might even have a mug of something and a piece of cake for you. Meanwhile, I'll get on with this manger. I want to finish it before milking time.'

At that moment Annie reappeared at the door of the farmhouse, noticeably tidier than before. As her father returned to his primitive carpentry, Perys called to her, 'Come and look at the motor-bike, Annie. Rupert sent it for me to use while I'm waiting to join the Royal Flying Corps.'

Seemingly unimpressed with the motor-cycle, Annie said, 'You're really going to become a pilot then?'

'Of course! I was certain even before I went up with Rupert. Since then I've been determined that nothing will stop me . . . but do come and look at the motor-bike, Annie. Isn't it a beauty?'

In truth, it was the first motor-cycle Annie had ever

really looked at, although she had seen one before. Edward Tremayne had owned one and had often been seen riding about the countryside, before he rode it into a ditch and caused such damage that it was never repaired. She agreed that Perys's motor-cycle was indeed 'a beauty'.

'Would you like a ride on it?' Perys asked, unexpectedly.

'Me? How? I mean . . . where would I sit, there's only one seat?'

'It has a pillion. You can sit side-saddle.'

Annie cast a meaningful glance towards the milking parlour. 'I really shouldn't. I'm supposed to be working in the house.'

'We'll make it a short ride. Just as far as the lane and back.'

Annie glanced towards the milking parlour once more before saying, 'All right then – but don't start the engine until we're away from the farm.'

Perys pushed the motor-cycle along the farm track until they were well clear of the buildings. Then, straddling the machine, he said, 'I'll kick-start it and as soon as the engine is running, sit on the pillion. But make certain your skirt is tight around your legs so it won't catch in the wheel – and hold on tight.'

'What do I hold on to, there's nothing—?'

Adjusting the levers on the handlebars, Perys kicked down on the starter pedal and the engine burst into life immediately.

'Hold on to me – and hold tight,' he repeated.

Seated on the motor-cycle, he held it steady as Annie settled herself on the pillion and gripped his waist gingerly.

The machine started with a jerk that brought Annie's arms encircling his body. Then they were wobbling alarmingly along the track with Annie screaming in mock terror as Perys fought to maintain balance. He eventually brought the motor-cycle under control, although Annie still clung to him tightly as though in imminent danger of falling off.

When they reached the lane that ran along the end of the farm track he successfully brought the machine to a halt and looked back over his shoulder to ask, 'Did you enjoy that?'

'I . . . I think so, but you frightened the daylights out of me when we started off!'

He grinned at her. 'It had *me* worried for a moment or two. Never mind, if you get off now I'll turn it around and give you a ride back home.'

'All right, but stop short of the farm. It's nearly milking-time and the cows will be close to the gate. I don't want you frightening them so much they'll give sour milk.'

Perys waited until Annie was settled on the pillion once more, then, engaging the first of the machine's two gears, he released the clutch and they set off on the return journey to Tregassick Farm.

It was all downhill and the motor-cycle got off to a less uncertain start. Unfortunately, when it was time to bring the machine to a halt, it was apparent that Perys had not yet fully mastered the art of motor-cycling. He managed to stall the engine when it was still in high gear, and at the same time the front wheel dropped into a deep rut in the track.

Before Perys could do anything to prevent it, the motor-cycle fell over. Fortunately, there was a high bank alongside and Annie toppled back on this.

Despite his best efforts to ensure that neither Annie nor the motor-cycle suffered harm, Perys found himself lying on the bank beside her.

'Are you all right, Annie?' he asked anxiously, as he sat up.

Much to his relief, she began giggling.

Looking down at her, Perys had an overwhelming urge to kiss her – and immediately substituted action for thought.

He took her by surprise, but she neither responded, nor resisted.

Nonplussed by her failure to react, Perys pulled back.

Still without moving, Annie looked up at him and she was no longer giggling. 'Why did you do that?'

'I . . . I'm sorry, Annie.'

'Why did you do it? Why did you kiss me?' She repeated her question, ignoring his apology.

'Because I wanted to. I think I've wanted to for a very long time.'

She studied his expression for some moments before saying, 'If you really mean that, then you've no need to be sorry about it. I'm not.'

He looked down at her in disbelief, before kissing her again. This time her arms went about him and she responded. Suddenly, she moved her head to one side and pushed him away.

'We'd better stop this before Pa finishes what he's doing and comes out into the yard. If he saw us like this I'd be in trouble. Besides, I've got work in the house to finish before Ma gets home.'

Perys's heart was thumping so violently he was

surprised Annie could not hear it. He stood up and Annie did the same, brushing grass and a few leaves from her dress.

'You . . . you won't mind if I call to see you again?'

'I'll be very upset if you don't, Perys Tremayne.' Smiling at his genuine relief, she said, 'But if you want me to ride on that machine again you'd better bring a cushion with you. That pillion is very uncomfortable.' Reaching out a hand, she touched his arm in a gesture of affection. 'Perhaps you should get in a little more practice before you take anyone else for a ride. I wouldn't like to think of someone else falling off the motor-bike with you.'

16

The driveway to Heligan was much smoother than the rough track which led to Tregassick Farm. Turning into it, Perys was about to open up the motor-cycle throttle when a young woman stepped out from behind some bushes, causing him to brake sharply and stall the engine once again.

As the woman approached him, Perys said, angrily, 'That was a stupid thing to do. You might have got us both killed. Who are you, anyway?'

'Eliza Dunn,' the girl replied, with no hint of contrition, 'and there's no need to talk to me like that. You wouldn't speak to Annie Bray in the same way, I'm sure. I stepped out to stop you because I need to talk to you.'

Perys could think of nothing Eliza might need to discuss with him and he said so, adding, as an afterthought, 'Unless, of course, it's something to do with your father?'

'It's nothing to do with him, he's coming along fine. He doesn't know I'm at Heligan and it's better that it stays that way . . . but we can't talk here. There's an old shed a little way off the drive, a bit farther on. Unless you'd like to take me somewhere else on your motor-bike?'

There was a boldness about Eliza that perturbed Perys, even while it stirred a certain reckless excitement within him. However, he settled for discretion.

'I think it might be better if we stay here and talk.'

Fingering the metal pillion of the machine he was still straddling, Eliza asked, 'Have you given Annie a ride on your motor-bike yet?'

Perys was startled and he wondered whether there was any hidden meaning behind Eliza's question. He dismissed his concern immediately. She could not possibly have seen he and Annie on the motor-cycle and managed to reach the Heligan driveway before him.

Eliza was not expecting a reply. 'I heard the sound of a motor-bike and could tell it was on the Tregassick Farm track. I thought it might be Edward. He has a motor-bike, you know? He gave me a ride on it more than once.'

'I believe he had an accident and damaged it before I came to Heligan.' Even as he replied, Perys wondered why Edward would choose to take Eliza riding on his motor-cycle. The fact that she had used Edward's Christian name in such a familiar fashion had not escaped him.

He doubted very much whether such familiarity from a village girl would meet with the approval of his arrogant distant cousin.

But Eliza was talking once more. '. . . I was hoping it *was* Edward. I need to speak to him.'

'Edward is not at Heligan. He hasn't been here for some time, as I am quite sure you know.'

Perys felt uncomfortable talking about Edward, especially with Eliza. He was aware of the gossip linking them and the possible implication of her need to speak with him.

'I knew he'd gone away from Heligan, but when I heard a motor-bike up this way I thought he might have come back.'

'I'm afraid he hasn't, so if there's nothing else you want to say . . .'

At that moment Perys heard the sound of hooves on the lane. A moment later a number of horses turned into the Heligan driveway. Riding the lead horse was Martin, with others tied in a line behind him. He was returning from having them shod in the smithy at the nearby village of Pentewan.

When Martin saw Perys with Eliza, he appeared startled. Passing them by, he gave Perys a perfunctory wave, but his expression was one of disapproval.

Remembering his earlier conversations with Annie, Perys would have been much happier had her brother not seen him talking to Eliza. But there was nothing he could do about it now.

Returning his attention to Eliza, he said, 'Now I've told you Edward is not at Heligan, I'll be getting back there. I suggest you don't make a habit of jumping out in front of motor-vehicles or you'll get yourself killed.'

'I doubt if that would upset any of the Tremayne family – not even Edward,' Eliza retorted, bitterly.

She had momentarily allowed her feelings to override prudence and Perys could not help feeling sorry for her. If she was in the sort of trouble he suspected, Perys doubted very much whether Edward would face up to his responsibilities and take care of this young Mevagissey girl.

Looking at her now, memories came flooding back to him of what it felt like to be deeply unhappy about something and being unable to confide in anyone.

'Look, Eliza, if you're in trouble you can tell me. If I can help, I will.'

For a few moments Perys thought she might be about to disclose what was worrying her. Instead, she shook her head. 'Why should *you* want to help me? From what I've heard said, it was your fault he went away in the first place. If you hadn't been so ready with your fists he'd still be here and I wouldn't need to be looking for him.'

She was angry, but Perys realised there was no sense becoming involved in an argument with her.

'Then there's no more to be said. I'll be getting back to Heligan.'

Adjusting the controls on the handlebars of the motor-cycle, he was about to kick-start the engine when Eliza said, 'Wait a minute . . . please!'

Looking up at her, Perys once again felt great sympathy for the girl. For just a moment he had seen an expression of desperation on her face.

'If you really want to help, could you give me Edward's address? I'll write to him.'

'All I know is that he lives somewhere in Devon,' Perys explained. 'That isn't a great deal of help, I know, but I'll find out what it is and give it to you.

Where will I be able to find you? You won't want me calling at your house with it.'

She shook her head emphatically. 'I work in a house at Heligan Mill every morning and finish at twelve o'clock. Soon after that I'm at the edge of the village, where the path from the mill comes out on the road. If you get the address you can give it to me there. When do you think you'll have it for me?'

'Give me a day or two. I can't ask for it outright – but I *will* get it for you,' Perys promised.

He knew he would probably not be helping Eliza a great deal – and doing his distant cousin no favour at all. However, he owed Edward nothing.

Moving closer to the motor-cycle once more, Eliza gave him another of her bold looks. 'I suppose you wouldn't like to give me a ride to the edge of the village? There's a path through the woods that Edward used to take with me—'

Kicking the engine into life, Perys gave her an incredulous smile and shook his head. 'I'm off to Heligan, Eliza. I'll have the address for you as soon as possible.'

17

A few days later, with a piece of paper on which was written Edward's address tucked in a pocket, Perys was about to set off to pay a visit to Tregassick Farm before meeting with Eliza. He was almost at the door when the telephone in the high-ceilinged hall began ringing. He reached it just ahead of the maid who came hurrying from the rear of the house.

It was Rupert and he was jubilant. 'Perys, I have some news for you. The German ship we saw, the *Dortmund* – our warships caught up with it and sank it!'

It seemed the action had taken place the day after the ship had been sighted, but the Royal Navy had kept it quiet because they wanted the Germans to believe their raider was still at large.

From survivors, information had been gleaned that it was intended the *Dortmund* would mount a fast and unexpected attack on the British ships guarding the narrowest section of the English Channel. It was hoped that such an action would draw off the naval vessels blockading the German ports in the North Sea and so allow the German battle fleet to put to sea.

'Your keen eyesight has saved a great many British lives, Perys. What's more, I have been recommended for an award – the DSO!'

'That's wonderful news!' said a delighted Perys. 'But you deserve it. Flying backwards and forwards alongside the *Dortmund* when it was shooting at us required both skill and courage.'

'It would all have been in vain had you not made such an excellent sketch of the ship,' Rupert pointed out. 'Had Admiral Trispen not recognised it immediately, no one would have believed us. I did suggest you should receive an award too, but it would appear there is no appropriate medal for a civilian who shows conspicuous courage when caught up in a war situation. Indeed, I have been told I am fortunate not to be court-martialled for having an unauthorised passenger in the aeroplane in the first place!'

'You won't get into trouble?' Perys asked, anxiously. 'It's not likely to jeopardise your DSO?'

'No. I told the commanding officer at Upavon that not only were you intending to join the RFC, but that I needed you in the aeroplane with me to look for a likely airfield, because of your detailed knowledge of the Cornish countryside.'

'But . . . I know nothing of Cornwall beyond the Heligan area,' Perys said.

Rupert chuckled. 'I know that, and so do you, but the War Office does not, and we won't enlighten them. Besides, by the time anyone gets around to seriously querying your right to be in the aeroplane you'll be in the RFC too.'

'Have you heard something?' It was the turn of Perys to be excited.

'As a matter of fact I have. You are to report to Nick Malloch at Brooklands at nine o'clock on the fifth of October to begin your flying course.'

Startled, Perys said, 'But that's next Monday!' It was now Thursday.

'That's right,' Rupert said, cheerfully. 'And Aunt Maude is expecting you on Saturday. I have also managed to pull a few strings in order to have you examined and issued with your flying licence as soon as possible after your course. If all goes well you have an interview with the RFC appointments officer at the War Office on November the sixth. I have said you will have your licence by then.'

'Do you *really* think I will qualify for my licence at the first attempt?'

Rupert could detect the excitement in Perys's voice, but he had another surprise for him. Abruptly changing the subject, he asked, 'How are you getting on with the motor-cycle?'

'It's great fun. I've learned where the brakes are and haven't fallen off since yesterday!'

'Then I have no doubt you will make an excellent pilot.' Rupert sounded amused. 'As you know, Perys, the machine was bought for me by my father. I spoke to him last night. He is so delighted that my name has been put forward for a DSO that he has said I can have his motor-car. It's a Rolls-Royce and absolutely superb. And in view of the very important part you played in identifying the *Dortmund*, without any official recognition, I said I would like you to have the motor-cycle. He thinks it a splendid idea.'

'You mean . . . I can keep it as my own?'

'Yes – if you want it, of course.'

'If I want it! Rupert, how can I thank you? You've been so very generous.'

Perys was choked with emotion and dared say no more. He had experienced very little kindness in his life. It was all too much for him.

'Well, if you feel so disposed, perhaps you will put in a good word for me with Morwenna while you are in London. I've not seen her since leaving Heligan. I was hoping to get to London to see her this weekend, but I have orders to rejoin my squadron in France. I set off in the morning. Before I go I will put what I have said to you in writing and send it to Maude, just in case you forget where you have to go and when.'

Perys knew he was not likely to forget a single word. Rupert's instructions were so important to him that they were already burned indelibly in his brain. After stammering out his thanks, he wished Rupert 'Good Luck in France,' then hurried outside the house to find *his* motor-cycle. He wanted to share his incredible good fortune with Annie.

18

Although Perys had tried to keep himself busy at Heligan in recent days, he had thought a great deal about Annie and of what had occurred between them when they had fallen off the motor-cycle together. Although it had not been planned, he was aware it had not been mere spur-of-the-moment opportunism on his part either. There had been a feeling of inevitability about it that he recognised. Had they not fallen off the motor-cycle, they would have kissed at some other time and place.

Perys had spent very little time with girls during his school days, but he had met enough of them to realise his feelings for Annie went deeper than friendship. He hoped she might feel the same about him, but did not know how he should go about finding out. He could not contemplate simply asking her directly.

Today, he cut the engine of the motor-cycle before

reaching the Bray farm, in order not to frighten the livestock as he had on his previous visit. Propping the motor-cycle against the bank alongside the track, he walked the remainder of the way to the farmhouse.

His arrival took Annie by surprise. She was cleaning out the pig-sties and was dismayed that he should see her in such a dishevelled and grubby state. However, this was not the reason why she made no attempt to greet him and did not reply when he called out to her.

Puzzled and not a little hurt, Perys made his way to the sty where she was working. Ignoring him, she continued her work. Perys began to feel ill-at-ease. Eventually, he asked, 'Are you having second thoughts about what happened when you had a ride on the motor-bike, Annie, or is it just that I've come visiting at a busy time for you?'

'I have work to do, if that's what you mean,' she replied, ignoring the first part of his question.

'Can I help?'

'There's not room for pigs and *two* people in a sty.'

'Well, perhaps I can clean out one of the other sties,' Perys said, patiently. 'If the work is finished early, perhaps we can go for another ride?'

'Do you go about the countryside offering rides on your motor-bike to every girl you meet? Or is it just me and Eliza Dunn? Did you manage to fall off with her as well?'

As she was speaking, Annie jabbed so hard with the large five-pronged farm fork she was using that it struck sparks from the stone floor.

Perys had suspected that Annie's off-hand attitude

might have had something to do with the fact that Martin had seen him talking to Eliza. Now he was left in no doubt.

'Eliza has never had a ride on the motor-bike – not on mine, anyway.'

'You're not denying you were with her after you left me that day?'

'It would be foolish of me to deny it when Martin saw me talking to her – but talking is *all* I did, and it wasn't of my making.'

Perys was uncomfortably aware that he had Edward's address in his pocket ready to give to Eliza when he left Annie today, but he could not tell her about their conversation.

'As a matter of fact I was very angry with her. She stepped in front of me and might easily have caused me to have an accident.'

'I've no doubt she was eager to show you how sorry she was,' Annie said, acidly.

'On the contrary, she was indignant that I should have complained about her stupidity.'

Only slightly mollified, Annie asked, 'What was she doing up at Heligan anyway?'

Perys did not like lying to Annie, but he felt that telling her the truth could be very embarrassing for the unfortunate Mevagissey girl.

'I think she'd gone up there to meet someone, probably one of the Heligan servants.'

'Eliza would only walk that far from home to meet a man, and her sights are set higher than house-servants,' Annie said, meaningfully, but Perys felt her anger with him had dissipated somewhat. He repeated his offer to help her clean out the pig-sties.

'Even if they are cleaned out quickly there's no chance of my coming for a ride with you,' said Annie. 'Ma wouldn't allow it. She has lots of jobs waiting for me in the house.'

'Never mind.' Perys managed to hide his disappointment. 'At least if I'm working with you we can talk – and I have a lot to tell you.'

In spite of what Annie had said earlier, there *was* room for two in a pig-sty, and as they worked Perys told her of Rupert's telephone call.

'This award that's being given to Rupert . . . it's for bravery, isn't it?'

'Yes.'

'Then you must have been in danger too.'

'The Germans were firing at us, yes, but they weren't very good shots.'

'You didn't say anything about that at the time.'

Perys shrugged. 'There was really no reason why I should. They missed us.'

'And this is the sort of thing that will be happening to you every day once you become a pilot and join the Royal Flying Corps?'

'I don't suppose I'll meet up with many German ships in France.'

'You know very well what I mean, Perys. When you're up in your aeroplane there will be people shooting at you.'

'I suppose so – after all, there's a war going on. But I would rather be in the air, where my survival depends to a great extent on my own skill, than fighting on the ground.'

'I wish you didn't need to go and fight at all,' Annie said, unhappily. 'I wish *no one* needed to go. Martin

119

has been talking again about leaving Heligan and joining the army.'

'A lot of the men at Heligan are doing the same,' Perys pointed out. 'Two of the gardeners and one of the grooms left this week.'

'When are *you* leaving?'

'On Saturday. That's why I wanted to see you today. I'm taking the motor-bike up to London on the train. I'll be starting my flying lessons on Monday.'

'So soon!'

Annie's dismay was not feigned and her concern gave Perys a warm feeling. 'Yes, but once the course is over and I've had my interview at the War Office I'll probably come back to Heligan until I'm sent for. That's if they want me, of course.'

'They'll want you,' Annie said, confidently.

Unhappy at the thought of Perys going off to war, she was relieved he would not be going away for ever when he left for London on Saturday. Her mother had told her more than once that she should not allow herself to become too fond of Perys. She had reminded Annie that he was a Tremayne – despite the unfortunate circumstances of his birth – and pointed out, yet again, that members of the gentry did not marry the daughters of struggling tenant farmers.

The conversation between Perys and Annie was brought to an end by Harriet Bray. Coming from the house, she was horrified to see Perys helping to clean out the pigs, declaring that it was not work for 'a gentleman'. Telling Annie she wanted her to help in the house, Harriet invited Perys inside for something to eat and drink.

Mindful that he had promised to meet with Eliza

and give her Edward's address, Perys declined her offer after receiving an assurance that he might return the following evening, ostensibly to discuss with Martin the subject of enlisting in the army.

19

The spot where the path from Heligan Mill joined the road was opposite the Mevagissey cemetery, a burial ground sited on an impossibly steep hillside. Eliza was nowhere in sight and Perys thought she might still be working. But he would need to give the address to her today if she was to have it before he left Heligan.

Propping his motor-cycle against a high, grassy bank, he took a stroll along the path that led to the mill. There was a deserted farmhouse along here. He thought he would pass a few minutes looking it over.

There was a small barn between the road and the old farmhouse. Set into the hillside alongside the path, it contained a quantity of the new season's hay. As he passed by he thought he heard a sound inside.

It made him curious. There were unlikely to be animals inside because the hay was piled above the level of the small, barred windows set high in the walls.

He listened for a few minutes and heard voices

inside the barn; the low voices of a man and a woman. Then he heard other sounds and realised he was listening to a couple making love.

Vaguely amused, he walked on and looked at the deserted farmhouse, but the door was secured and he decided to return to his motor-cycle. He was halfway between the barn and his machine when he heard a sound. Looking around he saw a man he recognised as a Heligan gamekeeper emerge from the barn. A married man, his wife was a large, loud and aggressive woman who was employed at Heligan House as a washerwoman.

When the gamekeeper saw Perys he turned and hurried away in the opposite direction.

A short while later a woman came out of the barn. It was Eliza Dunn. By this time the gamekeeper had disappeared from view and Perys was standing by his motor-cycle.

Assuming he had observed nothing, when Eliza reached him she said, 'Sorry if I've kept you waiting. I was taken short and couldn't wait. It must be this cold easterly wind. Do you have Edward's address?'

'Yes, I have it.'

Perys was not certain he should give it to her in view of what he had just seen, but he decided that despite her faults, he liked Eliza more than he did Edward.

'Well, give it to me then. I'll be late enough getting home as it is.'

'Think yourself lucky I'm here at all,' Perys retorted, stung by her attitude. 'I am doing you a favour – and it's not one that would be appreciated by the family.'

'I don't care about your family, any more than they

care about me. I don't suppose Edward is going to be very pleased with what I have to tell him, either, but he will look after me.'

Perys doubted very much whether Edward had ever cared for anyone other than himself, but he did not put his thoughts into words.

'Here, take the address. I have better things to do than stay here listening to you.'

When Eliza took the piece of paper from him, Perys began manhandling the motor-cycle in readiness to return the way he had come.

'Wait! You don't really need to hurry away, do you? I'm sorry if I sound ungrateful, but it is particularly cold today. Couldn't we go somewhere out of this wind and talk . . . or something?'

Raising an eyebrow, Perys said, 'Don't you think you're in enough trouble, Eliza?'

'If I'm already in trouble it can't get much worse for me, can it? Anyway, why should you worry? I've heard you're going off to war soon. It'll give you something to think about when you're with all the other soldiers, fighting in France.'

Perys did not correct her assumption that he would be joining the army. Instead, he said, 'I'll be on my way now, Eliza, I've got things to do.'

'And Annie Bray to see, no doubt. If she's not careful she'll end up like me, and it would serve her right. She wouldn't look down her nose whenever she saw me then, that's for certain.'

'That's not likely to happen. Her name's not Eliza, and I'm certainly not Edward,' Perys said, aware that Eliza had just confirmed what he had suspected about her condition.

'Names have got nothing to do with it. She's a woman – for all her holier-than-thou ways – and you're a man. That's all it takes.'

Despite her boldness, loose morals and worldly way of talking, Perys believed Eliza was a very unhappy young woman. Not for the first time, he felt sorry for her.

Suddenly and unexpectedly, Eliza stepped forward and, before he guessed her intention, she kissed him warmly on the mouth. Stepping back, she said, 'Thank you for the address . . . if you ever *do* want to see me, I walk home this way every day.'

Starting up the motor-cycle, Perys said, 'Goodbye, Eliza. I hope Edward lives up to your expectations.'

He rode off, heading back towards Heligan, wondering what Edward's reaction would be when he received a letter from Eliza with the news Perys felt sure she had to impart. One thing, at least, was certain. He would not be pleased.

Perys would have been less happy himself had he been aware that Annie's father was at that moment checking some of his sheep in one of the steep-sided fields farther along the path towards Heligan Mill. He saw Eliza and Perys together and, fully aware of Eliza's reputation, he was shocked when she kissed him.

Walter was a quiet man who made a habit of keeping things very much to himself. He would say nothing immediately to Annie or his wife of what he had just witnessed, but he decided there should not be such a warm welcome for Perys at Tregassick Farm in future. He did not want his daughter to be talked about in the same way as Eliza Dunn.

* * *

Perys walked to Tregassick Farm that evening in the company of Polly, the Heligan housemaid. He smiled to himself at the thought that Maude would have been horrified had she known that he was accompanying a servant girl to the home of a coachman to spend a social evening.

Since she and her two daughters had departed from the great house the routine had become far more relaxed. The servants were still deferential towards Perys, but there was not such a sharp divide between them as there had been when Maude and the girls were present.

Perys was not, and never could be accepted as 'one of themselves' by the servants, but they were aware that he was also less than a fully accepted member of their employer's family. It was not the easiest of situations for either side, but at least Polly was more relaxed in his presence than had been the case when they first met. Walking along together in the dusk, she pleaded with Perys to persuade Martin not to leave Heligan and enlist in the army.

'I'll do my best, Polly,' Perys promised her, 'but I know how Martin must feel. Many of the men who work on the estate have already gone – some from the house too, as you well know. There must be many others from the surrounding area who are known to Martin. He won't want people pointing at him and wondering why he is staying behind.'

'I know he'll probably need to go sometime,' Polly replied, unhappily, 'but the thought of it horrifies me. I . . . I would like us to be married before he goes away. I want to be his wife and be able to show him how much I love him.'

126

It was a plea from the heart and Perys felt desperately sorry for her. 'He is a very lucky man to have someone love him as much as that, Polly.'

'I'm a servant, so is Martin. I doubt if we'll ever be anything else. The only thing that can make either of us special in any way is to find someone to love so much that what we are to the rest of the world doesn't matter.'

There was silence for a while before Perys said, 'You are a very special girl, Polly.'

'When you love someone – *really* love them – and you know they love you, you become special, no matter who you are.'

While Perys was digesting this heartfelt sentiment, Polly said quietly, 'Annie is a very special girl as well. I hope you won't hurt her too much.'

Looking at Polly sharply, Perys said, 'Hurting Annie is the very last thing I want to do.'

'I'm glad.' Polly was relieved he was not angry with her for making such an outspoken remark. In spite of Perys's position as a fringe member of the family who employed her, he was still a Tremayne, and she was not fully at ease talking so frankly with him.

Because of this, she hesitated for a moment before saying, 'You know that your cousin Edward tried his luck with her?'

'No, I *didn't* know. Are you sure of this, Polly? Annie has never said anything to me about it.'

'She wouldn't, but I'm sure that's why Master Edward behaved the way he did towards Martin on the day you arrived. It would have been his way of spiting her for having nothing to do with him.'

Perys found he was angry. The more he heard of

second cousin Edward, the less he liked him. He sounded thoroughly obnoxious and well deserved the bloody nose he had given him, but Polly had more to say.

'You've heard that he took up with Eliza Dunn, the daughter of the man you and Martin saved?'

'I have heard rumours, yes.'

'Oh, it was more than just rumour.' Now Polly had decided to confide in Perys there seemed to be no stopping her. 'Some of us servants saw them together – so did one of the woodsmen. He saw a lot more than Master Edward would have wished him to see.' When Perys did not reply, Polly added, 'I used to be friends with Eliza when we were growing up. She was always one for the boys. Not like me. Once I'd found Martin I never wanted anyone else. I thought Eliza was after him at one time, but when I confronted her with it she told me she'd never get involved with someone who was just a servant. I got cross with her for talking about Martin like that and asked her what sort of man she thought she'd find for herself. She said she didn't care what he was like. That she'd give herself to the highest bidder!'

Perys thought that in Eliza's eyes second cousin Edward would undoubtedly rank high on her list of 'bidders'. However, he was convinced that in the end she would find herself paying a far higher price than he.

20

Perys's visit to Tregassick Farm that evening was pleasant enough, even though he was unable to spend any time alone with Annie. Much of the time was spent talking with Martin about the young coachman's wish to enlist in the army.

An added poignancy had been lent to the subject in the few hours since Perys had paid his earlier visit to the farm. Two telegrams had been delivered to homes in Mevagissey. Each informed the next-of-kin of regular soldiers of the First Battalion of the Duke of Cornwall Light Infantry, that the son of the house had been killed in action in a hard-fought battle in France.

Similar telegrams had been delivered to almost a hundred and fifty other homes throughout the county.

The news sent shockwaves through the small community centred upon Mevagissey. Suddenly war was no longer a game being played by soldiers in some far-away country. Cornish husbands, sons and fathers were dying violent deaths on foreign soil, far from their homeland.

It was a story that was being repeated in thousands of homes across the land. The grim spectre of war reached out and touched even the most remote villages and hamlets with an indelible grief that would be repeated ten thousandfold before the growing conflict was finally brought to an end.

Martin had attended school with one of the dead soldiers and he was shaken by the news. It did not lessen his resolve to enlist but he was ready to listen to what Perys had to say to him.

When Perys questioned Martin about the things he most enjoyed doing, he was surprised to learn that Hugh Tremayne, his great-uncle and the owner of Heligan, had bought a Rolls-Royce Silver Ghost motor-car in 1910. Martin had been on a training course to qualify as a Rolls-Royce chauffeur and mechanic. He had driven the magnificent motor-car until 1913, when the Heligan owner decided he preferred to travel by horse and carriage when in his home county. The Rolls-Royce was still garaged in one of the Heligan stable buildings and Martin kept it in sound mechanical order.

The disclosure of Martin's hitherto unknown skill prompted Perys to suggest that he too should apply to join the Royal Flying Corps. He declared that Martin's driving and mechanical skills could be put to good use in the new service.

Martin was not as immediately enthusiastic as Perys had thought he might have been. His reason for wanting to enlist was in order to fight the enemy, not maintain motor vehicles, or even aeroplanes.

'Someone has to do it,' Perys pointed out, 'and the safety of the flyers depends upon the skills of those who look after their aeroplanes.' Aware that he had failed to impress Martin, he added, 'Rupert told me that many of those on maintenance and other work often transfer to flying duties as observers – they are the men who fire the guns carried by the aeroplanes. That should be exciting enough for anyone. He also said that many observers eventually go on to qualify as pilots.'

Martin had been one of the Heligan employees who had gone to look at Rupert's aeroplane and expressed envy of those who flew in such machines.

'Do you really think I might become a flyer if I joined the RFC?' Martin suddenly sounded interested in Perys's suggestion.

'I'm sure you could, if you decided that was what you wanted,' Perys replied confidently. He pushed to the back of his mind the fact that he was putting his own interpretation on what had been said to him when he and Rupert had discussed his own enlistment.

He was also aware that Martin was determined to enlist, whatever anyone said to him. If he could be persuaded to join the Royal Flying Corps in some form of maintenance capacity, he might enjoy the work and remain on the ground. By so doing he would be much safer than if he were an infantryman caught up in heavy fighting, such as that currently taking place in France and Belgium.

Perys hoped that Polly, Annie and her mother would appreciate this when they learned he had encouraged rather than discouraged Martin to enlist.

*   *   *

Annie was *not* convinced by his argument. She said so as she and Perys walked together along the lane towards Heligan, later that evening.

Although Walter Bray had ensured that Perys and Annie were never together while Perys was at Tregassick Farm, he had gone outside to deal with a cow that was having a difficult labour.

His departure was the signal for Polly to look at the clock and announce that she would need to leave. The Heligan housekeeper put a ten-thirty curfew on live-in servants. It was now almost ten o'clock. Perys said he too needed to leave as he had much to do before travelling to London the following morning, and Martin announced his intention of walking to the house with them.

Unaware of her husband's recently acquired doubts about Perys, Maude Bray did not object when Annie said she would go too. She believed there would be no opportunity for mischief if they walked through the night as a foursome.

However, once away from the farm the couples soon parted company. Martin walked on ahead with Polly, who had no wish to be locked out of the house. Time permitting, they would be able to kiss and embrace outside the servants' entrance before the others caught up with them.

Once they were out of sight and sound, Perys and Annie discussed Martin. Annie only accepted that the advice Perys had given to her brother *might* be sound when he told her that sooner or later the country would need to conscript men for the armed services. If this happened Martin would be given no choice of how best he might serve his country.

Changing the subject, Annie asked, 'Are you excited about going off to learn to fly, Perys?'

'Very,' he replied, honestly. 'It's what I want to do more than anything else in the world. But I'm sorry to be leaving Heligan. I've had a very happy time here.'

'You won't be leaving for ever? You'll come back? You said so . . .'

'I hope I will, Annie, but a great deal depends on my Great-Uncle Hugh. He allowed me to stay here because he thought I would be joining the county regiment. Whether he'll allow me to treat Heligan as a place in which to spend my leave once I'm in the RFC is another matter.'

'If he doesn't, I'm sure you'd be welcome at Tregassick,' Annie said.

'Would you like to have me staying at the farm, Annie?'

'We'd all make you welcome.' Annie tried to evade his question, but Perys persisted.

'That isn't what I asked you, Annie.'

'What do you want me to say, Perys?' While she had no doubts at all about her own feelings, common sense told her nothing could possibly come of such a relationship. Their backgrounds differed too much.

'I hoped you might say you *want* me to come back to Cornwall, because you really want to see me again.'

'I didn't think I needed to put that into words.' Annie was glad it was dark. It meant Perys could not see the stupid, unwanted tears that had sprung into her eyes.

'I need you to tell me,' he continued. 'I . . . you

matter to me more than anyone I've ever known, Annie. I want you to tell me that if I come back, you'll be here . . . waiting for me.'

Annie tried desperately hard to be sensible. 'You'll always be a very special friend, Perys, but you've told me yourself that you haven't known many girls. You've also never known what it is to have a home, or a family. Since you came to Cornwall you've met me and been welcomed into my family. You've found a way of life you think you want – and I'm sure you do want it . . . at this moment. But tomorrow you're going off to London. You'll meet up with all the friends of your cousins, and when you're a pilot they'll all want to know and entertain you. It will be a very different life to the one you've had up to now. Totally different to the quiet life we lead at Tregassick. Once that happens you won't want to be tied to anything, or anyone, here.'

'That isn't so, Annie,' Perys argued. 'You are right in what you say about my never having had a home life, or knowing many girls, but I've known enough to realise that what I feel about you is different.'

Annie desperately wanted to tell Perys that she felt the same way about him, but she held back. Her mother was aware of her feelings for him and had discussed the situation with her. Harriet had pointed out the many – the *very* many – difficulties that stood in the way of such a relationship.

Although Annie had strenuously disputed the point with her mother, she had absorbed sufficient of her arguments to make her cautious when speaking to Perys.

'I don't think either of us should commit ourselves,

Perys, but I have no plans to go out with anyone in the foreseeable future. I'll still be here when you next visit Cornwall. We can talk about it again then, if you still want to. If you don't . . . well, I would like us to remain friends.'

She hoped she sounded far more nonchalant than she felt inside.

'We'll always be friends, Annie, but I hope that one day we'll be a whole lot more.'

In the darkness his hand found hers and she did not pull away from him.

When Perys set off to ride the motor-cycle to St Austell railway station the next morning, he found Annie waiting for him at the end of the Heligan driveway. She was carrying a bag containing a couple of pasties, some home-produced cheese and a few freshly baked scones.

'Ma thought you would like these.' She passed over the bag, trying to avoid meeting his eyes. She was far more upset at the thought of him going away, perhaps never to return to Cornwall, than she wanted him to realise.

Perys too was at a temporary loss for words as he carefully tucked the food inside the motor-cycle's pannier-bag. Finally securing the buckle, he said, 'Thank your mother for me, Annie. It's very thoughtful and kind of her.'

'She got up early this morning especially to make the scones for you,' Annie pointed out. 'I'm glad because it's given me the opportunity to come and say goodbye to you properly.'

It was a reference to the previous evening. As they

approached Heligan House they had met up with Martin, who had just left Polly. He walked a discreet distance along the driveway, in order to give them a degree of privacy to say their farewells. However, when they reached the main door, Perys heard the butler pushing home the bolts on the inside, unaware that he was not in the house. Perys had to bang on the door hard before the butler began to draw the bolts once more.

Annie had bidden him a hasty goodnight before hurrying away to return home in company with her waiting brother. Had the butler seen her, rumours would soon have begun circulating in Mevagissey, putting her in the same category as Eliza.

'I'm glad to have this opportunity to see you again as well, Annie. I was so annoyed with the butler last night. Had I been Edward, I would probably have dismissed him on the spot! Just thinking about it kept me awake for half the night.'

'Then perhaps it was just as well Martin was waiting for me.'

'Yes, and this morning I have a train to catch.'

'Of course, I'm sorry, Perys. I mustn't make you late.'

'It doesn't mean you have to rush away immediately, Annie.'

In order to put the food in the pannier-bag, Perys had propped the motor-cycle against the wall at the end of the driveway. Now, feeling awkward in his thick motor-cycling clothes, he reached out for her.

She came to him and responded eagerly to his kiss, but when he tried to kiss her for a second time, she pulled away, saying, 'You have a train to catch. You mustn't miss it.'

136

'I'll be back as soon as I can, Annie. In the meantime, do you think your parents would mind if I wrote to you?'

'I don't see why they should.'

'Good! I'll be able to tell you everything that's happening and what I expect to be doing in the future.'

He knew he had to go. The train would not wait for him. He kissed her once more, but briefly this time. Then, straddling the motor-cycle he kick-started the engine, put it into gear and, wobbling alarmingly, kept waving to her until he passed out of her sight.

He was sorry to be leaving Annie, but he was also very excited with the way his life had changed since coming to Cornwall. He was now the owner of a superb motor-cycle; was going to receive tuition to become a pilot then join the Royal Flying Corps; and he was leaving a girl – his girl – behind him.

His student days were well and truly over. He was setting out in life as a man.

21

As the rider of a motor-cycle, Perys found London to be a frightening place. He had been to the city before, but today it seemed busier and noisier than he remembered.

Travelling from Cornwall on the train he had studied a map drawn for him by Morwenna before she left Cornwall, but the reality was far more confusing than it appeared from her simple drawing.

After becoming hopelessly lost, he eventually found his way back to the route mapped out for him. Nevertheless, the journey from Paddington to Knightsbridge took twice the time he had anticipated. However, he eventually arrived in the elegant and fashionable square where the three-storey house was situated.

The door was opened to him not, as he had been expecting, by Arabella, but by Morwenna, with her mother standing close behind her in the hallway. It was apparent they had been looking out of the window, awaiting his arrival.

'We were beginning to become concerned for you,' Morwenna said, as he greeted her with a kiss on the cheek.

Greeting Maude in a similar fashion, he said, 'It was entirely my fault. I am afraid I was overawed by London and the volume of traffic you have. I managed to get myself terribly lost. But where is Arabella?'

Morwenna and her mother exchanged brief glances, but it was Maude who replied, 'Arabella is at the hospital where she is training. I am delighted to say she has thrown herself heart and soul into becoming a nurse.'

'No doubt she was inspired by the example Morwenna set for her when the Russian ship foundered off Mevagissey,' Perys said. 'But you are looking tired, Morwenna.'

In truth, Morwenna looked shockingly weary, and Maude was suddenly serious. Resting a hand on her daughter's shoulder, she said, 'Morwenna finds herself in the unenviable position of being the most highly trained nurse on her ward at Saint Thomas's Hospital, and the number of wounded soldiers being brought back from France is threatening to overwhelm the whole hospital system. She has been working around the clock for days. Last night she collapsed and the matron insisted that she stay home and rest for the weekend.'

'I really can't be spared,' Morwenna said. 'There is so much to be done.' Suddenly and startlingly her eyes filled with tears as she added, 'It is truly pitiful to see so many badly wounded men. They have been

139

through a dreadful experience and are embarrassingly grateful for even the smallest things we are able to do for them. Sadly there is so little that can be done for many of them.'

'You really must not take it to heart so, my dear,' Maude said, putting an arm comfortingly about her daughter. 'You are working as hard as is humanly possible. The greatest disservice you can do these poor men is to wear yourself out. But enough of such matters for this evening. We'll have the handyman take your motor-cycle to the shed in the garden at the back of the house, Perys, then we'll organise a meal for you. You must be famished. How was Heligan when you left Cornwall?'

Arabella did not return home that night. She telephoned to say she was studying late and would stay at the house of a friend who lived very close to the hospital. Maude raised no objection. It was a friendship of which she approved, the girl's father being a titled Minister of the Crown.

Putting down the telephone, Maude informed Perys that Arabella sent her love to her 'favourite second cousin'. The fact that Maude passed on the message was an indication to Perys that Arabella's infatuation with him was no longer a problem. It had no doubt resulted from her boredom at Heligan, where there was little to do. Here in London she had the excitement of her training and the stimulating bustle of England's capital city to take her mind off him. It was a great relief.

That evening, after they had eaten, they were all relaxing in the sitting-room when Maude suddenly rose from her chair and left the room without a word, returning a few minutes later bearing a letter.

Handing it to Perys, she said, 'I received this from your grandfather a couple of days ago. I think you should read it.'

Perys took it from her with some trepidation. Previous letters from his grandfather had tended to either remonstrate with him about the details of a school report, call for an explanation in respect of a complaint about his conduct, or upbraid him for growing out of a school uniform too quickly.

This letter was very different. True, it had been sent to Maude and not to him, but at least three-quarters of the content was on the subject of Perys. What his grandfather had to say about him left Perys dumbfounded.

Maude had quite obviously told the old man of Perys's part in the rescue of the Russian seamen, as well as the incident involving the German warship, and had detailed his current plans.

For the first time ever, the elderly Tremayne had praise for his grandson. The approval was only partially diluted by a comment that behaving in such a fashion was 'not before time'.

What was equally surprising to Perys was the offer of financial aid made by his grandfather. He suggested he should reimburse Rupert for the money he was to spend on Perys in obtaining a pilot's licence for him, but his new-found generosity did not end there. He promised that, should Perys be successful in his application to join the Royal Flying Corps, he would deposit sufficient money in his grandson's meagre bank account to cover such items as uniform, any accommodation that might prove necessary, and the mess bills he was likely to incur during the weeks, or months, before his training was completed and he began receiving an officer's salary.

When he finished reading the surprising letter, Perys looked up at Maude in disbelief. 'What on earth have you said to Grandfather to persuade him to do and say all this?'

'No more than the truth, Perys. I told him how much I, the girls and Rupert thought of you, and told him you are a credit to the Tremayne family.'

Deeply moved, Perys rose from his chair and as he handed back the letter to Maude, he leaned over and kissed her warmly on the cheek. 'Aunt Maude, you are wonderful. I wish we had met years ago.'

Flustered, but by no means offended, Maude said, 'Young man, I am too old for flattery. I merely told your Grandfather what I believe to be true. You *are* a credit to the family, and one day I have no doubt your true worth will be recognised.'

Recovering her composure, Maude looked pointedly at Morwenna and said, 'Now, we have all had a long and tiring day. I suggest we go to our rooms and have an early night.'

22

The following day was a Sunday and Perys and Morwenna took advantage of the current fine weather to take a walk in London's Hyde Park, while Maude attended a church service.

Many other couples were also exercising in the park, and a short distance inside the entrance a number of speakers were practising their oratorical skills upon cosmopolitan audiences.

Perys and Morwenna paused for a few moments to listen to a suffragette advocating the formation of a front-line regiment of women. Her proposition was being loudly derided by almost every listener in her largely male audience, and as he and Morwenna moved on, Perys asked, jocularly, 'How would you fancy being in the front-line of a battle, Morwenna?'

'If it proved necessary I expect I could cope,' she replied, somewhat surprisingly. 'In fact, if I knew that those who actually *start* wars were going to be in the firing-line opposing me, I could no doubt shoot very well and with great determination. Unfortunately, such men rarely expose themselves to the dangers they cause for others.'

'You are probably right,' Perys agreed, aware he had touched upon a subject about which Morwenna had very strong views. 'All the same, I don't think I would like to think that you, or any other woman come to that, were up at the front, exposed to such dangers as our soldiers.'

'I, and many thousands of other women, are not happy at the thought of those we know and care for being killed and wounded in battle,' Morwenna retorted. 'But it is happening just the same. Anyway, you will need to get used to women being close to the battle-lines. Many, among them women like the one we just heard speaking, are already in France, driving ambulances carrying wounded soldiers from the front to the hospitals in Paris. Others are working in field hospitals and first aid stations. I hope it will not be long before I too am there.'

Coming to an abrupt halt, Perys reached out and, taking hold of Morwenna's arm, brought her to a standstill.

'What are you saying, Morwenna?'

'I am saying that I have applied to join the Queen Alexandra's Imperial Military Nursing Service.'

'But are you quite certain it's what you want to do? By all accounts you are doing a truly wonderful job here in London.'

'What I *really* want to do is become a doctor. I will, one day, but the training takes so long that the war would be over before I qualified. In the meantime, such skills as I have are urgently needed – but not in London. Most of the men arriving at our hospital owe their lives to the skills of the nurses and doctors working in field hospitals. *That* is where I am needed. I am an experienced theatre nurse. My qualifications are not being put to full use here. I should be in France.'

For some minutes Perys thought of what she had said before replying. 'What does your mother think of the idea?'

'I haven't told her yet – and I would rather you said nothing until it is too late for her to prevent me from going.'

'I'll say nothing,' Perys promised, 'but I hope you've thought about it very carefully. It will be dangerous work. You are courageous even to consider it.'

'It is the soldiers I have been caring for who possess courage, Perys. They see their friends being killed, maimed and wounded all around them, yet they carry on fighting, knowing they are likely to be next. They deserve to know that if they *are* wounded they will receive the best possible attention. I want to be close at hand to ensure it is there for them.'

'Have you been thinking about this for long?' Perys asked.

'No, because I was too young to join the Queen Alexandra's, but the needs of war are so great that it is experience that counts now, not age.'

They were approaching the Serpentine, the lake in the centre of Hyde Park. On the water were a number of boats occupied by young men and women. Most of the men were in uniform, but their happy laughter gave an air of unreality to the conversation taking place between Perys and Morwenna.

Suddenly, a middle-aged woman stepped into their path. Smartly dressed, she was wearing a wide-brimmed hat decorated with a variety of artificial flowers, and in one hand she carried a bunch of white feathers. Each feather had a safety-pin fastened to it.

Addressing Perys, the woman said sharply, 'I have a present for you – and for all the other young men who should be in uniform, fighting for their country.'

Taken by surprise, Perys made no move to prevent the woman stepping forward with the intention of pinning a white feather to his lapel.

She was thwarted by a suddenly furious Morwenna. Snatching the feather from the woman's hand she broke it in two and flung it to the ground. Not content with this, she then grabbed the bunch of feathers and flung these down too.

Angrier than Perys had ever seen anyone, Morwenna confronted the woman. 'How *dare* you?! What do you think gives you the right to brand someone a coward?'

Drawing herself up to the full extent of her insignificant height, the woman made an attempt to restore her dented dignity. 'It is the duty of us all to support our country. Those who fail deserve to be pointed out as cowards.'

'Well, although it is none of your business, my companion begins flying lessons tomorrow in order to become a pilot in the Royal Flying Corps. *That* is your coward. But I have a question for *you*. Why are you not wearing a uniform? What are you doing for your country?'

Taken aback, the woman said, 'I? I am a woman, and not a young woman, either . . .'

'You are young enough to contribute something. I am a nurse at Saint Thomas's Hospital where we are caring for a great many soldiers who have been wounded in France. Present yourself there and you will be found something to do that is far more useful than handing out white feathers to men you know nothing about. Not only that, when you have seen the appalling sight of hundreds of young men with shattered minds and bodies, their lives destroyed by war, I doubt very much whether you will be quite so eager to send other young men to suffer a similar fate.'

Giving the now thoroughly shaken woman a last, withering look, Morwenna turned her back on her. 'Come, Perys, if we cannot walk in the park without being accosted by foolish, misguided women I think we should return home.'

As they walked away, Perys looked back. The woman in the flowered hat was looking after them, still in a state of shock. She had made no attempt to retrieve her white feathers. He felt almost sorry for her, but his over-riding feeling was one of admiration for Morwenna.

When he expressed this to her she replied somewhat tremulously, 'Now it is over I would rather we did not talk about it, or I will probably start shaking. I have never before spoken to anyone in such a manner.'

'She thoroughly deserved all she got,' Perys said. 'And thank you for taking my part. You said all the things I would have lain awake tonight thinking I *should* have said.'

'I meant every word of it,' Morwenna said, adding vehemently, 'This is a *wicked* war. There are times when I feel like weeping for some of the wounded soldiers I am tending.'

As though to back up her statement, tears suddenly welled up in her eyes and Perys took her hand and squeezed it comfortingly.

She gripped his hand tightly in return and did not release it until they reached the Knightsbridge square where the Tremayne home was situated.

23

The following morning it was still dark when Perys set off for the famous motor-racing track at Brooklands. He allowed himself plenty of time, determined not to be late for the first day of his pilot training. If he did not get lost along the way he would be there long before the appointed time of nine o'clock.

In fact, he reached Brooklands almost an hour too early, but aeroplanes were already taking off, landing, and circling the race track at speeds far less than those achieved by the cars which formerly raced there.

The only aeroplane Perys had been close to prior to today was the BE2c flown by Rupert. That had been a lean, elegant aircraft. Those he saw now were very different. They appeared to consist of a decidedly flimsy framework of wings, wires and struts, suspended in the midst of which was a gondola containing two men and an engine.

A further difference was the position of the engine.

Situated *behind* the two flyers, the propeller pushed the aeroplane through the air, whereas with the BE2c it pulled it along.

Just outside the perimeter of the Royal Flying Corps compound, but within the racing circuit, was a large hangar, built mainly of corrugated iron. Alongside it was a more permanent building, apparently an office. Above the door a sign read: 'THE MALLOCH FLYING SCHOOL, proprietor N. Malloch'.

Parking his motor-cycle beside the office building, Perys removed his leather hat and goggles, peeled off his gauntlet gloves and knocked at the door.

There was no response. He tried the door and when it opened he peered inside. It was empty.

He was disappointed, but a clock on the wall inside the office showed there were still more than forty-five minutes before he was expected. He decided to have a look around.

The hangar had sliding doors that formed the whole of the front of the building. Perys thought this must be where the aeroplane he was to fly would be kept.

Hoping to see it, he tried a small door built into one of the larger ones. Like the office door, this too was open. There was not one, but *three* aeroplanes inside, although one was in pieces. Of the other two, one was similar to those he had just seen flying around the perimeter of the race track. He would learn that this was a Maurice Farman 'Longhorn', so called because it had a structure in front of the gondola that gave it the appearance of possessing long horns. He thought it looked even more fragile here than it had in flight.

The second aeroplane he did not recognise, but would later get to know as an Avro 504 two-seater. It was impossible to identify the third aeroplane, or what it had once been. At the moment it was little more than a heap of broken struts, wire, canvas, metal and an engine.

While he was standing in the doorway looking at the aeroplanes, a tall, slim, dark-haired man in his thirties stood up from behind the Avro 504, where he had been adjusting a stay on one of the wings.

'Can I help you?' His voice carried a Scots accent.

'I'm looking for Mr Malloch.'

'It's Nick Malloch, and you've found him.' Advancing towards Perys and extending a hand, he added, 'You'll no doubt be Perys Tremayne. Welcome to my aviation school.'

As they shook hands, Nick said, 'I've heard a great deal about you, Perys. Rupert told me the story of your flight along the Cornish coast. He's quite convinced he owes his DSO to you.'

'Rupert is very generous in more ways than one,' Perys replied.

'He's also a damned good pilot. Do you realise that had you been in the RFC at the time you'd have probably got a DSO too?'

'Would I? I hadn't really thought about it. All I had to do was make a drawing of the German ship. It was Rupert who did the flying.'

'Well, it shouldn't be long before you'll be flying as well.'

'How long?' Perys asked, eagerly.

'There's an Aero Club examiner coming down to Brooklands on Friday of next week to test some of the

RFC boys. If the weather holds – and it looks as though it might – you should have enough flying time to try your luck with him. Mind you, you'll need to burn the midnight oil on theory and such like.'

Perys was disappointed. He had believed it should take no more than a week to master the art of aviation. After all, an aeroplane was only a machine, like a motor-bike, and he had mastered that in no more than an hour. Well, *almost* mastered it.

'Rupert says some of the pilots who are being sent to France have no more than thirteen hours' flying time in their log books.'

'Most of the thirteen-hour pilots are dead within a couple of weeks,' Nick said, bluntly. 'Rupert is a good friend of mine and he's paying for your course. I intend to see that he – and the RFC – get value for money. If I had my way we would be following the example of the French and many of the colonial governments. They demand a great many more flying hours than we do before a pilot is sent up on combat duties. You won't get it once you join the RFC, but I'll make damn sure you're a good pilot before you go to them and learn bad habits.'

'Is that what you did for Rupert?'

'I did – and he's one of the best pilots in the RFC as a result.'

'Then I'll try not to let you down,' Perys promised.

'Keep that thought in mind,' Nick said, adding, 'I'll know within a couple of days whether or not you'll ever make a pilot. If I don't think you will then I'll tell you. It won't necessarily mean you won't make it as a pilot in the RFC, only that I'll be protecting my own reputation for turning out some of the best pilots in the country. Now, let's go to the office. I'll give you a couple of files containing notes you'll need to read and learn by heart. Halfway through the morning I'll come in and question you about them. Then you can come out to the hangar and sit in the cockpit of one of the aeroplanes and we'll run through the controls.'

'Which aeroplane will I be learning in?' Perys asked, hoping it might be the Avro 504. He was to be disappointed.

'You'll be learning in the "Longhorn".' Nick pointed to the aeroplane which, with the exception of the two-seater cockpit, appeared little more than a wooden frame held together by an excessive number of taut wires.

Correctly interpreting Perys's expression as one of disappointment, Nick said, 'That's the one the RFC will expect you to fly in order to prove to them you are a pilot, so that's the one you will need to learn to fly and qualify in. If I think you're doing exception-ally well I might let you have a couple of circuits on the Avro. I've fitted it with dual controls myself because I personally think it's an excellent training aeroplane. Now the RFC are beginning to take an interest in it, too. It's an easy aeroplane to fly – though not so easy to fly well.'

At that moment Perys made a decision to master the Maurice Farman 'Longhorn' as quickly as possible in order that he might graduate to the Avro. He thought the 'Longhorn' embarrassingly fragile and primitive alongside the far more workmanlike Avro.

He spent the morning in the office, poring over the files Nick had given to him and writing copious notes copied from them. It felt like being back at school once more, although he decided that aeronautics was far more interesting than any of the subjects he had studied there.

Mid-afternoon, Nick entered the office as he had at least half-a-dozen times earlier. On each occasion Perys had been hard at work. Now, the flying instructor asked, 'How is the work coming along? Do you think you know a bit more about aeroplanes?'

'I'm finding it all very interesting,' Perys replied, 'but there's a lot more to flying than there is to learning to ride a motor-bike.'

'That's quite true,' Nick agreed, 'but you won't learn to fly an aeroplane merely by reading about it. Come on outside and have a look at the "Longhorn".'

'Are we going up for a flight?' Perys asked, eagerly.

'In a while. First I want you to sit in the aeroplane, get the feel of it, learn where everything is and, more importantly, what it does.'

Perys was so keen to familiarise himself with the aeroplane that he tripped and almost fell as he left the office, prompting Nick to remark drily that if he broke a limb it would undoubtedly set his flying ambitions back for some months.

The Maurice Farman 'Longhorn' had two cockpits with duplicated controls. Seated in the forward of the two, Perys decided it had fewer gadgets than the BE2c flown by Rupert. Apart from a couple of dials and switches there was only a single 'joystick' control, topped by a handlebar contraption.

These simple controls, plus two foot pedals, would take the aeroplane into the air, and they were sufficient for the pilot to keep it there and bring it safely back to earth again. In addition, under battle conditions they were expected to enable the pilot to outmanoeuvre an enemy and occasionally fire a gun at him too.

For half-an-hour, Nick explained the controls and the procedure Perys would need to learn by heart in order to fly the aeroplane, repeating it over and over again until Perys felt he could almost say it word for word.

Not until then did Nick say, 'Right, put on the flying gear that's behind the door in the office. We'll go for a flight.'

Twenty minutes later the Farman 'Longhorn' was bumping across the grass from the hangar, with Perys seated in the open forward cockpit, feeling far more exposed than he had in the BE2c. Then the sound of the eighty horsepower engine increased to an impressive roar, and with the undercarriage rumbling noisily beneath them, the 'Longhorn' gathered speed along the grass runway.

Suddenly the rumbling ceased and Perys realised the aircraft had left the ground – but the banked carracing track that surrounded the wartime airfield still rose above them, seemingly dangerously close and getting closer!

For a couple of heart-stopping moments, Perys shut his eyes and awaited the crash that seemed inevitable. When it failed to happen he opened them again – and Brooklands was behind them.

A speaking-tube linked pilot and passenger and Nick's metallic voice commented, 'She's a bit sluggish today. Could do with a bit more tuning.'

Determined not to allow his instructor to realise how apprehensive he had been, Perys asked, 'Where are we going?'

'High. I'll take us up to about five thousand feet and let you have a little play. Then, if you do anything particularly diabolical, I'll have height enough to put it right. While we're climbing, put your feet on the pedals and take a light hold of the control stick. You'll begin to get the feel of controlling the plane. The most important thing you'll learn is to maintain a firm but light touch. Until you're an experienced pilot – a *very* experienced pilot – never take liberties with your aeroplane and never panic. Keep a cool head whatever happens and ninety-nine times out of a hundred you'll be able to right whatever's gone wrong. Lose your head and you're finished. Make that your cardinal rule. Repeat it to yourself a hundred times each day until it's as familiar to you as your own name.'

It took the 'Longhorn' almost half-an-hour to climb to the height at which Nick wanted to fly. During this time he put the aircraft through various manoeuvres, each movement of the controls transmitted to Perys via the dual-control system.

Perys was surprised at how readily the aeroplane responded to the slightest movement of the controls and he quickly realised that Nick was indeed an experienced and skilful pilot. He also soon became used to the sound of the wind singing in the myriad wires that held the Maurice Farman together, but it was much colder than he recalled it being in Rupert's plane.

Peering over the side of his cockpit as they flew even higher, the countryside resembled a detailed, contoured map. Roads, fields, houses, horses, motor-vehicles – even people, as tiny as ants from this height.

Suddenly, Nick's voice came through the tube beside his ear. 'How are you enjoying the flight?'

'Wonderful – but a bit chilly.'

'Would you like to try your hand at flying it for yourself now?'

Would he!

'All right, Perys, she's all yours. I've taken my hands and feet off the controls.'

It had all happened so quickly . . . *too* quickly. Perys suddenly felt he had neither the know-how nor the confidence to fly the aeroplane. For a few brief moments he froze, not daring to move the controls even a fraction, lest he cause the plane to do something disastrous.

Then a sudden gust of wind caused the aeroplane to tilt, and Perys automatically moved his hand on the joystick in order to correct the movement. He overcompensated and the aircraft tilted in the other direction.

For a few minutes the plane wallowed its way through the air before steadying. Although Nick later denied playing any part in the recovery, Perys believed the instructor had brought his own skills to bear in order to bring the aeroplane under control.

For the next few minutes the plane maintained a steady course, then, with Nick giving quietly voiced instructions, Perys succeeded in banking and turning to head back the way they had come. He was delighted.

The next thing he was told to do was reduce speed and begin a descent. Had they been any lower the manoeuvre might have proved fatal. Perys reduced speed too much, at the same time pushing the nose of the aeroplane down at an angle that was far too steep. Only Nick's skill succeeded in bringing the plane out of a nosedive.

As a result, Perys's next attempt was more cautious and the aircraft began a steady descent.

'You'll need to turn to your left . . . gently now, you know what to do . . .' The tinny voice came through the tube and Perys cautiously worked the controls, this time hands and feet together.

As the aeroplane banked he had a moment of alarm as full realisation came to him of how close to the ground they were, but he completed the turn and Nick's voice said, encouragingly, 'That was perfect. I'll take over now and bring us down – but keep your feet and hands lightly on the controls to get the feel of it.'

Brooklands was not the easiest of places at which to land, the aircraft having to negotiate the steeply banked motor-racing track around the aerodrome perimeter before dropping on to the airfield at just the right moment. An added incentive for the pilot to concentrate fully on his landing was the presence of a sewage-farm on the line of take-off and landing. It had claimed many embarrassed and evil-smelling victims during its existence – and would claim many more.

But Nick Malloch was a skilful pilot who knew Brooklands better than he knew his own back garden. He made a perfect landing, then allowed Perys to taxi the aircraft to the hangar where they and a mechanic manhandled the machine inside.

As the two men stripped off their flying clothing inside the office, the instructor asked, 'Well, Perys, how did you enjoy your first flight under instruction?'

'It was absolutely fabulous,' he replied with honest enthusiasm, 'I can't wait to get up there on my own.'

When Nick made no reply, Perys said, anxiously, 'I know I didn't do very much actual flying, but how do you think I did?'

Giving Perys an enigmatic look, Nick said, 'As you say, you've hardly done any flying yet, but do as I tell you, don't get too cocksure of yourself, and you'll be a good pilot by the time you leave here.'

24

On the second day of Perys's flying course, Nick suggested he should move into the cottage occupied by himself, his wife and their two small children.

The cottage was only a short distance along the road from Brooklands, and as they were currently enjoying a period of ideal flying weather, Nick wanted Perys to put in as many flying hours as was possible without neglecting the theory. The journey to and from London each morning and evening took a large slice out of his working day, as well as tiring him for both flying and studying.

When Perys explained this to Maude it was agreed he should stay with Nick and his family during the week, returning to Knightsbridge from Saturday afternoon to Monday.

In truth, Maude was relieved. Arabella had slipped on some stairs in the hospital where she worked and sprained her ankle. She would be at home in the evenings when Maude was engaged in fund-raising activities on behalf of numerous wartime charities.

Maude believed the infatuation her youngest daughter had nursed for Perys had run its course, but she was relieved to have the risk of having it rekindled removed.

For his part, Perys was delighted to spend more time with Nick and the many flying friends who were in the habit of calling at the house in the evenings. There was now rarely a moment of the day when some aspect of flying was not being discussed.

There was another advantage to the arrangement. Now Nick was able to supervise Perys's study in the evenings, he felt able to give him more flying hours during the day. At the end of three days, Perys had succeeded in putting in a total of eight hours of dual flying.

As they came in to land for the final time on the third day, Nick spoke through the tube. 'All right, Perys, you've held the controls often enough while I've brought the "Longhorn" down, now you can do it by yourself.'

Perys felt a sudden thrill of fear. 'You mean . . . you want me to land . . . now?'

'That's what I said. It's all yours. I'll be leaning back with hands and feet off the controls. You're in charge.'

Perys snapped a glance back over his shoulder and saw Nick sitting in the rear cockpit with eyes closed and arms folded – and he broke out in a cold sweat.

He needed to turn the aeroplane in order to approach Brooklands from downwind, and turned so sharply he felt certain Nick would say something. However, the only sound from the speaking-tube was a faint whistling that sounded remarkably like the latest popular dance tune.

Perys was able to right the aeroplane easily enough, then he tried to remember everything that Nick was in the habit of saying aloud when he was bringing the 'Longhorn' down to earth.

Check speed . . . don't put the nose down too far on the approach . . . height . . . steady . . . adjust the trim . . .

Suddenly the high banking of the racing track loomed ahead and Perys had a sudden moment of panic. I'm too low . . . we're going to hit it . . . no, we're clear, but if I don't touch down soon we're going to over-run! Get it down . . . Quick!

The landing was so heavy that Perys felt certain the undercarriage would collapse, but then the wheels began rumbling over the grass and he cut back the engine. They were down safely!

His exhilaration was only slightly dampened when Nick said, 'We bumped down so hard I thought for a moment we were going to have the wheels up in the cockpits with us.'

'Was it really that bad?' Perys asked, anxiously.

'I've known a lot better landings,' Nick said, honestly. 'On the other hand, I've seen a great many first landings that were a hell of a lot worse – more than one from experienced pilots, too. Come on, take us over to the hangar. Time we went home.'

The whole of the following day was spent practising take-offs and landings and Nick would not allow even the smallest error to pass uncorrected. As he explained in very strong terms to Perys, most flying accidents occurred during these two essential procedures, adding, 'Any fool can fly an aeroplane once it's in the air. It takes skill and know-how to get it there and bring it safely back down again.'

By mid-afternoon Perys had lost count of the times he had landed and taken off in the 'Longhorn', then Nick's voice came through the tube. 'I think you've finally got the idea, Perys. Let's celebrate with a trip to the seaside. Head south, south-east, and gain a bit of height.'

Perys was only too happy to follow the orders of his instructor. Brooklands was going through a busy period. Trainee RFC pilots were circling the racing track and practising their own landings and take-offs. He thought the airfield resembled a bee-hive, with aeroplanes buzzing around it like giant bees.

Once the 'Longhorn' gained sufficient height, Perys continued on his designated course, occasionally carrying out a manoeuvre ordered by Nick, such as a stall, or, far more frightening on the first occasion, putting the aeroplane into a spin and getting out of it again.

When they were little more than half-an-hour's flying time from Brooklands, Nick called Perys's attention to the view around and below them. They were approaching the sea and, as they passed over the coast, Perys pointed out another aeroplane flying on a converging course, but closer to the ground than the 'Longhorn'.

'Well spotted!' Nick said, 'Let's go down and have a look at him.'

Perys banked the aeroplane and with a thrill of excitement pointed the nose of the 'Longhorn' downward. The wind sang in the wire rigging as the flimsy

Farman gathered speed. As the two aeroplanes drew closer to each other a number of thoughts crossed his mind.

What would they do if the other aeroplane proved to be a German? They carried no weapons. If it *was* a German, would it have a gun?

He need not have worried. As they drew nearer he could see the British markings on the other plane. The aircraft itself was similar to their own, but without the extension in front of the cockpit which had given rise to the nickname 'Longhorn'.

Nick called out that it was a 'Shorthorn', belonging to the Royal Naval Air Service. 'He's probably on patrol,' he added, 'but he's not keeping a very good look-out. All right, Perys, I'll take control for a few minutes and wake him up a little.'

Reluctantly, Perys relinquished control of the aeroplane, wondering what Nick had in mind.

He soon found out. They were quite a distance above the other aeroplane which was ambling along at a comfortable speed. Now Nick put the 'Longhorn' into a dive, gradually gathering speed. Perys realised they would be diving dangerously close to the other aeroplane. He could imagine the effect it would have on the two occupants of the Royal Naval plane when they suddenly appeared out of nowhere, cutting straight across their flight path.

The result was all he thought it would be. The other pilot did not see them until they came down in front of him. He took immediate and violent avoiding action, diving to one side and away from them.

He recovered quickly enough and immediately recognised their own aeroplane for what it was.

The two aeroplanes converged once more, but this time, when they were close enough, they flew alongside each other. The naval pilot shook his fist at them, but his wide grin took the sting out of the gesture.

The planes flew side by side for a couple of minutes before Nick's voice came through the tube again. 'All right, Perys, take over now. We've had our fun for today. Let's go home.'

With a final reciprocated wave from their occupants, the two aeroplanes parted company, the Royal Naval 'Shorthorn' resuming its patrol, and its older and slightly more cumbersome 'brother' setting a course for Brooklands.

25

The following day Perys flew solo for the first time. It came without warning. He and his instructor had travelled to the airfield in Nick's car, as usual, and Perys entered the office to put on his flying clothes while Nick went into the hangar to speak to his mechanics. When he returned to the office, instead of following Perys's example and putting on his flying clothes, Nick sat down at his desk and began poring over some paperwork.

Disappointed, Perys asked, 'Aren't we going flying right away?'

'I'm not,' was the reply, 'but you are. Away you go, before the RFC lads come out to play and get in your way.'

Perys had been aware that this moment could not be too far away, but coming like this it took him by surprise. Nick had said nothing to him about it on the way to Brooklands that morning.

'What is it you want me to do?' he asked, hesitantly.

'Nothing you haven't done many times before,' was the reply. 'Take off, fly around the track for a few circuits, then land. Take off again immediately and do the same again. After a while, if you feel confident enough, go off and take a jolly somewhere – but don't lose yourself. Choose a course, stick to it, and fly a reciprocal course home again.'

Perys taxied the aeroplane across the runway with considerable trepidation. He had practised all this before, and performed it well, but at the back of his mind had always been the thought that if anything *did* go wrong, Nick was always there to take over.

Now there was no one. He had to do it right the first time.

The knowledge that Nick trusted him to fly on his own was reassuring, but before he took off he looked across to the office. Both Nick and the mechanics had abandoned their work to come out and watch him.

The take-off went surprisingly well and Perys realised that the loss of weight of one man helped the performance of the 'Longhorn' a great deal.

For the same reason, the landing was somewhat less than perfect, but although Perys was not satisfied with it, the aeroplane suffered no damage and when he glanced towards the office Nick gave him a cheery wave.

The second landing was better and the third as good as any he had made with Nick in the aeroplane with him.

When he made his fourth landing, Perys saw that Nick and the mechanics had stopped watching and gone back to their respective tasks. He decided it was time to enjoy his flight.

He had already decided where he would go on his first solo flight and had even worked out the course and the distances involved. In preparation for this moment he had written a brief note and placed it inside a small shell case, attached to a home-made parachute.

It was his intention to fly over his old school in Oxfordshire and let them know that one of their less illustrious students was doing something useful with his life after all.

By the time Perys reached the school, lessons were over for the morning but, as had been the routine when he was there, most of the boys were out on the sports fields. They were either preparing for inter-house Rugby Union matches, or practising in order that the participants might one day graduate to a house team.

Perys's first pass over the fields brought all activities to an excited halt. His second, much lower this time, added consternation to the excitement. At the very moment he threw out his message, Perys thought he saw the face of the headmaster looking up at him, but he could not be certain.

Looking back as he climbed to clear the school buildings he saw such a scrummage to collect his parachute message that he could identify no one.

The return flight to Brooklands was uneventful, but back at the airfield an accident occurred. It was one that would remain in his memory for ever, even after he had witnessed the full horrors of war. It was undoubtedly caused by the RFC's poor method of training, something that Nick felt very strongly about.

The Royal Flying Corps had gone to France in the first days of the war. Despite the opposition of some diehard senior army officers who still believed wars could be won by sword-wielding gentlemen on horseback, the flyers had swiftly proved their worth in reconnaissance duties. Indeed, it was soon conceded, albeit grudgingly, that without them the German army might not have been thrown back from the very gates of Paris.

With this recognition came a belated realisation that Britain lagged woefully behind the other powers in the number of flying machines in service, and men qualified to fly them. In order to rectify this situation as quickly as possible, hastily recruited trainee pilots were rushed through a skimpy flying course. They learned only as much, or as little, as was necessary to obtain the qualifications required to pilot the increasing flood of aeroplanes being turned out by dozens of factories and workshops throughout the land.

As Perys brought the 'Longhorn' down, he observed a 'Shorthorn' aeroplane turning outside the perimeter of the motor racing track with the obvious intention of coming in to land. The somewhat jerky movements of the plane as it manoeuvred into position led Perys to the conclusion that it was probably a trainee pilot making his first landing under instruction.

Not wishing to risk distracting the novice pilot, Perys put the 'Longhorn' into a wide banking turn. By the time he returned to his original position the other aeroplane should have landed.

Because he was making such a wide turn, Perys

did not witness the actual crash. Not until he began his second descent did he see the 'Shorthorn' on the ground *outside* the racing track. It was lying on its side in a crumpled heap, the wings on one side pointing up to the sky. The accident must have only just occurred, but civilians and RFC personnel were running towards the scene from all directions.

A horrified Perys watched as the aeroplane erupted in a fireball that sent flames and smoke leaping into the sky ahead of him.

The would-be rescuers stopped running, standing about helplessly, waiting for the fire-engine from the airfield to arrive on the scene.

Perys's flight took him directly over the crashed aeroplane and through the smoke billowing up from it, but he needed to concentrate on his own landing and soon the tragic scene was behind him.

When he climbed from the 'Longhorn', he was shaking. His first words to the flying instructor were, 'There's been a crash. A "Shorthorn" . . . it's on fire!'

Nick nodded sympathetically, but when he spoke it was in a matter-of-fact manner. 'This is a training airfield, Perys, crashes are not uncommon. You've been lucky not to have witnessed one before this. When the RFC first moved here there were two or three a week – sometimes as many as one a day. Is it going to put you off flying?'

Perys was silent for what seemed a long time before replying, 'No. It will probably make me a better pilot and teach me to concentrate on what I'm doing for every minute I'm flying an aeroplane.'

Resting a hand on Perys's shoulder, Nick said sympathetically, 'If the accident has done the same

170

for all the trainee pilots here today then two good men won't have died in vain. Come on, I'll buy you a drink on the way home and you can tell where you've been . . .'

That night Perys wrote a long letter to Annie. He told her about London, about Brooklands, about Nick and his flying experiences to date. He did not mention the crash he had witnessed that day.

It was something he would try, without success, *not* to remember for as long as he was training to become a pilot.

26

At the end of his first week of flying training, Perys returned to Knightsbridge and the home of Maude and her daughters. He discovered the whole family was far more closely involved with the war than he and the trainee RFC pilots who spent their days circling above the race track at Brooklands.

In Europe, the British, French and Belgian armies were locked in a desperate defensive battle against the Germans, who were fighting their way towards the Belgian town of Ypres. Casualty figures on both sides were appallingly high. British casualties alone could be counted in tens of thousands, and hospitals in battle-torn France were unable to cope. As a result, trainloads of wounded soldiers were carried to the Channel ports and ferried to England, stretching the resources of the London hospitals to breaking point.

Nursing training had been temporarily suspended. Although still limping, Arabella had returned to the hospital after a plea from the matron. Young, would-be nurses suddenly found themselves performing duties that only a week before would have been considered far beyond their capabilities. Now such limitations were ignored. They had *some* knowledge of nursing. It would have to be sufficient for the time being.

Morwenna returned to the house on Sunday morning having been on duty all night, but she stopped only long enough to bathe and change out of the blood-soiled uniform she had been wearing for twenty-four hours. She looked desperately tired, but insisted there was no question of resting for a while. 'If you saw the state of those poor men you wouldn't be able to rest until every one of them had been treated and made comfortable. Some are in a pitiful state. I'll have something to eat quickly, then get back to the hospital.'

'I'll take you there,' said Perys. 'You can ride side-saddle on the pillion of the motor-bike. We'll need to go fairly slowly, but it will be quicker than by bus.'

At the hospital it was immediately apparent to Perys that Sunday was not going to be a day of rest for the doctors or nursing staff. Another train loaded with wounded soldiers had arrived at the nearby Waterloo station. All available transport, including that offered free of charge by sympathetic taxi-cab drivers, was being utilised. Some, more mobile than others, chose to walk, tearfully relieved to be home and away from the hell they had left behind them in France and Belgium.

Morwenna wasted no time in thanking Perys and hurried inside the hospital. As Perys was about to ride away, a soldier walking to the hospital wearing a uniform still caked with the mud of the trenches, with a bandage around his head and an arm in a sling, suddenly collapsed without warning, his knees simply buckling beneath him.

Abandoning his motor-cycle against the railings outside the hospital, Perys hurried to the soldier.

'Here, let me give you a hand.' Putting an arm about the wounded man, Perys lifted him carefully to his feet. As he did so he was aware of an unpleasant odour emanating from the soldier's clothing. It was the stench of dirt, mud, blood – and something else. Something indefinable. It was a stench that would one day become familiar to Perys. Although no one ever put a name to it, he always felt it to be the smell of death.

He helped the soldier into the hospital. Here the situation was chaotic. There were far more wounded men than the doctors and nurses could properly cope with and they had insufficient helpers.

Perys found a male nurse to take the wounded man off his hands, then went to the aid of a female nurse who was struggling to support one end of a stretcher.

Before long, he found himself as fully involved as the hospital porters in helping with the wounded men. It was a task that lasted for the whole of that day.

The hospital staff coped as best they could with at least ten times as many patients as they were equipped to deal with, and by the end of the day they had managed to transfer a great many of the wounded men to other hospitals in and around the capital city.

Now things were quieter, Perys went looking for

Morwenna. He found her thoroughly exhausted and ready to go home, having worked for a full thirty-six hours.

They travelled home on the motor-cycle. Maude was waiting for them, having already tucked her younger daughter up in bed.

When she had dealt with Morwenna in a similar fashion, she came downstairs and sat with Perys, who was having a drink while a servant prepared a meal for him.

'Was it very bad at the hospital?' she asked, aware from the expression on his face that he had found helping out there a traumatic experience.

He nodded. 'It was tragic to see the state of the wounded men. Many were no older than me. One can only guess what they've been through in France.'

'The first thing Arabella did when she reached home was burst into tears,' said Maude. 'She has had a busy and upsetting day, but by the sound of things managed to cope very well. I am extremely proud of my two girls.'

'With very good reason,' Perys agreed. 'The sad thing is, I fear there will be many more days like this before the war is over. Listening to the soldiers talking today it is likely to last for a long time. There is a fiercely fought war going on in France and Belgium. It seems the Germans are just as determined to win as we are.'

'Has what you have witnessed today made you rethink your decision to join the Royal Flying Corps and go to war yourself, Perys? No one would blame you if it has.'

'Quite the opposite, Aunt Maude. No one could fail

to be appalled by what I have seen, but it has made me angry – and determined. Angry that the Germans should deliberately start such a war and cause all the suffering I've seen today; determined to do whatever I can to help bring it to an end as quickly as possible.'

Maude wondered how many of the maimed and wounded young men Perys had seen that day had gone to war with exactly the same thoughts and aims in mind. Remembering the anguish she had suffered when her own husband had been killed in a war only fourteen years ago, she thought of the pain and despair there would be in so many households in the country at this moment.

Her friends in the War Office were grimly hinting that the experienced soldiers in the British army had been almost wiped out. The hope for future victories rested with the largely untried men who were volunteering in their tens of thousands to take their places.

Perys was one such young man – and one she and her two daughters had grown extremely fond of during the short time they had known him. She hoped with all her heart they would never need to grieve for him.

27

During his second week of training Perys put in so many hours of flying time that Nick complained light-heartedly that the fee he was receiving from Rupert would not cover the fuel Perys was using.

Perys was flying the Avro now. A couple of hours dual with Nick had been sufficient for the instructor to satisfy himself that Perys was proficient enough to take the aeroplane up by himself. It also meant Nick could take other pupils up in the 'Longhorn' while Perys was flying.

Towards the end of the week, Perys received disappointing news. The examiner who was to have come to Brooklands to test the flying skills of Perys and a number of other pupils had been involved in a flying accident. Although he survived the crash, he had received serious injuries and would be unable to carry out his duties for some considerable time.

The only consolation for Perys was that Nick

Malloch allowed him to stay at his home for an additional week and continue his solo flying. What was more, he had just obtained a BE2c aircraft, on which Perys put in a number of flying hours.

The aeroplane had been in private ownership since it was built, but the owner had sold it to Nick, who now had three serviceable aeroplanes at his disposal.

When the new examiner arrived at Brooklands, a week later than planned, it was discovered he was an old friend of Nick.

By this time Perys had clocked up a total of forty-five solo flying hours in three different aeroplanes. It was an impressive amount of flying time for a trainee pilot. He had also carried out aerobatics in the BE2c when playing follow-the-leader with Nick flying the Avro.

It was an exhibition of flying that filled the watching RFC trainee pilots with envy. There were so many of them that, with too few planes at their disposal, they were sometimes forced to wait all day in order to enjoy a mere half-an-hour in the air. They would be expected to obtain their pilot's certificate with only a fraction of the flying time clocked up by Perys. Another far more sobering thought was that many of the RFC pilots would be killed in action without ever achieving the number of flying hours Perys had to his name.

The Aero Club examiner first asked Perys some cursory questions, then Perys took up the Maurice Farman 'Longhorn' to carry out a few elementary manoeuvres around the perimeter of the motor-racing track.

As he was taxying off the examiner asked Nick, 'How do you rate this one?'

Nick responded immediately. 'I wouldn't dream of telling him, but he's a natural. Probably one of the finest pilots I have ever turned out.'

Shifting his glance from the 'Longhorn' to the man standing beside him, the examiner said, 'That's high praise indeed coming from you, Nick.'

'It's fully justified, I can assure you,' Nick replied. 'I thought his cousin, Rupert Pilkington, was good, but Perys will be better.'

Once again the examiner moved his glance from the aeroplane to the flying instructor. 'I know Rupert well. He's one of the very best. This boy *must* be good.'

'He is,' Nick said simply.

Perys did not let his instructor down. After his obligatory manoeuvres, the examiner turned to Nick and said, 'I think you're right. He handled that aeroplane as though he's been flying for years.'

Relieved, despite the confidence he had in his pupil, Nick grinned. 'You should see him performing aerobatics in the BE2c. I wouldn't fancy my chances were I an enemy with Perys on my tail.'

'Did you say there was some urgency about granting him his ticket?' As the examiner spoke he was writing something on the form attached to the clipboard he held in his hands.

'Yes, he has an interview for the RFC at the War Office next week. As a qualified pilot his acceptance will be assured.'

'I'll see his licence has priority, but don't worry about it. He'll be interviewed by Colonel MacAllen – Lord MacAllen. I'm having dinner with him this weekend, I'll see that Perys is given a mention.'

*   *   *

When Perys stood before Colonel MacAllen the following week, it quickly became evident that he had been mentioned to the Royal Flying Corps recruiting officer by more than one interested party.

After poring over the documents laid on the desk before him, the colonel looked up at Perys and smiled. 'You seem to have impressed a great many people in a very short time, young man. You have also seen action with your relative, Captain Pilkington, I believe?'

'Yes, sir. It was a very exciting first flight.'

'Quite!' The colonel chuckled. 'I think you and the Royal Flying Corps will suit each other very well – especially after the three weeks you have spent under the instruction of Nick Malloch. I expect great things from you, Tremayne. I doubt very much I will be disappointed.'

'You mean . . . I am accepted, sir? When will I be able to start?'

Colonel MacAllen held up a hand in mock protest. 'You will need a little patience, young man. Pilots are urgently required – and you are certainly a pilot, but you are not yet a Royal Flying Corps pilot. You will need to learn something of service etiquette, discipline and drill. We are now in November. Despite the urgency of the present situation, I doubt whether any new recruits will begin training until the New Year.'

Perys found it difficult to hide his disappointment.

Observing this, Colonel MacAllen said, 'I appreciate your eagerness to serve your country, Tremayne, but the best I can do for you is to make a recommendation that once your basic training is completed, your flying ability is assessed. If it is found to be satisfactory – and

Mr Malloch seems convinced it will be – I will recommend that you are sent on an advanced flying course immediately. With luck, you should be in France with a front-line squadron by the spring of next year. I doubt very much whether there will be any serious fighting before then.'

Looking back at the documents on the desk before him, he said, 'I see we have a London address for you. Is there anywhere else you might be when we send for you?'

'Yes, sir. I hope to spend a week or two at my great-uncle's house in Cornwall. The address should be somewhere in my file. It's Heligan House, at Saint Ewe.'

28

Perys had hoped to leave for Cornwall immediately after obtaining his pilot's licence, but in spite of all Maude's efforts to contact Great-Uncle Hugh Tremayne, it was proving difficult. Perys would need his approval in order to return to the house.

He wrote to tell Annie of his plans, then impatiently awaited news from his great-uncle.

During his time at Knightsbridge, Perys helped out at St Thomas's Hospital where many men wounded in the battlefields of France and Belgium continued to be admitted. He also spent a few days at Brooklands with Nick Malloch, adding to his flying hours and even accompanying trainee pilots on dual-flying flights.

The latter was something he did not enjoy, but it went some way towards repaying the debt he owed to Nick. Then, during the last week in November, a number of things happened.

The first was that Perys received a letter instructing him to report to the Central Flying School at Upavon, on Salisbury Plain, in Wiltshire, a few days after Christmas.

The second incident of note was that Arabella told him, in a dramatically serious manner, that she had fallen hopelessly in love with a young trainee doctor. She was convinced that this new love would be the man in her life 'for ever'. She begged Perys to forgive her fickleness.

Doing his best to hide his relief and trying to match her gravity, he informed his young cousin that he put her happiness before all other considerations. He hoped the man in question would prove worthy of her.

Arabella's reaction was to fling her arms about his neck and tell Perys what a wonderful person he was. For a few moments he was afraid he might have over-played the role of a jilted but understanding 'lover'. However, Arabella then regaled him with a list of the virtues of the man chosen to be the final love in her young life. Not least among them was the fact that he was the heir to an ancient baronetcy.

Two days later Maude received the long-awaited letter from Hugh Tremayne. Delighted that Perys was to join the Royal Flying Corps, the owner of Heligan declared that in view of Perys's part in the flight that had earned Rupert a DSO, he was to look upon Heligan as his home whenever the opportunity arose for him to pay it a visit. Hugh Tremayne himself would be spending little time there, preferring the comforts of another property he owned in Devon. All he asked was that Perys should inform the Heligan housekeeper in advance of his intended arrival.

Perys would have set off for Cornwall immediately, but there was also news from Rupert. An impasse had been reached in the war in Europe. The Germans had thrown everything into their initial assault upon France in anticipation of a swift and decisive victory, but their aims had been thwarted by the fierce resistance put up by the French and British armies.

Both sides had suffered horrific losses in the initial conflict. Forced to draw back from the gates of Paris, the German army had retreated to a defensive line that would change little during the ensuing four years, despite slaughter on a scale never before witnessed in warfare. Already the casualties were so high that neither side had sufficient trained men left to launch a major offensive in the immediate future.

This, together with the prospect of bad weather, meant that the Royal Flying Corps could temporarily scale down its activities and allow its pilots a period of leave. As a result, Rupert expected to be back in England during the second week of December. He intended paying a call on Morwenna and her family in Knightsbridge.

As a result, Perys postponed his planned visit to Heligan House.

When Rupert arrived at the Tremaynes' Knightsbridge house, driving his very impressive Rolls-Royce motorcar, Perys thought he looked older than when they had last met.

Rupert was equally concerned for Morwenna. After greeting Maude and the two girls, he stood back and looked critically at her.

'You look tired, Morwenna. You've been working far too hard – and don't tell me I am imagining it. You nursed one of my wounded pilots. He returned to France and told me he had met with you and that you were absolutely rushed off your feet for the whole of the time you were on duty. He also said you were an absolute angel to all the men on your ward.'

'I remember him well,' Morwenna said. 'He was one of our earliest casualties. We often spoke about you. I didn't realise he would be returned to duty so soon. He had chest and shoulder wounds, as I recall. How is he?'

A pained expression crossed Rupert's face. 'He was killed on his first flight back with us. Shot down by German anti-aircraft fire while on a reconnaissance flight.'

'I'm sorry . . .' Morwenna was genuinely upset. 'He was such a pleasant young man.'

'And a first-class pilot,' said Rupert. 'But don't let's talk of the war. I am only home for a few days. I would like to celebrate by taking you all out to dinner this evening. What do you say?'

Rupert's invitation met with a mixed reception. Morwenna and Perys were enthusiastic, but Arabella was unable to accept. She was on night shift at the hospital. Maude also had to decline. She was chairing fund-raising meetings on both the evenings Rupert would be spending with the family.

Rupert's disappointment was apparent to everyone and Maude said, quickly, 'You must not allow the absence of Arabella and me to spoil your evening. Make the most of your time away from the war, Rupert. Both Morwenna and Perys have worked very hard in recent weeks. You must go out and enjoy yourselves while you can. Indeed, I *insist* that you do. Who knows when you are all likely to be in the same place at the same time again? This is a special occasion, one to be celebrated in style. You must book a table at a first-class restaurant for dinner and have the bill sent to me.'

Rupert had planned for something a little less ostentatious; nevertheless, it was a generous gesture on Maude's part and he said so.

'Nonsense!' was Maude's reply. 'I am proud of you – every one of you – and am happy to have an opportunity to express my admiration.'

Aware that Arabella was deeply disappointed at being excluded from the evening's celebrations, Maude turned to her and said, 'I am equally proud of you too, dear, but we both have work to do. Never mind, you and I will go shopping at Harrods when next we have a free day together.'

Aware that her mother would be anxious to prove as generous to her as she was being to Morwenna, Arabella accepted the alternative happily.

29

During the remainder of that day Perys was aware of occasional whispered conversations between Morwenna and her mother, and also, occasionally, with Rupert.

He tried to ignore them. After all, Rupert and the Knightsbridge Tremaynes had known each other for very many years, while he had only recently come into their lives. There would be things they wanted to say to each other that did not concern him.

Nevertheless, although he tried hard to excuse such secretiveness, it left him with a feeling that however kind they were to him, he was still an outsider.

Then, when Maude had left for her meeting and Arabella and Morwenna were out of the room, Rupert gave Perys an explanation for their secrecy.

'Perys, you could not have helped noticing that Maude, Morwenna and myself were being unforgivably rude by whispering in corners, but I can now explain. I thought it might be rather nice if we could make it a somewhat more balanced dinner party tonight. I suggested to Morwenna that she invite one of her friends at the hospital for dinner and offered to pay for the extra guest. However, Aunt Maude agreed that it was a splendid idea and insisted that she pay for the evening, no matter how many of us there were. Morwenna telephoned one of her special friends, a girl named Grace Ballard. She has accepted an invitation to join us for dinner.'

Having written only the previous day to tell Annie how much he was looking forward to seeing her again later that week, Perys was not particularly enthusiastic about acting as a partner to one of Morwenna's friends. But Rupert's next words explained his reason for suggesting such an arrangement.

'By inviting a companion for you I am not being entirely altruistic, Perys. I hope it will mean I have more of Morwenna's attention. I would dearly like to have a serious discussion with her, so you are really doing me a very great favour, old chap!'

Perys had realised when they met at Heligan that Morwenna and Rupert looked upon each other as more than friends and second cousins, and he owed Rupert a great deal. Besides which he felt guilty about the thoughts he had entertained about their whispering.

'You have no need to apologise for taking me out to dinner and providing me with the company of a pleasant young woman – and I am sure that's what she will be if she's a friend of Morwenna.'

Despite his acceptance of the situation, some of Perys's guilt returned when Grace Ballard turned out to be a very attractive and well-educated young woman. She was quite obviously delighted to be going out to dinner in the company of two pilots, one of whom was already a decorated hero.

When Grace questioned him about his own flying future, it was evident to Perys that she had been very well briefed about him.

But conversation with his arranged companion was not difficult. They soon discovered they had a great deal in common, not least the fact that Grace's home was in the village of Asthall in Oxfordshire, only a short distance from the school Perys had attended.

When Perys told her he must have flown over her home on his way to drop the parachute message to his one-time headmaster, Grace became quite excited. Her mother had actually written to tell her about an aeroplane she had seen flying very close to the house. It was the first plane her mother had ever seen and Grace said she would be thrilled to learn that her daughter had actually dined with the pilot!

The evening was a highly successful and enjoyable occasion and Perys's earlier misgivings were quickly forgotten.

After dinner, Rupert drove the happy party to the Embankment. There he parked his motor-car and they paired off to walk beside the River Thames. Despite the late hour the river and the road beside it were still very busy.

As Perys leaned on the wall, watching the boats go by, Grace looked to where Morwenna was walking arm-in-arm with Rupert and said, 'They *do* make a handsome couple and they are very happy together. I hope this ghastly war does nothing to part them. But

Morwenna and I will soon be in France ourselves – perhaps she will see more of Rupert there.'

'*You* are going to France?'

'I'm sorry, Perys, has Morwenna said nothing to you about joining the Queen Alexandra's Imperial Military Nursing Service? I do hope I haven't spoken out of turn.'

'Morwenna told me she intended to apply to join. I wasn't aware matters had progressed beyond that.'

'We are both going,' Grace said. 'We had our interviews together only last week. We were not told right away whether or not we were successful, but they are desperate to recruit experienced nurses and Morwenna and I were the most highly qualified of the applicants.'

'What makes you think your duties might take you to France?' Perys asked.

'We made it clear at our interviews that we felt we would be most usefully employed in a field hospital operating theatre. That is where lives are saved – or lost.'

'I think you both have a great deal of courage,' Perys said, admiringly. 'Your parents should be very proud of you.'

'*You* speak of courage when before many weeks have passed you will be fighting the Germans from an aeroplane? The mere thought of leaving the ground in one of those machines would fill me with terror. To have to fight in one once I was in the air . . . !'

'You would feel quite different about it after your first flight,' Perys said enthusiastically. 'It is a magic world up there. There is a sense of freedom about flying that I have never experienced anywhere else, and probably never will.'

'I don't doubt you are right,' Grace said, unconvinced. 'I prefer to keep both feet on the ground and have you *tell* me how wonderful it is . . . But Morwenna and Rupert are returning. It must be almost time to go home. It has been a truly enjoyable evening, Perys. I do hope we will meet again . . . perhaps sometime over the Christmas period, when you return from Cornwall?'

Perys realised yet again that Morwenna had briefed Grace fully about his plans. He wondered how much she had disclosed about his past?

'Yes, it would be very nice if we could meet again,' he said, as she took his arm and they fell in beside Morwenna and Rupert to walk along the wide pavement of the Embankment.

30

Keeping a secret in a small rural community is well-nigh impossible, and Mevagissey was no exception. By late November the whole village knew Eliza Dunn was pregnant. Speculation was rife as to the identity of the father.

For a while suspicion fell upon Esau Tamblyn, a large, slow-speaking young fisherman who was somewhat simple and who had long been Eliza's most ardent admirer.

Esau was perfectly happy to have his name linked in such a fashion with that of Eliza, but she was not. Soon, other more persistent rumours began circulating. Those who knew her well gave the latest gossip more credence than any that had gone before.

It was now suggested that the father of her unborn child was no one from Mevagissey. Heligan began to be mentioned – and a certain young gentleman who had stayed there and who rode a motor-cycle about the countryside.

The certain young gentleman was named as Perys Tremayne.

The rumour reached Annie's ears via a village woman. She came to Tregassick Farm one day to order a goose for Christmas. Coming into the farm kitchen where Annie and her mother were working, she accepted the offer of a cup of tea while she told the two women the latest Mevagissey gossip.

When Annie angrily told the woman she had no right to spread such malicious rumours, the woman said mildly, 'Oh, 't'aint no rumour, m'dear. I put what I'd heard to Eliza Dunn herself and said that, of course, I didn't believe it. She, bold as brass, snapped back at me, "Oh! And why not? Are you saying I'm not good enough to carry a Tremayne baby? If that's what you're saying then you're wrong." Well, you can't have it more plain than that, can you? She's a hussy, but she's got her head screwed on the right way. I saw her wearing a coat the other day, the likes of which I've never seen in Mevagissey before. It weren't bought out of no fisherman's earnings, I can tell you that!'

'We've had Perys Tremayne here in this kitchen sitting in the very chair where you are. I think I'd trust him far more than I would the word of Eliza Dunn!'

Annie was still angry and the village woman gave her a searching look before saying, 'Well, I don't know the young gentleman myself, but one thing's certain – Eliza Dunn didn't get pregnant all by herself.'

'No, but you don't need to go to Heligan to find someone who *could* be the father.'

Annie was aware the innuendo would strike home. The woman's son had been one of Eliza's lovers a year or so before.

Harriet knew it too. She also knew the woman was an inveterate gossip. In a bid to prevent Annie from saying any more and getting herself talked about for having leaped to Perys's defence so strongly, she said, 'I thought young Master Perys was a nice young man . . . but don't let's waste the opportunity of a nice chat by discussing Eliza Dunn. Annie, go to the dairy and bring in some more milk, there's a dear, we're running short.'

Turning back to the Mevagissey woman, she said, 'Now, tell me what's happening down in the village. How is the fishing . . . ?'

Later that evening in the Tregassick farmhouse, Walter and Harriet Bray had just completed the evening ritual of wondering 'what Martin is doing right now', while Annie washed up the dishes.

Martin had been accepted by the Royal Flying Corps as a motor transport driver and mechanic and had been called up for training a week before, much earlier than the family had anticipated.

Suddenly, Annie untied her apron, hung it on a hook behind the kitchen door and announced, 'I'm going down to Mevagissey.'

Startled, Harriet said, 'At this time of night? What on earth for?'

'I'm going to find Eliza Dunn and have it out with her for what she's saying about Perys. It isn't fair for him to have his name blackened by her while he's not here to defend himself.'

Walter looked questioningly at his wife and she briefly explained about the visit from the Mevagissey gossip, adding to her daughter, 'I can understand you being upset by what she said, Annie, but by going down to the village and making a fuss about it you'll get yourself talked about.'

'I don't care!' Anger had been bottled up inside Annie all day. She had decided she would direct it where it belonged – at Eliza. 'She's no right to tell lies about Perys, making people believe he's the one who made her pregnant.'

Her father remained silent until Annie was about to leave the kitchen to find her coat, then he asked, quietly, 'What makes you think Eliza's lying, Annie?'

Taken aback, she replied, 'Because she *is*, that's why. He would never have had anything to do with the likes of her. You should know that, you met him more than once.'

'I don't know anything of the sort, girl. In fact, I know he *was* seeing her.'

'You mean that time our Martin saw them talking on the driveway up at Heligan? Perys explained to me about that.'

'No, Annie, I'm not talking of what anyone else has seen.'

'What do you mean?' Annie did not take her father's words lightly. He was not in the habit of speaking ill of anyone; neither did he pass on gossip.

'I saw Master Perys and Eliza together down by the track to Heligan Mill one day – it was just before he went away. He'd been up here on that motor-bike of his and must have gone straight from here to meet her.'

Annie looked at her father in disbelief. 'The day he came here . . . ?' She remembered the occasion. It had been later that same day when he had told her how much she meant to him. '. . . He probably needed to go to Mevagissey for something and just met up with her by chance.'

She desperately hoped her father would agree with her, but he shook his head.

'No, Annie. He'd left his motor-bike along the lane to go and meet her. They went back to it and were standing together just past the old barn. I saw him hand something to her. It might have been money, but I couldn't really be sure. Then . . .' he paused for a moment, aware that what he was about to say would upset Annie even more than she already was '. . . and then they kissed.'

There was a sharp intake of breath from Harriet, but Walter continued, 'So you see, Annie, the rumours aren't as far-fetched as they seem.'

Annie looked at him for a few minutes, her expression a mixture of disbelief and anguish.

'I'm sorry, Annie—'

Before he had finished speaking she turned and fled from the room and Walter and Harriet heard her running up the uncarpeted stairs to her room.

'I'd better go up and see if there's anything I can do.' Harriet rose to her feet to go to her daughter but Walter put out a hand to restrain her.

'Best let her be, Harriet. Let her get it out of her system. I always knew no good would come of her getting mixed up with anyone from the big house, but I didn't realise it had gone this far.'

For Walter, having everything out in the open had

come as a great relief. But he had another guilty secret, one that had been causing him a great deal of heart-searching during the past few weeks. Upstairs in the bedroom, in a locked deed box, were five unopened letters addressed to Annie. Letters he knew must have come from Perys. His actions in intercepting them and hiding them from her had troubled him greatly.

Now he felt he had been justified in taking such action.

31

The weather showed signs of deteriorating. Although it had been Perys's intention to make the journey from London to Heligan on his motor-cycle, he changed his mind. With the machine stowed in the guard's van, he travelled to Cornwall by train.

He was very excited at the prospect of seeing Annie again, although he was concerned that she had not replied to the four or five letters he had sent to her during the weeks he had been away from Cornwall. However, he had telephoned the housekeeper at Heligan to tell her the expected time and date of his arrival. He knew that within an hour every servant in the household would have the details and hoped Polly would pass on the news to Annie.

As the train pulled slowly into St Austell railway station, Perys opened the carriage window and looked out. He had nursed a faint hope that Annie might have found an excuse to come to the station to meet him, but he looked in vain. There were perhaps half-a-dozen women standing on the platform. Annie was not among them.

One of the passengers disembarking at St Austell was a soldier who lowered himself clumsily to the platform, supporting himself with the aid of two crutches.

Perys felt a pang of guilt at the realisation that the wounded soldier had endured a long journey in a crowded third-class compartment, while he had travelled in the near-empty luxury of a first-class carriage. However, it was not long before the wounded soldier was surrounded by laughing and crying relatives, young and old, and borne away in the midst of them, while Perys was left alone, watching his motor-cycle being unloaded at the rear of the train.

Once clear of St Austell, Perys bowled happily along the valley towards Heligan, enjoying the near-deserted road that was such a marked contrast to the noisy and crowded streets of London.

When he neared the lower lodge house that guarded one of the entrances to Heligan House, he decided he would call in to say hello to Annie before arriving at his destination.

It was with a great sense of excitement that he turned in to the track that led to Tregassick Farm. As he approached the farm buildings he cut the engine of the motor-cycle and coasted into the farmyard. This way he would not frighten the animals and birds. He also hoped he might take Annie by surprise.

Perys was successful in that his arrival did not cause consternation among geese and chickens in the farmyard, but no one came from the house to greet him.

Leaning his machine against a stable wall, he walked up to the farmhouse door. He was met there by Harriet, who had glanced out of a window and witnessed his arrival.

Smiling happily at her, Perys said, 'Hello, Mrs Bray. I've just arrived at Saint Austell by train. I thought I'd call in to say hello before going up to the house.'

The warmth of his greeting was not reciprocated. 'That was nice of you, Master Perys,' Harriet replied, with no indication that she was pleased to see him. 'I hope you enjoy your stay up at Heligan.'

Puzzled by her attitude, Perys's smile faded. 'Thank you . . . but is Annie around the farm?'

'I'm afraid she's away from Tregassick at the moment.'

'Away? You don't mean she's in Saint Austell? I've just come from there. I could have given her a ride back home . . .'

'She's not in Saint Austell, Master Perys, she's off staying at the family farm of a young man she's known since she was a girl. He's in the army and she's staying with the family so as to be near him until he goes off to war.'

Perys was unable to hide his dismay. 'You mean . . . Annie and this . . . this farmer's son have been walking out together? For how long?'

For a moment he thought Harriet was going to tell him it was none of his business. Instead, she said, 'It's not so much a question of them "walking out". They've known each other since they were small, when his family had the next farm, up at Tregiskey. They moved away a few years ago, but there's always been an unspoken understanding between our families about

200

Jimmy and Annie. He joined the army as soon as the war started. Now he's being sent to France. He came to see Annie and asked that she come to stay at his family's farm so she would be there when he left.'

The story was *almost* the truth. When the two families occupied adjoining farms, they had hoped Jimmy and Annie would one day marry, but they had not met for a couple of years until recently, when Jimmy and his sister, Rose, who had been Annie's best friend, called at Tregassick. It was immediately apparent to Harriet that the reunion had rekindled Jimmy's interest in her daughter. When Rose suggested Annie should come and stay with them for a few days, it seemed to Harriet an answer to the problems associated with Perys's expected arrival at Heligan.

The farm where she was staying was only a few miles distant, in nearby Fowey, but as Perys did not know this it might as well have been a thousand miles away.

Deeply upset by the reasons behind Annie's absence and by the noticeable coolness of her mother, Perys mumbled, 'I'm sorry to have troubled you, Mrs Bray.' At a loss for words, he could only add, 'Please tell Annie I called and . . . and say I hope she will be very happy.' He turned to leave, but suddenly turned back again. 'Did Annie receive my letters? I wrote some four or five to her.'

'I know nothing of any letters. If they *did* arrive she didn't say anything to me about them.'

Perys was very despondent as he rode away from Tregassick Farm. He had come to Cornwall only because Annie was there and he wanted to be with her. Without her there was very little reason for his presence at Heligan.

His mood was not helped when he found the servants at Heligan House were no warmer towards him than Harriet had been. There seemed to be no men servants at the house and his bag was taken to his room by a maid. On the way he asked about Martin and was told he had left to join the Royal Flying Corps.

He immediately enquired after Polly and was told in a disinterested fashion that she was 'somewhere about the house'.

It was not until the following day that Perys met up with Polly – and even then it was not of her making. He encountered her in a passageway on the first floor, when he was on his way downstairs and she was heading for the top floor of the house with clean linen for the servants' quarters.

'Polly!' Perys showed his delight at the meeting. 'I was beginning to think you were deliberately avoiding me. How is Martin?'

'He's all right, thank you, Master Perys. We had a letter from him only yesterday. He's in Wiltshire, looking forward to finishing his training. He's grateful to you for the advice you gave him about joining the Royal Flying Corps. He likes what he's doing. He says it's far more interesting than the army would be.'

'Good. I too shall be in the RFC immediately after Christmas. I hope we'll meet up.'

There was an awkward silence between them for a few minutes before Polly said, 'I must get this linen up to the servants' floor, Master Perys.'

'Before you do that I want you to tell me what has

happened to turn Annie and her family against me, Polly. I thought she and I had an understanding, but I have come back to Cornwall to see her, only to learn she has apparently taken up with someone else.'

Ill-at-ease, Polly said, 'I think you must speak to Annie about that, Master Perys, not me.'

'I would, Polly, but she's not at the farm, as I am sure you know.'

'Please don't get me involved in this, Master Perys. I'm finding things difficult enough as it is, what with Martin going away so quickly, and all. Things are changing so fast here, sir. I liked them the way they were.'

'I was happy with the way things were too, Polly. I especially remember that night when we all walked back to Heligan from Tregassick. I thought Annie and I had arrived at an understanding, yet I've returned to find that everything has changed – and I don't know why. When I called at Tregassick Farm, Annie's mother behaved as though I was a stranger. It's the same here. The servants are polite, but no more than that. Even you have been trying to avoid me— no, don't deny it. If we had not met accidentally now you would have kept out of my way for as long as you possibly could. What am I supposed to have done wrong, Polly? You must tell me . . . no one else will.'

Polly was very unhappy about becoming directly involved in a quarrel between a member of the family that employed her and the sister of the man she was going to marry. Nevertheless, she felt Perys deserved an explanation, at least.

'It's Eliza Dunn. She's pregnant.'

'That should come as no surprise to anyone. What has it to do with Annie and me?'

'People around here believe you're the one responsible,' Polly blurted out.

'Me!' Perys could not hide his astonishment. 'But . . . you know that's not true, Polly. It was you who told me of what she had been up to – and with whom – long before I first came to Heligan.'

'I know, sir. I told Annie so, but it seems . . .'

She hesitated and Perys prompted, 'It seems what, Polly?'

Reluctantly, Polly said, 'Annie heard that Eliza had been spreading a rumour that *you* were the father of her baby. She was going to go down to Mevagissey to stop Eliza telling such lies, but then her pa told her they probably weren't lies, because . . .' She faltered once more before saying, in a rush, 'He'd seen you and Eliza kissing.'

'He'd seen *what*? When is this supposed to have happened, Polly?'

'On your last day here. The same day you, me, Martin and Annie all walked back from Tregassick. Annie's pa also said he thought you'd given Eliza some money.'

Memories of the meeting with Eliza came back to Perys. He was horrified, but it was important that he set the record straight with Polly, at least.

'Annie's father jumped to some very wrong conclusions, Polly. It's true I *did* meet with Eliza. I also gave her something she had asked me to get for her – she asked for it on the day she waylaid me, when Martin saw us together. As for the kiss . . . *She* kissed *me*, Polly. I think it was a thank you kiss, and it surprised me as much as it must have surprised Annie's father. As for her saying I am the father of the child she's expecting, it's a blatant lie, and one I will have Eliza put a stop to right away.' Angrily, he turned away, but almost immediately swung back to confront the servant girl once more. 'Do you believe I have told you the truth, Polly?'

She hesitated for only a moment. 'Yes. Yes, I do. I told Annie so. I also told her what you once said to me, that you'd never ever do anything to hurt her.'

'And what did she say to that, Polly?'

'She said that only made it worse. I think she *wanted* to believe you, but she knew her father wouldn't lie to her about something like that.'

'No, Polly, I don't think he would either, but he read far more into what he thought he saw than what actually happened. I'll go and have a word with him once I have spoken to Eliza.'

32

When Perys set off from Heligan on his motor-cycle he was feeling angrier than he could ever remember. It was not a blind, hot fury, but cold, controlled anger, focused upon one person – Eliza Dunn.

Arriving at the path that led to Heligan Mill, he left his motor-cycle in the same place as before. Then, remembering the last time he was here, he checked the hay-filled barn where Eliza had enjoyed a liaison with the Heligan gamekeeper.

There was no one there today. Perys guessed that the gamekeeper and other of Eliza's lovers would be keeping their distance lest any breath of scandal should link them with her present condition.

Leaving the barn he saw Eliza approaching along the path from the mill. As she neared, her pregnant state was quite evident.

She had been looking down at the path as she

walked, seemingly deep in thought. She did not look up until she neared the barn.

Seeing Perys she at first appeared startled. Recovering quickly, she smiled disarmingly at him. 'Well, this is a pleasant surprise! Is this a chance meeting, or do you have something particular in mind?' As she spoke she glanced meaningfully towards the hay barn.

Perys thought she looked desperately tired, but he was not in a mood to feel sorry for her. 'Don't play games with me, Eliza. You have done quite enough of that. I am here to speak to you about the rumours you have been spreading about me – and your baby.'

'I haven't spread no rumours,' Eliza said, defensively. 'If people want to talk about me then that's their business. I'm just not bothered.'

'Then you had better *start* bothering yourself and ensure that everyone in Mevagissey – and beyond – knows that I am *not* the father of the baby you're carrying. What's more, you'll inform them that I have never had anything to do with you.'

'I don't see why I should!' Eliza spoke defiantly. 'I'm not asking anything of you. Anyway, if what I hear is right, you'll soon be away from here for good, so it won't matter what they say about you.' Suddenly and shrewdly, she added, 'Or is it because the rumours are upsetting someone else? Annie Bray, perhaps?'

'They are upsetting *me*, so I suggest you start denying them right away.'

'And if I don't?' Eliza demanded. 'What will you do about it? Go round telling everyone you've nothing to do with this . . . ?' Patting her bulging stomach, she said, scornfully, 'That's what they'd expect you to say – they'll be even more convinced it's yours.'

'I won't go around denying anything,' declared Perys. 'I shall first of all go to speak to the wife of the Heligan gamekeeper and tell her what I witnessed between you and her husband the last time I was here. Then I shall write to my cousin Edward and tell him what I know.'

Eliza paled. The gamekeeper's wife was a large, loud woman, prone to violence, especially against her husband. But her real fear was that Perys would give Edward grounds to absolve himself of any responsibility for the child she was expecting.

Suddenly, her eyes opened wide with fear, but it had nothing to do with the threats Perys had just made. Following her gaze, Perys swung around and saw a giant of a young man hurrying towards them. He was quite obviously angry and his anger appeared to be directed at Perys.

'What are you doing here with Eliza?' he demanded. 'Haven't you caused her enough grief?'

'It's all right, Esau, he's not bothering me,' Eliza spoke hurriedly, in an attempt to calm him.

'You would say that, Eliza. You don't like getting anyone into trouble, but he's got to learn to leave you alone.'

Perys realised from Esau's manner and speech that the other man was simple, but Perys had met with Eliza for a purpose. Before parting from her he intended that she should be in no doubt about the seriousness of his threat.

'Esau . . . is that your name? Look, be a good chap

and leave us for a few minutes until I have finished talking to Eliza, then you can be the first to hear what she has to say.'

'Oh no, I'm not going to leave you alone with her.'

Perys sighed. 'Please tell him, Eliza.'

Suddenly and unexpectedly, Eliza's eyes filled with tears. It had an immediate effect upon Esau. Rounding on Perys, he said, angrily, 'Now your bullying has made her cry. I told you—'

He swung a punch at Perys that would have pole-axed a bullock, but Perys ducked and it went harm-lessly over his head.

'That's enough, Esau, I have no quarrel with you.'

Instead of replying, Esau swung another wild punch. This time Perys only just succeeded in avoiding it.

'Don't push me too hard, Esau. Stop right there—'

Another punch was thrown, and this time it brushed Perys's ear in passing. He decided it was time to end the fight before one of Esau's great fists found its target. Stepping inside Esau's next wild swing, Perys landed two heavy punches to the big man's stomach. As he folded forward, Perys landed an uppercut that caused the man to stagger backwards and sit down heavily upon the path.

Eliza's scream galvanised Esau into life. Scrambling to his feet, he lunged at Perys once more.

The big man took two punches to the jaw, one of which caused him to bite his lip, which immediately began to bleed profusely. Then he was on the ground again and Perys appealed to Eliza.

'Tell him! Tell him the baby has nothing to do with me, before he gets badly hurt.'

Eliza acted swiftly. Dropping down beside Esau, she wrapped her arms about him, saying, 'No more, Esau. The baby is nothing to do with him. I swear he's never had anything to do with me. Never ever.'

Her words seemed to have the desired effect. Esau made no move to rise. Instead, he put a hand up to his mouth. When he took it away he looked stupidly at the blood staining his fingers.

'Oh, my poor love!' Producing a handkerchief, Eliza held it to Esau's mouth. Looking up at Perys, she said, 'You can go now. I'll do what you ask.'

'If you'd said so earlier none of this would have been necessary.' Nodding his head in the direction of the bleeding man, he added, 'Take good care of him, Eliza, there can't be many men around Mevagissey willing to fight for you.'

Perys waited for nightfall before going to Tregassick Farm. He wanted to be certain of finding Walter Bray at home.

He arrived while husband and wife were eating their evening meal. Harriet tried to use this as an excuse for not inviting him inside the farmhouse, but Perys insisted that what he had to say would not wait until the next day.

In the kitchen, Walter was still eating when Perys entered. Declining Harriet's half-hearted offer of a cup of tea, he said, 'No, thank you – and please, finish your meal, Mrs Bray. I am sorry to have interrupted you in such a fashion, but it concerns a matter that is very important to me.'

Harriet sat down at the kitchen table and began picking at her meal in a desultory fashion. Perys ignored the chair pulled out for him by Walter. Instead, he stood where they could both look at him while they ate.

'When I was staying at Heligan in the summer you made me very welcome here. I became very fond of you. I also became more than just fond of Annie – and I told her so. To be perfectly honest with you, she is the reason I have returned to Heligan. It was a great shock to me when I came to Tregassick yesterday and learned that Annie had an understanding with someone else and had gone off to stay with his family. I was also puzzled, Mrs Bray. You made it quite obvious that I was no longer welcome at your farm and I couldn't understand why.'

Harriet offered a mild protest, but Perys ignored it.

'When Polly explained what it was you believed about me, I realised why you had behaved in such a way. But you are wrong, you know.'

When neither the farmer nor his wife replied and avoided looking directly at him, Perys said, 'I went to Mevagissey today and confronted Eliza with what was being said about me. Unfortunately, someone named Esau came upon the scene to take Eliza's part. I was forced to knock him down. I am sorry about that, but there was nothing else I could do at the time.'

Walter stopped with a fork poised halfway between plate and mouth. 'You knocked down Esau? Esau Tamblyn? Why, he's nigh on twice your size.'

'He's twice the size of most men I know,' Perys agreed, 'but what I did served its purpose. In order to prevent him from taking matters any farther, Eliza admitted to him that I have nothing at all to do with

211

the baby she's carrying. I hope that by now she will have said the same thing to a great many more of her neighbours in Mevagissey. The baby she is having *is* nothing at all to do with me. Indeed, I hardly know the girl.'

Harriet threw a quick glance at her husband and, correctly interpreting the significance of the look, Perys said, 'Now I have made certain Eliza puts the record straight in the village, I wanted to come here to do the same – and to explain what it was you thought you saw, Mr Bray.

Looking ill-at-ease, Walter said, 'It wasn't what I *thought* I saw, Master Perys. I was up in the field by the path to Heligan Mill when you kissed young Eliza Dunn.'

'You did not see *me* kissing Eliza. What you saw was Eliza kissing me – and there is a difference. A big difference. She had stopped me in the driveway to Heligan a few days before and asked if I would get something for her, something that could only be got from the house. That was the day Martin saw us talking. I did what she asked and when you saw me I had just handed it to her. I suppose that kissing me was her way of saying thank you. Whatever the reason, it surprised me just as much as it must have shocked you.'

Walter was an honest man. When he thought about what Perys had just said, he knew the young man was telling the truth about who kissed who.

'If I got the wrong impression, I can only say I'm very sorry,' he said. 'But what with that and Eliza going about telling everyone about you and her . . .'

'Eliza will be going about putting everyone right

as quickly as she can,' Perys said, tight-lipped. 'The most important thing to me is that you know the truth – you, Mrs Bray and Annie. Especially Annie. I have had nothing to do with Eliza, nor would I. Had she not asked me for a favour I doubt if I would ever have met the girl again after speaking to her in the Heligan driveway. And believe me, I sincerely wish I never had.'

Satisfied he had put the record straight with Walter and Harriet, Perys still had another matter he wished to resolve.

'Do you know when Annie will be returning to Tregassick?'

'No,' Harriet said. 'It could be a week or so, or it might not be until Christmas.'

Her reply was not what Perys had wanted to hear, but he had one more question to ask – and it was the one most important of all to him.

'Do you really believe she will marry this farmer's son?'

Perys had convinced the farmer and his wife that he was not responsible for Eliza's condition and had not lied to either them or Annie, but he still belonged to a wealthy and aristocratic land-owning family. Such young men did not contemplate marriage with daughters of small-time tenant farmers. It was Walter who replied to this question.

'I very much hope so. They're made for each other. Our Annie has been brought up the way a farmer's wife should. They've got our blessing and his folk feel the same way.'

Watching from the farmhouse doorway as the dejected figure walked to where he had left his

213

motor-cycle, Harriet said, 'I feel sorry for the lad, Walter. He's a nice young man.'

'I wouldn't argue with that,' Walter agreed, 'but the future of our Annie will be more secure with Jimmy Rowe.'

33

At the Rowe farm, a letter from her mother reached Annie the day after Jimmy had left for France. Aware that Perys was at Heligan, Annie had decided to stay on at the farm with her childhood friend for a while longer. She did not feel able to cope with meeting Perys again just yet.

The letter threw her into a state of confusion. Harriet Bray had received very little schooling, and although the letter had been a laborious task for her, it did not make it clear to Annie what was happening at Tregassick.

It did, however, inform her that Perys had called at the farm and that Eliza had now admitted that she and Perys had never been lovers.

In view of what her father claimed to have seen, Annie was extremely confused. She was also distressed. Jimmy Rowe had left the previous day to rejoin his regiment, the Duke of Cornwall Light

Infantry, and was expected to embark for France almost immediately. Before his departure, it was evident that he firmly believed he and Annie had an unspoken agreement about a future together. Jimmy's parents thought so too. They spoke openly of having Annie return to stay at the Rowe farm in the event of Jimmy coming home on leave at any time.

Jimmy's mother had also pointed out an empty farm cottage as being a place where the parents would one day live when Jimmy took over the running of the farm and he and Annie occupied the farmhouse.

Annie was not happy with such an assumption of her future role as the wife of Jimmy. She knew she should have put the record straight immediately, but was reluctant to cause Jimmy distress on the eve of his departure to war. There would be a more suitable opportunity to enlighten him on his return.

The letter from her mother only added to her confusion. Although it failed to make anything entirely clear, Annie believed her mother was equally uncertain about the present course of events. Had it not been so, she would have made no mention of Perys's visit to Tregassick, or Eliza's denial that he was the father of her unborn child. Such news could have waited until Annie's return.

Having said her farewells to the Rowe family, Annie walked to the nearby small harbour town of Fowey with the intention of travelling as far as St Austell on the motor-bus service that had recently begun to operate between the two towns.

However, once in Fowey, she recognised a fishing boat unloading at the town quay as being from Mevagissey. She knew a couple of the men on board and was able to take passage on the boat for a much quicker journey to the fishing village.

On the way she chatted with the crewmen and elicited the surprising news that Eliza Dunn and Esau Tamblyn were likely to be married before her baby was born.

'Does that mean that *he's* the father?' Annie asked, incredulously.

'It means he *thinks* he is,' said the skipper of the fishing boat, 'but then, so do many others. The difference between them is that only poor Esau is simple enough to want to marry her.'

'I wonder if she'll go through with it?' Annie pondered aloud. 'I was quite sure she was after a grander catch than a simple fisherman.'

'Well, they do say that needs must when the Devil drives,' the fisherman said. 'Eliza won't be the first to marry when she's carrying someone else's child.' He suddenly chuckled, 'There'll be a lot of local men who'll breathe a sigh of relief when Esau and Eliza walk out of church together.'

Annie's return to Tregassick took her father by surprise. He had come in to the house from the cold of the farmyard to warm himself with a cup of tea before returning to his chores.

After Annie had kissed and hugged both parents and told them of her means of transport, Walter said, 'You must have smelled the tea, girl. Sit yourself down and get warm. There's a fresh wind blowing – you would have been frozen on a fishing boat from Fowey.'

'No, I sat under cover most of the time, while Jack

Henna told me what has been going on in Mevagissey. Most of the news concerned Eliza Dunn.'

Walter and Harriet exchanged glances and Harriet said, 'That's hardly surprising. She's been the subject of a lot of talk up here, too.'

'What was it caused her to admit Perys wasn't the baby's father? I doubt if it would have been an offer of marriage from poor Esau.'

Again it was Harriet who gave her a reply. 'As you know, Master Perys was up at Heligan House. When he heard from Polly what Eliza was saying about him he went straight down to Mevagissey to see her and get things sorted. He did, too. Since then Eliza has been at great pains to tell folk that Perys had nothing at all to do with the baby she's expecting.'

'I've never *really* believed he did,' Annie said, 'not in my heart of hearts. But you saw him kissing her, Pa, so he certainly had more to do with her than he wanted us to know about.'

Walter suddenly appeared ill-at-ease and Harriet said, 'He explained that to us, Annie. When Eliza stopped him in the driveway up at Heligan, the time our Martin saw them, it seemed she was asking him to find out something for her. He did what she asked and when he met up with her to tell her what she wanted to know, *she* kissed *him*. He said it took him by surprise at the time. Your pa agreed that when he thought about it, that *is* what happened. She kissed him, and not the other way around.'

As Harriet spoke, Annie was looking at her father in increasing disbelief. 'But Pa . . . you said you saw them kissing. You made it sound as though they were kissing each other.'

'Ah . . . well . . . I didn't mean it to sound like that. I had to admit to Master Perys that it happened just the way he said it did.'

Annie was very close to tears. 'How could you have led me to believe what you did, Pa? Everything I've done since then has been because of what you told me. I even went to the Rowe farm so I wouldn't have to meet Perys again. He must be so hurt by the way I've behaved towards him. How *could* you do such a thing?'

'You mustn't take on so about it, girl. It's all turned out for the best. If things had carried on the way they were you'd have been the one who would have ended up hurt. It's much better for you to settle down with a nice young man like Jimmy. Someone who'll have his own farm one day.'

'What makes you think I *want* to be a farmer's wife? What makes you think I want Jimmy?' Annie began putting on the coat she had taken off only a few minutes before.

Alarmed, Harriet said, 'What are you doing, child? Where do you think you're going?'

'To Heligan. To tell Perys I'm sorry for the way I've behaved and to explain why I wasn't here to meet him when he called.'

'Now you just stop there. I'll not have you running off after someone who lives up at the big house . . .'

Walter started up from his chair, but he suffered from arthritic knees and was slow in his movements, while Annie was young and determined. She was running out of the farmyard by the time he reached the farmhouse door and his shouted demands that she 'Come back!' did nothing to slow her.

At Heligan House, the housekeeper was frostily disapproving when Annie called at the front door and asked to speak to Perys.

'*Master* Perys is not here,' she said, acidly. The door would have been closed in Annie's face had she not asked, 'Can you tell me when you are expecting him to be back?'

'I doubt if he has any reason to return to Heligan. He has gone off to London again, to join the Royal Flying Corps.'

The housekeeper's statement dismayed Annie, but before she could ask for his London address, the door had closed. There was nothing Annie could do except leave and make her way home.

She had hardly passed out of sight of the house when a figure emerged from a shrub-lined path at the side of the driveway. It was Polly.

'I saw you from an upstairs window,' the maid said by way of explanation for her presence. 'I thought you might be looking for me.' Suddenly fearful, she asked, hesitantly, 'It's not . . . it's nothing to do with Martin . . . ?'

'No, Polly, it has nothing to do with Martin,' Annie hastened to reassure her future sister-in-law. 'I came here hoping to speak to Perys, but I'm told he's gone back to London.'

'He went back this morning,' Polly confirmed. 'He was very unhappy, Annie. He came all this way specially to see you. When he heard you'd gone off to stay with Jimmy's family and that you were going to marry him, he was very upset. He was able to sort Eliza out – and rumour has it that he laid into Esau too – but it was you he'd come to Heligan to see. He

220

told me yesterday there was nothing at Heligan for him now. He's gone back to London, but he's not going to be there for long. He's a pilot now and he'll be in the RFC, same as Martin, as soon as Christmas is over.'

'He's *passed* his pilot's exam? Oh, Polly, why hasn't he written to tell me what he's been doing? None of this mess would have happened if he had.'

Polly showed her surprise. 'But he *has* written, Annie. He told me so himself. He wasn't quite sure whether there were four or five letters, but he was definite about writing and I don't think he was lying.'

'No . . .' there was a break in Annie's voice. 'No, Polly, I don't think he was . . .'

When Annie arrived back at Tregassick Farm it was already dark and both her parents were once more in the kitchen.

Harriet was the first to speak. 'You shouldn't have run off like that, Annie. It upset us – your pa in particular.'

'I was upset too,' Annie retorted. 'I still am. Perys has gone back to London. He'll be in the RFC immediately after Christmas and he'll go to war thinking I'm going to marry Jimmy.'

'That'll be best for everyone,' Walter said. 'Jimmy'll make a good husband. No good could possibly come from you throwing yourself at the likes of Perys Tremayne.'

'How would you know?' Annie demanded, angrily. 'Would it be because you've read the letters Perys sent but that never reached me?'

'*Annie!* How dare you accuse your pa of doing

something like that? You just say you're sorry – this minute!'

'Well, *someone* has the letters and I'll find out who it is by checking with Postmaster Gilbert tomorrow.'

Before Harriet could say anything more, Walter said, 'There'll be no need for that. Yes, I took the letters because I guessed who they were from, but I didn't read any of 'em. They're upstairs locked in the deed box, still unopened.'

'*Walter!*' This from a shocked Harriet. 'I'd have staked my life against you doing anything like that. It's . . . why, it's unforgivable!'

'I thought it was for the best,' Walter said, not meeting his wife's shocked look. 'After what I'd seen going on between him and Eliza Dunn . . .'

'After what you *thought* you saw,' Annie said, tearfully. 'Or was it what you *wanted* to see? It seems to me Eliza didn't need to spread any lies about Perys – you've done a good enough job of it for her.'

'I've told you, I did what I thought was best for *you*,' Walter repeated, doggedly, well aware he was in the wrong.

'I'll never, *ever* trust your judgement again!' Tears were running down Annie's cheeks now. 'I'll never forgive you for what you've done, either. Perys came all this way especially to see me, now he's gone back believing I'm to marry Jimmy. Jimmy's family think so too . . .' Trying hard to maintain control of her voice, she said, 'I'll have my letters now and go off to my bedroom to read them. I don't want to have to look at you any more.'

Walter took a key from one of the pockets in his waistcoat and handed it to her, saying, 'You know where the box is kept.' The guilt he felt made him speak far more gruffly than he intended.

When Annie had left the room, Harriet rounded on her husband. 'Walter Bray, we've been married for a very long time and I felt I knew you. I never thought the day would come when you would behave in such an underhand and dishonest way – and towards your own daughter, too. I'm thoroughly ashamed of you.'

Harriet rarely showed anger, and on the infrequent occasions when there had been a difference of opinion within the family, she had invariably taken her husband's part. Her strong criticism of him on this occasion increased the misery that gripped him now.

In truth, the decision to keep Perys's first letter from Annie had been taken on the spur of the moment. He never expected there to be more than one. But having kept the first he felt that subsequent letters might have referred to earlier ones, thus causing questions to be asked about them. However, despite his decision, he could not bring himself to destroy the letters. They had gone into the deed box, for which he held the only key.

'I did what I thought was best for our Annie,' he said, miserably. 'I didn't want her getting hurt by someone who was just out to have a bit of fun with her.'

'So you decided *you'd* be the one to hurt her,' Harriet commented. 'It's going to take our Annie a very long time to forgive you. It's going to take me a while too, even though I think I understand why you did it. Not that I agree with you. You should have said something to me before deciding on such a thing.

223

You've split this family as nothing ever has before, Walter Bray.'

Rising to his feet, Walter said unhappily, 'I've got animals to bed down for the night. I'll be back in for supper.'

'You'd better hope there'll be some on the table for you,' Harriet said, unfeelingly. 'I'll be going up to see our Annie between now and then. She'll need some comforting, I've no doubt.'

Harriet waited for a full half-hour before going upstairs. A ribbon of pale light shone from the gap beneath Annie's bedroom door, but when she knocked there was no reply.

Knocking again, Harriet said, 'It's me, Annie. Can I come in?'

When there was still no reply, Harriet lifted the catch and pushed open the door. The lamp was turned low and Annie was lying fully clothed on the iron-framed single bed, her face turned to the wall.

'Annie, my love, you shouldn't be up here on your own like this. Come down to the kitchen and we'll have a talk, just you and me. Your pa is out in the yard. He'll be there until supper time.'

Annie made no reply. Unhappy to see her daughter so distraught, Harriet sat on the edge of the bed and stroked her hair, something she had often done on the occasions when Annie was ill as a small girl.

'What your pa did was wrong, girl, very wrong, but he thought he was doing it for the best. He'll likely be proven right in the end. Young Master Perys is a Tremayne. He's none the worse for that, but when it comes to choosing a wife he'll be looking among the wealthy families in the county. Gentlemen only look to young country girls for what they can get from them. A bit of fun, that's all you'd be to him. Your pa and I have seen it all before, Annie, too many times. We both want more for you than that.'

Annie shifted on the bed. Turning a tear-stained face up to her mother she thrust a bundle of letters at her. 'Read these. Take them down to the kitchen and when you've read them make *him* read them. When you've both done you can come back up here and tell me that what he's done is for the best. Until then, I just want to be left alone.'

34

When Walter returned to the house later that evening there was no smell of cooking in the air. He entered the kitchen and found Harriet huddled on a chair beside the window. Five letters were scattered on the table beside her.

'What's going on?' he demanded. 'Have I upset everyone so much I'm to be starved?'

When Harriet looked up, her eyes were red-rimmed and watery. 'I'm sorry, Walter, I just didn't feel like cooking. Sit down and get warmed up. I'll put a pasty in the oven and make up the fire – it won't take long.'

Pointing to the sheets of paper on the table, he asked, 'Are those Annie's letters?'

Harriet nodded, unhappily. 'She wanted us to read them. I already have. You can look at them while you're waiting for your supper. In the meantime, I'll make you a cup of tea.'

'I don't want to read no letters from that young man!' Walter spoke emphatically. 'He's caused enough trouble in this house. Anyway, he's gone away now. The best thing we can all do is forget about him.'

Harriet shook her head. 'I doubt we've heard the last of him, Walter. As for causing trouble in the house – I think it's us who've done that. Annie certainly thinks so and I'm inclined to agree with her.'

It seemed Walter would continue the argument, but Harriet said, 'Just read the letters before you say any more. We'll do any talking that's needed afterwards.'

Walter's education had been minimal and he was a very slow reader. He had not completed the first letter by the time a cup of tea was placed on the table in front of him. The tea was still untouched when he finished reading the last.

For some minutes he remained silent, seated with the fingers of his hands locked together on the table in front of him, chin sunk on his chest.

The letters had been an outpouring of Perys's happiness that Annie had given him a half-promise that she would wait for him. The happiness had changed to concern when he received no reply to any of his letters. The final letter had informed her of his intended visit to Heligan. In this, Perys had spoken of all the arguments that might be used to prevent them from marrying. They were the very arguments that Walter – and Harriet, too – had used to try to convince Annie that nothing could ever result from their relationship.

In this letter Perys had written at some length of the fact that he would never be fully accepted by the family whose name he bore. Because of this he believed his future lay in his own hands. He told her that for the first time in his life he had felt comfortable – at

Tregassick Farm, with Annie and her parents.

Finally, Perys had asked Annie if she would consider making the arrangement between them more permanent and public. If she agreed, he would tell his family that he intended marrying Annie as soon as he reached an age when their consent would not be needed. He was aware he was able to offer her little in the way of security immediately, but he felt certain there would be a commercial use for his skills as a pilot once the war was over. He was also convinced they could be very happy together.

It was apparent to anyone reading the letter that it was from a sincere and honest young man who genuinely loved Annie.

Walter Bray did not doubt Perys's sincerity. Nevertheless, when he spoke, it was to say, 'He's too young to know his own mind, Harriet. Why, he's hardly out of school!'

'And how old were you when you asked me to marry you, Walter?' Harriet retorted. 'He's old enough to pilot an aeroplane and fight for his country. Not only that, he's willing to tell the world how he feels about our Annie. That's why he came to Heligan, all the way from London.'

Walter fell silent again for a long time before saying, 'Our Annie . . . does she feel the same way about him?'

'You don't need me to give you an answer to that question, Walter. Of course she does. That's what all this fuss is about.'

'What of Jimmy? He'll have to be told.'

Tight-lipped, Harriet shook her head. 'That's where our interference has caused the biggest problem of all. Annie doesn't love Jimmy, but she likes him well enough. He's gone off to France to fight in this war thinking he's left a girl back home who'll marry him when he returns. Our Annie won't disillusion him while he's out there fighting and likely risking his life every day. She says she'll wait until he comes back and she's able to explain it to him face-to-face. I admire her for that, Walter. It makes me very proud of our daughter. Far more proud than I am of you right now for getting her into this mess in the first place.'

Walter was upset, both by his wife's words and by what he had read in the letter from Perys. 'What if I go and speak to Jimmy's folk? Tell them what I've done and how she really feels about things?'

Harriet shook her head. 'We've interfered quite enough in our daughter's future.' Heaving a big sigh, she added, 'We're living in the past, you and I, Walter. When we were Annie's age we did what our parents told us. They ordered our lives in a way that isn't acceptable to the young people of today. We must leave this to Annie now. Leave her to do things her way. If she wants our help she'll ask for it.'

'And if she doesn't?' he asked.

Harriet shrugged. 'If she doesn't then we'll need to stand back and bite our tongues.'

'That isn't going to be easy for me to do, Harriet. I care for her far too much.'

'Be certain she *knows* that, then step back and leave her to make her own decisions about her life. She'll make mistakes, as everyone does, no matter what their age, and they'll hurt us quite as much as they do her. Yet if we interfere again and are proved as wrong as I believe we are over this affair, everyone will be hurt a whole lot more and we might lose our Annie for ever.' Her expression softened and she gave her husband a sympathetic half-smile. 'It's going to be hard for both of us, but we have to accept that our Annie is not a young girl any more, Walter. She's a woman.'

35

For a number of days after his return to London, Perys found it difficult to settle at Maude's Knightsbridge home. Aware that he was unhappy about something, Maude and her two daughters encouraged him to take part in their preparations for Christmas.

The two girls were still nursing, but France was experiencing atrocious weather, which meant that troops in the opposing armies now faced a common foe. Both were preoccupied with the problem of survival.

Spasmodic fighting still erupted along the network of opposing trenches which extended on a line almost six hundred kilometres long, but no major offensives were planned for the immediate future. As a result, the tidal wave of casualties which had threatened to overwhelm hospitals during the late autumn had slowed to a trickle. Morwenna, Arabella and their friends were able to resume a normal working routine once more.

This Christmas had assumed particular importance to Maude. Morwenna had told her of her acceptance by the Queen Alexandra's Imperial Military Nursing Service – the QUAIMNS – fully expecting her mother to be horrified. Instead, Maude told her daughter she was proud of her spirit and courage in wanting to work where she could most help wounded soldiers, regardless of the dangers she would face.

Maude was also determined that Perys should enjoy a memorable Christmas among relatives who cared for him.

Christmas morning was a busy time for the whole family. The two girls were on duty, and Maude and Perys went along to the hospitals where they worked, distributing cigarettes and chocolate to wounded soldiers, the comforts purchased by Maude at her own expense.

The family celebrations took place that evening and proved far more successful than Maude could have anticipated.

One reason was that Rupert shared the evening with them. He had telephoned the night before to ask if he might pay a fleeting visit to the family. He would be in London, prior to returning to his squadron in France on Boxing Day. He was delighted to accept Maude's invitation to dinner.

It was a meal the family would share with the young trainee doctor with whom Arabella was currently infatuated. And Grace Ballard, Morwenna's friend who had been Perys's partner for their enjoyable evening out with Rupert, would also be with them.

Ian Cameron, the young doctor, was a rather shy

man who was spending Christmas a long way from his Scottish home. He proved to be a talented pianist and provided much of the evening's entertainment, occasionally accompanying Grace who possessed a fine voice.

It was during one of Grace's songs that Morwenna and Rupert slipped quietly out of the room. Everyone pretended not to notice, but after they had been absent for some fifteen minutes or so, Maude excused herself from the company and she too left the room.

The others were aware she had gone in search of the young couple and Perys said, 'Do you think we should try to find them and warn them?'

Amused by his concern, Grace smiled, 'Would you know where to look?'

When Perys was forced to admit he would not, Grace added to his mild embarrassment by asking, 'What do you think they are likely to be doing?'

'I . . . I really don't know,' he confessed.

'Well, I probably know Morwenna better than anyone else,' Grace declared, 'and whatever she and Rupert are doing, it will be nothing her mother need worry about. Quite the reverse, I would say.'

In spite of Grace's confident assertion, as the minutes passed Perys became increasingly concerned. Then, some twenty minutes after Maude had left the room, she returned. With her were Rupert and Morwenna.

Calling for the attention of those already in the room, Maude said, 'I must apologise for deserting you for so long, but when I tell you the reason, I am certain you will forgive me.' She smiled at Morwenna and Rupert before continuing. 'As I am quite sure you realised, I went off in search of Morwenna and Rupert. I found them in the conservatory. When I spoke to them I was very happy indeed that I had not disturbed them before. Rupert had just proposed to Morwenna—'

She was interrupted by the congratulations bestowed on the couple by Arabella and the guests. When they had run their course, Maude continued, 'Morwenna accepted his proposal, of course, but my approval was required before it could become an official engagement. Needless to say I am absolutely delighted to give them my whole-hearted blessing. Indeed, I am quite overcome. This is a truly memorable day. Perys, will you accompany me to the cellar. Such an occasion can only be celebrated with the help of the very best champagne.'

After offering Rupert and Morwenna his warmest congratulations, Perys followed Maude down some stairs to the cellar. Along the way she asked him, 'Were you aware that Rupert was going to ask Morwenna to marry him, Perys?'

'No,' he replied truthfully, 'but it comes as no great surprise. I have known for a long time how he felt about her.'

'I have always hoped they might one day marry, but until recent months I was beginning to believe it was no more than a fond parent's dream.'

Maude continued her happy chatter about the 'realisation of a mother's dream' until they reached the cellar. She selected six bottles of vintage champagne, and with Perys carrying four bottles and Maude two, they returned upstairs.

As she put down her bottles and locked the cellar

door behind her, Maude asked, 'How are you getting on with Grace?'

'She's a very lovely girl,' he replied honestly. 'Great fun to be with and she's dedicated to the work she does. In fact, just the sort of girl I would expect Morwenna to have for a best friend.'

'Do you see her only as Morwenna's best friend, Perys? Nothing more?'

The loss of Annie still hurt and Perys said, 'I have to make my way in life before I can think seriously about becoming involved with anyone, Aunt Maude.'

'Nonsense! You are still very young, of course, but so too is Morwenna. And you are a young man with considerable prospects. Your grandfather is a very wealthy man and you are his sole heir.'

Astonished by her words, Perys shook his head. 'My mother was virtually disinherited when I was born, as I am sure you know. Grandfather has always made it quite clear that I am an embarrassment to him – someone to be kept out of sight and out of mind. Besides, there are a number of nieces and nephews on my grandmother's side of the family who are much closer to them than I. No doubt they will be the beneficiaries of anything my grandparents have to leave.'

Maude gave Perys a sympathetic look. 'Your grandfather is a stubborn and intractable man, Perys. The family were well aware of the attitude he had adopted towards you, but we were reluctant to interfere lest he cut you off completely. We were wrong. However, your grandfather – yes, and your grandmother too – are beginning to be aware that they face a lonely old age. I believe they regret not taking a greater interest in you in the past.'

With the door safely locked and the key tucked in a pocket, Maude smiled at him. 'There, that is another happy thought for this very special Christmas.'

On the morning Perys was due to set off to report to the Royal Flying Corps training depot in Wiltshire, he had an early morning visitor. Grace arrived at the Tremaynes' Knightsbridge home still wearing her nurse's uniform. She had come direct from night duty at St Thomas's Hospital.

When Perys expressed his surprise at seeing her, she explained, 'I wanted to see you off and wish you good luck. I also wanted to give you this.' Handing him a small, velvet-covered box, she said, 'It's a Saint Christopher medallion. He's the patron saint of travellers. I hope he will keep you safe, always. I had it specially made for you.'

Opening the box, Perys saw a gold medallion on which was a scene showing the saint fording a river, carrying a child on his shoulders. Turning the medallion over, he saw his name engraved on the reverse.

'This is beautiful, Grace, but you really shouldn't have spent your money on me . . . it must have cost you the earth.'

'The cost isn't important, the sentiment is. Stay safe, Perys.' Her smile was forced as she added, 'Wherever you are you will always know there is someone thinking of you. I will pray for you each night.'

Deeply touched by her words and her gift, Perys said, 'I will remember that, Grace, thank you.' He kissed her self-consciously, aware of the beaming approval of Maude and her two daughters.

Their farewells were equally warm and sincere and,

when he started on his way, he turned to wave to the quartet who were standing outside the house.

Then, putting Knightsbridge behind him, he set off to begin a new life. As a pilot in the Royal Flying Corps.

36

During the weeks he spent in the training depot at Upavon, Perys began to think the War Office had posted him to an infantry training unit by mistake.

There *were* lectures on various aspects of aeronautics, but they covered such basic subjects that Perys realised he had learned more during the first couple of days with Nick Malloch than he would during the whole of this particular course.

Those who, like Perys, were civilian volunteers for the Royal Flying Corps, would not be allowed to wear uniform until they moved on to flying training. Others, who were already army officers, were required to remove all insignia of rank and were treated as 'cadets'.

The days were spent mainly in learning drill, under the instruction of army sergeants to whom drill was the one thing that raised the British soldier above all his contemporaries. There was also a certain amount of physical exercise – and kit inspections. Perys felt the latter to be a total waste of valuable learning time. He doubted whether ensuring that the soles of his spare boots were highly polished was calculated to strike fear into the hearts of German airmen.

Something of his thinking showed in the attitude he adopted towards the army-style regime. As a result, one drill sergeant in particular singled him out for special attention. It was, perhaps, inevitable that such conflicting attitudes to the training methods would lead to a clash between the two men.

It came on a day when an aeroplane from the nearby airfield flew low over the parade ground, making Sergeant Middleton's bellowed orders even more unintelligible to Perys. He turned the opposite way to the others in the squad and was immediately taken to task by the irate instructor.

'What *is* the matter with you, Tremayne? If you can't get your feet to do what they're supposed to when you're down here on the ground, they're hardly likely to be any use to you when you're up in the air. You'll never make a pilot if you drill for a hundred bleedin' years!'

Perys had become increasingly frustrated with both the drill and the sometimes vicious stupidity of the men who appeared to enjoy the harsh discipline inflicted upon the cadets in their charge. Throwing caution to the wind, he said, 'I am afraid I must correct you . . . sir. I am already a qualified pilot.'

It was one of the anomalies of initial training that prospective officers were obliged to address their non-commissioned instructors as 'sir'.

The sergeant had automatically written Perys off as

being one of the many recruits who had joined the Royal Flying Corps direct from school, with little knowledge of anything beyond the classroom. Now he said, 'What do you mean, you *are* a pilot?'

'I mean that I have my pilot's licence and have clocked up more than fifty hours of solo flying time, in three different types of aeroplane . . . sir.'

One of the squad tittered and Sergeant Middleton looked at Perys suspiciously, believing him to be enjoying a joke at his expense.

'And where did you do all this flying of yours, may I ask?'

'Brooklands, sir.'

Aware that the sergeant was uncertain whether or not he was telling the truth, and beginning to enjoy himself, Perys added, 'Mind you, when I was acting as observer to my cousin and we were shot at by a German warship – that was the occasion when he won a DSO – we were actually flying over the English Channel.'

Now a number of the squad members were having difficulty stifling their laughter and the sergeant had no doubt that Perys *was* trying to make him appear foolish.

'Do you think it's clever to try to make a fool of me, Tremayne? Well, some of your friends may find you amusing, but let's see if the adjutant shares their sense of humour. Fall out and report to the adjutant's office. I'll be along there to lay charges against you when I've finished with this lot.'

Aware he had gone too far and suddenly fearful that his commission as a Royal Flying Corps pilot might be in jeopardy, Perys asked, 'What charges . . . sir?'

'Insubordination – now move . . . *at the double*!'

As Perys ran across the parade ground, heading for the adjutant's office, he heard the sergeant barking orders at the squad of would-be RFC officers, determined to reassert his authority over them.

When he reached the building which housed the offices of the commanding officer, adjutant and initial training administration, a sergeant informed Perys that the adjutant was not in his office. Perys was instructed to wait outside, standing 'to attention' until his return.

He had been waiting outside for some ten minutes when the officer in charge of the initial training annexe left the building and saw him standing there, rigid.

Major Thomas Kemp, DSO, was an ex-Royal Engineers officer who had gained his pilot's licence prior to the war, as had most senior RFC officers. Sent to France with one of the first squadrons to accompany the British Expeditionary Force on the outbreak of war, he had also been one of the first pilots to be wounded. Forbidden to fly an aeroplane until he had fully recovered, he had been sent to Upavon to take charge of the training annexe.

Seeing a crestfallen Perys standing stiffly to attention, he frowned, 'What are you doing here, young man?'

'I understand I am to be taken before the adjutant, sir, charged with insubordination.'

Raising an eyebrow, Major Kemp said, 'It all sounds terribly serious . . . Were you insubordinate?'

'I don't think so, sir. Sergeant Middleton told me that if I couldn't get my feet to do what I wanted them to on the ground, I'd not manage them in the air and

241

would never make a pilot. I told him I already held a pilot's licence . . .' After a moment's hesitation, he added, 'I also mentioned a particular exploit I had in the air. I think he thought I was lying and trying to make him look foolish.'

'Sergeant Middleton . . . Isn't he the Coldstream Guardsman?'

'Yes, sir.'

'Hm!' Thomas Kemp had always doubted the necessity of teaching Guards-style drill to prospective airmen. 'What's your name, lad?'

'Tremayne, sir. Perys Tremayne.'

Major Kemp frowned. 'Tremayne? Are you from Cornwall?'

'Part of the family have a home there, sir. I was staying there recently.'

'I thought I had seen the name somewhere. Come into my office.'

The major turned and went back inside the building. Mystified, Perys followed him.

Passing through the outer office, the commanding officer said to the surprised administration sergeant, 'Find the file for cadet Tremayne and bring it to me straightway, Sergeant.'

Once inside his own office, Major Kemp dropped into a chair and faced Perys across the width of his desk. Perys was standing rigidly to attention once more and the commanding officer said, 'Stand-at-ease, Tremayne. Relax and tell me something about your flying. Who taught you and how many hours have you put in?'

When Perys had replied to his questions, Major Kemp leaned back in his chair and said, 'You had one of the best instructors in the country, Tremayne. He must be. He taught *me* to fly when I was more than twice your age and had stopped learning new tricks many years before. If you clocked up fifty-three hours with Nick then you are a more experienced pilot than a great many front-line flyers.'

The administration sergeant entered the office and placed a document file on his desk, together with a bulky manila envelope.

'Ah yes!' Major Kemp pushed the envelope to one side with the words, 'I *thought* you were the young man I had in mind.' Not bothering to explain more fully, he opened the file and began to read some of the documents from it, occasionally looking up at Perys in a speculative manner.

When he had shuffled through all the papers, he said, 'You have certainly made your mark on the aviation world, Tremayne – even *before* you are commissioned into the Royal Flying Corps. I don't think I have ever seen a more complimentary report from a flying instructor, and Nick Malloch isn't a man to bestow praise lightly. I see there is also a recommendation from Colonel Lord MacAllen. As for your adventure with Captain Pilkington . . . it was worthy of a medal. Talking of which, I believe that last year you took part in the rescue of the master of a Russian ship off the Cornish coast?'

Startled, Perys said, 'That's right, sir, but how do you know?'

Major Kemp smiled. 'It seems your sailor was related to an official at the Russian Court. As a result, Tsar Nicholas has awarded you the Medal of St George, for bravery. Not to be outdone, the Royal

Humane Society have given you their Bronze Medal for the same incident.'

The significance of the two medals was lost on Perys. He had won various awards at school, and looked upon the two he had just been told about as being in the same category.

Major Kemp was quick to enlighten him. 'Have you been measured for a uniform yet, Tremayne?'

'Yes, sir, but I have been told not to order it until I have completed initial training and have received a commission.'

'Then we will have to see what can be done to accelerate that day, Tremayne.'

Perys looked puzzled and Major Kemp explained, 'The War Office forwarded your medals with a memo, Tremayne. They say every opportunity must be taken to boost morale among trainee officers. I am to present the medals to you at a full parade of all trainee pilots at the Central Flying School. As they are intended to be worn on your uniform, together with any decorations you may be awarded in the future, I think we had better see that you are put into uniform as quickly as possible. What aircraft have you flown?'

'The "Longhorn", a BE2c and an Avro, sir,' Perys said, not certain why he had been asked the question.

'Fine! I have a BE2c at my disposal, across in the Central Flying School. I'm not allowed to fly it myself, just yet, but you can take me up for a flight and show me what you can do. Come along, I'll have the orderly take us across there in the motor-car.'

At the Central Flying School airfield, a BE2c was quickly wheeled from a hangar. Perys was fitted out with a flying suit and soon afterwards was taxying out to the airfield. He had felt apprehensive about acting as pilot to such an experienced RFC airman, but once in the air the sheer exhilaration of flying again took over and he put the BE2c through its paces.

Eventually, Major Kemp, who was in the forward cockpit, signalled for him to land back at Upavon. Reluctantly, Perys complied and twenty minutes later they were climbing from the aeroplane to the ground.

Patting Perys on the shoulder, the Major said, 'I am pleased to see that Nick Malloch's judgement is as sound as ever, Tremayne. You are a natural pilot. Putting you on the normal trainees' flying course would be a waste of time and money. Come along to my office. We'll see if I can find the exam papers for the theory you've learned so far. Nick will have taught you about such matters in far more detail. You can sit in my office to take the exam. Before that, give the details of your tailor to the admin sergeant. He can make a telephone call and arrange for your uniform to be ready for the weekend. I will present your medals at the church parade on Sunday, and you can join the advanced flying course on Monday.'

Perys was overwhelmed by his unexpected good luck but was temporarily brought down to earth when he reached the administration hut.

He had gone ahead of the commanding officer, who had stayed behind to detail the duties of his driver for the following day. Sergeant Middleton had been searching for Perys, furious that he had not been out-side the adjutant's office when the sergeant arrived from the parade ground. When he saw Perys, and without awaiting an explanation, he launched into an angry tirade, assuring Perys in no uncertain terms that his career in the Royal Flying Corps was at an end before it had even begun.

His angry outburst faded when Major Kemp came into view around the side of the building.

'Attention, Tremayne!' the drill sergeant barked, at the same time springing to stiff attention himself, his hand jerking up to perform a quiveringly perfect salute.

'All right, Sergeant Middleton, at ease if you please. Tell me, what is this business with Tremayne all about?'

Surprised that the commanding officer should know anything about the matter, the sergeant repeated what Perys had already said, adding, 'He was just making the stories up, sir, to belittle me and amuse his friends in the squad.'

'I think not, Sergeant; you see, all he said happens to be true. Indeed, he has just been awarded two decorations for bravery. I will be asking General Sir Charles Allerton to make the presentation at church parade on Sunday. I will expect a good, smart turnout for the occasion. In view of this, I presume you will wish to withdraw your charges, Sergeant?'

The commanding officer's stern glance left the drill sergeant in no doubt about what he was expected to say.

'Of course, sir. Had I been in possession of all the facts at the time . . .'

'Quite. Thank you, Sergeant Middleton. You may go back to your duties. Shall we go inside and find that examination paper, Tremayne?'

37

Five days after his flight with Major Kemp, Perys joined an advanced flying training course in the main section of the Central Flying School. His commission as a second lieutenant in the Royal Flying Corps had been confirmed and he felt proud but conspicuous in his new uniform, tailored for him in a remarkable forty-eight hours, thanks to the persuasive powers of Thomas Kemp.

He was mildly embarrassed by the two medal ribbons displayed on the breast of his uniform jacket. The dark blue and gold of the Russian Medal of St George over his left pocket, and the navy blue of the Humane Society medal on his right breast. Both attracted considerable interest wherever he went.

But for Perys, everything else was secondary to the fact that he was now flying once more, even though much of what he was doing was elementary compared with the advanced aerobatics he had practised with Nick Malloch.

His flying knowledge and abilities were soon recognised by the instructors at the Central Flying School and he was often detailed to run 'errands', using one of the school's aeroplanes.

Three weeks into his course, Perys was called to the office of Major Kemp, no explanation being given for the summons. Perturbed because he could think of no reason why the major should want to see him, Perys entered the office apprehensively.

His reception was immediately reassuring.

'Ah, Tremayne, come in! Take a seat.' Leaning back in his chair, Thomas Kemp beamed at Perys. 'How are you enjoying the advanced flying course? Having no trouble with it?'

'None at all, sir, it's good to be back in the air once more.'

'I thought you would feel that way. I can tell you that your chief instructor regards you very highly. He has asked whether he might take you on to his staff at the end of the course.'

Perys was dismayed. He had not joined the RFC in order that he might spend the war teaching others to fly.

Correctly reading his expression, Thomas Kemp smiled. 'It's all right, Tremayne, I told him I felt you would want to serve your country in a more positive role. I feel the same way and have finally managed to persuade the War Office that my talents and experience should be put to use on active service. I have been placed in command of a front-line squadron, with effect from the first of April.'

The date was more than a month ahead, but Major Kemp explained, 'I won't be allowed to fly until then, but I thought I would go across to France and have a look at the squadron before I took over. How would you like to fly me there?'

'Me, sir?' The question took Perys by surprise. He was still officially under training.

'All available pilots at the school are fully committed. You're as capable as anyone I know of making the flight. If you were to miss the remainder of the course you'd still be a better pilot than any of your contemporaries. Of course, if the thought of such a long flight worries you . . .'

'It would be no problem at all, sir,' Perys said, hurriedly. 'I'll be delighted to fly you there. When do we leave?'

'Good man, I didn't think I had misjudged you. We might as well leave tomorrow. I'll have one of the spare BE2c's made ready. If the weather is in our favour we will fly to Saint Omer, stay there for a night, then go on to the squadron's airfield, close to Ypres – that's in Belgium. We'll spend a couple of days there so I can get to know the pilots and have an idea of what's going on, then we'll come back here in time for the weekend.'

The weather was good when Major Kemp boarded the BE2c the following day, loading a rifle and a shotgun into the aeroplane with him. A great many of the Central Flying School turned out to see them off. Flying was still something of a novelty, even here, and a flight of some hundred and sixty miles, much of it over water, was regarded as an adventure.

Perys had no doubt about his ability and that of the BE2c to make the flight safely, and his confidence was not misplaced. Just under three hours later, he was taxying the aircraft towards the buildings of the French headquarters of the Royal Flying Corps at St Omer.

Climbing stiffly from the forward cockpit, Thomas Kemp said, 'Thank you, Perys. That was a very enjoyable flight.' It was the first time he had called Perys by his Christian name, and he confirmed the satisfaction he felt with his pilot by adding, 'When we return to the CFS you have my authority to put up your wings. You have earned them.'

The affixing of the cloth 'wings' above the pocket of a uniform jacket was the dream of every trainee pilot. It was the membership badge of an élite club and told the world that here was an élite fighting man. His words delighted Perys.

The next day, Perys flew the major to the advanced airfield close to the small, war-shattered Belgian town of Ypres, where Number 2 Squadron was based. This was the squadron Major Kemp would be commanding.

Once on the ground with the engine switched off, the sound of artillery fire was much in evidence. It was taking place not too far away. The RFC officer who had come out to greet them passed it off nonchalantly.

'They always have a little duel about this time of day. I think they use it as an opportunity to train gunners on both sides of the lines. Fortunately for us, they haven't yet brought any guns up to this part of the front with sufficient range to reach the airfield.'

Perys remained at the forward airfield with the major for two full days, during which time he was taken to the ruined town of Ypres and also visited the trenches of the front-line with Major Kemp, meeting the artillerymen for whom the squadron's aircraft performed duties as spotters. Both men also met with the pilots of Number 2 Squadron, who were particularly curious about Perys's lack of wings and his two unusual medals.

The days passed by very quickly and soon it was time to set off on the return flight to Upavon. As Major Kemp was to be their next commanding officer, a number of the squadron's officers assembled to see him on his way.

But there was one man who watched the aeroplane taxying out for take-off who had not made himself known to Perys. Seated at the wheel of a staff car, Martin Bray told himself for the umpteenth time that it would have been embarrassing for both of them had he done so. Perys was an officer, while Martin was only a motor transport driver. Men serving in the ranks did not show undue familiarity towards their superiors.

There was another reason why Martin had been uncertain about approaching Perys. He had received a number of letters from Polly, and although she had not gone into great detail, she had made him aware of much of what had occurred when Perys last visited Heligan.

His knowledge of the situation was sketchy, but Martin knew that Annie and his parents had fallen out over Perys. He also knew that Annie was supposed to be marrying Jimmy Rowe, although Polly reported that his sister was not at all certain she was doing the right thing. As a result, she was deeply unhappy.

His letters from his mother had made no mention of a visit from Perys, and he had received no mail from Annie, although he had written to her. In his letter he had mentioned the time they had spent together with Perys and asked, in a guarded way, whether life was happy with her.

There was always the possibility that she *had* replied to tell him what was happening. Since arriving in France, Martin had moved from squadron to squadron before arriving at the present airfield. Mail was always slow in catching up with servicemen who did not remain in one place for long.

He would have liked to have heard from Annie before meeting with Perys and discussing her with him. He had always believed Perys's affection for her went far deeper than anyone realised.

38

As the BE2c taxied away from the farewell party, Thomas turned in his cockpit and motioned for Perys to lean towards him. When Perys did so, the major shouted in his ear, 'When we take off, climb in a spiral, staying close to the front-lines. Gain as much height as you can.'

'Why?' Perys shouted in return. He needed to be clear about the major's intentions. Conversation would be impossible once they were in the air.

'I want to see the extent of the trenches. Number Two squadron is largely involved in reconnaissance. I want to see for myself what sort of a task it is going to be, and we couldn't have a finer day for it.' He did not explain that a major offensive was in the offing and constant updating of reconnaissance photographs would be of vital importance to the success or failure of the planned assault on the German lines.

Perys nodded agreement. There was hardly a cloud

in the sky and visibility was excellent.

Once in the air, Perys kept the BE2c climbing. He began to level off at five thousand feet, but Major Kemp motioned for him to continue climbing. Perys obeyed his orders. It was possible to see the twin lines of trenches snaking side-by-side into the distance. It was also possible to see the flashes of gunfire from artillery positions behind both lines.

They were some distance behind the German lines and the major was looking over the side of the cockpit when he suddenly turned to Perys and made excited gestures, calling his attention to something beneath them. He shouted too, but Perys was unable to make out what he was saying above the roar of the engine.

Banking in order to get a better view of what the other man was pointing at, Perys could at first see nothing. Then, far below them he could see a British aeroplane of the same type as their own, flying a zig-zag path towards the line of trenches. It was being harassed by three aircraft bearing German markings and it was immediately apparent that they were forcing it to fly ever lower.

Major Kemp gesticulated wildly for Perys to take the BE2c down. Reaching into the cockpit, he came up brandishing the rifle he had placed there before setting off from England. With a sudden thrill of fear, Perys realised that the other man intended that they should go down and take on the three German air-craft!

He put the nose of the plane down in a steep dive. As the wind whistled with increasing fury in the wires between the wings, Perys tried to remember all Nick Malloch had taught him about combat in the aerial games they used to play. He was also thinking about the pictures he had seen of German aircraft. If he could identify those they were diving upon he would know the guns they carried. This would, in turn, give him an idea of the best position from which to mount an attack, if such a word could be used to describe Major Kemp potting at the Germans with a rifle and a shotgun!

As they neared the other aircraft, the British aeroplane appeared to be in serious trouble. Its propeller was still turning, but a thin stream of blue smoke was trailing from the engine. It was doubtful whether it could remain in the air for very much longer.

The sudden arrival on the scene of Perys's BE2c caused a degree of consternation among the German airmen that was out of all proportion to his ability to change the course of such a one-sided battle. The BE2c's dive carried it past the rearmost German aircraft at considerable speed, but this did not prevent Major Kemp from firing off two quick shots before they were out of range. It was highly unlikely the shots caused any damage, but the sheer shock of being overtaken at such close range caused the German pilot to take violent avoiding action, immediately putting his plane out of the fight.

The BE2c was now flying *beneath* another of the German aeroplanes and this time Major Kemp's shots did strike home. The two British flyers could not know that one of the rifle bullets caused a painful wound to the German pilot's buttocks. It was sufficient to make him decide to give up the chase of the damaged British aircraft.

Now the odds were reversed, although the pursued

British aircraft was in no condition to take any further part in the fight. Fortunately, they had reached the twin line of trenches – and German pilots had strict orders not to operate beyond their own lines. The remaining German broke off the fight in the knowledge that his original quarry could not remain in the air for long.

The pilot of the damaged British aircraft was fighting hard to keep the plane in the air, at least until it was able to crash-land behind British lines.

It was a battle he lost. The faltering engine died when the aeroplane was low over the German lines and it landed in no-man's land, equidistant between the two opposing sets of trenches.

As the aircraft tilted on to its nose, a cheer went up from the German lines, but the crashed aeroplane neither broke up nor caught fire. Moments later, two men in flying suits scrambled out and began running awkwardly towards the British trenches.

The cheers from the German troops changed to howls of disappointment and they began shooting at the two airmen. The shots were immediately returned from the British lines. Caught up in the crossfire, the men dropped to the ground, taking cover in a shallow shell-hole.

Completing a climbing turn, Perys grasped the situation and nosed his BE2c down towards the frontline German trench. Immediately, most of the guns firing at the two stranded airmen were turned on the British aircraft. As the plane banked for another run, Major Kemp returned the German fire with his rifle. Perys thought wryly that he seemed to be enjoying himself.

Skimming along just above the trenches once more, Perys was alarmed to see a small group of German soldiers, led by an officer, leap over the parapet of the trench and begin running towards the airmen. Banking the aircraft once more, and flying dangerously close to the ground now, he headed for the Germans who were intent on capturing the British flyers.

They heard the aircraft heading towards them and dropped to the ground in the nick of time. However, not all the soldiers were preoccupied with self-preservation. The tiny glass windshield in front of Perys suddenly disintegrated and he realised it had been struck by a bullet that must have missed his head by a hair's breadth.

But his latest pass over no-man's land had drawn the attention of the two stranded airmen to their danger, and they gained a few precious yards before dropping to the ground once more.

Perys strafed the would-be captors one more time and on this occasion Major Kemp resorted to using his revolver, with little more success than he had achieved with his rifle. Nevertheless, a number of German soldiers remained sprawled on the ground and Perys guessed they must have fallen casualty to fire from the British trenches.

By now a British rescue party had ventured into no-man's land. With their aid, the airmen were nearing the safety of the British lines – but Perys had other matters to worry about.

The BE2c had been struck by a great many German bullets and the engine began popping and spluttering alarmingly. Perys thought the fuel system had been damaged. Fortunately, he was able to nurse the aircraft over the British lines. Clearing the ruined outbuildings of a totally destroyed farm, he set the BE2c down in a field that was pock-marked with shellholes. It was a heavy landing and the undercarriage collapsed. However, the aircraft was right-way-up and both men scrambled clear quickly for fear that it might catch fire.

As soon as they were at a safe distance and the aeroplane showed no sign of bursting into flames, Major Kemp turned to Perys and gripped his hand in both of his own.

'Perys, that was a bloody marvellous display of flying! It would have done credit to the most experienced pilot. I am proud of you.'

Although he tried hard not to let it show, Perys was beginning to feel very shaky, but he managed a grin. 'I thought you were enjoying it, sir.'

Slapping Perys on the back, the major said, 'I knew I was right to choose you to pilot me. Come on, let's find a command post and call up the squadron's airfield. They will recover the aircraft and have it back as good as new in a few days. In the meantime I shouldn't think we'll have any trouble borrowing another from Saint Omer.'

As they stripped off their flying suits, a lieutenant accompanied by a couple of soldiers came hurrying towards them. Saluting Major Kemp, the lieutenant said, 'Well done, sir. I've been sent to escort you to the command post. Brigadier Sir Henry Palmer is waiting for you there.'

'Brigadier Palmer is waiting for *us*?' Major Kemp queried.

'That's right, sir . . . Oh, I thought you would know. He was a passenger in the aeroplane that came down in no-man's land. It seems headquarters have something planned. He wanted to see the German defences for himself before committing the troops to an attack. He's a very good officer that way.'

The command post was an elaborate dug-out, heavily protected with sandbags. Entering the lamp-lit interior, the brigadier was the first man Perys saw. He was hatless, but even so he was recognisable by the red tabs on the lapels of the uniform jacket he had on beneath his flying suit.

Glancing briefly at Perys, he held out his hand and addressed the more senior of the two RFC officers. 'Major! I am delighted to meet you. I think Lieutenant Colonel Anderson and I owe our lives to you.'

'Not to me, sir, but to Second Lieutenant Tremayne. I haven't been passed as fit for flying after being wounded some time ago. Tremayne was the pilot who showed the Germans what an aeroplane is capable of when properly handled.'

The brigadier released Thomas Kemp's hand and turned to Perys. Eyeing him critically for a few seconds, he said, 'But he is hardly more than a boy . . . and where are his pilot's wings?'

'He hasn't been awarded them yet.' Major Kemp was enjoying the brigadier's disbelief. 'Second Lieutenant Tremayne is still undergoing training, but he was so keen to join the Royal Flying Corps that he learned to fly before volunteering. The man who taught him is probably the finest instructor in England. When he declared Tremayne one of the best young pilots he has ever turned out, I took him up to

259

test his skills for myself. As a result I immediately put him on an advanced flying course and chose him to fly me here from England. As a matter of fact we were on our way back when we saw you in trouble. I think our departure might be delayed somewhat now.'

'And damned glad I am about it too,' said the brigadier. 'I am delighted to meet you, Tremayne – but not nearly as pleased as I was to see you a while ago.' Extending his hand, he said, 'I owe my life to you, young man, and I certainly won't forget it.' Shaking Perys's hand vigorously, he added, 'Well, now you have had an unexpected taste of action, do you still think you will enjoy life as a pilot?'

Perys stuttered something to the effect that he was looking forward to joining a front-line squadron, but Thomas Kemp interrupted him. 'Actually, it is not Tremayne's first taste of action, sir . . .' He told the brigadier of Perys's encounter with the German warship that resulted in the award of a DSO to Rupert.

'I see you have two medals yourself, young man. You must have been awarded those before joining the service. I recognise the life-saving medal. What is the other?'

Perys told him as briefly as possible about the foundering of the Russian ship and of his part in the rescue of the ship's captain.

Suitably impressed, the brigadier said, 'I have a feeling you are making it sound far more mundane than it really was, young man. The Russians don't give away their medals for no reason – and neither do we, but we can't have it said we are less generous than the Russians, can we?' Turning to Major Kemp, he said, 'I am going to recommend the award of an immediate Military Cross to this young man. Does that meet with your approval?'

'Wholeheartedly,' said Thomas Kemp, enthusiastically.

His approval was echoed by the lieutenant colonel who had been piloting the brigadier, who said, 'Had you not suggested it, sir, I would have submitted a recommendation to the same effect. There are some men to whom things just seem to happen. I believe Tremayne is one of these.' He did not add what was in his mind, that such men either became heroes or were soon killed in action.

'Splendid,' said the brigadier. 'I will have it put through immediately. It will be awarded in time to give encouragement to the others on Tremayne's flying course. Now, the captain in charge of this part of the line told me he has some whisky hidden away. I suggest we get him to produce it in order that we might drink to our salvation, and to a long and successful career for this young man.'

39

Dear Polly,

Sorry I haven't written for such a long time, but one of the other squadrons became desperately short of drivers and I was loaned to them. I have hardly had half-an-hour to myself since then. They called it a 'bomber' squadron and we were working day and night.

Anyway, I'm back with my own squadron again now and you'll never guess who flew in just before I went away. Perys Tremayne! He piloted our new commanding officer on an inspection visit.

There was great excitement while he was here, too. Three German aeroplanes were attacking one of ours which happened to be carrying the area brigade commander. His plane was forced down in no-man's land and he would either have been shot or taken prisoner had it not been for Perys. He was able to save the brigadier before he too was shot down. Fortunately,

*he crashed behind our own lines and wasn't hurt,
except for a few cuts. He was awarded an immediate
Military Cross. He was quite a hero and I feel very
proud to know him.*

*I didn't speak to him while he was here – after all
he's an officer and I'm not – but there's a very strong
rumour that he'll be joining the squadron soon. I
thought you would like to hear about him. I expect
Annie would too, even though she is to marry Jimmy
Rowe. She and Perys were good friends . . .*

The remainder of the letter was of a personal nature
and Polly had retained those pages before passing on
the first few to Annie.

In her bedroom at Tregassick Farm, Annie read the
letter for the seventh or eighth time. It had taken some
weeks to reach Cornwall, as the forces' letters sometimes did, but the timing of it was not important. What
mattered to Annie was the way she felt about the contents. She was far more concerned for Perys's welfare
and the fact that he had crashed his aeroplane, than
she was about the dangers and hardships to which
Jimmy was exposed in the trenches on the front-line.

Jimmy was not an educated man, yet his few, brief
letters had painted a vivid picture of the filth and horror
of life in the trenches. It seemed that infantrymen were
being used as sacrificial pawns in the war games being
played by their staff officers – elderly generals who
sought to fight a complex twentieth-century war using
tactics which should have died with the charge of the
Light Brigade at Balaklava.

The only note of optimism in Jimmy's letters had
nothing to do with victory over the Germans. He and

his comrades were fully aware that this was not a realistic goal in the foreseeable future. Jimmy made it quite clear to Annie that all his hopes for the future rested with her. He told her in his letters that only thoughts of her enabled him to cling to sanity in the slaughter of this most horrific of wars.

Despite his lack of learning, Jimmy had succeeded in conveying to Annie the depths of his despair. She felt desperately sorry for him and agonised that her concern should not be for him, but for Perys. She decided to write to Martin and ask if he knew Perys's address. She would say that she wished to write and congratulate him on the award of his Military Cross.

Writing to her brother helped to clarify a great many matters for her. Chief among them was the certain knowledge that she did not love Jimmy. She was fond of him, very fond, but it was not enough. Yet she could no longer be certain about Perys's feelings for her. After all, they had not known each other for very long and it had been six months since their last meeting. What was more, she had not replied to the letters in which he had poured out his feelings for her. He had left Heligan believing that she was to be married to someone else.

Only one thing *was* clear to her. She could not marry Jimmy Rowe, knowing how she felt about Perys.

Breaking the news to Jimmy would not be easy. She thought about this aspect of her problem for many days, unable to discuss it with her parents. Eventually, she decided to visit Heligan and speak with Polly.

It was a pleasant spring evening when the two young women walked along the Heligan driveway as they talked. Becoming increasingly upset as she poured out her feelings and thoughts, a distraught Annie finally said, 'What shall I do, Polly? How can I resolve this mess?'

Sympathising with her friend, Polly said, 'I'm not quite sure what you can do, Annie, but I can tell you what you can't do. You can't marry Jimmy.'

'But how can I tell him? I know from his letters that he's having a horrible time out there. He doesn't deserve this on top of everything else. How can I destroy all his hopes for the future while he's suffering so much?'

Looking at Annie pityingly, Polly asked, 'Have you talked to your ma about it?'

Annie shook her head. 'I can't say anything about it to her. She believes that if I get mixed up with Perys I'm going to end up the same way as Eliza Dunn.'

Polly shook her head. 'You and Eliza are very different, Annie. But you have to do something. I only wish I could help.'

'You *have* helped, Polly, just by listening to me. Because of it I've been able to come to a decision. I know now what it is I must do.'

When Polly looked at her questioningly, Annie said, 'I must go to see Jimmy's ma and pa and tell them the truth. They won't like me very much, but at least they'll know I can't possibly marry Jimmy feeling the way I do about Perys.'

40

Proudly wearing the medal ribbon of the Military
Cross with the other medals below his wings, Perys
completed his advanced flying course in April 1915.
At the request of Thomas Kemp, he would soon be
leaving England to take up a posting with the Royal
Flying Corps operational squadron commanded by
the major and stationed near Ypres.

Before setting off to the battle-front, Perys was able
to enjoy a few days' leave. At Maude's insistence, he
spent them at her Knightsbridge home.

Grace also had a few days' leave from St Thomas's
Hospital and she and Perys saw a great deal of each
other. Grace and Morwenna had been given their
dates for joining the Queen Alexandra's Imperial
Military Nursing Service, but they first needed to
serve out their notice at the hospital. They would actually be leaving together, at the end of April.

One evening, when Morwenna was accompanying
her mother to a charity dinner in Kensington, Perys

invited Grace to dinner at the St Ermin's Hotel restaurant. It was where they had dined with Rupert and Morwenna at their first meeting.

The evening began well. The restaurant was not too crowded and the presence of such a young RFC pilot accompanied by a strikingly attractive young woman brought many admiring glances from fellow diners. It also ensured the young couple received attentive service from the waiters.

Perys was seated facing the door. Just as he and Grace were about to begin their meal he gave an involuntary start.

Concerned, she asked, 'What's the matter?'

'I am sorry, Grace, it was an over-reaction. A distant cousin of mine has just come into the restaurant. He is in uniform and with a couple of fellow officers. I wasn't even aware he was in the army.'

'Do you want to call him over?'

'That's the very *last* thing I want. I would be quite happy if he didn't see me, but I think it's already too late for that.'

'Would it be the cousin you punched on the nose when you and Morwenna were in Cornwall?'

'She told you?' Perys was taken aback. Then he remembered that Morwenna and Grace were very close friends and it was hardly likely they would *not* talk about him.

'She said he was unforgivably rude to you and treated one of the servants abominably. Is he likely to come and speak to you?'

'I doubt that very much, but he seems uncomfortably interested in us. I wish I could hear what he's saying about me to his friends.'

Reaching across the table, Grace grasped his hand for a brief moment. 'Don't allow him to spoil our evening together, Perys. Not tonight.'

Perys's glance shifted from the other table to Grace and he smiled. 'I'm sorry. They won't spoil anything for us, I promise. Let's raise a glass to our next evening out together, wherever and whenever it may be. I know – we'll make a promise that the next time we are both in London we will come here for dinner again.'

Perys was able to keep his gaze from wandering to the table occupied by Edward and his friends, although he was aware when Edward left his two companions and was absent from the dining-room for many minutes. On his return he seemed pleased with himself.

Eventually, Perys and Grace finished their meal, relieved that there had been no untoward incident with Edward.

When they left the restaurant, Perys walked to the foyer to wait for Grace who had gone to the cloak-room. He was standing looking disinterestedly at one of the paintings adorning the wall when he was approached by an army captain. He recalled that the officer had put in a brief appearance in the doorway of the restaurant, accompanied by a sergeant and a corporal, while he and Grace were eating.

Addressing Perys, the captain said, 'Good evening, Lieutenant. Are you in London for the evening, or are you enjoying a spot of leave?'

'I am on leave, sir,' said Perys, believing the captain to be making polite conversation. At the same time, he wondered why he should bother to speak to a junior officer.

'Are you with a front-line squadron?' the captain asked.

'Not yet, sir. I have just completed my flying training.'

The captain nodded. 'Then you were no doubt with a regiment before joining the RFC?'

Perys realised he was being questioned, but could not understand why.

'No, I came directly into the RFC. Is there a reason for your questions, sir?'

'There is, Lieutenant. I am on the staff of the Provost Marshal at the War Office, just a short distance away. I would be grateful if you would accompany me there.'

'Accompany you . . . but why? I am escorting a young lady on an evening out. Here she is now.'

Grace came towards them, smiling. 'I am sorry if I have kept you waiting, Perys. I am glad you found someone to talk to. Are you ready to go now?'

'I am afraid Second Lieutenant Tremayne will need to accompany me, miss. I have a few questions to put to him.'

The fact that the provost captain knew his name confirmed to Perys that someone was deliberately causing trouble for him – and Perys had no doubt who that 'someone' was.

Taken aback by the captain's words, Grace said, 'Perys is escorting me for the evening. Why do you wish to take him away?'

'I am afraid it is a military matter, miss. However, I will ensure you are not left stranded. I will arrange for a taxi-cab to take you wherever you wish to go.'

Perys had always looked upon Grace as an unassuming, gentle girl, somewhat overshadowed by her more positive friend, Morwenna. He was about to see her in a very different light.

Suddenly angry, she snapped at the provost captain, 'I will *not* be abandoned in such a manner, Captain. Where do you intend taking Perys?'

'To the War Office, miss, where I am stationed—'

Grace did not allow him to finish what he was saying. 'Then you will telephone Major General Ballard. I believe that in addition to other responsibilities, he is in charge of the army's provost section. Tell him what you are doing – and why – and ask him to please come to collect me here, or at the War Office, because if you go there I shall certainly come too.'

The provost captain was startled. Major General Sir Giles Ballard was a senior officer at the War Office and responsible for many more important departments than the army's provost section.

'You are acquainted with General Ballard, Miss?'

'He is my father.'

Grace's statement took Perys by surprise – but it thoroughly dismayed the provost captain. A comparatively minor incident had suddenly assumed proportions which could have serious implications for his career.

Fully aware of his misgivings, Grace offered him a lifeline. 'Do we call out my father, Captain, or will you explain what all this is about?'

The captain was a realist. If he sufficiently antagonised the daughter of Major General Ballard he could say goodbye to all hopes of advancement within the provost section.

'Shall we take a seat over there . . . ?' He pointed

270

to a corner of the lounge where a number of comfortable armchairs were clustered about a small table. 'I fear people are becoming interested in us.'

The trio moved to the corner. Perys and Grace shared a sofa, while the captain sat facing them across the table. Addressing Perys, he was the first to speak.

'I received a telephone call informing me that a young Royal Flying Corps pilot, fresh from his training course, was here in the hotel dining-room, wearing ribbons of decorations to which he was not entitled. When I arrived you were the only RFC officer in the restaurant and by your own admission are fresh out of training, yet you are wearing the ribbon of the Military Cross – as well as two other ribbons I do not recognise.'

'One is Russian,' Perys explained. 'The Medal of the Order of Saint George. The other is the Royal Humane Society Medal. Both were given to me for rescuing the captain of a Russian ship which sank off the Cornish coast last year.'

'And the Military Cross?'

Before Perys could explain, Grace said, 'Perys qualified as a pilot *before* joining the Royal Flying Corps. Because of this the officer in charge of training asked Perys to pilot him to Ypres in Belgium. While there they became involved in the rescue of Brigadier Palmer and his pilot who had crashed in no-man's land. Perys was awarded an immediate Military Cross. My father knows all about it – in fact, he is of the opinion that Perys should have received an even higher award. You may check with him, if you wish.'

'That will not be necessary, Miss Ballard. You have satisfied me that the information I have been given is erroneous. Please accept my sincere apologies. You too, Lieutenant Tremayne – indeed, I am proud to have met with you. I hope you will understand that I had to take action on the telephone call that was made to the War Office.'

'May I ask the name of the caller?' Perys said. Although greatly relieved that the matter had been satisfactorily settled, he was angry that it should have occurred at all.

'It was an anonymous call,' admitted the captain.

'But the caller mentioned me by name?'

'Why, yes, he did.'

Now Perys was quite certain he knew who had made the call. 'I think you will find your anonymous caller seated at a table in the restaurant at this moment, in the company of two friends. His name is Edward Tremayne and he is a Second Lieutenant in the Duke of Cornwall Light Infantry.' The captain's eyebrows rose and Perys added, 'We are cousins – at least, *second* cousins. Shortly before the war began I gave him a bloody nose. He has never forgiven me. I noticed he was absent from the table for some minutes earlier in the evening. It is probable he was making a telephone call to you.'

'Now you mention it, I thought I recognised the voice. I believe he has a junior post at the War Office. I will go and have a word with him now. The provost section does not exist to settle family feuds. Thank you both for your understanding. I trust this unfortunate incident has not spoiled your evening together.'

It was a fine night and Perys and Grace decided to walk back to the hostel at St Thomas's Hospital, where she had a room. On the way, his anger over the incident at the hotel almost gone, Perys said, 'You never told me your father was such a senior army officer.'

Grace smiled at him. 'You never asked me about him. He has taken a much greater interest in *you*. He was almost as thrilled as I was by the award of your Military Cross. He is a great RFC enthusiast and believes you have an assured future in the service. We spoke on the telephone earlier today. He has asked me to invite you to our home in Oxfordshire as soon as you have a free weekend . . . I suppose that really means as soon as we both have a free weekend at the same time. Life is likely to be changing a great deal for both of us in the coming weeks and months.'

'Making plans will be difficult,' he agreed, 'as it already is for a great many people.'

'But we *will* see each other again, whenever it is possible? We will try to make it happen?'

'Of course.'

They were in the shadows, midway between two street lights, and it seemed a natural thing for them both to come to a halt and kiss.

Grace came to him eagerly. His response matched her ardour, but it needed a conscious effort to banish thoughts of the last girl he had kissed in this manner.

It was not easy.

But Annie was to marry someone else. It was time to put the past behind him.

41

Nine days after the evening spent with Grace, Perys arrived in France.

He had hoped to fly there from England, but other senior officers at the Central Flying School were less confident of his skills than Major Kemp had been. Perys had only just completed his advanced flying course, therefore he had to travel with other newly qualified pilots drafted to front-line squadrons – by boat and train.

It was a long journey. Perys was the only man joining Major Kemp's squadron, and by the time he reached the nearest railway station to the airfield he was tired, hungry and not in the best of humour. It did not help to be told that transport from the airfield might take anything up to two hours to arrive.

In fact, a vehicle arrived in less than an hour, but by this time night had fallen and the railway station was in darkness, for fear of an unlikely attack by German aircraft.

Perys had to wait until mail for the squadron had been loaded into the van, before climbing inside the cab beside the driver. Impatiently, he asked, 'How long will it take us to reach the airfield?'

'A lot longer than it would in daylight, sir. We'll be running on dimmed lights and the road isn't too good . . .'

But Perys had stopped listening to what the man was saying. 'I know that voice,' he said. 'It's Martin, isn't it? Martin from Heligan.'

'That's right, sir, but I'm Driver Bray now – Air Mechanic First Class.'

'We'll leave all that for when we're on the airfield, Martin.' Reaching across the cab, he shook hands with the ex-Heligan coachman. 'I knew you were in the RFC. I was at Heligan for a short while before Christmas.'

'I know, sir. Polly wrote and told me.'

'Is she well, Martin, she and . . . the family?'

'They were all fine when I last heard, sir, but I've been moving about a bit since I left England. I'm not sure all the mail has caught up with me.'

'It isn't only here there are problems with the mail,' Perys said, ruefully. 'I wrote a number of letters to Annie that failed to arrive.'

'Oh, they got there in the end,' Martin said, hoping Perys would not question him too closely. 'Polly mentioned it. There was some sort of misunderstanding, I believe. Annie didn't get the letters until after you'd been and gone from Heligan. Polly said she was very upset about it.'

They had left the railway station behind now and Martin spoke without shifting his gaze from the road, barely discernible in the dim light from the shielded headlamps.

'She never received them . . . ?' Perys suffered a brief moment of consternation. If she had not received his letters, then perhaps . . . Then he remembered she was to marry the farmer's son. 'It's probably just as well she never had my letters before I arrived. After all, I believe she's to be married.'

In the darkness of the van's cab, Martin's gaze flicked momentarily from the road to the man beside him. 'Might they have caused trouble?'

'Possibly. I grew very fond of Annie when we were all at Heligan together.'

'I always thought she felt the same way about you,' Martin said.

'Then why was mention never made of this farmer's son she's marrying? According to your parents a marriage between them was planned long before I came on the scene.'

'It's certainly what Ma and Pa would like. They've never made any secret of it, but it came as a surprise to me when I heard that Annie and Jimmy were going to marry. Rose – Jimmy's sister – is Annie's friend, her best friend, but I was never aware of anything between our Annie and Jimmy. Still, there must have been something going on, I suppose, because both Ma and Polly have written to tell me about it.'

'When you next write to Polly will you ask her to pass on a message to Annie from me? Tell her that I hope she will be very, very happy with this Jimmy.'

'I'll do that. But changing the subject for a moment, there are a couple of things I'd like to say before we reach the airfield . . . sir. It might be better for both of

276

us if you don't let on that we know each other. The men I work with would resent it and make more of it than there is. It wouldn't do you any good either, sir. A couple of the pilots who are officers now were once just ordinary airmen like me. They've been told off in no uncertain terms about being too friendly with men they once worked with.'

'Very well, Martin, if that's the way things are, that's the way we'll behave – when we're on the airfield. When we're on our own like this I'd like things to be the way they were during those happy days at Heligan. But you said there were a *couple* of things?'

'Yes. I'm very grateful to you for suggesting that I should join the RFC. I've seen something of life in the trenches, up at the front. I don't think I could survive in the way they have to. All the same, I believe I might be doing something more useful than driving a van around the countryside.' There was another quick glance at Perys before Martin added, 'What I'd really like to do is fly . . . perhaps not as a pilot, I don't think I'll ever be good enough for that, but I'm sure I could do the job of an observer. I know you won't be able to do anything about it right away, not until you've settled in a bit, but there aren't enough observers in the squadron to go round right now. Sometimes the pilots choose one of the ground crew to go up with them. If ever the occasion arises I'd be very grateful if you'd consider taking me.'

'Of course I will, Martin, but, as you say, I'll need to settle in a little first.'

Perys's settling in period was much shorter than he had anticipated.

He was informed on his arrival that it was Major Kemp's policy to give new pilots a minimum of fourteen days' familiarisation before they were sent up on active duties. The commanding officer made this ruling in a bid to curtail the alarming loss of pilots and observers that the squadron had experienced prior to his arrival.

He decided that before a pilot became operational, he should be familiar with the area in which he operated, know the spots where German anti-aircraft guns and aircraft were at their most dangerous, and be able to find his way back to the airfield after an operation, no matter where he happened to be.

Unfortunately, Perys had only been with the squadron for two days when three pilots and two observers were seriously hurt in a vehicle smash when they were returning to the airfield after a night out in the local town. He was told he would need to be available immediately.

The squadron had been given the task of reconnaissance and aerial photography, both of which were of prime importance with a spring offensive in the offing. Aerial photography was dangerous work. While taking photographs of enemy lines it was necessary for the pilot to fly a straight and even course, in order that the photographs so obtained could later be joined together to give a full picture of the trench system of the German army. Any significant changes would be assessed by senior officers at army headquarters in a bid to guess what the Germans might be planning.

The loss of so many of the squadron's experienced aircrew was a chance for Perys to inform the commanding officer of Martin's ambitions. As a result, the ex-Heligan coachman was given the opportunity he had hoped for, although he would not initially be flying with Perys. He was allocated to an experienced pilot for the same reason that Perys flew with an experienced observer.

The first two operational flights undertaken by Perys posed no problems. He photographed a section of the German trench system that was well established and had few anti-aircraft defences.

His third flight was very different. A pilot sent to photograph a particularly sensitive section of the German lines had failed to return from his mission and was presumed to have been shot down. As this part of the line featured in a planned assault, it was essential that a full set of photographs be obtained. Perys was detailed to carry out the task attempted by the missing man.

In view of the importance attached to the information sought by army headquarters, Perys was given an escort of four 'Longhorns'. Two flew above him to guard against enemy fighter planes, the other two below. One of these was in radio contact with the ground.

Despite the primitive and experimental nature of the equipment being used, the object of the radio link was to bring artillery fire to bear on any German anti-aircraft fire that posed a particular threat to the operation. Unfortunately, the radio aircraft was hit by German fire almost immediately and forced to abandon its assignment. Perys last saw it descending rapidly towards the British lines, trailing smoke.

As a result of the loss of this plane, the German anti-aircraft batteries were able to range upon Perys's aeroplane without fear of retribution.

Their shooting was uncomfortably accurate. When one near miss threw the BE2c off course, Perys decided to lose a thousand feet of height before resuming his photographic duties. It meant the photographs would need expert interpretation, but Perys decided this was preferable to remaining on course at the previous height and risking the loss of *all* the photographs, together with himself, his observer and the aeroplane.

The observer, a full lieutenant with considerably more experience than Perys, thought so too. He made this clear in the report he gave when they landed safely. In the mess later that evening he insisted on paying for Perys's drinks, announcing to one and all that he would be happy to remain as Perys's regular observer.

The lieutenant did remain with Perys for a few more days, but then he returned to England for a week's leave. He was replaced by Martin Bray.

42

Following Perys's recommendation, Martin had spent a week flying as an observer with two different pilots. Their reports on his capabilities led to him being placed on acting observers' duties with the squadron.

When he was allocated to Perys, it was immediately apparent to Major Kemp that the two formed a very effective team. On their first flight together they were photographing a section of the front-line when they were attacked by a German fighter plane.

Although the very nature of their sortie decreed they should maintain a steady course, the German pilot was an experienced and aggressive airman. Any attempt to ignore him would have proved fatal to the British flyers.

In an aerial duel that lasted for fifteen minutes, each pilot tried to manoeuvre himself into a favourable attacking position, without giving his adversary an advantage that would bring the conflict to a swift and fatal conclusion.

Both men were skilful pilots, and to the watching soldiers on the ground on both sides of the front-line, it was like witnessing a duel between two eagles engaged in a deadly territorial contest.

Then the German pilot made his first and only mistake. For a few moments his aeroplane flew above and behind his opponent, giving Martin a clear shot at him.

It was enough.

Half a drum of bullets tore through the fabric of the aeroplane beneath the German pilot's seat. He was dead even before the plane began falling in a nose-down spiral.

Martin had downed his first enemy aircraft. It was a feat which earned both men a mention in dispatches. Martin's proud letter to his parents at Tregassick Farm, informing them of the award, gave them their first indication that their son was now a flying man.

However, the encounter with the downed German had not been an entirely satisfactory experience for Perys. It made him more aware than ever before that the capabilities of the BE2c fell far short of those of the German aeroplane. His success, if not his very survival, was a result of the excellent instruction he had received from Nick Malloch, coupled with Martin's accurate shooting. Most other RFC pilots would have been shot down in the first few minutes of the encounter.

He discussed the matter with Major Kemp a few evenings later, when the squadron commanding officer was giving Perys a lift into the nearby town to enjoy an unexpected twenty-four-hour break from flying due to bad weather which had closed in on the front.

'The German aircraft *are* superior to our own aeroplanes,' agreed the commanding officer. 'I put in a report saying so to RFC headquarters weeks ago.'

'It's not only their aeroplanes,' Perys persisted. 'Our pilots are sent to France with little more than an elementary knowledge of battle tactics and aerobatics. The Germans not only have better aircraft, they have pilots who are more expert in handling them.'

'Again, I agree with you,' said Major Kemp, 'but don't exaggerate the flying skills of German pilots. *Inexperience* is responsible for the deaths of far more British pilots than the enemy. Properly trained, a British pilot is more than a match for his German counterpart, whatever aeroplane he is flying – as you recently proved – but so far we have not had time to train them sufficiently before they're needed urgently on operations. I know it's wrong and a very senior RFC officer agrees with me. He is currently badgering the War Office to improve both recruiting and RFC training methods. He's on the look-out for good instructors. If you would like to put some of your ideas into practice . . .'

Perys shook his head vigorously. 'I'm not ready to take on training duties just yet. On the contrary, I'd like to take a more active role. I believe the formation of a number of fighter squadrons is being considered. Much as I enjoy being in your squadron, sir, I would like to volunteer to move to one of them.'

'You don't know how delighted I am to hear you say that, Perys. I have asked to be given one of these new fighter squadrons. The trouble is, the powers-that-be haven't yet agreed on the type of aircraft they want, although it will probably be a single-seater. When they've finally made up their mind and the squadrons are formed, I expect to be given one. When that happens I'd like to take you with me – as one of my flight commanders.'

Perys could not hide his astonishment. 'A flight commander? I'm not even a full lieutenant yet!'

'Oh, hasn't anyone told you? Your promotion came through a day or two ago. Besides, you have as much experience and more flying ability than any other pilot in the squadron – so you had better put up that extra pip when you get back to your billet.'

Some days later, still with the reconnaissance squadron, Perys was to witness an event that, although he was not aware of it at the time, would have a profound effect upon his private life.

He and Martin were making a routine reconnaissance flight behind the German lines, looking for any unusual movement that might indicate an imminent enemy attack. All seemed fairly quiet, with nothing out of the ordinary taking place. However, half-an-hour into the flight, Perys banked the aircraft and went lower, in order to evade shells from a German anti-aircraft battery which had gauged their height with uncomfortable accuracy.

As he levelled out once more, Martin turned in the forward cockpit and gestured downwards. His vision blocked by the lower wing, Perys banked again in order to see what had caught Martin's attention.

Close to the ground a greenish smoky substance was being discharged from dozens of tube-like chimneys seemingly rooted in the ground. Drifting across no-man's land to the allied trenches, the cloud so formed gradually became a blue-white mist.

'Perhaps one of our artillery shells has started some sort of a fire!'

Martin's shouted suggestion lacked conviction and Perys shook his head. Not until figures could be seen scrambling from the Allied trenches and fleeing for their lives did Perys realise what they were seeing.

'It's poison gas!' he shouted.

He remembered hearing a rumour that a soldier taken prisoner by the British had disclosed that the German army intended using poison gas against the Allied armies. This information had been relayed up the line of command to the commander-in-chief, who dismissed it as deliberate scaremongering. He pointed out that the Germans were signatories to an international agreement forbidding the use of such a weapon in war. It would *not* be used.

Anti-aircraft fire was once more being directed at the BE2c with disturbing accuracy, but Perys banked the plane again in order to obtain a better view of the ominous, drifting cloud now gradually dispersing behind the Allied lines.

He reached a sudden decision. The commander-in-chief and his staff were wrong. What he and Martin were seeing *was* poison gas. He would land as quickly as possible and report what he had seen to the nearest command post.

Perys's opinion of the significance of what he had seen was received with the same scepticism as the information imparted by the German prisoner. Frustrated, he took off again to make his report back at the air-field.

Within an hour it had been tragically confirmed that what Perys and Martin had seen was indeed poison gas. The troops they had seen fleeing were French colonial troops and their terrified abandonment of their position left a whole section of the advance trenches undefended. These were swiftly occupied by German troops, but the extent of their success seemed to have taken them by surprise. They failed to take full advantage of it by bringing up more troops and consolidating their gains immediately.

Nevertheless, it was only the tenacity and outstanding courage of Canadian troops, hastily deployed to contain the German advance, that prevented a far more serious situation developing, despite many of these troops also suffering the effects of poison gas.

Among their number was a small platoon of British soldiers, engaged on an ammunition delivery detail. One of the soldiers in the platoon was Private Jimmy Rowe.

43

It took Annie some days to work up the courage to go to the Rowe farm in order to break her news to them. She knew it would not be an easy thing to do and felt miserable about it. She was also aware that it would mean the end of her life-long friendship with Rose, Jimmy's sister.

But once she had decided exactly what she would say to the Rowes she set out for their farm. Giving her parents no prior warning, she merely put on her coat and left Tregassick.

When her mother called after her to ask where she was going, Annie replied, 'To the Rowe farm.'

To her mother's shouted demands for an explanation, Annie would only reply that she would 'know in due course'.

Walter, coming in from the fields, saw her disappearing along the track and hurried into the farmhouse to find out what was happening.

When Harriet told him, he at first shared her concern. Then, after giving it a few moments' thought, he said, 'Annie hasn't had a letter from young Jimmy for some time. She'll have been getting worried about him. She's gone to see if the Rowes have heard from him.' Smiling at his wife, he said, 'That's what our Annie's up to, Harriet, you mark my words. Things are beginning to work out the way we want them to. I knew she'd come to her senses sooner or later. She's finally got young Tremayne out of her system.'

Harriet did not share her husband's confidence. She believed there was some other less acceptable explanation for Annie's unexpected visit to the Rowe farm, but she kept her thoughts to herself.

When Annie arrived at the Rowe farm she walked into a household in a state of turmoil. When Winnie Rowe, Jimmy's mother, saw her, she let out an anguished shriek. 'Annie! Thank the Lord you're here! But how did you get here so quickly? Charlie Clemo only set off on his horse to tell you half-an-hour ago.'

Charlie Clemo was a well-known Methodist minister on the local circuit. Puzzled, Annie asked, 'To tell me what?'

'Oh my dear soul, of course, you wouldn't know. It's our Jimmy.'

Guiltily aware of the reason she had come to the Rowe farmhouse, Annie said, apprehensively, 'Jimmy? He's not . . . he's not been killed?'

'No, but he might well have been, from all accounts. The son of the doctor down at Fowey is in the same regiment. He's an officer. He telephoned his father last night from London to say he'd been wounded, and to ask the doctor to come up and tell us about our Jimmy. He's been wounded too – badly wounded. He's in a hospital in London. The doctor said we were to tell you that Jimmy's asking after you. He felt it would help him a lot if we was to take you up there to see him.'

This was the worst possible news Annie could have received. There could be no question now of saying what she had come to tell the family. Besides, she had known Jimmy all her life and was genuinely concerned for him. She suddenly felt inextricably trapped by the tragic and unexpected situation which had arisen.

'You say he's badly wounded . . . *how* badly?'

'The doctor's son said he's been gassed. He's also got shrapnel wounds – one in his head. He said Jimmy can't see right now, although I don't know whether or not that's because he has a bandage covering his eyes, or something. But now you're here we can go and catch a train right away, Annie. Me and Rose were only waiting for you to arrive. Jimmy's pa will stay on to look after the farm.'

'But . . . I can't go dressed like this. Besides, what about Ma and Pa . . .' Annie felt a desperate need to think about what was happening.

'I'll get word to them. Have a message telephoned through to Polly at Heligan. At such a time as this I'm sure the old housekeeper up there won't choose to be difficult. Come on now, we'll take some of Rose's night-clothes for you. A change of dress, too. You and she are much the same size.'

It was the first time any of the trio from Cornwall had left their native county. Winnie Rowe, in particular, such a positive character at home, found the busy railway terminal at Paddington awesome, and the streets outside the station took her breath away.

Standing by one of the station entrances, they were wondering what to do now they had arrived in the capital city, when a policeman approached them. It was evident they were from the country and thoroughly bemused. He asked if he could be of help.

Winnie, confused by the bustle all about her and becoming increasingly distressed, replied, 'We've come up from Cornwall to see my son. He's been wounded in the war . . . gassed. He's in hospital here.'

'Which hospital, ma'am?'

'It's called Saint Thomas's, but I don't know exactly where it is.'

'Don't you worry about that, ma'am, we all know Saint Thomas's. I'll get a taxi-cab for you. The driver will know where to take you.'

Stepping out into the road, the policeman held up his hand. With much squealing of brakes, a taxi came to a halt beside the small party. The vehicle had a closed-in section for the passengers, but only a windscreen in front to protect the driver from the elements.

Speaking to the driver, the policeman said, 'These three ladies are up from the country to see a soldier who's been gassed in the war. He's in Saint Thomas's Hospital.'

'If you open the door to let 'em in, I'll have 'em there in no time.'

The policeman opened the door for the three women, but Winnie held back. 'I can't ride in *that*! It was bad enough riding in a train for the first time. I should be frightened nigh to death.'

'You'll find nothing to get you there faster, nor safer,

missus,' said the taxi-driver. 'It'll take hardly more than ten minutes, then you'll be able to tell your son all about it – I presume that's who it is you're going to see?'

'That's right, my Jimmy. This is his sister, Rose, and Annie, the girl he's going to marry.'

'I'm sure it'll do his heart good to see you all. In you get, missus, and we'll be on our way.'

Trying hard to overcome her misgivings, Winnie climbed inside apprehensively, saying, 'I don't know about seeing us. The doctor who told me about him being in there said he's blind, as well as being gassed, but he'll be glad to have us there with him for a while, I'm sure of that.'

Annie and Rose followed Winnie into the taxi-cab. Before closing the door behind them, the policeman said, 'I hope your boy will soon be fit and well again, ma'am.'

There was barely time for Winnie and the others to call out a thank you before, with much crashing of gears, the taxi-cab moved away into the busy street.

None of the three Cornishwomen had experienced anywhere quite like London. The traffic was an alarming and diverse mixture of horse-drawn carts and carriages, steam- and petrol-driven vehicles, and bicycles threading their way in and out of the traffic. As Winnie commented, 'There's more folk on the streets than in Bodmin on market day!' Throughout the journey she was convinced the taxi-cab was in imminent danger of a collision with one or more of the vehicles that weaved about them in all directions.

The driver, a cheerful cockney, was aware of her fear. Sliding open the window that separated him from his passengers, he first questioned her about the extent of Jimmy's wounds, then began pointing out places of interest along the route.

Winnie was particularly impressed with Buckingham Palace, but wondered why even a king would need as many rooms as they must have in such a huge building.

Eventually, soon after passing the Houses of Parliament, the taxi-cab crossed Westminster Bridge and they arrived at the main entrance to St Thomas's Hospital. Bringing the vehicle to a halt, the driver helped the three women to the ground, together with the small bundles they were carrying.

It was now that Winnie asked the question which had been causing her increasing concern, as she wondered how much a journey in such a fine and modern vehicle would cost her.

'That's all right, missus,' said the taxi-driver, generously. 'Use the money to buy something for that brave son of yours. I hope he's soon well enough to go back to your farm in Cornwall.'

The taxi-cab drove away while Winnie was still trying to find words to thank the driver. She was left saying to her daughter and Annie, 'Well! Who'd have believed that folk could be so kind – and the driver wasn't even Cornish!'

While the taxi-driver had been both kind and helpful, the busy hospital staff were less so when they were told the reason for the visit of the three women. One of the hospital receptionists informed Winnie that wounded soldiers were not allowed visitors until they were well enough to leave the hospital and go to convalescent homes.

'But . . . one of Jimmy's officers telephoned Cornwall to say he was here. We've come all this way specially to see him.'

'I'm sorry.' The receptionist refused to be moved by Winnie's plea. 'This is not a hospital rule, it's one that has been imposed upon us by the army.'

The receptionist was aware that the ban on visitors was in place to prevent the public from becoming aware of the scale of casualties and the horrific wounds inflicted upon soldiers of the British army. It was believed it would be detrimental to public morale and so have an effect upon the vital army recruiting campaign currently being waged throughout the British Isles.

Nevertheless, Winnie had come all the way from Cornwall to see her son, and she would not readily accept defeat. Strongly supported by Rose, and to a lesser extent by Annie, she doggedly insisted that she be allowed to see Jimmy.

The conversation had become heated when a nursing sister passing through the reception area glanced in their direction and came to a halt. Looking at Annie uncertainly, she asked the receptionist the cause of the altercation.

'It's these people, Sister Tremayne. They say they've come up from Cornwall to see one of our patients, a Private Rowe. It seems one of his officers sent word to them to say he'd been wounded and was in our hospital. I've told them that soldiers are not allowed visitors, but they refuse to take my word for it. There's no need for you to become involved though, Sister, you won't be with us for very much longer . . .'

'I leave tomorrow,' Morwenna replied, but she was

looking at Annie as she spoke. 'I remember you. You were one of those who came to see Rupert – Mr Pilkington – and his aeroplane when he came to Heligan.'

'That's right, Miss Tremayne. I'm Annie Bray. My father has the farm just by Heligan . . . Tregassick. My brother was coachman at Heligan until he left to join the Royal Flying Corps.'

'Is that who is in the hospital?'

'No, it's Jimmy Rowe. He's Mrs Rowe's son and Rose's brother.'

'I see. Well, what the receptionist told you is perfectly true, but what is Private Rowe to you?'

Before Annie could reply, Winnie said, 'My Jimmy and Annie are to be married. That's why she's come to London with me and Rose. After travelling all this way we can't leave without at least seeing him.'

Morwenna glanced at the receptionist and said, 'You are quite right of course to point out the rules regarding visitors for wounded soldiers, but I will take full responsibility and personally escort these ladies to the ward.'

'Well, I've done my duty,' said the receptionist, huffily. 'If you say they *can* see him . . .' She shrugged in offended indifference.

'I do,' Morwenna said, brusquely. 'Now, Annie, if you and the others would like to come with me . . .'

Winnie hurried after Morwenna gratefully, the others following on behind. As they passed along one of the hospital corridors, Winnie said anxiously, 'This is very kind of you, Miss Tremayne. I do hope it won't get you into any trouble.'

Morwenna smiled. 'I don't think you need concern

yourself too much about that. I am only at Saint Thomas's for one more day before leaving to join the Queen Alexandra's Imperial Military Nursing Service. Besides, Private Rowe is on my ward. We have spoken often of Cornwall . . .' Suddenly serious, she asked, 'You *do* know how badly he is wounded?'

'I know he's been gassed,' Winnie replied, 'although I don't know exactly what that means. I've also been told he can't see too well either, but I haven't been told how long that's likely to last.'

'Oh!' Morwenna came to an abrupt halt and the others stopped too. 'I think we had better have a little chat before you meet him. He has suffered shrapnel wounds as well as being gassed. The shrapnel struck him in the head and body and a piece would seem to have severed an optic nerve. I don't know which came first, the gassing or the wounds, but he was probably exposed to the gas for rather a long time. It has seriously damaged his lungs and he has difficulty breathing.'

Horrified, Rose began quietly weeping, and as Winnie struggled to take in the news of Jimmy's condition, Annie asked, 'His sight . . . will he ever get it back?'

Morwenna shook her head. 'I am afraid he is permanently blinded. In fact, with all the wounds he has suffered he is very lucky to be alive at all.'

Bitterly, Annie wondered whether Jimmy thought himself 'lucky'.

'Oh, my poor, dear soul!' Winnie was fighting back her own tears. 'And he was so proud to be going off to be a soldier.'

'He has every reason to be proud,' Morwenna said.

'You should be proud of him too. He and all the others in the ward are brave men who have served their country well . . . but this is the ward. Dry those tears before we go in. It is important to your son and the other soldiers that your visit doesn't distress them.'

It took a few minutes for Winnie to compose herself, but she eventually said she was ready. Opening the door, Morwenna led the way.

It was a sobering experience for the three women. The ward held some of the most seriously wounded soldiers, many the victims of German gas attacks. Others had suffered severe and often ghastly wounds. To Annie, walking at the rear of the small visiting party, it seemed the scene might well have been a glimpse into Hell.

Halfway down the overcrowded room, Morwenna paused at one of the beds and glanced at a clip-board attached to the metal frame at its foot. Turning to Winnie, she said, 'Here he is. This is your son, Mrs Rowe.'

Had the nursing sister not been with them, Annie doubted very much whether they would have known the man lying in the bed was Jimmy. Heavily bandaged around his eyes and upper face, an attempt had been made to leave part of one ear free in order that he might hear. What little they could see of his skin was an unhealthy, almost yellow pallor and his breathing was laboured.

Fighting back her tears, Winnie leaned over him. 'Jimmy, can you hear me, boy? It's your ma.'

'Ma?' Jimmy clutched at the air until Winnie grasped his hand in hers. 'Ma! Is it really you? What are you doing here?'

His speech was slow, his voice little more than a whisper.

'Doctor Martin from down at Fowey came up to the farm to let us know you were here. His son had telephoned him to tell him. So here we are. Me, Rose and Annie.'

'Annie? Annie's here?'

His excitement caused him to wheeze, and for some minutes he fought for breath in an alarming fashion. Morwenna moved forward in an attempt to calm him.

When he had recovered she stepped back again and Jimmy reached out once more. 'Annie . . . where are you?'

Annie took hold of his hand. Gripping it so tightly she winced, he pulled her towards him. 'Annie . . . you don't know how glad I am that you're here. I've thought so much about you just lately.'

Annie felt overwhelming pity for the wounded man lying in the hospital bed. At the same time she was embarrassed that he should be paying her attention to the exclusion of his mother and Rose, whose presence he had not even acknowledged.

She spoke with him for a few minutes, although afterwards she could remember nothing that had been said. Then, gently but firmly releasing his grasp on her hand, she said, 'We haven't got long, Jimmy. Your ma and Rose want to speak with you.'

'You'll come and see me again?' he begged.

Annie looked up at Morwenna, who shook her head.

'No, we were very lucky to be allowed to see you today, Jimmy. But you'll soon be home, back in Cornwall.'

'I hope so, Annie, I really hope so. You don't know what it was like there, at Ypres . . . but I'll feel better when I've got these bandages off and can see again. Then I'll get my lungs sorted out.'

Realising that Jimmy had not been told he was permanently blinded, Annie felt pity for him flood over her once more.

Winnie and Rose held Jimmy's hands and spoke to him for a few more minutes, then Morwenna said they would have to leave. Winnie did not want to go, and Jimmy begged to be allowed to hold Annie's hand once more, but Morwenna gave them only a couple of minutes before she ushered them from the ward.

A tearful Winnie alternately thanked Morwenna and cried for her son all the way to the hospital reception area. Aware that it was too late in the day for them to return to Cornwall, Morwenna asked where they were staying while they were in London.

When Annie said they had given the matter no serious thought, Morwenna gave them the address of a boarding house which she said was clean and cheap. It was a large house where many relatives of the hospital's patients stayed.

Before they parted company, Morwenna said, 'I envy you returning to Cornwall. I think Heligan is my favourite place anywhere in the country.'

Suddenly plucking up the courage to ask about something that had been troubling her for some minutes, Annie said to Morwenna, 'May I ask you a personal question?'

The request took Morwenna by surprise, but she replied, 'Of course. What is it?'

'I've noticed you are wearing an engagement ring.

It's very beautiful. Was it given to you by Master Perys?'

'Perys? No, by Rupert, the pilot of the aeroplane that landed at Heligan. What made you think it might have been given to me by Perys?' Morwenna was intrigued by Annie's interest.

'I remember Martin, my brother, saying you took his part against Edward when there was all that trouble up at the big house.'

'Of course! I had forgotten that – and Martin's involvement.' Morwenna smiled at her. 'Perys and I are friends as well as second cousins – very good friends – but his affections are with Grace, a friend of mine. I would not be surprised if he gave *her* a ring before very long . . .'

The three women left St Thomas's Hospital that evening feeling very depressed, but Annie's state of mind was not due entirely to the tragic condition of Jimmy Rowe.

44

The telephone call to Heligan asking that Walter and Harriet Bray be informed of what Annie was doing and why, was taken by Polly. She decided she would speak to the housekeeper and ask her for time off to go to the farm.

Her visits to Tregassick had been less frequent since Martin had joined the Royal Flying Corps. It was no one's fault. She was kept busy at Heligan House. Squire Tremayne intended turning the house over to the army as a convalescent home for wounded officers as soon as it could be made ready. The servants would be kept on, but they could expect to be far busier than in pre-war days. They were currently rearranging the rooms and packing and storing many of the valuables.

The news of Jimmy's wounds caused consternation at the Bray farmhouse.

'Perhaps they'll send him to Heligan,' suggested Walter.

'I doubt that very much,' Polly replied. 'Heligan is to be a convalescent home for officers – and that excludes poor Jimmy. But, much as I would like to stay talking to you and exchange news of Martin, I was told to hurry straight back. The inventory of what will remain has to be completed tonight and I still have a couple of rooms to work on. Tell Annie to let me know when she gets back. I'll make certain I find time then to come and speak with you all.'

News of Annie's return reached Polly via one of the elderly estate workers a few days later. He had been asked by Walter Bray to tell her.

She made her way to the farm later that same evening. She had some news of her own to pass on to the family. A letter had arrived from Martin that morning, telling her he had been promoted to the rank of acting sergeant and was now flying as an observer with Perys Tremayne!

Her pride for his achievement was tempered by fear of the increased danger he would be facing in his new role. However, Martin's pay was now more than double the amount he had been earning when he was employed at Heligan. It was more than enough to support a wife and a family.

Martin hinted that it might be possible for him to make an occasional flight to England. Should such an opportunity arise, he would send a telegram asking her to obtain a special licence in order that they might be married right away.

It was an exciting prospect and one to share with Martin's family.

The fact that Jimmy had been wounded was likely to detract from what she had to tell them, but Polly hoped his wounds might not be too serious. Besides, if Annie had already told her parents – and Jimmy's – that she was not going to marry him, her own news might come as a welcome relief to everyone.

It was a wet evening and the walk through the woods to the farm was muddy, but Polly had left Heligan House prepared for the weather. Her rain-coat and hat were soaked and her wellington boots filthy, but the rain had done nothing to dampen her spirits.

However, her hopes of being able to tell of Martin's letter were dashed immediately she entered the farm-house.

Opening the door to the kitchen she was surprised that no lamp had been lit to dispel the evening gloom. The family was gathered in the room and were grouped as though they had been talking together. Polly thought they had probably not yet got around to lighting the lamp.

She realised it was more than this when their greeting was totally lacking in enthusiasm.

Stepping out of her muddy boots, Polly paused in the process of unfastening her raincoat.

'Is something wrong?'

'It's Jimmy,' said Harriet, shaking her head in a pained expression.

'He's not . . .' Polly hesitated before completing the question, '. . . he's not dead?'

'No, poor soul,' Harriet replied, 'but he's suffered as no young man should. Not only was he gassed by the Germans, but then he was blown up by a shell that wounded him in half-a-dozen places and robbed him of his sight. He's blinded.'

Polly was genuinely horrified. 'That's *dreadful*! What will happen to him now?'

She looked at Annie and, correctly interpreting the unasked question in her glance, Annie shook her head almost imperceptibly. Polly realised Annie had mentioned nothing to her family of her decision not to marry Jimmy. Polly's heart went out to her.

But one thing was quite clear. This was not the moment to break her own news to the Bray family.

It was not until two days after the visit to Tregassick Farm that another opportunity arose, but on this occasion too, Polly was thwarted.

Unable to keep her own unhappy feelings bottled inside her for any longer, Annie had come to Heligan House in the evening to speak with her future sister-in-law. When she described how she felt when she was taken to see Jimmy, and his reaction to her presence, she broke down.

Polly was deeply sympathetic, but could think of absolutely nothing to say to console her.

'It's a dreadful thing to happen to him, Annie, but what are you going to do now?'

'What *can* I do?' Annie asked, helplessly. 'He's suffered so much I feel guilty for even *thinking* I wouldn't marry him.'

Polly looked at her, aghast. 'It's not just a question of hurting someone, Annie. You're talking of marrying someone you don't love! It would utterly destroy you – and trying to live a lie will destroy Jimmy too in the long run. You just can't do it!'

'I can't *not* do it, Polly. Jimmy is such a mess that rejection by me could kill him. Besides . . .' Just for a moment she faltered. Then, gathering herself, she said,

303

'Perys has found someone else. Someone of his own class.'

'How can you possibly know that?' Polly asked.

Annie said unhappily, 'When we got to the hospital in London, Morwenna Tremayne was there. She's a nursing sister. It was she who got us in to see Jimmy, even though visits from relatives and friends aren't allowed. I saw she was wearing an engagement ring. I thought it might have been given to her by Perys, but she said the man she was going to marry was the pilot who flew the aeroplane to Heligan when Perys was here. Isn't he another distant cousin?'

Polly frowned, not understanding, and Annie continued, 'She also told me Perys is to get engaged to one of her friends, so you see, whatever *I* do will make no difference to Perys now. And it doesn't really matter to anyone else what I do.'

Annie's statement upset Polly. 'Even if what you've said is true – and I don't really believe it because it's not what Martin says in his letters, and he should know better than anyone because he's flying with Perys now – it's certainly not reason enough to marry a man you don't love.'

'I may not love him in the way you love Martin, Polly, or even the way I love Perys – and I do – but I've got to face reality. Apart from Perys, I am more fond of Jimmy than any other man I know, and he needs me. *Really* needs me. I can't let him down. Not now.'

'What about *you*, Annie? How will you be able to live with Jimmy, knowing it's not him you love?'

'I'll learn to stop loving Perys, Polly. I have to anyway if he's going to marry someone else. Besides, it was just a foolish dream to think there could be anything more than a brief friendship between us. Pa was right, Perys and I live in two different worlds. I'm sure people can fall out of love just as easily as they can fall *in* love. And Perys is not really one of the Tremaynes of Heligan – he once said so himself – so I doubt if we'll ever see or hear anything of him again. I've just got to get on with my life.'

'Do you really believe that marrying a man who is as ill as you say Jimmy is, is "getting on with your life", Annie? It sounds more like opting out of it to me!'

In her heart, Annie knew Polly was right, but it was something to which she would never, ever admit.

'It's my decision and no one else's, Polly. Jimmy desperately needs me and I won't let him down. I'll make him happy and by doing it I'll find my own happiness too, you'll see.'

Polly disagreed very strongly with Annie's views, but she knew that further argument right now would be useless. She was also aware that what she had said about Martin flying with Perys had not registered with Annie, but this was not the right time to tell her of the happy plans she and Annie's brother were making for their future together.

Yet again it would have to wait for another day.

45

Jimmy spent more than three months in various hospitals before he was discharged from the army at the end of August 1915, and allowed to return to the family farm at Fowey.

He had finally accepted that he would never see again and would always suffer the effects of damaged lungs, but he had not yet succeeded in coming to terms with his disabilities.

Annie had gone with Winnie Rowe to fetch him from the military hospital at Aldershot, to which he had been moved, but after seeing him safely back at his home she returned immediately to Tregassick. Walter Bray was gathering in the harvest and needed all the help the family could give him. So many men had left to go to war he was unable to call on hired help. Even Polly put in whatever time was left at the end of her long day's work at Heligan.

Harvesting was still in progress when Annie

received a visit from Jimmy's sister, Rose. As Annie had done on previous occasions, Rose had sailed to Mevagissey on a fishing boat from Fowey. Annie knew instinctively that her visit had to do with Jimmy and she feared the worst.

'No, he's all right,' Rose reassured her. 'Well . . . as right as anyone can be who's suffered as he has. It's not his wounds, Annie, it's his state of mind we're all concerned about. He's saying that he's got nothing to live for any more. He can't see, so someone has to take him wherever he needs to go, but he doesn't seem able to walk more than a dozen paces without gasping for breath. He's giving up, Annie. He's even started saying it'd be better for everyone if he'd been killed instead of wounded. Ma's so worried about him she asked me to come and see if you'd get over to our place and speak to him as soon as you can.'

A call to go to Jimmy was something Annie had anticipated ever since she and Winnie had collected him from hospital. It had been apparent to her then that he was determined not to allow anything to rouse him from his misery. Although it left her feeling guilty, she had been relieved to leave him at his parents' farm and return home to Tregassick.

However, she realised there would come a day when she would need to face up to a future with Jimmy. It now seemed that time had arrived – yet she made one final, albeit weak attempt to defer the moment.

'I can't go until we've finished harvesting. Pa has no one else he can call on except Ma and me.'

'I'll stay here and do your work, you know I can,' Rose said immediately.

Annie looked at her mother who had been listening in silence to the conversation. She hoped she might raise an objection. She did not.

'You must go to him, Annie. Jimmy was so proud to be going off to war. Who could have imagined he would end up like this?'

'Who indeed?' Annie said, bitterly. 'All right, you stay here, Rose. I'll go right away.'

If Jimmy was pleased to see her, it was not immediately apparent. He was seated alone in the farmhouse's front room with the curtains drawn.

In answer to Annie's question, Winnie Rowe explained, 'I drew the curtains because the bright light might hurt his poor eyes.'

'Why have him sit in here at all?' Annie asked. 'Why can't he sit in the kitchen where people are coming and going for much of the time and where he can join in any conversation that's going on? Wouldn't you prefer that, Jimmy?'

'Who wants to talk to a man who can't see and who can hardly stand up from a chair without fighting for breath?' Jimmy replied, in a tone of voice that indicated utter defeat.

'Are you telling me you *enjoy* sitting in here on your own, not wanting to be a part of what's going on around you? You'd prefer to spend the rest of your life wallowing in self-pity, is that it?'

'*Annie!* How can you be so cruel as to talk like that to our poor Jimmy?' Winnie was shocked.

'It's even more cruel to sit him down on his own in a darkened room with nothing but his thoughts for company,' Annie retorted. 'What he needs is understanding, not pity. Give him something to do— no, I don't need reminding that he's blind and not yet fit enough to do a full day's work, but he can do some things. Find out what they are and help him get started.'

Bristling with indignation, Winnie said, 'It's all very well for you to talk, you don't have to look after him . . .'

'No, that's right, and unless he gets a grip on himself I never will . . . But why are we talking as though he can't hear us? Isn't he at least capable of *thinking* for himself?' Turning her back on the farmer's wife, she spoke directly to the subject of their discussion. 'You've heard what we've been saying about you, Jimmy. What do *you* think? Are you happy to sit here doing nothing day after day, or are you going to face up to the way things are and build a new life for yourself? I tell you one thing, I have no intention of marrying a man who has to be helped into church and who intends to go through life accepting everyone's pity. If you want to marry me, Jimmy Rowe, you'll need to stand beside me at the altar and walk back down the aisle with me on your arm. If you don't, there'll be no wedding.'

Appalled, Winnie said, 'I've never heard anything so cruel! Why—'

'I'm not talking to you,' Annie snapped, 'I'm speaking to Jimmy, and he can answer for himself.'

'You'll still marry me, Annie?' Jimmy turned sightless eyes towards her. 'Even though I'm . . . the way I am?'

'Only when you're capable of walking down the aisle beside me.'

Rising from his chair and shaking off his mother's arm when she went to help him, Jimmy stood uncertainly. 'If you'll still take me as your husband then I'll do it, Annie. What's more, show me what work I can do and I'll do my best to support you.'

'Then we can start planning a wedding. When it will be depends entirely upon you.'

With Jimmy ensconced in the kitchen, Annie made her way to Rose's room, where she was to stay for the night. Winnie followed her upstairs.

'It wasn't necessary to speak to our Jimmy the way you did, Annie.'

'It was entirely necessary. It was either that or leave him to rot away in a darkened room. That would have been even more cruel.'

'You know very well he'll never be capable of making money to support a wife. There's nothing he can do here to earn himself a living.'

'If we marry we won't be living here,' Annie declared firmly. 'There are a couple of gamekeepers' cottages over by Tregassick that are empty right now. They used to be occupied by Heligan gamekeepers, but now they've gone off to war their families have moved into Mevagissey. I've said I'll take one over and Polly will move into the other when she marries Martin. It's close enough for Jimmy to take on some of the work at Tregassick and we'll all be there to help him.'

Winnie was horrified at the thought of letting Jimmy move away from the farm worked by the Rowe family. 'Why move over there? He knows his way about the farm here. He'll need to learn where everything is all over again – and he can't see.'

'He'll have all the help he needs from me, Ma and Pa,' Annie said, firmly. 'If he stays here he'll always be treated as an invalid. When he comes to Tregassick he'll be expected to earn a living for himself – and for me and our family, should we ever have one. *That's* what Jimmy needs and he'll be all the better for it.'

Annie had decided she must put aside the doubts she still held about marrying Jimmy. She had declared her future now. It was not the one she had always dreamed of, but she told herself this was real life, not a dream world. She would need to face facts and accept what fate had decreed for her.

46

Annie's wedding to Jimmy was not the happy occasion she had so often imagined the ceremony to be.

It was due to take place at the nearby St Ewe Church, but before the banns were called there was an argument between the vicar of Mevagissey and the incumbent of St Ewe about which of their parishes had responsibility for Tregassick Farm. Technically, the farm lay within the Mevagissey parish, but it was administered by the Tremayne Estate, and the Tremayne family worshipped at St Ewe. The vicar of Mevagissey gave way only when Annie threatened to have the marriage ceremony performed in a Wesleyan chapel if the two clerics failed to agree.

Jimmy, his mother and Rose came to Tregassick the day before the ceremony. Jimmy's father would ride over first thing in the morning after tending the animals.

Tregassick Farm would have been overcrowded

had the Rowe family stayed there, so they were accommodated in the semi-detached cottage that Annie and Jimmy would occupy after their marriage. It was only a short distance away and the Rowes would eat at Tregassick.

After depositing their clothes at the cottage, Jimmy and his family arrived at the farm. It was an uncomfortable evening. Winnie complained unceasingly about her son's new home. It was too large for a newly-wed couple; was sparsely furnished; water needed to be fetched from a well situated in a nearby field; there were no clearly defined paths about the property; the privy was sited too far from the house; the adjacent cottage was empty and so there would be no neighbours nearby for Jimmy to call upon if he was taken ill while Annie was absent from the house . . .

Her final assessment was that 'her Jimmy' would have been far better off had the young couple made their home at the Rowes' farm.

Winnie arrived alone for breakfast at Tregassick the following morning. She said it was unlucky for the bridegroom to see his bride before the ceremony, and Rose had stayed to attend to Jimmy.

She resumed her tirade against the cottage almost immediately, pointing out the problems 'her Jimmy' would have summoning a doctor to 'such an out of the way place'.

After listening in smouldering silence, Annie suddenly turned on her fiercely. 'You're right, of course. None of this is suitable for Jimmy. Not the house, the place where it is – or me. Shall I tell Jimmy the wedding is off, Mrs Rowe, or would you rather do it yourself?'

Winnie looked at Annie in dismayed disbelief. 'You . . . you can't call off the wedding only hours before it's due to go ahead!'

'Better that than have you forever saying that Jimmy should never have married me in the first place. It's going to be hard enough for us to make a go of it as it is with all the problems he has. I'd rather call it off right now and let Jimmy return home with you.'

'I . . . I wasn't suggesting the wedding should be called off,' Winnie blustered, 'I was only pointing out—'

'You were putting up a very good case for me and Jimmy not to get wed, Mrs Rowe. So good that you've well-nigh convinced me it wouldn't be right for us to be married. I suggest you go back to the cottage now and tell Jimmy you've persuaded me to call it off. I'll get into my work clothes and go out and help Pa. There's a whole lot of work needs doing on the farm.'

Aware she had pushed Annie too far, Winnie said, 'I'm sure I wasn't trying to upset things between you and our Jimmy. I was only pointing out that things won't be easy here. I was thinking of Jimmy – and you too, seeing the way he is.'

'Jimmy needs someone to point out to him the things he *can* do, Mrs Rowe, not try to convince him he can't do anything. He's *alive*. A lot of men from around here who went off to war are dead. That's the first plus for him. Jimmy and me will build on that.'

'Well!' Winnie made it clear she was deeply offended. 'I was only saying what I thought was best for *both* your sakes. But once you're married he'll be your responsibility, not mine. I don't think I could eat any breakfast now. I'll go back to the cottage and send Rose over . . .'

When she had gone, Annie's mother said, 'You were very hard on her, our Annie. She was only thinking of Jimmy, I'm sure – and he *is* going to be a big responsibility for you.'

'Don't you think I know that already, Ma? It's something we're going to have to cope with – me and Jimmy, no one else. I'll learn to live with it, but only if I'm left to get on with things in my own way. It's certainly not the way I thought married life was going to be . . .'

Despite her determination to put on a brave front, Annie's voice broke. Turning away, she hurried from the kitchen.

Harriet felt deep compassion for her daughter. For a moment she wondered what might have happened had she and Annie's father not pushed her towards Jimmy; had they allowed the relationship with Perys Tremayne to take its course . . . She decided it was something she would rather not think about right now.

The wedding of Jimmy Rowe and Annie Bray came close to disaster. Standing at the front of the church, awaiting the arrival of the bride, Jimmy was suddenly overcome by the emotion of the occasion and began desperately and noisily fighting for breath.

His best man was a childhood fisherman friend from Mevagissey. A boating accident had left him with a badly crippled arm which prevented him from going to war. When Jimmy collapsed he was unable to support him, and the unfortunate bridegroom fell heavily to the stone floor where he continued to fight for breath.

Concerned, the wedding guests hurried to his assistance. This was the scene which greeted Annie when she entered the small church on the arm of her father.

The organist, who did not have a view of the front pews, immediately struck up the chords of the wedding march, adding considerably to the confusion.

It was almost half-an-hour before Jimmy recovered sufficiently to stand at the altar, supported by the best man on one side and Annie on the other. He felt the humiliation of his collapse very keenly.

Aware of his distress, Annie's heart went out to him. Supporting his arm in the crook of hers, she linked her fingers in his and squeezed them reassuringly, hoping to stop his shaking.

When the ceremony came to an end the newlyweds returned to Tregassick in a farm wagon, but the excitement of the day had been too much for Jimmy. He collapsed once more and was put to bed in the Bray farmhouse.

A doctor was summoned from Mevagissey and he gave Jimmy a strong sleeping draught that would knock him out for at least twelve hours.

It was not the wedding night either of them had anticipated, but it gave Annie a good indication of what married life with Jimmy was going to be like.

Lying alone in bed that night her tears were for Jimmy, for herself – and for what might have been.

47

News of Annie's marriage was given to Perys by Martin as they walked to their aeroplane from the briefing room on a late autumn evening.

Perys received the information in silence. He had long ago given up any idea of a miracle happening that would bring him and Annie together again, and yet . . .

'I wish I felt she was doing the right thing,' Martin said, unhappily.

'Is there anything to suggest she isn't?' Perys asked. 'No one's forcing her to get married. It's entirely her own decision, surely?' He spoke more sharply than he had intended.

'That's just it,' Martin said, 'I don't think it *is* her decision. I don't mean that anyone has actually forced her to marry Jimmy, but because of his wounds, she didn't feel she could back out of it.'

'What makes you think she might have wanted to?' Perys asked.

'It was something Polly said in one of her letters. She won't usually tell me any of the unhappy things that happen at Tregassick, in case I worry about what's going on there, but she did say that she and Annie had had a long talk about it. She wouldn't say in so many words that Annie didn't want to marry Jimmy, only that she couldn't have backed out had she wanted to, what with both families – and Jimmy in particular – expecting there to be a wedding. If she'd tried to get out of marrying him, everyone would have said it was because he'd been so badly wounded. Polly says Annie told her Jimmy had said he'd have nothing to live for if she didn't wed him. Knowing our Annie, she'd have felt duty bound to marry him.'

They had reached the aeroplane now and Perys said, 'I hope there's more to it than that, Martin. Feeling she must marry because she's sorry for him is hardly the recipe for a happy life – for either of them.'

'I agree,' Martin replied, as he began checking the munition drums in his cockpit, 'but it's too late now for anyone to try to change her mind. She's not Annie Bray any more, she's Annie Rowe.'

The late evening photographic reconnaissance proved far more difficult than either man had anticipated. The Germans were increasingly dominating the skies above the front-line because the latest aircraft being delivered to their squadrons were fitted with a revolutionary new device – a gun that was synchronised to fire through the propeller. It made the German aircraft formidable. The pilot pointed his aeroplane at a target, pulled a trigger – and machine-gun bullets did the rest.

It was only Perys's flying skill that enabled them to survive a determined attack pressed home by a lone German pilot, but the photographic sortie had to be aborted.

Perys returned to the airfield feeling extremely disgruntled, but he was met on the ground by Major Kemp who informed him that four new pilots and two observers had arrived at the squadron, bringing at least a temporary end to the dire shortage of flyers they had been suffering.

'It means I can send you away for a few days, Perys,' said the squadron's commanding officer, as he and Perys walked back to the administration building.

'Send me where, sir?' Perys was alarmed. 'You're not taking me off active duties?'

'It's a purely temporary arrangement,' Thomas Kemp reassured him. 'I want you to take your BE2c up to RFC headquarters at Saint Andre. Some senior officer has come across from London, no doubt to see what the war is all about. I've been asked to provide an aircraft and pilot to show him around. You're the best man for the job. You can go via Saint Omer and drop Acting Sergeant Bray off there. He's being sent on a course so that he can be officially classified as an observer and his promotion can become permanent.'

The news that Martin was to become a qualified observer was good news. Perys knew his friend would be delighted. In a conversation some time before, he had been concerned that he was likely to revert to being ground staff if he were transferred to another squadron. Perys had passed his concerns on to Major Kemp, together with his opinion that Martin was a first-class observer and thoroughly at home in the air, but nothing more had been said on the subject until now.

'You'd better take your best uniform with you,' Thomas Kemp was still talking to Perys. 'Senior officers from England expect to do a great deal of socialising while they're here. Right, off you go and get yourself ready. By the way, don't take any chances while you're in the air with whoever you'll be taking around. The army won't want to lose him. More importantly, I can't afford to lose either my best pilot, or a BE2c.'

Perys had almost reached the door when Major Kemp added, 'When you've finished what you have to do at headquarters, take a couple of days off. Go to Paris and let your hair down a little. They tell me the show at the Folies Bergère is worth a visit. Have a look at it and when you return you can tell me all about it.'

Martin was excited at the possibility of becoming a fully fledged observer. On the way to their aircraft that afternoon, he said, 'Do you think that when I put up my observers' half-wing I might manage a few days' leave to get to Cornwall?'

'I don't see any reason why not,' Perys replied. 'And Polly will be absolutely delighted and proud of you, I've no doubt.'

'If it can be arranged I'm aiming to be a bit more ambitious than just *seeing* her,' declared Martin. 'If I can get a few days' leave I'll send a telegram to Polly and ask her to get a special licence so we can be married right away.' Martin hesitated for a few moments before adding, 'If it all works out as I want it to, I have another favour to ask of you, sir. I hope you won't be offended.'

'Offended? Why, what is it, Martin?'

'If I can arrange the marriage and you can get to Cornwall . . . would you consider being my best man?'

The question took Perys by surprise, but he was greatly touched by the request. 'I am deeply honoured, Martin. I don't need to tell you that it might *not* be possible but, if it is, I shall do my damnedest to do the necessary for you.'

'Thank you, sir. That would make both me and Polly very happy.'

48

Having dropped off Martin at St Omer, Perys reached
the airfield close to the Royal Flying Corps headquarters at St Andre and taxied to the hangar area.
He brought the BE2c to a halt and switched off the
engine.

His arrival was expected. By the time he climbed
out of the cockpit and lifted out his suitcase, a staff
car was beside the aeroplane. The driver, a corporal,
dressed far more smartly than his colleagues in the
forward airfields, hurried towards him, saluted stiffly
and queried, 'Lieutenant Tremayne, sir?'

'That's right, Corporal. Is my aeroplane all right
here?'

'It'll be fine, sir. The maintenance staff will put it
in the hangar and check it out, ready for the morning.'
Lifting the suitcase from the ground, he asked, 'Is this
all the luggage you have with you, sir?'

While the corporal was placing the suitcase in the

luggage compartment of the car, Perys removed his flying suit.

Once seated beside the driver, Perys asked, 'Where am I billeted for tonight, Corporal?'

'In the chateau, sir. You've been given a room there. It's usually reserved for senior officers, but General Ballard insisted that you be given a room there, to be close at hand when he needs you.'

Mention of the general's name startled Perys. 'General Ballard, you say?'

'That's right, sir. Major General Sir Giles Ballard. I believe he's over here from the War Office on some fact-finding mission. If you don't mind me saying so, sir, it'll make a nice break for you to be flying this side of the lines and not having to worry about having a German aeroplane coming at you out of nowhere.'

'Pardon . . . ? Oh, yes, it will be.' But Perys's mind was not on what the driver was saying to him. General Ballard was Grace's father. Perys believed he must have asked for him to be allocated as his pilot during his tour of France. He also believed that Major Kemp would have been aware of this. He wished the commanding officer had told him.

The driver was speaking again.

'I've been told to tell you that General Ballard would like you to join him for drinks before dinner, sir. That should give you plenty of time to have a nice hot bath. I'll speak to the housekeeper when we get to the chateau. She'll see that your uniform is pressed and ready for you before you meet with the general.' He grinned at Perys's bemused expression. 'Life here's a bit different from what you'll be used to up at the front, sir.'

'Yes . . . yes, I'm sure it must be.'

Perys wondered whether Grace was aware that he was to be her father's pilot on his visit to France – or whether she was even aware that her father was in France. He and Grace wrote to each other occasionally, but she was moved around a great deal, to where most casualties were suffered. They usually occurred in futile attacks that achieved nothing, against an enemy who was proving increasingly stubborn in defence.

Perys was never certain whether or not his letters were reaching her – and Grace had time to pen only the briefest of notes. No doubt General Ballard would have more up-to-date knowledge of his daughter's whereabouts.

Perys was already apprehensive about meeting with such a high-ranking officer before he entered the luxurious room which served as a mess for the senior officers. He was dismayed to see there was not an officer present under the rank of lieutenant colonel. He was by far the most junior, both in age and rank.

But Major General Ballard, although the most senior person present, was by no means the oldest. An ex-guards officer, he had earned rapid promotion serving with his regiment during the Boer War.

Seeing Perys standing uncertainly in the doorway, he broke away from the group about him and advanced towards the young man. Reaching him, he smiled, extended a hand and said, 'Lieutenant Tremayne! I am delighted to make your acquaintance at last.'

'Not nearly as pleased as I was to see him on the last occasion he and I met, Giles.' Following General

Ballard was Brigadier Palmer, the officer whose rescue from the Germans had resulted in the award of a Military Cross to Perys. Also shaking Perys's hand, he added, 'I owe my life to this young man.'

'I had no idea it was *you* he saved, Henry,' said General Ballard. 'I learned the story from my daughter, Grace. She and Lieutenant Tremayne are very good friends.' To Perys he explained, 'Brigadier Palmer and I were in the same regiment, in South Africa.'

'Well, if he's to be your pilot while you're here with us, you are in very safe hands, Giles,' said Brigadier Palmer. 'When I recommended him for his MC I was told he would one day be one of the RFC's finest pilots. A couple of mentions in dispatches since then would seem to bear out that promise – but allow me to buy you both a drink. I seem to remember you are quite partial to whisky, young Tremayne – and I have no need to ask what you will have, Giles . . .'

For the remainder of the time before dinner both senior officers went out of their way to make Perys feel at home in the august company present at the Royal Flying Corps' French headquarters. When word was passed around that Perys was a close friend of General Ballard's daughter, and had been instrumental in saving the life of Brigadier Palmer, his acceptance by the other senior officers was assured.

Later, after they had eaten, General Ballard asked Perys to take him to see the aeroplane in which they would be flying. Outside the chateau he suggested that they walk to where the BE2c was being kept. 'It's a fine night and it'll be good to get some of that tobacco smoke out of my lungs. It's bad enough when everyone is smoking *English* cigarettes. I would have thought that smoking the French varieties would make a man immune to poison gas before very long.'

Perys smiled in sympathy. He had noticed that General Ballard did not smoke.

As they walked together, the general said, 'Have you heard from Grace recently?'

'I had a brief letter a week or so ago,' Perys replied, 'but I don't think she has much time to write. She is being moved around so often that few of my own letters seem to have caught up with her yet.'

'Her mother complains about exactly the same things,' the general said. 'But Grace has been able to make a telephone call to me at the War Office on two occasions. When we last spoke she was expecting to be in Paris with a hospital train sometime this week. I told her I would send a letter to our Embassy there, giving her details of my visit to France. I hope she was able to pick it up and that I might find her waiting for me somewhere along the way.'

'I'm sure that would be very nice for both of you, sir. I hope I might also have the opportunity to meet up with her.'

'I would never hear the last of it if the two of you were *not* able to spend a little time together!' General Ballard gave Perys a sidelong glance when he added, 'Grace is very fond of you, you know.'

'And I of her,' Perys affirmed. 'I only wish she was working somewhere safer than a field hospital. Some are situated frighteningly close to the front, especially when a major battle is taking place.'

'Her mother and I are concerned for her too.' The general spoke as a father and not as a soldier. 'She could have remained at Saint Thomas's in London, but this is what she wanted. I could hardly insist it would be too dangerous when other nurses are out here doing the same thing.' He remained silent for a couple of minutes before asking, 'Have you and Grace ever discussed what the future might hold for the pair of you?'

Perys was aware that the general had been replaced by the father once more and he replied, 'I don't think either of us has looked beyond the duration of this war, sir. For Grace it must seem that every man who is sent into battle is going to eventually pass through her field hospital – and I have no illusions about my own chances of survival. I have been with my squadron for less than six months, but am already one of its longest-surviving pilots. No, sir, even *thinking* of a future would be tempting fate.'

'You are a level-headed young man, Perys – and a realist. As Grace's father that is very comforting. Nevertheless, although our casualty rate is horrifyingly high, a great many young men *are* going to survive the war. Young men like yourself, who have experienced war at its most desperate, will be the senior officers of the future. The RFC will have need of you.'

'Thank you, sir.' Perys realised the purpose of General Ballard's questions, but he had decided he liked Grace's father and felt he should be honest with him. 'Unfortunately, my service pay will probably be all I have to live on. It won't exactly keep a wife and family in luxury.'

The general gave Perys an appreciative glance. 'I know exactly how you feel. Do you know, I had very similar thoughts when I first met Grace's mother. She is the daughter of an earl – has Grace told you that? Well, she is. When I met her I was a young lieutenant on a salary far less than yours. We married – against her parents' wishes – when I was promoted to captain. For a few years things were hard, but we survived. More than that, we were happy. Very happy – and still are. Please don't misunderstand me, I am not suggesting you should rush off and ask my daughter to marry you. Indeed, Grace would be extremely embarrassed were she to know I was having this conversation with you. However, *should* you feel strongly enough about Grace to contemplate marriage, I am pointing out that you should not allow financial considerations to stand in your way. Money will not be the primary requirement for any man Grace might wish to marry. I hope I have made myself clear?'

Perys felt that General Ballard would hardly have been so forthcoming had he not believed that Grace was herself seriously contemplating marriage with him. He appreciated her father's forthright way of dealing with the situation.

'Thank you, sir, I really do appreciate being able to have this talk with you.'

'Good. Now, here we are at the hangar. Let's have a look at this aeroplane of yours . . .'

49

The next few days were busy ones for Perys. Major General Sir Giles Ballard had come to France with instructions direct from the Prime Minister to learn the truth about the shortages being experienced by men at the battle-front.

Some of the shortages were of a purely local or temporary nature. However, others, in particular the lack of artillery shells, were far more serious.

During his tour General Ballard was able to relieve the immediate situation slightly by ordering the relocation of some stocks, and persuading the French to part with some ammunition that was capable of being fired from British artillery pieces, but such amounts were not significant.

What was apparent was that the production of shells in Britain fell far behind that of France which, in turn, could not match the output of the German factories. It was a dire situation that needed to be redressed immediately and General Ballard worked well into each night compiling his reports and recommendations.

Sometimes there were as many as four conferences in a day, and when the BE2c landed at each location both Perys and the general had hopes that Grace might be there to greet them. They were to suffer disappointment until the final day of the general's tour of France.

Perys landed the BE2c at an airfield on the outskirts of Paris for the final meeting with high-ranking French government and military officials. It was to be held at the British Embassy in the city.

An Embassy car was waiting at the airfield, and after Perys had passed responsibility for the aeroplane to a British liaison officer, General Ballard insisted that he accompany him into Paris. When the meeting was over the general would be returning to England – by train.

It was the first visit Perys had made to the French capital and he was impressed both by the wide boulevards and the magnificent buildings that flanked them.

Learning that Perys had never been to Paris before, General Ballard delighted in pointing out places of interest along the way.

Eventually the motor car turned off the boulevards and passed through massive gates, beyond which was Great Britain's Embassy, shut off from the outside noise and bustle of the city.

There they found Grace waiting for them.

Her delight at discovering that Perys was accompanying her father was apparent to everyone who witnessed the reunion. The greeting for her father was less inhibited, but her expression when she greeted Perys told her father far more about her feelings for him than any words.

She looked at her father accusingly. 'You said nothing in your letter about bringing Perys with you.'

'That's because I did not know at the time whether he would be available to pilot me around France,' he protested. 'However, I could not have chosen a more considerate pilot. He kept me well clear of danger, allowing me no more than a high-altitude view of the front-line trench system. As a result of this glimpse of the front, I will return to London with a much greater awareness of the difficulties experienced by the troops on the ground. My only regret is that Perys refused to allow me to have a machine-gun mounted in my cockpit in order that we might go in search of enemy aeroplanes.'

'I should think so!' Grace pretended to be shocked. 'But how long am I going to be able to enjoy your company?'

'Well now,' said her father, 'I am about to go into a conference with some very senior French army officers. We will have a number of policy matters to thrash out. My hope is that all will be resolved by this evening. If it is, then I will take you both out to dinner and return to London on a train in the morning. Until this evening you will need to entertain each other, but I doubt if that will pose too much of a problem here, in Paris, especially as it is Perys's first visit.'

Perys and Grace had lunch only a couple of streets away, in a restaurant recommended by one of the Embassy staff. From the outside, with its peeling paintwork and indifferently cleaned windows, it seemed the sort of establishment that should be avoided. However, the food was truly delicious, and the presence of an English pilot and his nurse girlfriend prompted the chef to new culinary heights.

The other diners in the restaurant were equally eager to please them and more drinks were offered to the young couple than they could possibly consume.

Perys had a good command of the French language and, aided by Grace, who had spent some time in the country, he was able to refuse many of the offers without causing offence, by pleading that he would be flying again later in the day.

Eventually, the gourmet meal came to an end and the restaurateur earned the applause of the diners by refusing to accept payment for the memorable meal enjoyed by the happy pair. They finally escaped from the restaurant, but not until Perys had shaken hands with all the men present and been kissed by the restaurant owner's wife, the waitresses and every female diner.

Perys and Grace realised there was no sense in returning to the Embassy before late afternoon and they decided to take advantage of the Paris sunshine. After crossing the spacious and impressive Place de la Concorde, they walked along the north bank of the River Seine as far as the Île de la Cité and the splendour of the Cathedral of Notre Dame.

Uniforms were very much in evidence on the streets of Paris, yet the British pair still attracted a great deal of interest from those they met along the way, and there were smiles of approbation from most.

Returning to the Embassy in the Rue du Faubourg

St Honore at about four-thirty, they found Major General Ballard uncharacteristically flustered.

Speaking to Grace, he said, 'Darling, I am afraid there has been a change of plan. We will not be able to enjoy dinner tonight after all. Field Marshal French was visiting Paris today and he decided to attend the meeting. He read my report and wants me to travel with him to London tonight to place some of the points I have raised before the War Cabinet in the morning. We are leaving by train this evening. In fact, I should be on my way right now. The Embassy motor-car has been waiting for some twenty minutes. I am so very, very sorry, my dear.'

'I am too.' Grace seemed close to tears. 'I was so looking forward to spending an evening with you. But I do understand – and you must not keep the field marshal waiting.'

Field Marshal Sir John French was the commander-in-chief of the British army in France.

'Thank you, my dear. But, here . . .' Reaching into a pocket, the general thrust a wad of notes into her hands. 'When an opportunity arises, treat yourself and your friends to a really good meal.'

Holding out a hand to Perys, he said, 'It has been a very real pleasure to get to know you, Perys. You took care of me splendidly. I look forward to welcoming you to our home in Oxfordshire in the not-too-distant future.'

With this and a final hug and kiss for Grace, he hurried away to the waiting motor-car, leaving Grace standing on the Embassy steps. Perys thought she looked very vulnerable and forlorn.

'I am very sorry your evening has been spoiled,

333

Grace, but I know your father is equally disappointed. He was really looking forward to spending some time with you.'

'I realise it is not his fault,' Grace said, with a resigned shrug. 'He had no way of knowing Field Marshal French would be here, and Father is a soldier. It's his life. He can't say, "Sorry, Field Marshal, I am not coming back to London with you because I have promised to have dinner with my daughter, whom I haven't seen for months."'

Despite her apparent understanding there was bitterness in her voice, and Perys said, gently, 'You're right, Grace. He *can't* say that, much as he might wish to. Your father has worked hard on his report. Field Marshal French obviously thinks it is important. So do I. You do too, really.'

'Yes . . . yes, I do. It's just . . . oh, I don't know, it's so disappointing, especially as I have been given a few days off. One of the French nurses I work with has given me the keys to her flat here in Paris, in the hope that Father might have been able to spend a while with me . . .' She shrugged, unhappily. 'We have got to expect such things to happen in wartime.' Giving Perys a weak smile, she added, 'I suppose now that Father is on his way back to England by train you will need to get back to your airfield?'

'Actually, no!' Perys said. 'In fact, I too must obey the orders of a senior officer. My squadron commander told me I should take a few days' leave in Paris before returning to duty.'

It took a few moments for his words to sink in, then a disbelieving Grace said, 'You mean . . . you can stay in Paris for a while?'

'That's right. Look, I saw quite a pleasant hotel just along the road from here. Why don't I book in there and telephone the liaison officer at the airfield. I'll ask him to take care of my aeroplane for a couple of days and send my belongings along to the hotel. Then I can take you out to dinner tonight and we can make plans to spend some time together over the next few days.'

'Perys, that would be wonderful! But *I* will take *you* out to dinner with the money my father gave to me.'

'I won't argue with that, Grace. Now, let's see if they will allow me to use the Embassy telephone . . .'

50

The liaison officer at the Paris airfield told Perys the BE2c would be perfectly safe where it was for as long as he wished to leave it there. He would send a driver right away to deliver Perys's single piece of luggage to the Hotel Castigliane, where Perys had no difficulty in booking a room.

For their evening meal, Perys and Grace chose another unpretentious but superb restaurant that had been recommended by the French nurse who had given Grace the use of her flat.

Once again, the presence of an English pilot and nurse appealed to the romantic and generous nature of the Parisians. The proprietor insisted that the wine be enjoyed as a present from the establishment. Then, after a superb meal and a delightful evening together, the young couple discovered that their bill had been settled by one of the other diners who had left without making himself known.

Outside, in the narrow Paris street, Grace took hold of Perys's arm and hugged it to her. 'It has been a wonderful evening after all, Perys, exactly as Paris should be. This is a truly magical city.'

Perys agreed, then, becoming practical, he asked how she was planning to make her way back to the flat where she was staying.

'Oh, it's not very far away,' was her reply. 'I was hoping you would walk me there.'

'I would like that very much.' Perys was delighted at the opportunity to make the happy evening last for as long as was possible.

Their route took them alongside the river, which seemed to have attracted all the lovers in Paris. They walked hand-in-hand, arm-in-arm, with arms about each other's waists, or stood kissing on the wide stone walkways that followed both river banks. Others occupied shadowy recesses in the walls that rose high above the river walks to the roads above them.

'The war seems so far away from here,' said Perys, as a water bus glided past them with a party on board who were lustily singing a popular music-hall song of the day.

'Shh!' Grace put a finger to his lips. 'Talk of war is not allowed for as long as we are in Paris together . . . By the way, how long will you be able to stay here?'

'Three or four days. How about you?'

'I have another three days before I need to be back.'

Grace had forbidden all mention of war, but speaking of the time she and Perys would have together in Paris was in itself a reminder of what they would be returning to at the end of their time together. Sensing her sudden unhappiness, Perys freed his arm from hers and put it about her waist, pulling her closer.

They were passing beneath a bridge and, without a word being spoken, they stopped and kissed. When they resumed walking, with arms about each other, they said very little, each content in the nearness of the other.

Soon, Grace guided him towards a flight of steps that led away from the river. Leaving behind the Seine and the wide boulevards that flanked it, they walked through ever narrower streets until, beside a wide-fronted church, Grace stopped before a tall building.

Pointing to a door of impressive proportions, she said, 'This is where I am staying. Yvonne's flat is on the first floor.'

Reluctant for the evening to come to an end, Perys said, 'This has been a wonderful night, Grace. The most enjoyable I have ever spent.'

It seemed that Grace was equally disinclined to bring the evening to an end. 'Would you like to come up for a coffee, Perys? I haven't yet learned to make it as the French do, but I promise it will be reasonably drinkable.'

The stairs were narrow, uneven and complaining, but as soon as Perys followed Grace into the first-floor flat he realised that Yvonne possessed both money and considerable taste. The flat was luxuriously yet stylishly furnished.

When Perys aired his observations aloud, Grace smiled. 'The flat is a present to Yvonne from an elderly but extremely wealthy lover.'

Trying to hide his astonishment that Grace could

talk of such a relationship so casually, he said, 'Are you saying she gave up a comfortable life here to become a nurse?'

'That's right – and she is a very good nurse. Her lover lost his only son in the battle that was fought to keep the Germans from taking Paris and he is very proud of Yvonne. He delights in sending unexpected luxuries for her and all the nurses at the field hospital. They arrive in such quantities that we often share them out among our patients.'

'It would seem he is a very generous man,' Perys commented.

'Yes . . . now, would you like a cognac with your coffee? I believe that too is the best money can buy, although I am no expert.'

The cognac was as excellent as Grace had promised. It led to a second . . . and then to a third.

Perys was not used to drinking the quantity he had consumed that evening and he was feeling quite heady. When he eventually rose to his feet, he said, 'It's very late, Grace. I had better leave you to get some sleep now.'

'Yes, I suppose so.' Grace too seemed somewhat unsteady on her feet. 'It has been an absolutely wonderful evening, Perys. All I could have wished for.'

'I'm glad, that's just the way I feel about it.' He kissed her. Then he kissed her again . . . and again.

He was holding her very close to him when she spoke his name in little more than a whisper.

'Perys?'

'Yes?'

'You don't have to go . . . not if you would like to stay.'

'There can only be one answer to that, Grace, but . . . are you certain it's what *you* want? We've both had a great deal to drink – you might wake in the morning and hate me.'

Her head was against his shoulder and she shook it vigorously. 'No, Perys, I won't do that. I could never feel like that about you. Never. Working in the field hospital I see men come in every day who have had their lives cut short before they have known a moment of real love or fulfilment. Others never will, even though they survive – well, a survival of sorts. It has changed the way I was brought up to think, Perys. Some things are no longer important. Others much more so. I believe everyone deserves to experience true happiness at least once in their lifetime. I have come to realise it is something to be seized upon if the opportunity arises. A memory, at least, is something that can never be taken away. Do you understand what I am trying to say, Perys?'

'Yes, Grace. Yes, I do.'

He knew *exactly* how she felt. He had often entertained similar thoughts when a pilot or observer, fresh from training school and not long out of college, failed to return from an operational mission. It was something he needed to hide in the everyday life of the squadron: the feeling that he had witnessed a sadly wasted life before it had even begun to know the meaning of life, love and fulfilment.

'The only thing I wish now is that we could go out and find someone to marry us—'

His words were cut short when her finger pressed against his lips for the second time that evening. 'That doesn't really matter, Perys. I love you – and I think

340

you love me too. *That's* what matters. That's *all* that matters.'

When Grace woke the next morning, with Perys beside her, he was leaning on one elbow, looking down at her. She had the feeling he had been doing so for a long time.

'What is it? Is there something—?'

He kissed her, cutting off the unfinished question. When he drew away, he said, 'I love you, Grace.'

'In view of what we've been doing I am both happy . . . and relieved!' Smiling up at him, she stretched contentedly. 'Is this how everyone feels after doing *that*?'

'I wouldn't know about everyone, but I know how *I* feel.'

'How *do* you feel, Perys?'

'I feel . . . so hungry I could eat a horse.'

'Perys Tremayne! You are hopelessly unromantic!'

'Am I? Is that what you really think?'

He felt obliged to prove to Grace that she was mistaken . . .

The days – and the nights – passed all too quickly, as happy times are wont to do, but they were idyllic hours for both Grace and Perys.

For possibly the first time in his life, Perys knew what it was to be fulfilled and unreservedly happy. He and Grace enjoyed walking in Paris together, savouring everything that the great city had to offer. But the times that were most precious and which gave them the happiest memories were the hours they spent together in the flat.

Regrettably, all too soon it was time for each of them to take their memories in different directions.

During the dark hours of their last night together, passionate love-making gave way to tears and the abject misery that heralded imminent parting.

Not until the grey light of a Paris dawn drove away the darkness did the lovers put their nakedness behind them and don uniforms that carried with them the responsibilities of their respective callings.

Perys accompanied Grace to the crowded railway station. There they were obliged to keep their longing for each other confined to an occasional meaningful glance and a seemingly casual touching of hands.

Their moment of parting too needed to be restricted to a brief kiss and a quick, painful hug. Once the train pulled away from the platform, they were no longer lovers. They were Lieutenant Perys Tremayne, pilot in the Royal Flying Corps, and Sister Grace Ballard of the Queen Alexandra's Imperial Military Nursing Service.

51

The difficulties experienced by the armies on the Western Front during the final months of 1915 continued well into the following year. The wet and cold and mud, at times knee-deep, were ever-present discomforts experienced by the soldiers of both sides.

The more practical Germans coped better with front-line conditions than their British counterparts, but both sides found themselves fighting a natural enemy that was both persistent and unrelenting.

The pilots of the Royal Flying Corps maintained their presence in the air but, in the absence of a sustained offensive by either side, their operations lacked the urgency of earlier months. As a result, Perys and Grace were able to snatch one more weekend together in the Paris flat.

Then Grace was sent on a temporary attachment to a hospital for British soldiers in the small French coastal town of Wimereux.

By April 1916 the weather was improving and talk of a new offensive was in the air. Major Kemp sent for Perys and told him he had a special assignment for him.

'It seems the French have come up with a single-seater aeroplane – a new Spad that has excited someone at headquarters. It's a scout – a fighter – which uses the same synchronised method of firing through the propeller as the Fokker. If it proves to be as good as headquarters believe then it could be exactly what we are looking for and is likely to be produced in England. We could certainly do with *something* to turn the tide in our favour.'

'It sounds almost too good to be true,' Perys agreed, 'but where do I come into the picture?'

Major Kemp grinned. 'Not only do you have friends in high places, but you seem to have impressed some of our own people too. It has been suggested that you are the right man to put the Spad through its paces here, then take it to England and show senior officers and government officials its capabilities as a fighting plane.'

'You mean I am to be taken off active service duties?' After waiting out the frustrating winter months, Perys was not happy at the thought of being sent away from the front-line squadron at the very time it would be in most need of an experienced pilot.

'It will not be a permanent arrangement, Perys. If I thought it was likely to be I would object very strongly. But if this Spad fits the bill, we could soon have squadrons of aircraft in the front-line that will put an end to the Fokker scourge we are suffering right now. They might even allow you to bring the

Spad back with you – if you feel it's worthwhile.'

Perys's reluctance to leave the front-line squadron was tempered by the thought of putting a new and exciting aeroplane through its paces.

'When would I need to go – and where?'

'The factory producing the Spad is just outside Paris. Travel there over the weekend and you can begin familiarising yourself with the aeroplane on Monday. Once you feel comfortable handling the machine you'll fly it to the Central Flying School at Upavon. The timing is entirely in your hands – but you're to go nowhere near the front-line and the aeroplane is to be kept under guard at all times.' Looking serious, Thomas Kemp added, 'This is an important assignment, Perys. Certainly not one I would entrust with just anyone. The Spad is still on the secret list. If we can keep it that way it could play an important part in defeating the Germans in the air.'

Perys was aware of Thomas Kemp's strong views on the importance of fighter planes – 'scouts' – and the role they should play in the war. At the moment it was War Office policy to allocate one or two of the 'scouts' to each squadron. Kemp felt this to be an ineffective way of dealing with the 'Fokker scourge' and Perys agreed with him. It was the squadron commander's firm belief that the RFC needed an aircraft capable of matching the German fighter planes. When they had one, he believed special squadrons should be formed with the sole purpose of fighting and defeating German aeroplanes.

He stated these views forcibly whenever an opportunity arose, and he felt that senior officers in the Royal Flying Corps were beginning to recognise he was right. All they lacked was an aircraft capable of proving his theories.

Perys liked and respected Thomas Kemp and realised the squadron commander had put a great deal of trust in him by sending him on this assignment.

When he reached Paris, Perys tried to contact Grace, to tell her he would be in the vicinity for a few days. He put through a telephone call to the Wimereux hospital, only to be told she had left a few days before. What was more, no one was prepared to disclose her present whereabouts.

Perys found this particularly disconcerting. He knew from past experience that the withholding of such information usually meant she had been sent to a field hospital in an area where there would soon be a battle in which many casualties could be expected.

Once again Perys felt he was leaving the squadron at a time when his experience was most needed, but he had a task to perform, and fascination with the new French aircraft soon pushed all other considerations to the back of his mind.

He spent a somewhat frustrating day learning details of the aeroplane. Poring over a great deal of technical data written in French required laborious translation. It was irritating because he could see that the Spad was indeed a fine aircraft and he was impatient to test its capabilities for himself.

When it seemed a second day might be spent in a similar manner, Perys suddenly pushed all the paperwork away from him and announced that he was ready to *fly* the new aircraft.

It caused a great deal of consternation. As all the French officers present were considerably senior to himself, Perys expected to encounter strong opposition. Instead, one after another, the officers shrugged or made gestures that indicated that if this was what the English pilot wanted, then, so be it!

Settled in the Spad's cockpit, Perys felt excitement from the moment the aeroplane's powerful engine roared into life. It seemed to take to the air much more quickly than the BE2cs he was used to, and when he had climbed to sufficient height, he began performing aerobatics, each more demanding on the Spad.

The French constructors had set out a target for him on the ground, and swooping lower Perys pulled the trigger of the gun with some trepidation. Firing through a fast-moving propeller was a new and somewhat fearful experience for him. He was only too aware that the slightest error in the synchronisation would result in the propeller being shot to pieces. Such an accident would inevitably result in the end of the aeroplane – and its pilot!

The juddering of the plane when the gun was fired was at first disconcerting. It was also exhilarating. Perys's shooting was not particularly accurate, but this was partly due to the fact that he could not point the aeroplane directly at a target on the ground and maintain his course for long. In the air, in pursuit of an enemy aeroplane, it would be a very different story.

Back on the ground, Perys's praise for the aeroplane was matched by the congratulations of the French officers and the aircraft's manufacturers for his display of aerobatics. He decided he would write to Major Kemp that evening telling him of the Spad's capabilities and his belief that with this aircraft he would be willing to take on either Immelmann or von Richthofen, two of the top German flyers.

Tomorrow he would take the Spad to the Central Flying School in England and try to persuade the War Office that this was an aeroplane the Royal Flying Corps must have.

52

When Perys reached the Central Flying School, he was told that it would be at least a week before senior officers and government officials could be gathered together to assess the capabilities of the Spad. It was suggested that, in the meantime, he should take some leave.

When he put in a telephone call to Aunt Maude, her delight at hearing from him was perfectly genuine.

'You must come and stay in Knightsbridge, Perys,' she said. 'It will be a pleasure to have you here. I will make certain the handyman has your motor-cycle ready for you when you need to use it.'

Perys had left the machine in a shed in Maude's garden. Her handyman was a motor-cycle enthusiast. Although he could not afford to own one himself, he was quite happy to spend a great deal of his own time ensuring Perys's machine was maintained in perfect working order.

Perys travelled to London by train, arriving at Maude's home that evening. The door was opened to him by Maude herself and, much to his surprise, Morwenna. After being greeted warmly by both women, Perys said to Morwenna, 'This is a very pleasant surprise. I thought you were in France.'

'And so I was,' she replied, 'but I arrived in London today on a hospital train.' In a deliberately casual manner, she added, 'Grace was on the train, too.'

Perys's reaction was all that Grace herself would have wished. 'Grace was with you? I feared she had been sent to a front-line hospital. Where is she now? In London?'

Morwenna shook her head. 'She was, but her father has taken her home to Oxfordshire.'

Perys's deep disappointment was so apparent that Morwenna felt obliged to put him out of his misery immediately.

'When I arrived home and learned you were coming to stay, I telephoned Grace and told her. She insisted that you call her the moment you arrived.'

Perys looked pleadingly at Maude and she smiled. 'Speak to her right away, Perys. The number is on a pad beside the telephone. Make the call now, while I am having something cooked for you. By the way, Arabella sends her apologies for not being here to greet you. The parents of her young doctor friend are in London. They have taken Arabella and Ian out to dinner.'

Perys mumbled acknowledgement of the news, then hurried away to make the telephone call to Grace.

In Asthall, Grace had been on tenterhooks waiting for his call, seldom straying more than a few paces away from the telephone. When it finally rang, she snatched up the earpiece and gabbled out the telephone number.

'Grace! Is that you?'

'Yes, Perys. How are you? What are you doing in England?'

'I'm fine, Grace. I've brought a new aeroplane over here from France and don't have to be back at the Central Flying School until Monday. How about you?'

'I need to report back on Sunday . . . but my father would like you to come to Asthall to stay with us until then. Can you come . . . please?'

'I'm sure Aunt Maude would welcome the opportunity to have Morwenna to herself for a few days. Yes, I'd love to spend some time with you. I know it won't be the same as Paris . . . but when would you like me to come?'

'Can you come tomorrow, Perys? I miss you terribly. For both of us to be in England yet not to be together seems such a dreadful waste of time.'

'I couldn't agree more – but what about your parents? They see so very little of you these days they will want to have you with them as much as is possible.'

'They will have me to themselves for twenty-four hours, by which time they will be thoroughly bored because I spend so much time telling them about you. By coming here you will be doing them a favour. Please say you will.'

'I don't really need to be persuaded to be with you, Grace. I will be there tomorrow, probably late afternoon, or very early evening.'

Grace's joy must have been evident to her parents

because Perys heard her father's voice in the background. 'I gather Perys is coming to Asthall . . . !'

They spoke for only a few minutes more before Perys ended the telephone call in order to tell Aunt Maude of his plans.

The Ballard home was an impressive house of soft, yellow-grey stone on the fringe of the Cotswold hills. It was also only a short distance from Burford, where Perys had spent the last years of his schooling.

Proximity was the only thing the two places had in common. The early years at Burford had been very unhappy ones for him. When he arrived in Asthall, on the other hand, Grace made it abundantly clear that Perys was the most important person in her life.

Her parents too gave him the warmest of welcomes and Perys was made to feel immediately at home.

Later that evening, at dusk, Grace and Perys decided they would take a walk to the river. Her parents told the young couple they would not wait up for their return.

In their bedroom, as they undressed, Sir Giles asked his wife what she thought of Perys. Puzzled when she did not reply immediately, he repeated the question.

'I am not quite certain how to reply to that, Giles,' she said, eventually. 'He is a very likeable young man – very likeable indeed. Were we living in normal times I would be delighted to welcome him into the family.'

Sir Giles paused in the act of unfastening a cufflink. 'In normal times? What has that to do with his suitability as a son-in-law? Perys is already a brevet-captain and decorated for bravery at an age when most young officers would feel they had taken an important step on the promotion ladder were they detailed to walk their commanding officer's dog! Perys is a hero. He will probably finish this war with a rank he could never even dream of in peacetime.'

'If he survives the war,' Lady Susan said, grimly. 'You just referred to him as a hero. Heroes are not renowned survivors. Grace absolutely adores Perys. Should anything happen to him she would be inconsolable. I would wish to spare her that, Giles.'

'Have you ever thought that your parents might possibly have felt the same about you and me?' he asked, quietly.

'I know they *did* – and they were right to do so. We were very lucky, Giles. Can we dare hope that such luck will come to a second generation, when this ghastly war is claiming the lives of more young men than any conflict ever known?'

'We must keep hope for the future alive, Susan. Besides, Grace deserves an opportunity to enjoy the happiness you and I have known, even if – God forbid – it is short-lived. She loves Perys. I am convinced he loves her too. I believe this, and this alone should direct any decision we make about Grace's future.'

The few days Perys and Grace spent together at Asthall passed all too quickly. They parted with a promise to each other that they would try to overcome the communications problem with a view to once more spending a few days together in the Paris flat.

Perys departed from Asthall on the Sunday night, to ride his motor-cycle directly to the Central Flying School in Wiltshire, rather than return to London first.

He wanted to be certain the Spad was in first-class order for whatever the next few days would bring.

When he had ridden out of sight, Grace did her best to keep her unhappiness hidden, but she did not deceive her parents. Putting a comforting arm about her shoulders, Sir Giles said, 'Be brave, darling, and try not to worry. Perys is a fine pilot.'

'That's partly the trouble, Daddy. His very skill is going to take him into more and more danger.'

'Not for a while, Grace. He will be in no danger from the enemy for a month or two, at least.'

'What do you mean?' Grace turned to look at her father as he replied.

'Perys has brought a new aeroplane to England from France for us to look at. It will take a week or two for the experts to assess its worth. When they have done that Perys will be asked to fly one or two other new aeroplanes that are being developed, in order to compare the qualities of each of them. It makes sense for one pilot – one *proven* pilot – to try them all. Otherwise it would be necessary to assess both man and machine before arriving at a conclusion.'

Grace digested what her father had said before asking, 'Is Perys aware of what he will be doing?'

Sir Giles shook his head. 'I believe his commanding officer thought it better that he remain in the dark about what was planned for him. Otherwise, I fear that not even your charms might have persuaded him to leave his squadron for so long and take on a safe assignment in England.'

53

The 'safe assignment' given to Perys was to result in the most serious accident of his flying career to date, almost two months after leaving Asthall.

He had complained bitterly about being kept at the Central Flying School while his squadron was involved in fierce fighting in France. Nevertheless, he grudgingly accepted the explanation that it would be better for a single pilot to assess the qualities of each new aeroplane being developed in an attempt to counter the German Fokker.

Even after flying a number of new aeroplanes, Perys still enjoyed flying the Spad he had brought from France more than any of the others – but it was a purely personal preference. He readily conceded that the Sopwith 'Pup' was highly manoeuvrable and robust and would probably suit many British pilots more than would the French aeroplane.

Then he was asked to test a monoplane that had

been designed and built by a company which had manufactured bicycles prior to the war.

Perys expressed his doubts about this aircraft even before taking it up for a trial flight. He thought it appeared far too fragile for serious flight – and was proved alarmingly correct within ten minutes of taking to the air.

As he banked the aeroplane sharply to fly back above the watching officers on the airfield, he heard a sharp report from the direction of the wing on one side of the aircraft. It was swiftly followed by another. Two wire wing stays had snapped and the wing suddenly began moving in an alarming manner.

Perys levelled out as best he could and throttled back the engine, but he was having to fight hard to maintain control of the aeroplane. When he made a slow, wide turn, with the intention of returning to the Central Flying School airfield, the wing began flapping. Perys feared it was about to break away and send him plunging to the ground.

He decided he must land immediately.

A field ahead of him seemed fairly flat, but trying to land an aeroplane with one wing flapping like a bird proved well-nigh impossible.

He almost made it, but then the damaged wing tip touched the ground and the aeroplane performed a spectacular cartwheel, with pieces breaking off and flying in all directions. It finally came to rest with the now wingless fuselage broken in two and lying on its side. Hurriedly unbuckling his safety belt, Perys crawled from the cockpit, hoping the remains of the aeroplane would not burst into flames until he was clear.

He stood up to run but a fierce pain in his leg caused him to fall to the ground and he resumed his rapid crawl, this time with an increased, if painful, urgency.

When an ambulance from the Central Flying School reached him, he was seated on the ground well clear of the aeroplane which had not, in fact, caught fire.

A doctor who was with the ambulance quickly diagnosed a broken leg, the break being well below the knee. However, the doctor declared it was not too serious and assured Perys he would be flying again 'within a couple of months'.

By this time the senior officer who had been supervising the flying trials had arrived on the scene and heard what the doctor said. Looking at the wrecked aircraft he said, drily, 'You may be flying again soon, Tremayne, but it certainly won't be in this aeroplane.'

'No, sir,' Perys agreed, 'and I suggest you tell the company who made it to go back to making bicycles – and they can count me out as a prospective customer.'

Perys spent a month at Maude's Knightsbridge home while his broken leg was mending. Then he received a letter from Martin Bray which had been forwarded from the Central Flying School. Martin was coming to England to undergo a course in aerial gunnery at Hythe in Kent. When it was completed he would return to a front-line squadron, instructing other observers in the use of the Lewis gun, in addition to his own operational duties.

Before the course began Martin was taking some well-deserved leave and intended using the opportunity to marry Polly by special licence. The wedding was to take place in the first week of July. In his letter he reminded Perys of the promise he had made to act as his best man.

Perys's response was to telephone the Heligan housekeeper right away to tell her he was coming to stay. He asked her to inform Martin, through Polly, that he would be there to act as his best man.

As his leg was healing well, Perys decided to risk travelling to Cornwall on his motor-cycle. It was not the most sensible thing to do. The journey took him an entire day and he arrived at Heligan tired, stiff and with a sore leg. However, the house was now occupied by convalescent officers and the sight of them, many minus limbs, put his own injury into perspective.

The rooms retained for family use were at the rear of the house, and it was here, as he limped to his room, that Perys met with Polly. Ignoring the housekeeper's shocked disapproval, Perys embraced the young servant girl and planted a kiss on her cheek.

Releasing her, he smiled at the housekeeper and said, 'Martin flies with me as my favourite observer. Between us we have claimed a number of Germans and I am proud to be standing as his best man. What's more, when he marries Polly he will be getting a lovely wife – and she a fine husband.'

Following the woman, who was muttering darkly about 'Not knowing what things are coming to!', Perys left the scarlet-cheeked servant girl standing in the back hall and made his way to his room.

Martin arrived home the next day and came to the house to meet with Polly when her day's work was done. From the window of his room, Perys saw him standing outside the servants' door and went out to greet him.

'Martin! It's good to see you . . .' Suddenly observing the medal ribbon of a Military Medal on the other man's chest, he pointed to it and said, 'How long have you had that?'

Embarrassed, Martin said, 'It came through last week.'

'Does Polly know about it?'

'No, I thought I'd keep it as a surprise for her.'

'Haven't you seen her yet?' Perys was indignant. 'We'll have to see about that. Come to my room and I'll send for her.'

When Martin hesitated, Perys guessed the reason. 'You're not a servant now, Martin. You are a sergeant observer in the Royal Flying Corps – and a damned good one. Come along.'

Self-consciously, Martin followed Perys to his room. Here, Perys poured him a drink, then rang the bell to summon a maid. When she arrived, Perys told her to find Polly and send her to his room.

When the maid had gone, Perys said to Martin, 'I am going for a walk in the garden. I shall return in about fifteen minutes. Until then you and Polly should not be disturbed.'

Outside the room he met Polly hurrying towards his room. When she saw him she said anxiously, 'You sent for me. It's not . . . it's nothing to do with Martin?'

'Actually, it *is*,' Perys said, 'but go inside, Polly, you'll learn more about it there.' Perys closed the door behind her before limping away to spend the fifteen minutes he had given to the young couple in the garden.

Martin found him before the time had expired, explaining, 'Polly still has some work to do. The servants are kept busy helping to look after the convalescents. She did not want to risk upsetting the housekeeper in case she keeps her working late.'

As they walked together on the lawn beside the house, Perys asked, 'How are your parents – and Annie?'

'Ma and Pa are fine,' Martin replied. 'I'm not so sure about Annie.'

'Why, what's wrong?' Perys asked.

'It's Jimmy. He's proving to be a very difficult patient. It's hardly surprising, I suppose. If I was blind and had trouble breathing for most of the time I doubt if I'd be the happiest man in the world.'

'How is Annie coping?' Perys realised that Annie's well-being still mattered to him. He found this disturbing.

'Ma says she's very patient with him for most of the time, but she occasionally verges on despair. Jimmy's mother doesn't help much, apparently. Whenever she visits she fusses over him and complains that Annie tries to make him do too much. I don't know what the answer is, but it can't be easy for her. Why don't you pay her a visit up at the cottage while you're here? She'd like that.'

'I look forward to seeing her at the wedding,' Perys replied, non-committally. '. . . But here's Polly. It looks as though she has got off early after all. I'll leave you two alone, you'll have a lot to talk about. Come up to the house and see me tomorrow, Martin. I would come to the farm, but I can't walk very far just yet and a day on the motor-bike hasn't helped. I want to be your support on Saturday, not have you supporting me.'

Perys spoke to Polly as he passed her by, but she had eyes only for Martin. However, as Perys was about to enter the house, she shouted after him.

'Perys!' When he turned to her, she called, 'I thought you ought to know. There were a number of new convalescent arrivals today. Your cousin Edward is one of them.'

54

Perys considered finding Edward and making an attempt at reconciliation, but the next day while he was still contemplating the matter, he met with one of the convalescent officers in the gardens of Heligan. Perys recognised him as the administration captain who had been helpful when he had tried to join the Duke of Cornwall Light Infantry at Bodmin on the outbreak of war.

He was wearing the blue jacket of a convalescent soldier.

The captain did not immediately recognise Perys, but when he was reminded, he remembered the incident. Ruefully, he added, 'So much has happened since then I wonder I have any memory left at all. On occasions I *wish* I had none.' The infantry officer had one arm bent at the elbow and strapped tightly to his chest. 'But you have done well.' He nodded in the direction of Perys's medal ribbons. 'All those, and a captain too! You should be thankful you were turned down for the regiment! But what are you doing here? You are not convalescing, yet I notice you are limping quite badly.'

Not bothering to explain that he was a brevet-captain, Perys replied, 'I crashed an aeroplane on a test flight, but I'm well on the mend now. Heligan belongs to a great-uncle and I am staying here to attend the wedding of a member of the squadron. He was my observer.'

'Of course, I remember now, you're a Tremayne,' said the captain. 'Edward Tremayne came in yesterday. Is he a relative of yours?'

'Yes, a second cousin. I heard he was here. Unfortunately, he and I fell out just before the war but I feel I should make my peace with him, especially as he's been wounded.'

The captain suddenly smiled. 'I wouldn't say he was wounded, exactly. Perhaps "met with an unfortunate accident while under fire" might be a more accurate description of what happened.'

When Perys looked blank, the captain explained, 'Lieutenant Tremayne was on attachment to the Cyclist Battalion and had yet to see any action. When there was a German breakthrough he and his company were despatched to the front-line. While they were on their way a long-range German gun lobbed a shell across the lines. It landed close to the road on which your second cousin and his company were riding and caused him to lose control of his bicycle. He crashed in a ditch and was thrown off, damaging his elbow. He has problems moving the fingers of that hand and as a result it is feared he will be invalided

363

out of the army.' The captain made a gesture of mock sympathy. 'A tragedy, really. Who knows what he might have contributed to future battles had his full potential been realised?'

'Who knows, indeed?'

Perys knew he should have felt sympathy for his kinsman, but he found it difficult not to be amused at the thought of the haughty and arrogant Edward being injured when going into action on a bicycle.

The weather on Martin and Polly's wedding day was as perfect as the couple could have hoped. Many of the Heligan House staff attended. So too did a number of the convalescing officers; Polly was a popular housemaid.

Polly had no immediate relatives, but in the church at St Ewe were Martin's parents – and Annie. She was seated in the pew behind Martin and Perys.

Annie looked around when Perys and Martin walked down the aisle to take their places at the front of the church, and when their eyes met, Perys experienced the same sudden thrill as when he had seen her for the first time. He had to remind himself that she was now a married woman, and he was committed to someone else.

When the service in the crowded church came to an end, he found himself walking to the door beside Annie and spoke to her for the first time since they had parted, more than a year-and-a-half before.

'Hello, Annie, how are you?'

The mundane remark was not sufficient to bridge the gulf that had opened between them and she replied, 'I'm fine, Perys – but how are *you*? I believe you broke your leg in an aeroplane crash?'

'It's almost fully healed now, thank you, Annie. I shall be flying again in a week or so.' After a brief silence, he asked, 'How is your husband? Is he here today?'

'He didn't feel like making the journey to the service, so his mother stayed at the house with him. He'll be at the farm for the celebrations afterwards.'

It was a conversation that not even the most suspicious of listeners could have read anything into, but for almost the whole time Annie had kept her gaze on the ground, not looking at him. When they reached the church door she glanced up at him and he thought she looked strained and unhappy. Then she left him in order to join the family group being gathered together by a harassed photographer. Perys was left with a disturbing feeling that too much had been left unsaid between them. That they were both afraid of talking to each other.

This was a simple rural wedding and when all the photographs had been taken, the guests were conveyed to Tregassick Farm on well-scrubbed farmcarts.

Perys had hoped he might be seated close to Annie, but they travelled to Tregassick on separate carts.

Contrary to what Annie had told him, Jimmy was not present at the wedding party. Neither was his mother, and Perys thought Annie seemed uneasy, undoubtedly due to the absence of her husband. However, as she was helping with the catering, he had no opportunity to talk to her about it.

At dusk, the party was still in full swing when Perys decided to leave. He intended walking back to Heligan House. It was little more than a mile away, and although it would of necessity be a slow walk for him, he felt the exercise would strengthen his injured leg.

Before he left he looked for Annie, to say goodbye to her, but she could not be seen. He assumed she must have left earlier without him noticing.

Leaving the farm, he walked slowly and had only just reached the lane at the end of the track when he thought he heard a sound behind him. Turning, he saw someone walking quickly towards him. As they drew nearer he saw it was Annie.

She seemed to slow her pace as though realising for the first time who was ahead of her, but Perys came to a halt and waited for her to catch up with him.

She was the first to speak. 'Is it wise for you to be walking so far on that leg?'

'I need to get it back to full strength,' he replied. 'It's time I went back to the war.'

'I suppose it won't be very long before Martin has to return too.' Annie sounded unhappy at the thought.

'We'll probably both be leaving England about the same time,' he said.

'Polly's going to be very upset,' Annie added. 'No doubt your fiancée will be unhappy too – or are you married already?'

'Me?' Perys was startled. 'No, I am not married – nor am I engaged.'

'Oh! I thought you were getting engaged to a girl named Grace?'

'How do you know about Grace?' Perys knew he had never mentioned her to Annie. In fact, he had not seen Annie since he and Grace had met.

'Miss Morwenna mentioned her when we met at Saint Thomas's Hospital in London, when Jimmy came home after being wounded.'

'How did you come to be talking about me?' Perys asked.

'I saw she was wearing a very beautiful ring. I thought you might have given it to her. She said you hadn't, but that you would probably be buying one for her friend and she mentioned her name.'

When Perys said nothing, Annie asked, 'Are you to marry Grace?'

'I would like to think so, Annie, but at the time of which you speak I had only met her a few times. Before then, if anyone had asked whether I had a girl, I would probably have said yes . . . and I would have been talking about you. I didn't realise you were already promised to someone else.'

'It wasn't like that, Perys,' Annie said, miserably.

'Then how was it, Annie? Explain it to me.'

'There's no point in talking about it now, Perys. We can't turn the clock back. I'm a married woman. Married to Jimmy.'

'Are you happy, Annie?'

It was a question he knew he had no right to ask, and he was about to apologise when Annie replied, 'I would be far happier if Jimmy had his sight and his health.'

'Of course. I am sorry, Annie, I should not have asked such a question.'

Annie thought, unhappily, that in view of the way she had treated him, he had every right to question her, but they had arrived at the entrance to the track which led to the cottage she shared with Jimmy.

'This is my way home, Perys. I do hope you and Grace will be very, very happy.'

'Thank you, Annie. I hope Jimmy's health improves.'

There was a moment's hesitation between them, then she turned and made her way along the track. He had taken only a couple of paces in the direction of Heligan when she called out to him.

'Perys! Take care of yourself. I pray for both you and Martin every night.'

Having said this, she was gone, and he could hear her running along the track towards her home.

Had Perys been more familiar with the area he might have wondered why Annie had not walked across the single field that divided her home from Tregassick Farm. Had she done so she would have reached her destination in a fraction of the time it had taken her via the lane.

Halfway to Heligan, Perys began to regret deciding to walk back to the house. Then he heard a motor-car coming along the lane behind him. Quite as loud as the vehicle's engine was the sound of singing from its occupants.

Perys had admired a 1913 Argyll motor-car parked outside Heligan House on the previous day. Its owner was a wounded Scots naval lieutenant, whose father was part-owner of the company that had built the vehicle.

As it drew closer, Perys stood back to allow the Argyll to pass him by. As it did so, the headlights picked him out. There was a sudden screech of brakes and cries of, 'It's the pilot!', and the motor-car slid to a halt a short distance along the lane.

'What are you doing so far from home at this time of night, Captain?' asked the cheery driver. 'Would you care for a lift?'

Perys was happy to accept the offer, even though he realised the men in the motor-car – including the driver – had been drinking heavily.

He was less certain of the wisdom of his decision when the occupants inside the passenger compartment moved to make room for him and Perys found himself seated next to Edward Tremayne.

'Well, if it isn't Second Cousin Perys,' Edward sneered. 'You've been hobnobbing with servants again, I believe?'

'No,' Perys replied, evenly, 'I've been acting as best man to my observer – a rather splendid chap who has won a Military Medal and twice been mentioned in dispatches. What is *your* tally, Edward? By the way, I understand you are known as "Ting-a-ling Tremayne" in your regiment. Why would that be?'

This piece of information had been imparted to him by the Duke of Cornwall Light Infantry captain earlier. One of the passengers in the Argyll who had been listening with interest to the conversation and who knew the story of Edward's 'war wound', took it up immediately.

'Did you hear that, chaps? Edward answers to the name of Ting-a-ling. Ting-a-ling Tremayne.'

This provoked a howl of approval from the other officers in the Argyll, and for the next couple of minutes each of the convalescent officers gave a highly individualistic imitation of a bicycle bell.

When the vehicle crunched to a halt in front of Heligan House, Edward alighted from it and stalked off without a farewell to any of his fellow passengers. Perys realised there would be no reconciliation between the two of them during their stay at the house.

55

When Annie entered her cottage she found Winnie Rowe seated in the kitchen. Jimmy was nowhere to be seen.

'You've taken your time getting home!' declared a tight-lipped Winnie.

'I beg your pardon?' Annie retorted, indignantly. 'Today is my brother's wedding day and although Jimmy didn't want to come to the church, you were supposed to be bringing him to the farm. Where is he now?'

'He's in bed. He didn't feel like getting involved with all the folk who would be at Tregassick.'

'He didn't feel like it – or did you tell him he shouldn't go?' Annie put the question angrily.

Winnie shrugged. 'I certainly didn't try too hard to persuade him he *should* go. It's no fun for a blind and sick young man to be surrounded by folk enjoying themselves when he can't join in.'

'It would have been better for him than staying here and being made to feel sorry for himself. As for joining in the fun . . . he'll become involved whether he likes it or not. Martin and Polly will be home tonight and most of the guests are coming to serenade them on their first night together.'

The cottage where Jimmy and Annie lived was one of a pair of semi-detached cottages. The other had been rented by Martin and Polly.

'Why didn't you try to stop them from coming? Our Jimmy's a sick young man—'

'So you keep telling him,' Annie snapped. 'I'm going up to tell him what to expect.'

'He'll be asleep,' Winnie said. 'He's been in bed an hour or more.'

'Then he'll have had rest enough to get up and dress and go out and wish the newlyweds well.'

Annie realised she sounded cold and unsympathetic, even though her anger was directed not at Jimmy but at his mother. Winnie's interference and unnecessary molly-coddling of her son were constantly undermining Annie's attempts to promote a degree of independence in Jimmy, and pride in the achievements of which he was still capable.

'Well! I've never heard of such a thing. There's our Jimmy lying upstairs sick and all alone and you want to force him to get up and be dragged out into the night air – and for what? For something that can just as easily be put off until the morning!'

'Had you brought Jimmy to Tregassick as we planned, he'd be tucked up now having enjoyed a day when he'd been treated as a human being and not as something to be shoved into a corner and allowed to rot away. I've told you before, Jimmy is my husband and I'm going to see that he has as near-normal a life as is possible. I'll not let him go around believing he's some kind of freak. Now, Martin, Polly and the wedding guests will be up here soon. If you want to tidy yourself up before they arrive I suggest you do it now, while I get Jimmy up.'

'Not me! I'll not be a party to this. You've made it perfectly clear how you feel about me. I'll go to bed and try not to think of what's happening to poor Jimmy. Whatever made me think you'd make him a good wife I'll never know.'

Having made her thoughts clear to her daughter-in-law, Winnie stomped up the uncarpeted wooden stairs to the bedroom she was occupying in the young couple's cottage.

Left alone downstairs, Annie found she was shaking. She often disagreed with Winnie about her interfering ways, but this was the first time it had developed into such an acrimonious exchange. For some moments she wondered whether she should perhaps go upstairs and apologise to her mother-in-law. Common sense prevailed. If she suggested she was in the wrong, she would sacrifice what little authority she possessed over Winnie in respect of Jimmy.

When she heard her mother-in-law walking heavy-footed around her bedroom, Annie went upstairs to where Jimmy was in bed. There was a lamp alight in the room, turned down low, and Jimmy was curled up on his side in the bed. Speaking in a tone of voice far removed from that she had used when talking to Winnie, she said, softly, 'Jimmy, are you awake, love?'

'What do you want?'

'To see if you're all right and to find out why you didn't come to Tregassick. Everyone was asking after you.'

'I've no doubt things went well enough without me – better, probably. Anyway, I didn't feel up to being among lots of people I couldn't see. Ma reckoned I'd be better staying home.'

'Well, most of those who were at Tregassick are coming up here to see Martin and Polly into their new home. As you didn't come to the farm, I said you'd be outside to wish them well.'

'But . . . I'm in bed, Annie!'

'And this is a very special day,' Annie said, firmly, 'especially for Martin and Polly. Martin, in particular, will expect you to wish him well. But I don't want the pair of you talking for hours about the war. Remember, it's his wedding night.'

Annie spoke in a jocular fashion, knowing from experience that this was the most successful ploy to adopt when her husband was in one of his 'can't do' moods.

Jimmy continued to grumble about having to get out of bed, dress and be taken out into the cool night air. However, when the newly married couple and their guests reached the house in a celebratory mood and insisted that Jimmy have a share of the ale they had brought with them, his mood mellowed. Much to Annie's delight he seemed to be enjoying himself more than at any time since returning home from the hospital.

She wished Winnie was present to see the change in him for herself. But she was curled up in her bed, a pillow over her head, trying to exclude the sounds of the merry-making outside. She felt both anger against Annie and sympathy for her poor son. He had been dragged out of bed by an unfeeling wife and forced to join revellers who seemed intent upon carrying the party well into the early hours of the morning.

56

Martin and Polly enjoyed only five days of married life before he had to return to the School of Aerial Gunnery and she to her work at Heligan House. The only difference that married life made to Polly was that instead of retiring to a room in the big house when her work was done, she went home to the semi-detached house next to that occupied by Annie and Jimmy.

A few days after Martin went away, Polly was given the task of cleaning the room occupied by Perys. He was in the room at the time and, as Polly worked, they chatted. They spoke of the wedding, of married life in general – and of Martin.

'I wish he didn't have to go back to the war,' Polly said, unhappily. 'I used to lie awake worrying about him before we were married. It'll somehow be so much worse now.'

'I can't tell you there's nothing to worry about,

Polly,' Perys said, seriously. 'You're far too intelligent to accept that, but I know he would much rather be fighting the war up in the air than in the trenches – and that's where he'd be now if he hadn't joined the RFC.'

In a desperate bid to replace the front-line soldiers who were being slaughtered in their tens of thousands, the government had brought in conscription earlier that year and many local men had been drafted in to the army.

'That's what I keep telling myself,' Polly said, 'but it doesn't make me miss him any the less.'

Suddenly and unexpectedly she broke down and began to cry. For a few seconds Perys was at a loss about what he should do, then he crossed to the weeping housemaid and, feeling awkward and slightly embarrassed, put his arms about her.

After a few minutes Polly moved away from him. Making a determined effort to regain control of herself, she said, 'I'm sorry, Perys. I didn't mean to embarrass you. I just don't know what came over me.'

'It's all right, Polly. I understand – and so would Martin. He's a lucky man to have someone like you care so much about him.'

'Thank you.' Polly avoided looking directly at him. 'But, if you don't mind, I'd like to go and tidy myself up before I finish your room.'

'Of course . . . and I do understand, Polly, I really do.'

When she had gone, Perys thought that women like Polly, who had their men fighting in the war, carried a heavy burden as they went about their daily lives.

Now his leg was virtually healed, Perys was anxious to get back to his squadron. He had recently received a letter from Thomas Kemp, commiserating with him over his injury, but hoping he would soon be back in action.

He also informed Perys that he *was* to bring the Spad back with him. The French plane would be their principal fighter aircraft until more Spads, or perhaps Sopwith 'Pups', were delivered to the Royal Flying Corps in sufficient numbers for fighter squadrons to be formed.

It was what Major Kemp and other commanding officers had been advocating with increasing conviction as the war progressed, and all were convinced it would pay immediate dividends.

Perys had been awaiting the arrival of a medical board at Heligan to assess the convalescents. He intended asking them to examine his leg and pronounce him fit for duty.

Unfortunately, word reached the convalescent home that the board would be delayed. All available army doctors had been sent to France, where the British army was fighting a futile and costly offensive in the region of the Somme. Rumour had it that the British had suffered disastrous casualties throughout the course of the fierce battle.

Perys decided to return to the Central Flying School right away. Once there, he would make a couple of flights in one of their aircraft to confirm his leg would stand up to the rigours of operational flying, then have the School medical officer certify him fit for duty. He hoped to fly the Spad back to the squadron in time to take an active part in the present fighting.

When he told the Heligan housekeeper he would be leaving the next day, word was quickly passed around to the staff.

That evening, before she left for home, Polly came to his room. His luggage bag was half-packed on the bed, with clothes lying about it, and she said, 'So it's true then, you are leaving Heligan?'

'There's nothing to keep me here now, Polly. I've done my duty as best man at your wedding and my leg is better. It's time I was back with the squadron.'

'Were you going without saying goodbye?'

'Of course not. I would not have left before seeing you in the morning, but I haven't said anything because . . . well, I didn't want to make a big thing of it and set you off worrying about Martin all over again.'

'I never *stop* worrying about him.' Polly was quiet for a few moments before asking, 'Will you be seeing Annie to tell her you're leaving?'

Perys shook his head. 'She's a married woman now, Polly. She has her own life to lead.'

'It's not very much of a life, Perys. Jimmy either can't – or won't – do anything for himself.'

'It must be very hard for her,' Perys agreed, 'but she chose to marry him. She didn't have to.'

'I'd be happier if that were so,' Polly said, 'but she felt she *did* have to. She'd actually gone to Jimmy's house to tell his ma and pa she wasn't going through with the marriage when they heard about him being wounded. When she saw how bad he was hurt she felt she couldn't hurt him even more – so she married him, even though she doesn't love him.'

Perys looked at her in disbelief. 'You're just sur- mising this, Polly. It probably wasn't like that at all.'

'What I'm telling you is the truth, Perys. We talked about it a lot. Annie didn't want to tell Jimmy when he was in the trenches having a dreadful time, so she went to tell his ma and pa first. She hoped they might be able to think of some way of letting him know, without hurting him too much.'

'But . . . that's appalling, Polly. To be tied for life to someone as severely disabled as Jimmy would be hard enough if she loved him. If she really doesn't . . .' He stopped, suddenly lost for words.

'So will you be saying goodbye to her?' Polly persisted.

He shook his head. 'No, Polly, it wouldn't be a good idea, especially after what you have just told me. You know what people are like. They'd only have to see me heading towards Annie's cottage and the rumours would begin. The last thing I want is to have her talked about in the way folk around here used to talk about Eliza.'

'Annie is going to be very upset when she knows you've gone,' said Polly. 'But mention of Eliza reminds me . . . You know she has a little girl now and is married to Esau Tamblyn?'

'I knew about her marriage,' Perys replied, 'but I wasn't aware her baby was a girl.'

Continuing her story, Polly said, 'Esau joined the Royal Navy before conscription came in because he didn't want to get called up for the army. Just before Christmas his ship was sunk. Fortunately, Esau wasn't hurt, but he's a prisoner in Germany. To give Eliza her due, she's behaved herself and not gone back to her old ways – at least, not until Edward Tremayne came back to Heligan. They've been seen together a couple of times. The last time was on the path that runs from Mevagissey to Heligan Mill . . .'

Perys remembered the hay barn and Eliza's liaison with the Heligan gamekeeper . . . but Polly had more to say.

'Esau has always been a simple soul, Perys, but he's well-liked in Mevagissey. The fishermen who haven't gone off to war are angry that Eliza should be carrying on while Esau is a prisoner. Most of their anger is directed against Edward. I think you should warn him, Perys.'

'Edward will be leaving once a medical board has visited Heligan.' Perys was reluctant to commit himself to talking to his second cousin if it could be avoided. 'He'll be invalided out of the army and return to his family home.'

'A lot could happen before then,' Polly warned. 'There are some hotheads in Mevagissey who don't share the respect of Heligan servants for the family.'

'All right, I'll try to warn him off,' Perys said, with some reluctance, 'but I can't promise anything, Polly. I am not exactly Edward's favourite relative.'

'At least you will have *tried* to warn him,' Polly said, 'and I really *do* think you should.' Suddenly becoming brisk, she said, 'I must go now or I'll have the housekeeper searching for me. Thank you for being Martin's best man – and please, take care of yourself. I'm going to say goodbye to you now because I wouldn't be able to do this in the morning.'

Stepping closer, she gave him a hug and a kiss. Then, scarlet-cheeked, she hurried from the room, leaving behind her a slightly bemused Perys.

He smiled to himself at the thought of how horrified

Aunt Maude would be had she witnessed the display of affection shown to him by a Heligan maidservant.

Perys's meeting with Edward served only to confirm to him how obnoxious his second cousin was.

Edward was in his room and in response to Perys's knocking called out for him to 'Come in'.

When Perys opened the door and entered the room he found his relative lying on his bed, reading a book. At sight of his unexpected visitor, Edward put down the book, sat up slowly and swung his feet to the ground.

'What the hell are you doing in my room?' he demanded.

'I am here to do you a favour,' Perys said, 'although I really don't know why I should. I've come to pass on a warning I was given – about you and Eliza Dunn.'

Edward was startled but replied belligerently, 'I don't know what you are talking about. Even if I *did*, what I do is none of your business.'

'That is what I told my informant you would say,' Perys agreed, 'but I promised I would pass on the warning anyway. It seems that folk in Mevagissey know what is going on between the two of you and are not happy about it.'

'They can mind their own business too,' Edward declared. 'And just who is this "informant" – that little farmer's girl of yours?'

It was Perys's turn to be taken by surprise.

Observing this, Edward sneered, 'Oh yes, I know all about her. As far as I am concerned this is a case of the pot calling the kettle black. It must be most convenient for you both that her husband is unable to see what is going on around him.'

Perys knew Eliza must have told Edward about Annie, but he was no less angry with him for the manner in which he had repeated her gossip.

'I knew it would be a mistake to come and talk to you, but if anything happens I will at least have a clear conscience.'

'Tell that to the husband of your farm girl.' Edward was enjoying what he regarded as a verbal victory over Perys. 'And kindly close the door on your way out . . . Cousin.'

57

Perys arrived back with his squadron just in time to take part in their relocation to an airfield close to the French town of Albert.

The British army's offensive extended north of the River Somme and the squadron's aeroplanes were kept busy recording the progress – or lack of it – for the benefit of the generals at army headquarters.

Meanwhile, German fighter planes were reaping a grim harvest among the slow-flying reconnaissance aircraft.

Nevertheless, Perys and the French pilots who were also flying Spads proved their aircraft were a match for the much-feared Fokkers of the German air force, even though they were greatly outnumbered.

During the ensuing months they fought against daunting odds to enable the BE2cs to obtain the information required by Field Marshal Haig and his staff at General Headquarters.

Then, towards the end of the campaign, when the onset of winter was adding to the appalling discomfiture of the ground troops, another of the aircraft Perys had evaluated – the Sopwith 'Pup' – began arriving in France in rapidly increasing numbers. It quickly established itself as the equal of the Fokker and, at last, the dream of Major Thomas Kemp was realised.

The first fighter squadrons were formed, their sole purpose being to shoot down enemy aeroplanes and establish Allied superiority in the skies above France. Command of the squadron formed at Arras was given to the delighted Major Kemp. Perys, now a substantive captain, became his senior pilot and a flight commander.

The popular commanding officer's elation was of a tragically short duration.

The squadron came into being on a Wednesday. By Friday Thomas Kemp was dead, killed in a collision between the aeroplane he was flying and that piloted by a young second lieutenant flying his first operational mission.

It came as a severe personal blow to Perys, who greatly admired Thomas Kemp, both as a man and as his commanding officer. He doubted whether there was another flyer in the Royal Flying Corps capable of taking his place, but he was given little time to mourn the man who had been a friend and a much-respected senior officer. For ten days, while they awaited the appointment of a new commanding officer, Perys took over the squadron.

It was a difficult time. The pilots of the newly formed fighter squadron were largely unknown to each other. The only thing they had in common was that they were all young; this, and a burning ambition to shoot down German warplanes.

Although not the oldest of the squadron's pilots, Perys had more flying hours than any of the others and his leadership was readily accepted by them. Even so, the main subject of conversation in the mess each evening was of who would be appointed as the new commanding officer.

Ten days after taking temporary command, Perys returned from a morning sortie in which he and his flight had downed two German reconnaissance aeroplanes, to find the new commanding officer awaiting him on the airfield.

It was Rupert Pilkington, now a major.

The two men greeted each other warmly and Rupert said, 'I have just spent half-an-hour being briefed by your acting adjutant. He tells me I have been given command of a crack squadron. I hope you won't resent me coming here and taking over from you?'

'I couldn't be more pleased,' Perys replied, honestly. 'It's a relief to be handing over responsibility and I am thrilled that it should be you who is taking over the squadron. I am also thankful not to have lost any pilots during my brief tenure.'

'You have done a splendid job,' Rupert said. 'It has not gone unnoticed at RFC headquarters.'

As they walked together to the squadron administration office, Perys asked after Morwenna.

'She is fine,' Rupert said. 'We met up in London only a couple of weeks ago and I was able to catch up on all the family news.' Glancing at Perys, he added, 'You have heard about the tragedy involving Edward, of course? It was a damned peculiar business.'

'I have had no family news for months,' Perys replied. 'Aunt Maude usually keeps me up-to-date on what is going on but, as you know, she has been in America for some time, fund-raising for one or other of her many war charities. Tell me, what has happened to Cousin Edward?'

Remembering the warning he had tried to pass on to Edward, he feared the worst and was not as surprised as he might have been when Rupert replied, 'Edward is dead.'

Amplifying his blunt statement, he explained, 'It must have happened soon after you left Heligan. He was found dead in the harbour at Mevagissey. There was some mystery about his death at the time. The landlord of one of the Mevagissey public houses swore in the coroner's court that Edward had been drinking heavily there for much of the evening, but one of the convalescent officers who had also been drinking in the village said none of the officers from Heligan had seen him there. Whatever the truth of it, the verdict was accidental death. It was a tragedy, really. I know neither of us liked Edward very much, but he had been wounded fighting for his country and was within a few days of being invalided out of the army.'

Perys decided to say nothing of what he knew about Edward's 'war wound', or of the warning he had passed on to him from Polly. Nevertheless, he was uncomfortably aware of something Annie had said to him in 1914, when they visited the injured Henry Dunn.

She had said that the fishermen of Mevagissey 'looked after their own'.

Perys strongly suspected that they had once again proved this to be so.

58

In recognition of the number of German aircraft he had shot down during his command of the squadron, Perys was awarded a second Military Cross, one of three given to the squadron's pilots, and by the end of November 1916 the bloody battle of the Somme was over.

The end of the fighting was decided as much by conditions on the battlefield as by the sheer exhaustion of the combatants. The few insignificant square miles of ground won by the Allied armies had been churned into a wasteland of mud in a carnage that had claimed more than a million-and-a-quarter casualties.

The soldiers who had fought and died to no avail spoke many differing languages, but, spilled on the shell-torn earth, an enemy's blood was indistinguishable from that of a friend.

Winter would bring peace, of a kind, on the ground,

but in the air great changes were taking place, the Royal Flying Corps developing along lines that would shape its future for more than half-a-century.

Instead of squadrons made up of aeroplanes designed for a number of different purposes, they now had separate fighter squadrons: the 'scouts'; the bombers; and others whose purpose was reconnaissance and artillery spotting. Each would have an important but very different part to play in the aerial warfare of the future when tactics too would assume increasing importance.

Rupert and Perys trained their squadron as a unit, each pilot being responsible for covering another in combat. Each, in his turn, would be protected by another.

However, the main purpose of a 'scout' was to shoot down the enemy. Because of this the fighter pilot became glamorised as a 'knight of the sky', fighting a personal battle against an adversary. It was a mode of fighting that had not been seen since the days of King Arthur and his knights of the Round Table.

However, 1917 was to bring about other changes that would eventually bring this, the most costly of conflicts, to an end.

Germany was about to embark on an all-out war at sea and her submarine commanders were given orders to sink any vessel found in British waters, or which the submarine commander believed to be en route to a British port, regardless of the flag it was flying.

This unwise and draconian measure would bring a hitherto dithering United States of America into the war against the Germans. The vast resources of this mighty country would more than offset the collapse of Russia, Germany's Eastern enemy, which was about to tear itself apart in a bloody revolution.

In March 1917, when British and French generals were planning yet another offensive, Perys received a letter which left him stunned. Forwarded by Maude, who was now back in London, the letter had been written to Perys by his grandfather.

It began by saying that now Perys had passed the age of twenty-one, it was time for some changes in his life. Incredibly, his grandfather then expressed deep regret for the fact that his own Victorian upbringing and that of Perys's grandmother had left them unable to cope with the shame they had felt over the circumstances of Perys's birth. They had now come to realise that they had been guilty of a tragic injustice to him and were deeply ashamed of the suffering they had caused to both him and his mother.

Letters sent to them by Maude Tremayne and by Rupert had made them realise how much they had lost by their indifference towards him. Even more regrettable was the unhappiness they had caused him during the years when he most needed the support of a family.

Grandfather Tremayne went on to say that nothing he or Perys's grandmother could do would ever compensate for those lost years, but he had been in correspondence with his London solicitor with a view to ensuring Perys's future would be happier and more secure than his past.

Hardly able to believe the contents of the letter, Perys went on to read that his grandfather was making over to him all the properties he owned in England, together with monies deposited in his name in a London bank.

He added that he and Perys's grandmother had property and money enough in Italy to ensure they would live out their remaining years in all the comfort they needed.

Accompanying the letter was another from the London solicitor, listing the properties and land which had been made over to Perys, together with details of the monies and investments that would also be transferred to his own hitherto meagre bank account.

The grand total was staggering! Perys found it difficult to grasp that he was now a wealthy man with properties in a number of English counties. Among these was the home of his grandparents on the Sussex Downs and a number of farms in Cornwall. Perys was astonished to learn that among these were Tregassick and its neighbour which, with others, were being administered on his behalf by the Heligan Estate office.

Perys remembered Annie had once said that although the farm was administered by Heligan, it was owned by another member of the Tremayne family, but he never dreamed the owner was his grandfather. Now, of course, *he* was the owner. He wondered what the Bray family would think of the situation. He decided it was not necessary to tell them just yet.

Reading through the list of properties and possessions being passed on to him, Perys found his grandfather's hitherto parsimonious attitude difficult to excuse – but today was not a time for recriminations.

Seeking out Rupert, a still-stunned Perys told him of his astonishing and unexpected good fortune.

Rupert offered Perys genuine congratulations, adding, 'I am very, very pleased for you, Perys. My only regret is that it has taken the old boy so long to come to his senses. He should have listened to the family many years ago.'

'Do you know him very well?' Perys had never before thought to question Rupert about the relationship he had with his grandfather.

'I have met him a few times,' Rupert replied. 'He would occasionally visit the home of my parents.'

'What sort of a man is he really?'

When Rupert appeared startled by the question, Perys explained, 'He would never speak to me while my mother was alive – and I never even saw him afterwards. I had thought I might once, when I was in trouble at school for fighting – a not uncommon occurrence, I am afraid. The headmaster told me he had written to Grandfather Tremayne, asking him to come to the school and deliver a final warning to me about my behaviour . . .'

When Perys fell silent, Rupert prompted, 'I take it he didn't come to speak to you?'

Perys shook his head. 'He sent a letter to the headmaster saying, "Talking to the boy will achieve nothing. If he so much as *looks* as though he might misbehave, beat him."' Perys managed a wry smile. 'The letter actually did me a favour. I think the headmaster was shocked by Grandfather's attitude and was never quite so hard on me after that.'

Giving Perys a sympathetic look, Rupert said, 'Well, now the old boy has finally relented, do you have any ideas about spending your newly acquired wealth?'

'Yes. Well . . . two ideas come to mind immediately. The first is that when the next spell of bad weather grounds us, I'll take the squadron out for a night on the town.'

'And the second . . . ?' Rupert queried.

After only a moment's hesitation, Perys said, 'Now I am no longer a pauper, I intend writing to Grace and asking her to marry me.'

59

Perys was able to keep his promise to treat the squadron to a night out only a few evenings later. They went to Amiens. It was far enough away from the front-line to enable the squadron's pilots and observers to forget the war for a few hours. They enjoyed a superb meal and consumed enough wine, cognac and other drinks to make them all grateful that bad weather kept them grounded until the evening of the following day.

It was to be the last party the squadron would enjoy for a couple of months. For many it would be the last they would ever know.

The latest offensive was launched against heavily defended German lines near Arras, and air reconnaissance was considered essential if it were to succeed.

The task of the fighter squadrons was to ensure that reconnaissance aircraft were able to carry out their duties unmolested by German airmen.

They performed well – but at a terrible cost. Baron Manfred von Richthofen and his pilots flying the German Albatross aeroplane reaped a rich harvest in the skies above France as new and inexperienced British pilots were flung into the battle in unprecedented numbers. Some lasted only days in the skies above the battlefield, others a matter of hours.

At night, in the quiet of his darkened room, the distant thunder of artillery only faintly discernible when the westerly wind eased, Perys turned his thoughts from war to what he hoped would be happier times.

He had not yet received a reply from Grace to his proposal, but it was hardly surprising. Fierce fighting was raging all along the battle-front and casualties were appallingly heavy. All branches of the medical services were stretched to the limit.

Perys and Rupert were sharing a drink in the quiet of Rupert's office one evening in April 1917. Both men were feeling the strain of the offensive and Perys had been discussing with his second cousin the question of replacements for two flight commanders who had been lost in action that day. One had been shot out of the sky by Baron Manfred von Richthofen, the other by his brother, Lother.

The decision on one replacement was quickly reached. The other would need to be brought in from outside the squadron. The issue temporarily settled, both officers tried to relax. It was not easy.

'Have you heard from Grace since you sent off your proposal?' Rupert asked.

'Not yet,' Perys replied. 'I doubt if I will until things quieten down along the front. She'll be pretty busy.'

'I had a telephone call from Morwenna today,' Rupert said. 'She told me she will be well clear of the fighting for a while. I must say it is a great relief to me. She's in Paris at the moment, preparing men to return to England. When they are ready she'll travel with them to Le Havre, then accompany them to England on a hospital ship, the *Sultan*. Once the men have been safely delivered to hospitals in London she's taking some leave.'

'Will you be able to get across to England to spend a few days with her?'

'I'd like to,' Rupert replied, 'but with things the way they are at present I will need to lead one of the flights myself.'

'Things aren't looking too good,' Perys agreed. 'When I look around at those of the original squadron who are left, I am aware I am living on borrowed time.'

Rupert recognised the truth of Perys's statement, but he said, cheerfully, 'Nonsense, Perys. Not even von Richthofen himself could down you – and if he's wise he will give you a wide berth in the air . . . But here, let me refill your glass.'

A few days later Perys travelled by road to St Omer to meet with three pilots, two newly qualified from the Central Flying School in England. They were replacements for the squadron's lost pilots. With Perys and the third, more experienced, pilot, they would bring four Sopwith 'Pup' fighters back to Arras in order to bring the squadron up to almost full operational strength.

Perys spent twenty-four hours with the pilots,

briefing them on the situation at Arras and trying to instil in them some sense of the importance of flying as a tightly knit unit. In order to emphasise this he managed to fit in three hours in the air with them, practising formation flying.

The third pilot had served with the Royal Naval Air Service for two years. Answering an urgent call for experienced pilots to transfer to the RFC on either a temporary or permanent basis, he was to fill the flight commander vacancy in his new squadron.

After the day's flying practice was over, Perys met up with the new flight commander to discuss the role of the fighter squadrons and fill him in on details that would help him in his new duties.

They had been talking for some time when the naval pilot said, 'Actually, I heard news only this morning that almost makes me wonder whether I have done the right thing, or whether I might not have been of more use staying with the RNAS and taking on anti-submarine duties.'

'What brought on the doubts?' Perys asked, casually, more to make conversation than for any deep interest.

'All my belongings haven't arrived at Saint Omer, so I telephoned my old squadron at Calshot in Hampshire. The duty officer is an old friend. He told me that after the sinking of a hospital ship off Le Havre during the night, the squadron was out hunting the submarine that did it.'

The naval officer's information caused Perys to sit up and take an immediate interest. 'A hospital ship sunk off Le Havre? Do you know its name?'

Perys's sudden interest startled the naval officer. 'I

was told. It's something like . . . the S.S. *Sultan*, that's it . . .'

When Perys leaped to his feet, the naval pilot, alarmed, asked, 'Does it have particular significance?'

'Yes,' Perys said, grimly. 'One of the nursing sisters on board is my second cousin. She is also engaged to be married to Major Pilkington, your new commanding officer. Excuse me, I must get to a telephone.'

Leaving the shocked naval pilot staring after him, Perys hurried from the mess to the administrative section. There he was able to find a telephone. Less than ten minutes later he was talking to Rupert.

The squadron's commanding officer had not heard of the sinking of the hospital ship and was deeply distressed by the news. 'It's horrifying, Perys. Are you absolutely certain . . . ?'

'I am afraid there can be no mistake, Rupert. Navy aeroplanes have been out for most of the day searching for the submarine. Of course, it doesn't mean that anything will have happened to Morwenna . . .'

'Will you try to learn all you can about what happened, Perys? I can do little myself right now. The Canadians have taken Vimy Ridge and are holding it against fierce German counter-attacks. We're throwing in every aeroplane that can take to the air in order to help them.'

Reaching a swift decision, Perys said, 'Issue the daily orders for tomorrow, then take an aircraft up to Le Havre first thing and find out what's happening. I'll leave here with the new men at dawn. When I get to Arras I'll take over and run things until you get back. Don't come away from Le Havre until you have definite news of Morwenna. Leave me any instructions you feel are necessary and don't worry about the squadron. I took care of things when Thomas Kemp was killed and am bringing a good navy man to Arras with me as the new flight commander. Just get to Le Havre and stay there until you know that Morwenna is safe. I'll do all that's necessary at Arras.'

60

It was a very happy company of nurses and wounded soldiers who had boarded the hospital ship S.S. *Sultan* at Le Havre. For most of the soldiers, the war was over. Many had wounds that would affect their lives until the day they died, but for now this was not the most important consideration. They had survived. Many – far too many – of the men with whom they had gone into battle had not.

These men considered themselves to be among the lucky ones. They had journeyed to hell and beyond and had survived.

As medical orderlies carried stretcher cases into holds fitted out as spacious wards to receive them, nurses were kept busy ensuring that medical records for each patient were secured to the cot on which he was placed. If not, rough weather could cause havoc. One of the nurses was Morwenna – another was Grace.

A number of the men were being transferred to hospitals in England for specialised treatment. For such men the journey would be a particularly hazardous one and they would require constant attention from the nursing staff.

Eventually the bustle and confusion on the dockside began to subside until, at dusk, the last scheduled ambulance had departed and the hospital ship was almost ready to sail.

Looking out across the wide estuary of the River Seine, as she walked across the deck from the dispensary, Grace found it difficult to equate this mighty seaway with the river so beloved by Parisians, where she and Perys had strolled on their memorable first visit together to the French capital.

She had paused on the upper deck when Morwenna emerged from one of the cabins carrying a tray of clean dressings. Aware of the meetings Grace and Perys had enjoyed in Paris, she smiled at her friend. 'Let me guess. You are thinking of the Seine and its associations with Paris?'

Grace nodded. 'Paris – and Perys. I was wondering what he is doing right now.'

'Thinking of you, I expect,' Morwenna said. 'Do you think you will spend your honeymoon in Paris?'

Grace carried the letter from Perys in a pocket. It gave her a warm glow whenever she thought of it and she nodded. 'I would like that very much, Morwenna, especially if this war is over by then. Paris is a truly magical city in peacetime.'

At that moment a late ambulance drew up at the foot of the gangway to the ship. Two men emerged from the rear of the vehicle and turned back to help a third, who was supported by two crutches and had difficulty negotiating the step.

'I thought the last of the patients were already on board,' said Morwenna as the three men made their way slowly up the gangway. The leading man had lost the lower half of a leg and was obviously unused to using crutches.

'I'll go and help him,' Grace said, hurrying to the gangway.

Morwenna watched her for a few moments before going about her own business.

It was quite dark when the *Sultan* edged away from the Le Havre quayside and headed out of the harbour, nosing into the gentle swell of the estuary.

There was no black-out on the ship and no attempt at concealment. Huge boards on either side carried hundreds of red and white electric bulbs, forming the pattern of a red cross on a white background, indicating clearly that this was a hospital ship. In addition, spotlights had been rigged over the side to illuminate red crosses painted on the white hull.

The movement of the ship as it cleared the estuary was the cause of a great deal of hilarity on board. Nurses, in particular, had difficulty moving about, hampered as they were by their long skirts. There were loud cheers from their patients when they succeeded in successfully negotiating the length of an aisle between the beds.

However, by the time the ship had been ploughing through the swell for an hour, the men lying in their cots were beginning to find the movement of the ship less to their liking. When Grace went among them asking who would like a drink of cocoa, very few accepted her offer.

Grace had gone to the galley, situated amidships, to collect the cocoa for the hardy few when there was a violent explosion. She was thrown against a bulkhead and the ship shuddered as though struck a blow by a superhuman fist.

'What—?'

Before she could complete the sentence, the chef shouted, 'It's a torpedo. Quick . . . out on deck!'

Stumbling outside in the cool night air, Grace found a scene of frightened confusion. The ship was no longer underway and from somewhere below decks she could hear the sound of escaping steam and a great deal of shouting.

The ship's officers added to the noise by calling for crew members to swing out the lifeboats.

Miraculously, one of the first people Grace saw on deck was Morwenna.

'We've been torpedoed!' Morwenna shouted the news to her friend. She was in charge of the officers accommodated in the deck cabins, while Grace was the senior nurse in the forward hold.

Grace said, 'Yes, get your officers from the cabins to stand by the lifeboats. I'm going below to help bring my patients up on deck. Most are cot cases. Send any able-bodied men you can find to help me.'

They were the last words the friends would ever speak to each other.

Grace had disappeared below decks for no more than a minute when there was a second gigantic explosion, this time from the bows of the vessel. The *Sultan* seemed to rise in the air for a moment before settling down once more, but now the deck was sloping to one side and most of the lights on board had been extinguished.

Aware that the latest torpedo must have struck the ship in the vicinity of the forward hold where Grace had just gone, Morwenna ran to the hatch which was now minus the hood and framework erected to protect the entrance from the elements.

At the edge of the hatchway one of the ship's officers grabbed her arm. 'You can't go down there, miss. The ladder has been blown away.'

'But there are wounded men down there . . . and nurses.'

'I'm sorry, miss, listen for yourself.'

Above the pandemonium on deck and the cries of wounded men, Morwenna could hear the sound of rushing water. It came from beneath her feet. From the forward hold.

'There's nothing can be done for anyone down there, miss. You'd better be finding yourself a place in one of the lifeboats . . .'

Despite her horror at the knowledge that Grace must have been caught in the explosion, Morwenna still hoped that a miracle might have occurred . . . but now there was a great deal that needed to be done for those wounded men who had found their way out on deck.

The *Sultan* was settling in the water quickly and had developed a severe list, making it extremely difficult to fill and lower the lifeboats. Despite this, the surviving nurses, aided by doctors and crew, worked frantically in a bid to help the wounded men into boats.

One of the officers tried to persuade Morwenna to take a place in a lifeboat, but she brushed him aside. There were still many wounded men to be placed in the boats first.

She was busy at her task when there was a huge sigh of escaping steam and someone shouted, 'She's going down! Quick, get all boats away! Everyone else . . . into the water!'

There were no empty boats close to Morwenna, and one of the doctors nearby shouted, 'We'll be in the water in a minute. Get your cape and that skirt off or they'll take you under.'

When Morwenna hesitated, uncertainly, the doctor ripped the heavy cape from around her shoulders. Suddenly aware of the sense in what he had said, she swiftly unfastened her skirt as the ship began to roll over. She had a few moments of sheer panic as she tumbled from the stricken ship and cold water closed over her. Fighting her way to the surface, she trod water and sucked air into her lungs before becoming aware of the shouts about her. They were cries for help, but Morwenna was finding it difficult to remain afloat herself.

Suddenly, from nearby, someone shouted, 'Is there anyone here?'

'Yes . . . Help me!' Morwenna cried.

'Swim towards me. I'm on a grating of some sort . . . There's lots of room, but I can't make it go in any direction . . .'

Striking out towards the voice, Morwenna soon reached a wooden grating which was floating like a giant raft.

'I'm here . . . ! Here!'

A hand reached out for her and a few moments later she was hauled on board the grating. She lay gasping until her rescuer called for her to help him haul another survivor on board.

Morwenna was cold, wet and uncomfortable – but she was safe.

When morning came there were eight men and Morwenna on board the makeshift raft. They quickly discovered that one of the men had died during the night. After removing his identity disc, the body was dropped over the side, into the sea.

Even without the dead man the raft was still over-crowded and an occasional wave would wash over it, threatening to sweep the occupants away.

Now daylight had arrived those on board expected to be rescued quickly, but it was not to be. There was no sign of anything, or anyone, about them. They seemed to be alone on the water.

Close to midday they saw smoke that must have been pouring from the funnel of a ship, but it was so far away it was not even worth shouting in a bid to attract attention.

As the day wore on their hopes of being saved began to fade. Then, just when it seemed they were destined to spend another uncomfortable night on the raft, the survivors heard the throb of an engine. It gradually became louder and one of the men stood and shouted excitedly that it was a fishing boat.

For a few terrifying moments it seemed the boat would pass them by, but this time they *did* shout and one of the wounded men on board the raft removed his bright red hospital coat and handed it to a *Sultan* seaman. With two men holding his legs so he would

407

not overbalance and fall, the seaman stood up and frantically waved the coat, while others on the raft shouted as loudly as was humanly possible.

'They've not seen us. They're going past!'

Morwenna joined the men in their desperate shouting. Suddenly, a man came out of the fishing boat's wheelhouse and looked straight at them. A minute later the boat slowed, then turned back towards them.

Fifteen minutes later the desperately relieved survivors were on board the vessel, everyone talking excitedly at once. While coffee was being handed to them, one of the crew began preparing food.

They were safe.

Four days after the *Sultan* sailed from Le Havre with such high hopes held by all on board, Morwenna and the others who had been rescued from the raft returned to the French sea port.

The fishing boat which rescued them had taken them to a small fishing village, many kilometres along the coast. A message had been sent to the British military authorities that seven men and a woman from the torpedoed hospital ship had been rescued, but no names had been given to them.

All that was known was that they would be conveyed to the military hospital at Le Havre in two vehicles, a taxi-cab and an ambulance, both commandeered by the French police.

Rupert realised it was a forlorn hope that Morwenna would be the woman with the small party of survivors. Nevertheless, he was waiting at the hospital when the vehicles arrived.

The able-bodied men were first to alight from the taxi-cab, then three wounded men were helped from the ambulance. They were accompanied by a woman who backed out of the ambulance, directing the hospital orderlies as they lifted a soldier in a stretcher from the vehicle.

Rupert's hopes fell when he first saw her. Dressed in a rough-woven brown dress, her hair tied loosely at the back of her neck, it seemed she was a peasant woman.

Then the woman turned towards him and he recognised Morwenna.

Calling her name he pushed his way past two startled French policemen as she ran towards him. A moment later he was holding her and, suddenly, all the stoicism she had shown during recent days disappeared. Clinging tightly to Rupert, Morwenna broke down in tears.

61

Perys would always look back upon April 1917 as the worst month of his life. For a couple of weeks after the sinking of the *Sultan* he clung to the hope that Grace might have survived, perhaps been picked up by a German vessel and her rescue not yet reported.

As time passed his optimism faded. It left him altogether when he put through a telephone call to Major General Ballard at the War Office in London, to ask if he had heard anything of Grace.

General Ballard's reply was sombre. Sir Giles had many friends in neutral embassies in London, through one of which he had made enquiries in Berlin. They revealed that due to a strong British naval presence in the area after the sinking of the hospital ship, German vessels had given the waters off Le Havre a wide berth. Furthermore, the submarine responsible for sinking the hospital ship had not surfaced to rescue survivors and had since returned to its base.

There was no possibility that Grace might have survived. She, together with eight other women of the Queen Alexandra's Imperial Military Nursing Service, were deemed to be dead.

The loss of Grace filled Perys with a burning determination to avenge her death. The day after the telephone call to General Ballard, when he took his flight out on a patrol, they met up with four German Fokkers.

In the fierce fight that followed, all four German aeroplanes were shot down without loss to his own flight, Perys claiming two victories for himself.

Afterwards, in the mess back at the Arras airfield, while Perys was making a report to Rupert, one of the new young pilots who had been in the flight spoke of his thoughts while the aerial combat was taking place. He declared that Perys had fought with such a reckless ferocity that it had come close to unnerving him.

'You are lucky to have such a flight commander, take it from me,' said one of the few pilots to have been with the squadron since its early days. 'The worst type of flight commander you can have is one who is *not* a hundred per cent ferocious in combat. We took on four Huns today, shot them down, and all of us came back. That's the sort of man I will always be happy to follow into combat.'

Perys's champion was not alone in recognising his skill both as a fighter pilot and flight leader. Three weeks later, after Perys had succeeded in downing three more German aircraft, he was told he had been

411

awarded a Distinguished Service Order.

Although the RFC frowned upon the appellation of 'Ace', given to some of their flyers by the Press, Perys was rapidly establishing himself as one of their most successful pilots.

Soon after the announcement of the award, Rupert sent for Perys, who entered the office fresh from a sortie in which his flight had destroyed another three German aircraft.

Rupert listened to Perys's report in silence before sitting back in his chair and smiling at his second cousin.

'You have done exceptionally well recently, Perys. So well that your exploits are being reported in the British newspapers. In due course you will be going home to receive your DSO from a very senior RFC officer, and as a result of the publicity you're getting you'll probably be fighting off the newspaper reporters.'

Perys showed his discomfiture when he said, 'If it's all the same to you, Rupert, I would like to forego all the ballyhoo. Can't you arrange to make the award yourself – preferably over a drink in the mess?'

Rupert smiled at him. 'I am sorry, Perys, but you're something of a celebrity – and the British public have need of a hero right now. But look on the bright side. Your photograph will be plastered over the front pages of all the newspapers and you'll not be allowed to pay for a drink anywhere in London! Besides, that's where I want you to be as soon as we're into winter and the weather curtails flying. Morwenna and I want to marry before the year is out. Your presence at the ceremony is an essential part of our plan.'

'You want me to be your best man?' Perys was surprised; Rupert knew so many men of note that he felt quite certain he could find someone with a title, at least, to perform the duty for him.

'Not my best man, Perys – although you *were* my first choice. Morwenna has different ideas. She wants you to take her up the aisle and hand her over to me.'

It was a duty that would have been performed by Morwenna's father, had he been alive. Perys was deeply touched that Morwenna should want him to take his place.

'That's an honour I shall be delighted to perform, Rupert,' he said, honestly. 'Have you settled on an actual date yet?'

'We need to keep it fairly flexible and hope everything will come together at the right time. It will be easier now that Morwenna has been given a home posting after two years in front-line hospitals. It's largely a result of her ordeal when the *Sultan* was sunk, of course. She is being posted to a convalescent home and has applied to be sent to Heligan. The nursing corps is reluctant to send married nurses to operational areas, so it means Morwenna should be safe for however long the war lasts – although I can see no end to it just yet . . .'

'No.'

Perys thought unhappily that *his* proposal of marriage had come too late to save Grace. He had not yet spoken to Morwenna and was not even certain his letter had reached Grace before she boarded the ill-fated *Sultan*.

Aware that his mention of the hospital ship had

stirred up unhappy thoughts, Rupert rose to his feet and said, 'Right, Perys, let's go across to the mess. I'll let you buy me a Scotch to celebrate the news of my forthcoming wedding.'

62

Circumstances decreed that Perys was not officially presented with his Distinguished Service Order until January 1918, at a ceremony in London. Rupert's wedding to Morwenna took place three days afterwards.

The couple were married in a Knightsbridge church, where, for the first time, Perys met with Rupert's parents and other members of the Tremayne family from whom he had been isolated for so long.

In the main he was greeted warmly, although one or two of the older family members maintained a certain coolness towards him.

Perys's main regret was that the elusive Hugh Tremayne, owner of Heligan, was not present. He would have liked to thank him for allowing him to stay at Heligan whenever an opportunity arose. Unfortunately, his great-uncle was currently in Ireland and probably not even aware of the hastily arranged marriage of Rupert and Morwenna.

The wedding itself was a very happy occasion. Arabella, now engaged to her young Scots doctor, made a beautiful bridesmaid and Maude was as proud as any mother could be of both her daughter and her new son-in-law.

Morwenna had managed to shake off the distress she had suffered during the weeks and months following the sinking of the *Sultan*, but she had not forgotten. When she said goodbye to Perys after the wedding reception, tears sprang to her eyes when she said, 'My dearest wish is that Grace could have been here today, Perys. That would have made everything absolutely perfect.'

'Everything *is* absolutely perfect for you and Rupert, Morwenna. Grace would have wished, as I do, that it will always be that way for both of you.'

Rupert and his bride would be spending a few days at a hotel in East Anglia for their honeymoon. Meanwhile, while he was in England, Perys intended visiting as many of the properties ceded to him by his grandfather as possible.

In Cornwall he would stay at Heligan, but had already decided he would still not disclose to the Brays that he was now the landlord of their farm.

As Perys rode his motor-cycle along the driveway leading to Heligan House late in the afternoon, it was as much a homecoming as any he had ever known, yet nothing was the same as it had been on that first occasion, more than three years before, when he had arrived in the Tremayne coach.

Then, gardeners and labourers had doffed their caps to the carriage in which he was travelling. Now, the occasional convalescent officer, wearing the regulation blue coat, gave him a curious stare as he rode past.

He was mildly surprised that no one came out to greet him, but this was not entirely unexpected. Heligan was no longer solely the home of a frequently absent country squire with servants whose sole purpose in life was to pander to the needs of any member of the family who came visiting. It was a convalescent home, where the needs of recuperating officers were paramount.

Besides, in his telephone conversation with the housekeeper, Perys had said only that he would be arriving today. He had not given a time and was, in fact, rather earlier than might have been anticipated.

He carried his bag of luggage through to the room which was all prepared for his arrival and then set off for the kitchen in the hope of obtaining a cup of tea.

In a passageway he met with a young servant girl whom he recognised as having been a thirteen-year-old newcomer to the house during the time he was at Heligan recovering from his aeroplane crash.

She dropped him a surprised curtsey but would have hurried on had he not called her back. 'Where is everyone? You are the first servant I have seen.'

'The housekeeper is having a meeting with the nurse in charge and most of the servants are preparing rooms for a new batch of officers who are coming in today, sir.'

'Is Polly busy at the moment? I would like to speak to her.'

Unexpectedly, the young girl's eyes filled with tears. 'Polly isn't working today, sir. She's staying at Tregassick Farm for a while.'

Alarmed by the maid's reaction to his question, Perys realised immediately that Polly's absence must be connected with Martin, who was now serving as an observer with a bomber squadron based in France.

Fearing her reply, Perys asked the girl, 'What's the matter with Polly? Has something happened to Martin?'

'Yes, sir. She had a telegram yesterday afternoon. Martin has been reported missing, believed killed. Everyone's very upset about it, him having worked here for so long before he went to war.'

'Of course . . . I am very upset myself – but we mustn't give up hope yet, believe me. There are so many reasons why he might not have returned to his airfield.'

Perys was far less optimistic than he hoped he might sound. In the vast majority of cases a missing flyer turned out to be a dead flyer – yet he desperately wanted Martin to be one of the fortunate ones.

Making a sudden decision, he said to the girl, 'When you see the housekeeper, tell her I've arrived and will be back in the house later this evening. I am going to Tregassick Farm.'

63

The sound of Perys's motor-cycle entering the Tregassick farmyard brought Harriet Bray hurrying from the house. When she saw who it was she asked, apprehensively, 'Have you come—? Do you have news of Martin?'

'No. I only arrived at Heligan a short while ago and was told the news. I came straight here to see how Polly is and to ask if I might help in any way.'

Harriet looked desperately tired and Perys thought she had been crying very recently. She explained, 'All we know is what was in the telegram. Martin is missing, believed dead.'

Perys thought that in view of the recent heavy casualties suffered by the army and the Royal Flying Corps, it was all she was likely to hear for some time.

Squadron commanders would write to the next-of-kin of squadron members killed in action, but *when* they wrote the letters depended very much on how many men had been lost and how busy the commanding officer was. Martin's bomber squadron was likely to be heavily engaged in the current offensive.

'How has Polly taken the news?' Perys asked.

'She's asleep right now. I think she's exhausted herself with weeping.'

'I'm so sorry.' Perys had not been invited inside the farmhouse, but he was aware that at such a time as this the family would not wish to share their grief with an outsider. 'Please tell her I will try to find out more for her – and for you, of course.'

'Thank you. Now, if you'll excuse me I'll go back inside the house in case Polly wakes.'

Perys wheeled his motor-cycle well clear of the farm before starting it, in order not to wake Polly. He returned slowly to Heligan, trying to think what he could possibly do to make good the promise he had just made to Harriet Bray.

His first telephone call was to the War Office in London. He was fortunate enough to speak to an officer who was both sympathetic and also familiar with the manner in which the news of men who died behind German lines, or were taken prisoner by them, was notified to the War Office.

Unfortunately, the numbers of dead had reached such proportions that the system had been completely overwhelmed; so too with those who had fallen into German hands.

However, when Perys mentioned that the man in question was a Royal Flying Corps observer, the War Office spokesman said the fate of flyers was usually known much more quickly than that of infantrymen.

When Perys asked that Major General Sir Giles

Ballard be informed of his interest in the fate of Martin Bray, the War Office spokesman became even more helpful.

Next, Perys put a telephone call through to the acting commanding officer of his own squadron at Arras. This took much longer, it being almost two hours before he was successful. However, once the link was established, the officer promised to contact Martin's squadron and find out what he could about the mission on which he had been reported missing.

By the time his telephone calls had ended there was time only for Perys to enjoy a late evening meal and go to bed wondering what the next day would bring.

The acting commander of Perys's squadron was the first to telephone Heligan. He was able to tell Perys that Martin's squadron had been bombing a busy railway junction some miles behind the German lines. The aircraft had successfully completed their mission, but were surprised on the way back by an unusually large number of German fighter planes.

During the battle five British aircraft were lost, Martin's being one of them. Two had gone down in flames but it had been impossible to identify the particular aircraft at the time.

The prospects of Martin having survived were not looking good.

Then, shortly before five o'clock that afternoon, Perys received a telephone call from the helpful officer at the War Office. Identifying himself to Perys, he asked, 'This observer you were asking about, will you confirm that his first name is Martin and that he was flying with twenty-two squadron?'

'That's correct – you have news of him?'

'Yes, we received it here only some twenty minutes or so ago. He and his pilot were brought down inside the German lines. The pilot was quite badly hurt, but Bray seems to have suffered only minor injuries. At the moment he is in a prisoner-of-war transit camp at Le Cateau. He'll no doubt be transferred to a permanent camp in Germany very shortly.'

'Knowing he is alive is wonderful news!' Perys was highly elated. 'You are quite certain of this? There can be no doubt . . . ?'

'None at all. I have his service number here if you would like to check it, but only seven RFC men are on the list that came through – four dead and three prisoners. He is one of the lucky ones.'

After thanking the officer at the other end of the telephone, Perys's first thought was to rush out of the house, jump on his motor-cycle and hurry to Tregassick to break the news to Polly and the Bray family.

Then he remembered that one of the convalescent officers, a motor-cycle enthusiast, had suggested Perys's motor-cycle was in need of a 'de-coke' and had offered to carry out the task for him. The machine would not be back together until nightfall.

Perys felt unable to keep the news he had received to himself until then. He decided to hurry to Tregassick on foot to tell them what he knew.

When he reached the farmhouse there was no one in the yard, but the front door was wide open. Stepping inside to the small hallway, he called, 'Hello . . . Is anyone at home?'

When he received no immediate reply, he went

farther inside the house, and was heading along the passageway that led to the kitchen when the door opened and he was confronted by Harriet.

'I thought I heard someone . . .' Tremulously, she added, 'What is it, Master Perys? Have you had news of Martin?'

Suddenly, Polly appeared behind her and her fear was apparent. It would have been cruel to keep either woman in suspense for any longer than was necessary.

'Yes . . . and it's *good* news. I've just had a telephone call from the War Office. Martin is alive and well. He's been taken prisoner by the Germans, but he's safe and uninjured. You have no need to worry about him any more. As far as he is concerned, his war is over.'

Harriet turned to Polly, but the Heligan housemaid pushed past her and confronted Perys anxiously. 'Are you quite sure? There can be no mistake?'

'None at all, Polly. The telephone call came to Heligan and I hurried straight here. Martin is in a transit prisoner-of-war camp in France right now but in a day or two he'll be transferred to a permanent camp, probably in Germany. When he arrives there you'll have official notification giving you an address where you can write to him – and he'll be able to write to you.'

A variety of conflicting expressions fought for supremacy on Polly's face, then, suddenly, she flung herself at him and between tears cried, 'Thank you, Perys . . . Oh, thank you!'

'It's all right, Polly,' he said, in a bid to comfort her. 'Believe me, I am almost as delighted as you at the news. I couldn't wait to get here to let you know.'

Breaking away from him, Polly ran to Harriet and the two women clung to each other, tears of joy and relief running unchecked down their cheeks.

64

Perys left the two women debating which of them should run down the valley to the field where Walter Bray was working to break the good news to him.

He was taking a short cut across the fields to Heligan when the cottages of Polly and Annie came into view, standing side-by-side at the edge of a small wood. He realised that Annie too must be very upset about her brother. He decided he would call in and break the good news to her before returning to Heligan.

When he reached the cottages he stopped, uncertain which of them was Annie's. While he was trying to make up his mind, one of the doors opened and Annie herself stood in the doorway.

'Perys! What are you doing here? Do you have some news of Martin . . . ?' Her expression was one of fear, as that of her mother had been.

'It's all right, Annie, he's been taken prisoner by the Germans, but he's safe and well.'

'Oh! Oh, thank God! I have been so worried about him.'

She put out a hand to support herself against the door frame. She appeared so shaken that Perys moved closer. Concerned, he asked anxiously, 'Are you all right, Annie?'

'Yes . . . Yes. It's just . . . I've been trying not to think the worst, these last couple of days, yet whatever I did, I've been unable to think anything else.' Trying valiantly to fight back tears, she asked, 'Do Ma and Polly know?'

'Yes, I've just come from Tregassick.'

'I'll go there to see them in a few minutes.' Gesturing towards the cottage she had just left, she said, 'This is Martin and Polly's place. I live next door but found it so difficult to settle down to anything I came in here to tidy up. Polly hasn't been home since she heard.'

A stray thought came to Annie and she asked, 'How did you find out about Martin before Polly did?'

'I made a few telephone calls, to France and also to the War Office in London. Someone from there telephoned me back a short while ago and I went straight to Tregassick. I was on my way back to Heligan when I realised that you would be concerned about Martin too.'

'That was very thoughtful of you, Perys. It really is wonderful news. I . . . I . . .' Suddenly, Annie began to cry. She reached inside one of her sleeves, apparently seeking a handkerchief.

When she failed to find one, Perys pulled one from a pocket and stepped forward to give it to her. 'Here!'

Taking it from him she held it up to her eyes,

saying, 'I'm sorry, Perys. I . . . I just didn't realise what a strain it has been, worrying about Martin.'

'There is no need to apologise to me, Annie. I was very concerned about him myself.'

She looked up at him as he stood close. Their eyes met – and they held the glance. Perys experienced the same feeling that had come over him more than three years before, when they had fallen off Rupert's motor-cycle together.

He responded to it now as he had then. Taking a step forward he put his arms about Annie and kissed her.

He was never certain afterwards whether or not she responded initially. If she did, it did not last for long. Suddenly she began struggling against him. When he failed to release her immediately her struggles became more violent until she eventually broke free.

Pushing him away, she said angrily, 'What do you think you are doing, Perys? Why did you do that?'

'Why? I thought . . .' He broke off, lamely. There was nothing he might say that would justify what he had just done, but he tried. '. . . I suddenly remembered the time when we fell off the motor-bike together . . .'

'That was different. *Very* different. I wasn't a married woman then.' Still angry, she added, '*Was* that why you did it – or was it because you thought I'd be so grateful for what you'd told me about Martin that I'd behave as Eliza would? Perhaps Pa wasn't so very wrong about what he thought he saw you and her doing!'

'That isn't fair, Annie—'

'Fair? Is it fair to kiss a married woman in the hope that she'll show some gratitude for receiving news that her brother is alive? Is it?'

Annie's rage was so fierce and unexpected it dismayed Perys, but she had not finished with him yet.

'Quite apart from your lack of respect for me, it doesn't say much for the respect you have for the girl you are going to marry . . . Grace, isn't it?'

Perys realised she knew nothing of what had happened to Grace.

'What would she say if she knew what you had just done? What would *you* do if I was to tell her?'

Perys looked at Annie in silence for a few moments before saying, quietly, 'I only wish you were *able* to tell her, Annie. You see, she was reported missing last year when the hospital ship on which she was serving was torpedoed. Unlike Martin, she was never found.'

Turning away, he hurried off in the direction of Heligan before Annie could see how distressed he was – by everything.

Watching him walking away from her, Annie was almost equally upset. She realised her reaction to his kiss had been out of all proportion to the deed. She was aware also that her anger was directed as much against herself as at Perys. When he had held her she too had remembered the time they fell off the motorcycle together.

And as on that occasion, she had *wanted* Perys to kiss her. Her anger had stemmed from her own sense of guilt and confusion.

Turning, she ran back inside Polly's house. She would not be able to face Jimmy just yet, and knew she would need to compose herself before her mother came to tell her about Martin, as she surely would.

The following morning Polly called at the cottage to put on her maid's uniform and tell Annie she was returning to work at Heligan. She still looked pale and wan after the trauma of the past few days, but was happy in the knowledge that Martin was safe, albeit a prisoner of the Germans.

'I want to thank Perys properly too, for finding out about Martin so quickly,' she said. 'Fancy him telephoning all the way to France and London to ask about him. If it hadn't been for Perys we probably wouldn't have heard anything for weeks – and I could have been dead from a broken heart by then. Your ma said Perys even called here to tell you the good news before he went back to Heligan last night.'

'That's right, he caught me here when I'd just finished tidying up your place. I'm afraid I didn't quite appreciate how much trouble he'd put himself to in finding out about Martin.'

'He thinks a lot of Martin,' Polly said. She was in a happy, chatting mood today. 'He always has, when I come to think about it, right from the day when he stood up for him against Master Edward. Perys says Martin is probably the best observer he has ever had – and certainly the best gunner. Martin thinks a lot of Perys, too. He says he's one of the best pilots in the whole of the Royal Flying Corps. Mind you, Martin says that because Perys is always in the thick of the fighting, he would never be surprised if he heard one day that Perys had been shot down.'

Polly was retying a shoelace as she was speaking

and never saw the distress her words caused to Annie. Her task completed, she stood up. 'If I'm perfectly honest, Annie, although I don't like to think of Martin being locked up in a prisoner-of-war camp, I'm glad he's out of the fighting. Ever since he went back to France, after we were married, I'd wake every morning dreading that I'd get the telegram that came on Monday . . . But I'd better be getting off to work now there's no longer a reason for me to stay home.'

Later that day, Annie took Jimmy to Tregassick. He was now able to carry out certain tasks about the farm. He could milk the cows once they had been brought in, help with making cheese, and feed the chickens, geese and some of the other animals. He was also able to sharpen many of the tools in use on the farm.

He seemed to enjoy making a contribution, but when his mother came visiting she complained bitterly that the Brays were taking advantage of her son's disabilities and using him as 'cheap labour'.

However, Winnie Rowe was not at the farm today and all went well. Annie and Jimmy remained there all day, and were still there that evening when Polly came to the farm for supper. She had finished work at Heligan early, the usually stern housekeeper sending her home because she looked 'wisht'.

Not unnaturally, much of the conversation was of Martin, his family wondering what he was doing at the very moment they sat down for a meal together.

It was Annie who suddenly came up with an idea, as though it had just occurred to her. 'I know, why don't we invite Perys to come and have a meal here with us? He's seen far more of Martin than we have during the war years. He'd be able to tell us at first hand something of Martin's life in the Flying Corps, and what he's likely to be doing in the prisoner-of-war camp.'

'Invite one of the squire's family here to Tregassick to eat with us?' Walter Bray looked at his daughter in disbelief. 'What are you thinking of, girl?'

'You're living in the past, Pa. The war has changed things. Perys has already been to the house to eat with us – the last time was after he'd been Martin's best man. I'm sure he'd love to come. He'd certainly enjoy it much more than eating on his own up at the big house.'

'It doesn't really make any difference whether or not he'd like to come here,' said Polly. 'He's not at Heligan any more. He left this morning, saying it was time he got back to his squadron in France. I doubt if we'll see him at Heligan until the war's over – if we see him then. He'll have no reason to come.'

Of those sitting around the table, only Harriet saw the look of dismay that crossed Annie's face for a fleeting moment. She shifted her glance to Jimmy, who was spooning food into his mouth, seemingly oblivious of the conversation being carried on about him.

Harriet thought of all that had occurred after the first visit of Perys to Heligan. She would not have wished upon Annie the life she now had, but felt it might have become far more complicated for everyone around the table had Perys chosen to remain in Cornwall for a while instead of returning to his squadron.

65

Perys was a confused and unhappy man when he rode away from Heligan. He accepted that his behaviour towards Annie had been unforgivable. She *was* a married woman and she had a husband who had been blinded and disabled in the service of his country.

But he was also confused about his feelings when he was holding Annie. He had believed himself to be in love with Grace. Had she lived they would have married, and he was convinced they would have been very, very happy.

Yet when he held Annie outside Polly's cottage he felt an emotion he had known only once before – when he had kissed her all those years ago.

For a moment the previous evening he had imagined Annie might have felt the same way, but she had made it very clear that this was not so.

Perhaps it was fortunate for both of them. Had she shown him the slightest encouragement they would

have become involved in an affair that would ulti-
mately have destroyed their respect for each other.

By the time Perys arrived at the Central Flying
School, he had made up his mind to put the incident
– and Annie – behind him once and for all, and to
concentrate on the thing he did best – flying a fighter
plane in combat against the Germans.

He had hoped the Central Flying School might have
had an aeroplane for him to fly to St Omer, but he
was out of luck. He was issued with a travel warrant
to return to France by train and ferry.

After depositing his motor-cycle at Aunt Maude's
London home and spending a night there, he made
his way to Victoria station to catch the afternoon train
to Dover. From there he would board the night ferry
to Boulogne. It was likely to be a cold crossing. Snow
was falling in London and the sky gave every indication of more to come.

The train was already standing at the platform and
he settled himself in a first-class compartment with
only two elderly nuns as his travelling companions.

The whistle had just sounded for the train to move
off when Perys heard the sound of running feet on
the platform. The next moment, the door was thrown
open by an officer wearing the uniform of a lieutenant
colonel in the Royal Artillery.

Sliding a suitcase inside the compartment, he held
the door open to allow a young woman to scramble
inside. Then, as the train jerked into motion, the door
was slammed shut behind her.

Ignoring the disapproving looks of the nuns, the
young woman opened the window and, as the train
gathered speed, blew kisses to the artillery officer and

waved until the rails curved away from the platform and the station disappeared from view. Then she tried to close the window, but she had problems with the leather strap with which it was pulled up. Perys went to her rescue and by the time he succeeded in closing the window she had sat down opposite the seat he was occupying.

She had also left her suitcase on the floor. Anticipating her request, Perys lifted it to the rack above her head.

'*Merci, Monsieur Captain* . . . I thank you. You are very kind.'

She spoke English well, but with a strong French accent that he found quite charming.

'I see you are a pilot, Captain – and a *brave* pilot. You are going back to the war?'

The young woman smiled at him, ignoring the quite evident disapproval of the two nuns for her forwardness.

'I am,' he replied.

'Ah! It is so sad. My friend . . . the colonel. He too was in the war. Now he is teaching others to fight, here in England. He invited me to London for a few days. It is a *wonderful* city and we had great fun. It is good to be away from the war for a while, is it not?'

Perys agreed that it was. He guessed that the lieutenant colonel must have paid the young woman's fare. Her clothes were not those of someone used to first-class travel. Indeed, they were unsuitable for the present cold weather. She wore only a lightweight coat over a simple and not particularly warm dress.

During the journey to Dover, Perys learned that her

434

name was Gabrielle and that she lived in the town of Amiens, where Perys had taken the pilots of his squadron to celebrate the gift of money and property he had received from his grandfather.

Gabrielle was due to catch the same night ferry as Perys and she chattered quite happily all the way to Dover.

In view of the fact that they had travelled together on the train and would both be boarding the same ferry, it seemed natural for Gabrielle and Perys to remain together and that he should pay for a meal for her before boarding the dimly lit boat.

The temperature dropped even further with nightfall, and once on board the ferry it was immediately apparent there was a heating problem in the lounge where they sat on a padded leather seat.

It was not long before Perys became aware that Gabrielle was shivering. He was wearing a greatcoat and, standing up, he removed it and gave it to her. 'Here, it is not exactly chic, but it will keep you warm.'

'But no! I cannot take it. If I do, *you* will be cold.'

Despite her words, she shivered again, this time more violently, and she said, 'If you insist, we will *share* your coat. Come, sit. I will cuddle up close and it will keep us both warm.'

Perys sat rather stiffly beside her and she smiled up at him. 'I think it will be better if you put an arm about me so I can cuddle closer. Otherwise your coat will not cover all of both of us.'

Perys followed her suggestion without protest, aware of envious looks from the many other officers in the lounge. As Gabrielle snuggled up to him he was very aware of her perfume. He knew little of such

435

things, but felt it was probably one of the more expensive makes.

Once the cross-Channel ferry nosed out into the waters of the English Channel, the other passengers soon lost all interest in Perys and Gabrielle. The sea was rough and those who were bad sailors were soon in trouble.

Perys was not particularly uncomfortable with the motion of the vessel and his only concern was to keep a tight hold on Gabrielle.

The French girl was so indifferent to the weather conditions that she fell asleep. Without Perys's support she would probably have fallen from the padded bench seat.

The journey to Boulogne took almost three hours, by which time conditions in the lounge had deteriorated considerably as more and more passengers succumbed to violent movements of the ferry.

None of this made any difference to Gabrielle. When Boulogne was reached and the ferry was sailing in more sheltered waters, Perys had to wake her.

'We are there . . . so soon?' Seemingly reluctant to move, she smiled up at him. 'I felt very safe with you, Captain Perys.' Sitting up, she produced a powder compact, looked at herself in the small mirror and gave a sound of disapproval. 'I look terrible!'

Making no attempt to do anything about 'looking terrible', she closed the compact and put it away. Smiling at him once more, she said, 'You have been very kind, and a charming companion.'

He left the ship with her, carrying her suitcase in addition to his own bag, and as they walked to the station, she asked, 'Have you ever been to Amiens?'

'Once. I went there with the pilots of my squadron.' Amiens was, in fact, on the same railway route as Arras, but he would not be travelling directly to the Arras airfield. He first needed to go to St Omer, to report his arrival and possibly pick up a replacement aeroplane to take to his squadron.

'You must come to Amiens to see me . . . please! You will find me at the Restaurant Eugenie. It is where you will enjoy the best food and entertainment.'

'Thank you, I will try to pay you a visit,' he promised.

The warmth of her farewell when they reached her train quite literally took his breath away, and as she waved to him from an open carriage, he grinned, remembering she had been equally effusive when waving farewell to the artillery colonel at Victoria station.

66

Gabrielle was quickly forgotten when Perys returned to his squadron and picked up the routine once more. Rupert would not be returning for a while as he was attending a senior officers' course in England.

Meanwhile, new tactics were being planned for the next phase in the air war – and it was becoming increasingly apparent that they were necessary. The Germans were making a determined attempt to regain control of the air over the front-lines, seemingly able to concentrate large numbers of aircraft in specific areas at will. Perys's squadron had already been involved in some savage fighting with German planes.

To counter this very effective tactic, the RFC began carrying out their raids over enemy territory with fighter escorts in similar strength, making whatever odds they were likely to meet more even.

Then, in March 1918, while the British and French generals were trying to reach agreement on the next attempt to break the stalemate in the war, the Germans took the initiative and launched a major offensive. They attacked on a wide front that encompassed the former Somme battlefield south of Arras.

So successful and unexpected was this attack that the German armies fought their way forward for some forty miles before being brought to a halt. They stopped not so much as a result of the efforts of the opposing armies, but because they had advanced faster than their supplies could keep pace. This was due largely to the state of the ground over which they had to be carried. It was a landscape of mud and water-filled craters, the result of more than three years of constant warfare.

Nevertheless, the German advance caused a great deal of panic on the British-held side of the front-line. A number of airfields were hastily evacuated for safety.

Perys's squadron moved first to St Pol, then, when the German advance ground to a halt, it was resited on an airfield a few miles to the west of Amiens.

For a while, the fighting on the ground almost ceased as the Germans sought to consolidate their gains, but in the air it increased in intensity, both sides suffering heavy losses in men and machines.

In April 1918 one of the greatest pilots of the war was killed. German 'Ace' Baron Manfred von Richthofen, with eighty confirmed victories to his name, was himself shot down.

Not until late May did a spell of bad weather bring about a temporary lull in the savage air war.

Rupert had returned to the squadron some weeks before and he now decided the pilots of his squadron should have a night out together – in Amiens.

The idea was put to them over lunch and it received an enthusiastic response.

'Good!' declared Rupert. 'I'll lay on the transport, but does anyone know Amiens? Is there somewhere we could be guaranteed a good evening?'

There was silence for a few moments, then Perys remembered Gabrielle. 'Does anyone know the Restaurant Eugenie?' he asked.

His question provoked shouts and whistles from a number of the pilots and one of the young lieutenants commented, 'It's probably the best-known restaurant in this part of France. Good food, fine wine, hot music – and even hotter women!'

The acclaim that greeted this assessment of the Restaurant Eugenie decided the issue.

'Right,' Rupert said, 'I will telephone the restaurant now and make sure they can accommodate thirty noisy, thirsty pilots.' Giving Perys a quizzical look, he added, 'One day you can tell me how you learned of such an establishment.'

The pilots travelled to Amiens in two lorries, into which Rupert had thoughtfully placed a number of crates of beer.

He travelled in the cab of one of the lorries and, as senior flight commander, Perys travelled in the other. The laughter and singing in the back of both vehicles was an indication that the pilots intended taking full advantage of this rare opportunity to enjoy a celebration.

Had anyone asked them what they were celebrating, they would have received thirty different answers. The only reply that would not have been given was the true one. They were celebrating the fact they were still alive.

It was enough.

The lorries drew to a halt outside the Restaurant Eugenie and the pilots quickly crowded inside. It was a large establishment by French provincial standards, with a stage on which was assembled a sizeable band. It also boasted a well-stocked bar and a restaurant area in which a number of tables stood empty, awaiting the arrival of the English pilots.

There was also a disproportionate number of waitresses and 'hostesses'. Dressed provocatively, the latter were eager to share the tables of the pilots and accept drinks which contained very little alcohol, but for which they would receive commission from the restaurant owner.

Perys expected to find Gabrielle among these women, but she was nowhere to be seen. He shared a table with Rupert, the naval flight commander and one of the senior squadron pilots.

It was about fifteen minutes after they arrived that Perys looked up and saw Gabrielle enter the restaurant from a door at the back of the room. She was dressed, not as a hostess, but in a shimmering, pale blue, shoulderless evening dress.

Her entrance was the signal for applause from the restaurant's customers, but Gabrielle had seen Perys. Hurrying across the room towards him, she cried, 'Captain Perys! How wonderful to see you.' Giving him a hug, she presented both cheeks for him to kiss, then beamed at the others. 'And these are all your friends . . .'

She encompassed the other pilots with an expansive gesture, smiling at the remarks they were throwing in Perys's direction as a result of the familiarity she had shown towards him.

Speaking to Perys, she said, 'I will sing my first song especially for you. Afterwards, I will sing for your friends.'

It was apparent that Gabrielle was very popular with the customers of the restaurant. A few minutes later, Perys understood why. She had a fine, rich voice that charmed Frenchmen and Englishmen alike.

She sang for perhaps half-an-hour, mixing English and French songs, much to the delight of her audience. When she eventually left the stage to great applause, she came to Perys's table and sat beside him, giving him a degree of attention that made him the envy of his RFC colleagues.

Perys and Gabrielle chatted for a while before she said to him, 'Captain Perys, it is so hot in here, would you mind if we went to the garden at the rear of the restaurant? It is where we eat in the summer, but the weather is not yet suitable.'

The couple walked to the French doors at the rear of the restaurant, ignoring the raucous and envious shouts of the pilots, who were consuming wine in vast quantities.

Behind the restaurant they entered a very pleasant enclosed and paved garden. Closing the door behind them, Gabrielle turned to Perys. 'I am so happy to see you again. Ever since we parted at Boulogne I have wondered what you were doing. I hoped we would meet again one day – and now here you are.'

As she spoke she moved closer to him until she

was looking up into his face. Then, putting her arms about his neck, she kissed him full on the lips. However, when he began to respond, she suddenly moved away.

'No, Perys, not here and now. I must go back inside and sing once more in a few minutes. Afterwards I will go home. When you see me leave the restaurant, follow me, but do not attempt to speak to me. I will lead you to my home. Once inside the house – ah! There will be no one to see us. Such precautions are for my reputation, you understand?'

'Of course.'

Gabrielle was a very attractive woman, Perys had no ties, and he had come to Amiens half-hoping to meet with her again.

At that moment, the door through which they had left the restaurant was flung open and a thin, sharp-featured woman stood in the doorway. She gave Perys a withering look, but when she spoke it was to Gabrielle, and in French.

'What are you doing out here with the Englishman? Do you have no shame?'

'You are early tonight!' Gabrielle replied, also in French. 'I have sung once and came out here to breathe in some fresh air. Had I remained inside I would have been able to do no more than croak like a frog when the time came to sing again.'

'Is it necessary that you must always have a man with you when you come out into the garden – and that it should be an Englishman?'

'The English officer is not a complete stranger. We met when I was returning to Amiens after my last visit to my mother in Paris. Surely I told you about it? It was in that very cold weather. The train had no heating, I was shivering and the gallant captain loaned me his greatcoat. He is a true gentleman – and he is a hero, look at his medals.'

The thin woman looked at Perys suspiciously and said, bitterly, 'My son is a hero too, but now he lies at home in bed, more like a vegetable than a man.'

Although he had been taken aback by Gabrielle's lies about where they had first met, he said, in perfect French, 'I am sorry to hear of your son, madame. This war has destroyed the lives of far too many men, but what Gabrielle says is quite true, we have met before. It was then she said that if ever I was in Amiens I must pay a visit to the Restaurant Eugenie. My squadron recently moved here, so when my friends decided we must have a party, I thought it should be here. When Gabrielle and I met again we chatted, but there was so much smoke in the restaurant she needed to come out here for some air before she sang again. It was my idea that I should accompany her.'

The woman looked at Perys intently for a few moments, then, apparently satisfied, she nodded. 'It is almost time for Gabrielle to sing again. A drink will await you inside.'

Turning away, she re-entered the restaurant.

When the door had closed behind her, Gabrielle said, 'Madame Navarre owns the Restaurant Eugenie. She does not speak English – but I did not realise you spoke French so well.'

'And I did not realise we were on a train from Paris.'

Gabrielle smiled at him. 'I told her I had to go to Paris to see my sick mother. She needed to know nothing more. I must go inside now – but remember what I said earlier. I will not walk too fast for you.'

Perys had not intended to take Gabrielle up on her offer. At least, he wasn't *certain* he would. However, by the time she finished singing he had drunk far more wine than he was used to – and she was a very beautiful woman.

She was aware he was following her and when she turned into a house, the door was left ajar. When he entered, she was waiting and greeted him with a kiss that aroused him even more than her singing.

'We must be quiet,' she whispered to him, 'there are others in the house . . . Come.'

He followed her upstairs to a bedroom on the first floor. There was only the light from the sky outside, but it was enough to see the room was untidy, the bed unmade. But then Gabrielle was undressing and all else was quickly forgotten.

Gabrielle's love-making was more savage than passionate and left him gasping. Afterwards, she began nibbling at his ear and whispered, 'Your love-making is *wonderful*, my captain Perys. If I could, I would award you a medal for that, too.'

It was not long before he was aroused again but, as they were about to make love once more, they both heard the sound of the street door being shut noisily.

Gabrielle sat up as though someone had stuck a pin in her. 'Quick,' she gasped, 'you must dress and go. Hurry – but do not make a sound.'

She leaped from the bed and had a moment of panic when she could not immediately find her dressing-gown. Then she located it on the floor behind the door. Pulling it on hastily, she opened the door quickly and stepped outside, closing it behind her.

She was only just in time. A voice that Perys recognised as belonging to Madame Navarre demanded, 'You are in bed so soon? Have you been upstairs to see my son?'

'Of course,' Gabrielle lied. 'He was sleeping, so as I was tired, I came to bed.'

'The place for a wife to go to bed is with her husband. However, I realise he can no longer be the husband *you* would wish. I will go and see for myself that he is asleep.'

'I will come with you,' Gabrielle said, immediately.

'That will not be necessary,' Madame Navarre replied.

'Nevertheless, I will come.'

Outside in the street, Perys hastily checked that he had forgotten nothing in his haste to dress in the darkness of Gabrielle's room. Then he hurried back to the Restaurant Eugenie, aware that if he was fortunate, he might still ride back to the airfield in one of the lorries.

Later that night, as Rupert and Perys walked back to their respective billets from the lorries that had brought the pilots back to the airfield, Rupert said, 'I was very surprised when you returned with us tonight. I thought you had gone off with that young French singer and wouldn't be seen again until morning.'

Perys gave him an amused smile that was lost in the darkness. 'You know me, Rupert, work comes before pleasure.'

Undressing for the second time that night, this time in his room, Perys thought of what had happened in

Amiens. He doubted if he would ever see the lovely Gabrielle again.

He wondered how he would have returned to the airfield had they not been disturbed – or if Gabrielle's mother-in-law had not made so much noise entering the house and had caught them in bed together?

For Gabrielle, making love with him was probably no more than a brief adventure, and one she had undoubtedly embarked upon many times before, with no apparent regard for her maimed husband who was sleeping under the same roof. He wondered whether she would have remained with such a husband had his mother not owned the Restaurant Eugenie.

He compared her conduct with that of Annie. If Polly was to be believed, she had married Jimmy because she would not add mental hurt to the wounds he had received in war.

She had become angry over a kiss she must have known was far more meaningful than a momentary thrill.

Perys fell asleep wondering how different his life might have been had Annie's morals been more in line with those of Gabrielle . . .

67

In the late spring of 1918 life was not easy for Annie. Jimmy was going through a very difficult period of violent mood swings. One day he would be perfectly happy to accompany Annie to Tregassick and take pleasure in the work he was able to do there. The next, he would refuse to leave the house, complaining that life had treated him badly and he was incapable of carrying out even the most simple task.

On one such day, when Jimmy refused even to leave his bed, Annie was tidying the dressing table in the bedroom. Opening a drawer in which she intended placing a cheap crucifix she had worn to a church service the day before, she saw the letters Perys had sent to her after his first visit to Heligan, and which had caused such an upset in the Bray family.

Acting upon a sudden impulse, Annie removed the letters from the drawer and placed them in a pocket in her apron.

Later, downstairs in the kitchen, she took them out and read them until tears welled up in her eyes and she was unable to read on.

She had promised to go to Tregassick and help out with the last of the lambing. She had hoped Jimmy would accompany her, but she was aware from hard-learned experience that in his present mood he would do nothing she asked of him.

Rather than go back to the bedroom, she placed Perys's letters on a shelf in the kitchen and called up the stairs to let Jimmy know she was leaving the house.

She received no reply and had not been expecting one. When he was in one of his moods he listened only to the voices in his head, voices that could be heard by no one else.

The letters she had just read had unsettled her. Although she tried not to think about it, she could not help wondering what her life would have been like had her father not intercepted the letters.

When she entered the kitchen of Tregassick Farm, Harriet saw immediately that her daughter was unhappy.

'Jimmy not with you this morning?' she asked as she busied herself kneading dough with which she would make bread for the farm, with a few loaves left over to sell.

'He's not feeling too well this morning. I left him lying in bed. He'll stay there until he's feeling better – or fancies getting himself something to eat. Everything's to hand for him in the kitchen.'

Harriet was aware of what Jimmy's 'not feeling too well' meant and she was unhappy for Annie. In a bid to cheer her up, she said, 'Go out and look at the three lambs that were born in the night. By the time you come back I'll have a cup of tea ready. When your pa comes in we'll have a bit of breakfast.'

After Annie had gone out into the farmyard, Harriet continued kneading dough on the kitchen table, but her mind was on her two children. She thought, bitterly, that each was a prisoner in their own way. Of the two, Martin was probably the more fortunate. When the war came to an end, with victory for Britain and her allies, as it surely must now the United States of America had declared war on Germany, he would be released and return home to a hero's welcome. There was no such happy prospect in view for Annie. She was not able to look forward to a time when all would be well in her life. She had committed herself to Jimmy 'in sickness and in health'. Harriet knew her daughter well enough to be aware that it was a vow she had taken seriously.

Annie was gone longer than Harriet had expected, but when she came back to the house she looked happier than when she had left.

Speaking to her mother, she said, 'When I got to the barn one of the ewes was giving birth. She had a bit of trouble so I helped her. She's had not one but *two* healthy lambs.'

'Good for you, Annie. Your pa will be well pleased. He's relying on the sheep to bring in a little bit of profit for us. Heaven knows, we could do with some right now.'

She did not add that even the small wage they paid to Annie for helping about the farm was really more than they could afford right now. Annie had enough problems of her own.

'Here's your pa coming into the yard now. Tell him about the lambs, it'll put a smile on his face.'

Somehow, that morning seemed a happier one than usual for Annie. Two more ewes gave birth while she was on the farm. She enjoyed helping them and watching the lambs rise to their feet and take their first, shaky steps.

She was even happy cleaning out the pig-sties, work that Jimmy had learned to do.

At noon, she ceased work and went to the farmhouse kitchen to collect hot pasties to take to the cottage as a midday meal for Jimmy and herself.

She was there talking to her mother when Harriet peered through the window and said, 'Are you expecting a visit from Winnie today?'

'No.'

Following her mother's gaze, she saw Jimmy's mother picking her way through the mud of the farmyard, heading for the house.

'She doesn't look very happy,' remarked Harriet.

'She never does,' Annie replied, with glum resignation. 'It's usually because she doesn't think I'm looking after Jimmy properly. I'd better go out and meet her.'

But there was something in Winnie Rowe's walk that caused Harriet to say, 'No, let her come inside the house. If she has something to say to you she can say it in front of me.'

There was nothing unusual in the fact that Winnie came into the kitchen without knocking, but Harriet had been right in thinking she was visiting the farm looking for trouble. Winnie wasted no time before launching into an attack on Annie.

'I thought I'd find you here instead of where you ought to be – at home, looking after your husband.'

'Someone has to earn money if we're to keep food in the house,' Annie retorted. 'If he'd got out of bed this morning he'd be here with me. Anyway, I'm just on my way home with some pasties for dinner. Do you want me to bring an extra one for you?'

Annie was used to Winnie's rudeness and her constant complaining that Jimmy was not being looked after properly. For this reason she had come to dread her visits. Jimmy was always moody and far more difficult to cope with after she had gone home.

But this visit was to be like no other.

'I don't want any pasties and there's no need for you to take anything for our Jimmy. He's not there. I've sent him off home with our Rose. It's where he went in the first place when he came home from the war – and he should have stayed there.'

Her statement left Annie speechless.

Harriet had always tried to keep out of the arguments she knew went on between Annie and her mother-in-law, but she was unable to remain silent now.

'That's taking things too far, Winnie. Annie has always taken very good care of Jimmy. I can vouch for that because most days he's here on the farm with her, enjoying being able to do a little work.'

'You would say that, seeing as how Annie's your daughter. It must have been a great relief to you and Walter when you were able to marry her off on our Jimmy, but I'd have expected a bit more honesty from you, seeing as how we were once neighbours.'

'And what exactly do you mean by that, Winnie Rowe, I'd like to know?'

'You know very well what I'm talking about, Harriet, and it's no use you saying you don't. I'm talking about the goings on between your Annie and one of them up at the big house at Heligan. Did you think she might be expecting when you got her married to our Jimmy? That all the fine promises made to her by that young gent she was carrying on with would come to nothing?'

'I'm sure I don't know what you're talking about.' Harriet was shocked by the other woman's accusations.

'I do,' Annie said, angrily confronting Winnie. 'Unless I'm mistaken you've been reading letters that were not addressed to you.'

Unabashed, Winnie replied, 'If you didn't want folk to read them then you shouldn't leave them lying around. Of course, I don't suppose it would matter much, what with our Jimmy not being able to see what's been going on under his nose.'

'My letters weren't left lying around, they were put on a shelf in the kitchen, where only the nosiest of persons would have found them and put two and two together to make five. They were sent to me long before I married Jimmy. Before he joined the army, even. Only the most evil-minded woman would have made something out of what was written by a young man barely out of school, to a girl he hardly knew, but thought he was in love with.'

'That's your story,' Winnie said, derisively. 'I've no doubt you and your family will stick to it, but I don't believe you and I doubt whether anyone else will.'

'I think you had better get out of my house right now, Winnie Rowe, before I use language that the

453

Good Lord might never forgive me for. Our Annie is right, you are an evil-minded woman. Why I ever let her marry into such a family I'll never know.'

'Don't worry, I'm going,' Winnie said, defiantly. Jabbing a finger in the direction of Annie, she said, 'And don't you come trying to get Jimmy back. He'll be properly looked after from now on.'

With this, Winnie swept out of the kitchen, almost knocking over Walter Bray who stood looking after her in astonishment, a smile of welcome frozen on his face.

Later that evening, Polly called in to check that all was well with Annie. She had gone straight to Tregassick Farm after work and been told by a still upset Harriet what had occurred earlier that day.

She found a calm Annie putting the finishing touches to the spring cleaning she had been carrying out in her house since returning home that afternoon.

'Are you all right, Annie?' Polly asked anxiously.

Wielding a duster energetically, Annie replied, 'I'm feeling better than I have for a very long time, thank you, Polly.' Turning to her sister-in-law, she added, 'It's a dreadful thing to say, I know, but it's almost a relief not to have responsibility for Jimmy, even if it turns out to be only for a short while. He's been particularly difficult lately. Nothing I did seemed to please him.'

Making a resigned gesture, she said, 'It's not as though it's been a marriage in the real sense of the word, Polly. Not like yours is, even with Martin being in a prisoner-of-war camp. All I could do was try to take care of Jimmy – and I *did* try because he and I had been very good friends since we were both small.'

She shrugged. 'No matter what I did, it was never enough for his mother.'

'Will you go back to live at Tregassick now?' Polly asked.

'No,' Annie replied. 'Sooner or later Winnie will realise how difficult it is to take care of Jimmy and she might not be able to cope. This is still his home. It will be here if ever he needs it.'

68

'They downed Tim Miller today.'

A weary Perys gave the news to Rupert as he walked stiffly into the commanding officer's office and slumped into a chair. He had been in the air for three sorties on a long August day. Only the onset of dusk had brought the day's operations to an end.

Miller was the ex-navy pilot who had been one of the squadron's flight commanders and with whom Perys had formed a particular friendship.

'That leaves me the only surviving pilot of your original squadron, Rupert.'

Neither man dwelled on the death of the popular navy pilot. There had been too many like him. Talking of those who had been lost made a pilot feel vulnerable.

Rupert looked at Perys anxiously. 'If it were possible I would take you off flying duties for a while, Perys, but we need every pilot we can put in the air right now. You, in particular, are indispensable.'

The Royal Flying Corps was now defunct, the Royal Naval Air Service and the RFC having been merged into a single force – the Royal Air Force. With the change, the tactics of putting aircraft into the air in ever larger formations had been further extended. Perys, now a brevet-major, had led a full squadron into action and had proved a very successful leader.

'I am aware of the need to get everyone possible in the air, Rupert, but I wish we could pull a few more experienced pilots out of the hat. The youngsters we're getting are as keen as ever, but they're not lasting long enough to prove themselves.'

When Rupert made no immediate reply, Perys asked, 'How long do you think we'll need to carry on pushing our pilots this hard?'

'Until the end, I'm afraid, Perys. The Germans can see the writing on the wall. They've lost the war and they know it. All they can do is to throw everything they have at us in the hope they can retain some bargaining power when the end comes, and not be forced to accept the humiliation of an unconditional surrender.'

Perys nodded, grimly. 'That's much the way I thought it was. In the meantime good men like Tim Miller will die unnecessarily, all in the cause of politics. It's a crazy world, Rupert.'

Perys's own war came to an end the very next day. Escorting a squadron of bomber aircraft en route to attack strategic bridges behind the German lines, his squadron was set upon by a German fighter group that had once been led by Baron von Richthofen. Under its new commander, Herman Goering, it was still a force to be reckoned with.

For fifteen minutes the sky above the lines was filled with so many aircraft it resembled the flies to be found about a carcass on the plains of Africa. This was no test of the skills of individual combat. British and German pilots threw their aeroplanes about the skies in a bid to shake off an attacker, and in the hope that by so doing they would find themselves with an enemy momentarily in their sights.

Perys brought his confirmed 'kills' to thirty-three this day, but when he was bearing down on his thirty-fourth, his aeroplane suddenly juddered under the impact of a hail of machine-gun bullets. A moment later he was thrown forward in the cockpit as though punched in the back by a heavyweight boxer. Then he lost control of his aeroplane, which began spiralling earthwards.

He fought the fall, bringing to bear all the skill he had first learned from Nick Malloch. Miraculously, he regained a degree of control of the aeroplane and began a shallow dive that would take him over the British lines – and now he became aware that he was not alone.

Three of his squadron were with him, protecting him against any German bid to finish him off.

Perys had control of his ailing aeroplane, but he was finding it increasingly difficult to concentrate on the task that lay ahead of him – that of setting the aircraft safely on the ground. It was as though he was in a fitful dream, alternately dozing and waking, never quite certain which was fantasy and which was reality.

Suddenly, he realised there were trees ahead of him – much too close. Automatically, he pulled the control column back and only the aeroplane's undercarriage clipped the topmost branches.

When the plane dropped once more he knew he was about to crash. He cut the engine in the hope that this would prevent the petrol from igniting.

A split second later the aeroplane smashed into the ground with an impact that sent an agonising pain shooting through the muscles of his wounded back.

Then, mercifully, all went blank and he knew no more.

Perys became aware of voices before he regained full consciousness, but it took a few minutes of confusion to clear his mind and recognise that the voices he could hear were talking in French.

At the same time, he found he needed to make a conscious effort to breathe – and to keep breathing.

He opened his eyes. Even in his present state he recognised the concern on the face of the nurse who was looking down at him. He tried to smile, but was aware the expression would probably not be recognised for what it was.

'Where am I?' he croaked, in French. It was an unnecessary question. He was being cared for in some form of hospital.

'You are in the Amiens hospital. You were brought here when you crashed in your aeroplane because you needed urgent attention. The doctor thinks there is a bullet inside you, close to a lung. You will be going to the operating theatre in a short while. We have the facilities here . . .'

They were the last words Perys would hear for two days. When he woke again he was lying on his side.

He tried to move but it felt as though someone was twisting a knife in his back. He was also unable to move his left leg. On the verge of panic, he suddenly realised it was encased in a heavy plaster cast from hip to ankle.

'Welcome to the world once more, Major Tremayne.'

The words were in French and had been spoken by a man with a stethoscope dangling from his neck. He was surrounded by a group of young doctors and nurses.

'The pain in my back . . . A nurse said I had a bullet there.'

'It is there no more.' The French doctor picked something up from the top of Perys's bedside cabinet. 'There was a bullet, lodged dangerously close to your spine, and it had touched your lung. It is here, a souvenir for you. Fortunately, I was able to remove it without causing any permanent damage to anything important. Unfortunately, you also have a badly smashed leg. However, you were lucky to have been brought to me and not taken to your surgeons in a field unit. Had they seen you first they would undoubtedly have amputated your leg. I had rather more time to work on you.'

'Thank God for that!' Perys said, fervently.

'No, Major,' the surgeon said, 'you must thank *me*. I believe very strongly that amputation should be a last resort. In fifty per cent of the cases who have passed through my hands I have been correct. You are one of those fifty per cent.'

Perys realised he was speaking to an exceptional surgeon and he said, in French, 'I thank you most sincerely, sir. I think I would rather die than lose a leg.'

'That may yet be your fate,' declared the French surgeon, without emotion. 'But I think not. We will be keeping you here until we are certain you are on the mend. Then you will be handed over to your own medical services.'

Before moving away, the surgeon said, 'I see you are a flyer, Major. I greatly admire men such as yourself. I often think that had I not taken up medicine I would have liked to be a pilot – although I doubt whether I would have emulated men such as yourself. But for you the war is over, Major. Your leg will heal and you will be able to walk, but you will never again be able to fly. It is regrettable, Major. Very regrettable, but when this war ends you will be a live hero and not just a name carved on a memorial. For that you should be thankful.'

69

While Perys was in the French hospital he was visited regularly by Rupert, occasionally by pilots from his squadron, and once, to his great surprise, by Gabrielle from the Restaurant Eugenie.

After greeting him with a warm kiss, she produced fruit, confectionery – and a bottle of cognac which she slipped into his bedside cabinet, saying, 'Doctors and nurses do not always know what is best for a man. They tend his injuries, but forget the things that will make him happy.'

'How did you know I was here?' Perys asked.

'Some of your pilots came to the Restaurant Eugenie. They told me you had been shot down and brought here. I thought you had not come to the restaurant because you did not want to see me after the last night we were together, but when I heard you were hurt so badly . . .' She shrugged. 'I have a soft heart, especially for handsome men. Besides, the

Boche are being pushed back to Germany so fast there will soon be no British officers left to visit the Restaurant Eugenie. I will be singing only to men of Amiens, who come to the restaurant merely to talk business with each other. They would not notice if I stripped off all my clothes and began dancing instead of singing.'

Perys was amused by the imagery she painted and he laughed. It was the first time he had laughed for a long time. Although it hurt his lung, he felt better for it.

'What is it you want of me, Gabrielle?'

He felt that she was not telling him the whole truth about the reason for her visit.

'I want nothing, Perys . . . except, perhaps, one day I will come to London to sing and become famous. You would like to see me there? Perhaps I might stay with you for a while. It would be fun, I think.'

'I will certainly give you the address of someone who will know where to find me, Gabrielle, but I don't know where I will be living. Wouldn't your colonel be able to put you up? The one who saw you on to the train at Victoria station when we first met.'

He added the details when she looked at him blankly.

'Ah! You are talking of Colonel Harry!' She grimaced. 'He *would* help me, of course, but it would be possible only if his wife were not in London.'

Perys had realised soon after their first meeting that Gabrielle was quite amoral, but he could not help liking her. However, she had a husband.

When he spoke of him, she looked genuinely unhappy. 'He cannot live for very long, Perys. Indeed, although he eats and drinks, he is not *really* alive.

When he dies I do not think his mother will allow me to sing at the Restaurant Eugenie for very long. She does not approve of me.'

Gabrielle stayed talking to Perys for almost half-an-hour. Before she left he gave her Aunt Maude's address as somewhere she could write to him.

When she had gone he wondered how Aunt Maude would cope if Gabrielle turned up on her doorstep one day, instead of writing. He decided she would be able to cope quite adequately with such an eventuality.

Gabrielle had promised Perys she would visit him again, but it was a promise she did not keep.

After a five-week stay in the Amiens hospital, he was conveyed to an ambulance train that took him and some three hundred soldiers to Le Havre. There he was put on a hospital ship for passage to England.

As the ship set sail, Perys was aware that this was the route taken by Grace on the ill-fated S.S. *Sultan*. He could not rid himself of the thought that he might soon be passing over the very spot where she shared a watery grave with so many of those for whom she had been caring when she died.

Lying in the hospital ship cot, rocked by a gentle swell, he said a silent prayer for the girl he had hoped one day to marry.

On arrival in England, Perys was sent to a hospital in Portsmouth where his ultimate recovery was set back when he developed an infection in the lung which had been damaged by a German machine-gun bullet. He remained there for seven weeks, towards the end of which time he received an unexpected visit from Rupert and Morwenna.

Rupert was now a full colonel and had returned to England for a short but well-deserved period of leave before taking up an appointment with the Air Staff in London. He had motored to Cornwall and after spending a few days with Morwenna who was the senior nursing sister at Heligan, they stayed for a few days with Rupert's parents at their Devon home. They were now on their way to London where they would spend a few days together before resuming their respective duties.

'I believe you will soon be discharged from hospital,' Morwenna said, after the greetings were over. 'I spoke to the sister in charge of your ward. She says your lung is healing well, but it will be some time before you are able to walk without the aid of crutches.'

'I am much better than I was,' Perys agreed, 'but they tell me I must have a period of convalescence before I am declared fit for whatever the future has in store for me.'

'Yes, that is what the sister said. You will, of course, come to Heligan so I can keep an eye on you, Perys?'

'I haven't really thought that far ahead, Morwenna,' he replied, cautiously.

'It is *not* that far ahead. I will be returning to Heligan in four days' time.' She smiled at Rupert. 'I shall be *driving* there. Rupert has promised to buy me a small car. What is it to be, Rupert?'

'It's a super little Crossley two-seater, Perys. You'll love it when you see it.'

'I didn't know you were able to drive, Morwenna.' Perys was impressed.

Morwenna gave him a scornful look. 'I could drive

before I left England and would occasionally drive an ambulance while I was in France.'

'Morwenna drove the Rolls for part of the way here,' Rupert said, proudly. 'She's probably a better driver than I am. When I pick up speed in a car I keep waiting for it to leave the ground.'

Speaking once more to Perys, Morwenna said, 'Now you have my driving credentials I trust you will consider me a fit person to drive you to Heligan. I will call here for you on my way back from London and in the meantime make arrangements for the ward sister to have you ready for me.'

'I haven't said I *will* go to Heligan,' Perys protested.

'Where else would you go?' Morwenna demanded. 'Unless, of course, you have some particular reason for not wanting to convalesce there . . . ?'

'Of course not,' Perys said, hastily.

'Good. Then it's settled.' Morwenna smiled at him. 'The servants are all eager to take care of you – especially Polly. Her husband was your observer, I believe, and she tells me you were best man at their wedding. If I had not known this I would have suspected there was something going on between the pair of you. The girl is obviously very fond of you.'

'She is a very nice girl,' Perys commented.

'She is an extremely nice girl,' Morwenna agreed. 'And she is becoming very excited at the prospect of her husband being released from his prisoner-of-war camp in the near future.'

'Talking of nice girls,' Rupert said, tongue-in-cheek, 'you will remember Gabrielle, Perys – the singer from the Restaurant Eugenie? I believe she came to see you in the Amiens hospital?'

'Yes,' said Perys, uncomfortably aware of Morwenna's interest in what Rupert was saying.

Continuing as though he had not noticed Perys's embarrassment, Rupert said, 'She has created quite a scandal in Amiens. She had a very badly wounded husband, apparently. I believe he had been in a coma for some time. He must have died of his wounds only a day or two after her visit to you, but she didn't mourn him for very long. Six weeks later she married a captain from a Canadian regiment and is now on her way to Canada. The good folk of Amiens were scandalised.'

'Is this the young woman you told Mother about, Perys? The one who might possibly call on her for your address?'

'Yes. She spoke to me of coming to London. It would seem she has had a change of plan!'

'How intriguing!' Morwenna raised an eyebrow and added, 'You must tell me more of this French merry widow. Perhaps on the drive to Heligan. You *will* be coming with me?'

Perys nodded. Trying not to think what Annie's reaction to his return to Cornwall might be, he added, 'I can think of no place where I am more likely to make a full recovery.'

70

On the way from Portsmouth to Cornwall, Perys and Morwenna broke their journey on two occasions. The first time they called in to look at a small, near-derelict mansion which formed part of the Devon landholdings given to Perys by his grandfather. There they met the land agent who took care of these and other of his properties in the area.

The second stop was at the home of Rupert. Here, Morwenna was greeted warmly by her in-laws and Perys was given a hero's welcome. They stayed there for a night, during which time they learned that the Kaiser, Germany's ruler during the war years, had abdicated. It would appear that an armistice to end four years of unprecedented blood-letting was imminent.

In fact, the armistice was signed the next day and the sound of church bells greeted Perys and Morwenna in each of the towns and villages through which they drove on the road to Heligan.

Confirmation that the war was over was given to them when they arrived at Heligan, and Polly greeted Perys with a huge hug, even as she wept tears of joy at the thought that Martin would soon be home again.

Later, when she was more in control of herself, she spoke to Perys in his room – the room he had occupied during his recent stays at Heligan and which it had been agreed he could occupy during his convalescence.

'Miss Morwenna told me you would be coming here until you were fully recovered from your wounds. We spoke about you often. You, Martin and Colonel Pilkington.'

After a few moments of hesitation, she added, 'Annie was very concerned for you when she heard you had been shot down and badly hurt.'

Aware from Polly's surprised expression that he had over-reacted to her words, Perys said quickly, 'How is Annie – and her wounded husband?'

Polly's mood sobered. 'Things aren't going very well for her right now.'

'What's wrong? Is her husband still as ill as when I was last here? While I've been in hospital I've met with a number of men who have been gassed. Some have been very ill, but others were well on the road to recovery. Hopefully, he may be one of those.'

'That's not what's causing her problems,' Polly exclaimed, not looking directly at him as she spoke. 'It's the letters you sent to her after you came here that first time. Winnie – Jimmy's ma – found them and said some very nasty things to Annie. She finished up taking Jimmy back with her to the Rowe farm near Fowey.'

'You mean . . . she read Annie's private letters?' Perys was appalled.

'Winnie's like that,' Polly explained. 'She's a nosey busybody. The sort of mother-in-law every woman dreads having.'

'That is inexcusable!' Perys was perturbed at Polly's news, but he added, 'There was nothing in my letters to upset anyone – if they were aware of the story behind them. Do you think it would help Annie if I wrote to Jimmy's mother and explained why, when and how old I was when I wrote them?'

'I doubt it very much,' Polly replied. 'Winnie *might* believe you, but only if she wanted to. Besides, to be perfectly honest, Annie is a much happier person without having Winnie around telling her she's not looking after Jimmy properly. Annie tried very hard, but Jimmy was not the easiest of patients – as I'm sure Winnie has learned by now. You'll no doubt meet up with Annie again while you're at Heligan. She comes in every few days to bring in food she and her ma have cooked.'

Seemingly in a mood to chat, Polly added, 'Between you and me, I don't think the farm has been doing too well just lately. The weather hasn't been very good for farming. It's rained when they wanted sun and there's been no rain when it was most needed. When you get a year like that there's not much a farmer – especially one with only a small farm – can do about things. Not only that, Annie's pa has been paying her a wage he can't really afford in order to help her and Jimmy out with things. I think the farm is in serious trouble.'

When Polly had gone, Perys thought about the

troubles Walter was having with Tregassick Farm – a farm that he, Perys, owned. He also thought of the problems faced by women who had to look after husbands disabled in the war. It was something both Annie and Gabrielle had needed to face – but there the similarity ended.

During the course of the next few days, the end of the war was celebrated in every community throughout the land – and Cornwall was no exception.

The parties would continue for weeks, but the one that involved Perys was the party thrown by the Bray family to celebrate the homecoming of Martin.

Experimenting with a stick instead of the single crutch he had relied upon for support in recent days, Perys was hobbling around the outside of the house when he saw a man in Royal Flying Corps uniform standing at the edge of some bushes, close to the servants' door of the house.

It was Martin!

Calling to him and making his way towards him as fast as he was able, Perys greeted him with genuine delight. 'Martin! My dear chap, what are you doing here? Polly and I were talking about you only today. She said she wasn't expecting you home for another week or so!'

Martin grinned, delighted by the warmth of Perys's welcome. 'When the gates of the prison camp were thrown open I "appropriated" a motor-bike belonging to one of the guards. It got me most of the way to the French border. I walked for two days then came across a friendly French infantry officer. He took me to one of their airforce bases and they flew me to Saint Omer.

From there I was able to cadge a lift to the Central Flying School in Wiltshire. They advanced me some money – and here I am.'

'After all that you are standing outside Heligan, waiting for Polly to finish work?' A sudden thought struck him. 'Does she know you're here?'

Martin shook his head. 'I didn't want to inconvenience anyone.'

'Inconvenience anyone . . . !' Perys shook his head in disbelief. 'You come with me, Martin. We'll go to my room and I'll have Polly sent for.'

In a repetition of what had happened once before, Perys was leaving his room when he met Polly hurrying to answer his call.

'You sent for me, Perys? Joan said she was to tell me it was urgent.' She paused, tremulously. 'It's not . . . it's nothing to do with Martin?'

'It *is*, Polly, and in the nicest possible way. But the only way you'll learn about it is to go into my room.'

Polly's eyes widened even more, but before she could ask any more questions, Perys said, 'In you go, Polly. I'll find the housekeeper and tell her you've finished work for the day.'

Two days later, when Polly was still away from work, Martin came to Heligan to speak to Perys. His first words were to apologise to him for not asking about his wounds when they had met before.

Perys smiled at him. 'You had far more important things on your mind as I remember, Martin. Besides, I am coming along fine. I was very lucky to be treated by a brilliant French surgeon who had time to devote to me after I was shot down. Far too many men we both know were not as fortunate.' Suddenly serious, he said, 'Do you know, I was the last surviving founder member of my squadron.'

'I know how you must have felt. By the time I was shot down I was well aware I too was living on borrowed time. Thank God those days are over. But to celebrate my homecoming the family are throwing a party for me at Tregassick tomorrow. It won't be a grand affair, only family, farming neighbours and one or two particular friends from Mevagissey. We all agreed the party wouldn't be complete without you there.'

Perys knew that Annie would be at the party. He had not met with her since his arrival at Heligan this time. Remembering the last occasion on which they had met he felt that accepting the invitation would prove an embarrassment for both of them – and also for Martin and Polly.

'It's very kind of you to invite me, Martin, but I have no transport. Even if I had I would spend the whole of the party propped up against a wall somewhere. I haven't yet mastered the art of using this stick to help me around.'

Martin was not prepared to accept Perys's excuses. 'We'll find some way to get you to Tregassick – and there is no shortage of chairs there. It just wouldn't seem right to have a party without you. Had it not been for you I would probably have gone into the infantry – and I wouldn't have survived all those years in the trenches. There are very few men from around here who have, especially among those who joined up when I did. I'm not exaggerating when I say I probably owe my life to you. Anyway, that's what I think and it's what Annie told Ma and Pa.'

'Annie has said she wants me to come to your homecoming party?' Perys was incredulous.

'Of course.' Martin was puzzled. 'Is there any reason why she shouldn't?'

'I don't know. I thought . . . well . . . if Jimmy's mother has mentioned my letters to anyone, people might talk.'

'Everyone invited to Tregassick will be well aware how hard Annie worked to take care of Jimmy. They will also know that Winnie is a very difficult woman. In fact, the reason the Rowes moved away from this area was so they could make a new start in a place where Winnie wasn't known. Unfortunately, it didn't change her. Annie has sent a letter to her asking that she and Rose bring Jimmy to Tregassick for the party, but I doubt if Winnie will risk losing him to Annie again.'

Perys thought for a few moments about what Martin had said, then he nodded. 'All right, Martin, I would love to come to your party – but I am a convalescent. I'll need Morwenna's approval. That should be no problem . . . transport might.'

'Don't you worry about that.' Martin was delighted Perys had accepted his invitation. 'Some of the farmers will come in pony traps. I'll have one of them collect you. We'll make it a night to remember, I promise you!'

Perys was conveyed to Tregassick by a farmer named Wesley Pencarrow, who boasted to Perys that the Pencarrows had been farming the area for at least a hundred years before the Tremaynes took up residence at Heligan, and they still lived on the farm they had owned then.

When they arrived at the Bray farm it was immediately apparent that Martin had underestimated the number of those attending his homecoming party. Perys calculated there were at least two hundred guests. Horses and conveyances of every description crowded the farmyard and stretched back half the length of the long track leading to Tregassick.

As they approached, Wesley Pencarrow shook his head reproachfully and Perys asked, 'Don't you approve of such a party for Martin?'

'Martin's a fine young man,' said the farmer. 'A son to be proud of – and he's served his country well. If things were different I'd say no party would be good enough for him. But as things are . . .'

'If what things were different?' Perys queried.

'Well, it's well known that Walter Bray is going through a bad time right now, same as many farmers,' Wesley explained. 'Chances are he'll have to give up Tregassick when rent time comes around.'

'Surely things can't be that bad?' Perys protested.

'I've never known them worse,' was Wesley's reply. 'But this isn't the time to be talking of such things. We'm here to celebrate Martin's homecoming, and if he were my son I'd be doing exactly the same as Walter.'

The friendly farmer helped Perys down from the trap and walked with him slowly to the house, the guests along the way standing back respectfully to allow him to pass through.

Inside the house, Perys greeted Polly with an affectionate kiss and shook hands with Martin and a somewhat abashed Walter.

He did not immediately see Annie or her mother and guessed they were both busy in the kitchen.

Saying it would be quieter in the barn, close to the farmhouse, Polly and Martin took him there, found him a chair and, after providing him with food and drink, remained talking to him until Perys insisted that they circulate among their many other guests.

He was never short of someone to talk to, and among those who remained with him for some time was the tenant of the neighbouring farm – which was also owned by Perys.

Unaware that he was talking to his landlord, the farmer was quite ready to discuss the problems currently affecting Cornish farmers. He insisted he was coping better than most, but felt he would need twice the acreage he currently rented if he were to make a real success of farming in the post-war years.

Later that evening, when Martin escorted him to another barn where most of the men seemed to be congregating, Perys asked him whether he would be returning to Heligan as a coachman now the war was over.

'I probably won't have very much choice,' Martin replied. 'Had I not been taken prisoner I might have put myself up for a commission and considered staying in the RFC – or Royal Air Force, as it is now, of course, but there will be no place for non-commissioned aircrew in a peacetime airforce. What I'd really like to do is take up farming. It's what I've always wanted to do, ever since I was a small boy. Polly and me were able to put a bit of money by while I was flying and she was working, but it isn't enough to pay rent and stock a farm.'

When Perys suggested Martin might go into partnership with his father at Tregassick and use the money to buy new stock on this farm, Martin shook his head and confirmed what the neighbouring farmer had told Perys earlier.

'Tregassick isn't large enough to support two families. Pa's finding it hard enough to make ends meet with what he and Ma have here. It might be a bit easier for them now they're not having to help Annie with Jimmy, but it won't make a great deal of difference in the long run.'

'Talking of Annie,' Perys said, 'I haven't seen her all evening. Is she all right?'

'She's been kept pretty busy in the kitchen,' Martin explained. 'I suspect she's also keeping out of the way so she doesn't have to field too many questions about Jimmy. Most folk are well-meaning, but one or two are inclined to be a bit spiteful.'

Perys thought Annie might also be trying to avoid him. He decided it was time he returned to Heligan. Telling Martin his leg was beginning to ache, he suggested he should ask Wesley Pencarrow to take him back to the house.

It had been dark for some hours but a number of lanterns had been hung about the farmyard and in the various outhouses. As Martin passed out through the doorway he paused to speak to someone, and in the light of a lantern hung above the door, Perys saw it was Annie.

She looked thinner than when he had last seen her, but he thought she was even more attractive than he remembered and he felt the same thrill he always experienced when he saw her.

When Martin moved on into the farmyard, Annie came inside the barn and looked about her until she saw him.

Perys began struggling to his feet as she approached. Immediately concerned, she said, 'No, don't stand up, Perys. Martin said you are going back to Heligan because your leg is hurting you. Were you going without even saying hello to me?'

'I looked out for you all evening.'

It seemed to Perys that Annie had decided she would forget what had occurred the last time they had met, but he did not find it easy to do the same. 'I thought you were deliberately avoiding me.'

'Why should I do that?' she asked. 'If you are thinking of what happened the last time you were here . . . I over-reacted. I realised that within minutes of you leaving me – and I certainly shouldn't have mentioned Grace. I wouldn't, had I known. I'm sorry.' Looking at him with an expression he could not read, she said, 'Shall we agree to say no more about it, Perys? If we don't we're going to waste an awful lot of time apologising to each other and it would always stand between us. I wouldn't want that.'

'Thank you, Annie . . . I wouldn't want it, either.'

There was an awkward silence between them before Perys broke it by saying, 'I'm sorry to hear about you and Jimmy. Life hasn't been easy for you over the past few years, has it?'

'There are many far worse off than me,' Annie said. 'Besides, I should be the one asking how *you* are. Polly says Miss Morwenna told her you'd been through a very bad time.'

Smiling at her, Perys said, 'I'll give you exactly the

same reply you made to me. There are many far worse off.'

The smile seemed to break the ice between them and they chatted about more general matters, including the present state of farming at Tregassick.

Eventually, Perys said, 'Martin must be having trouble locating Mr Pencarrow.'

'If he doesn't come back in the next few minutes I'll go and find out what's happening,' Annie promised.

She did not have to leave Perys. Martin put in an appearance a few minutes later and explained that he had located Wesley Pencarrow. Unfortunately, the farmer had consumed rather more ale than was good for him. As a result, he was in no fit state to drive Perys home.

'I've got out our trap and harnessed up the pony,' Martin explained. 'I'll drive you to Heligan.'

'But you're the guest of honour,' Perys protested. 'You can't go off and leave everybody.'

'To be quite honest,' Martin confided, 'those who haven't already gone home are getting themselves so drunk I doubt if they can even remember what the party is all about.'

'What about Wesley Pencarrow? How will he get home?'

'There's no problem there,' Martin declared. 'We'll put him in his trap, slap the pony on the rump and it'll take him home. The publican at Saint Ewe has been doing it for years!'

'I'll come with you for the ride,' Annie said, unexpectedly. 'I've spent all day in the kitchen, I could do with some fresh air.'

479

On the way to Heligan, much of the talk was of the future, now the war had come to an end. When questioned, Perys told Annie and Martin of the reconciliation between himself and his grandfather, saying that he was no longer under pressure to earn a living.

'What a happy state of affairs,' said Annie, wistfully. 'But you deserve it. I hope it will make up for the many unhappy years you had before and during the war.'

'What would *you* do if you suddenly came into money, Annie?' Perys asked.

'Well . . . first of all I'd give Pa and Ma enough to make sure they wouldn't lose Tregassick. Then I'd give Martin and Polly the money to buy a farm of their own and raise the family I know Polly dearly wants. Then I'd see that Jimmy never wanted for anything. That might be more difficult because I wouldn't want Winnie spending it on things *she* wanted for him.'

'That's everybody around you catered for,' Perys pointed out. 'How about you? What would you do for yourself?'

After thinking about his question for a while, Annie said, 'That should be easy enough to answer, Perys – but it isn't. If everyone around me was happy, I think *I* would be quite contented.'

She did not disclose that the only thing she would wish for herself would be the power to turn the clock back to 1914. If this was possible she would plan a future for herself that would eliminate the disastrous mistakes she had made during the four years since then.

Annie believed she had replied to Perys's question

without disclosing her very real unhappiness. However, Perys had not missed the fact that she had used the word 'contented', and not 'happy'.

After delivering Perys safely to Heligan, Martin and Annie drove back to Tregassick in a silence which Martin was the first to break. He spoke with a degree of hesitancy, as though unsure what his sister's reaction would be.

'Perys was very sweet on you at one time, Annie. How do you think things would have turned out had Pa not hidden his letters to you?'

'Who knows?' Annie said, unaware of the bitterness in her voice. 'I would probably have had his baby and he might have lost interest in me. On the other hand, he might not. We'll never know. One thing is certain, I would never have married Jimmy. That was an awful mistake for both of us. He would have been happier had he gone straight back to the Rowe farm after being wounded, with his ma and Rose to look after him. Marrying me only made things worse for him. It wasn't only because he couldn't see or do things for himself, either. Because of his other wounds, he could never be a proper husband to me. No matter how much I said it didn't matter to me, it mattered to Jimmy. I've thought about it lots. I believe it was probably a relief to him when Winnie found Perys's letters and insisted on taking him back to the Rowe farm.'

71

The day after the party at Tregassick Farm, Perys took a slow and painful walk to the office of Roger Barton, steward of the Heligan estates and agent for their landholdings in Cornwall.

The office was attached to the steward's house, only a short distance from Heligan House itself, but Perys's leg was stiff this morning as a result of the previous evening's exertions. It took will-power in order to cover the distance involved.

Perys knew that if he told Morwenna of the discomfort he was in she could give him something to ease the pain – but she would also curtail his activities. He had lain awake for much of the night thinking about certain matters. There were a number of things that required his urgent attention.

Roger Barton was a tall, distinguished-looking man who at first thought Perys was a convalescent officer who had strayed into the grounds of the steward's house by mistake. Even so, he was extremely polite and, when Perys explained who he was, the estate administrator was apologetic, but happy to meet with Perys.

Helping him into his office and seating him on a chair, the administrator said, 'My dear chap, you should have sent for me. I would have come to the house to speak with you. I am not at all certain you should be walking any distance on that leg.'

'I am beginning to wonder about it myself,' Perys grimaced. 'But I needed to speak to you and to look at the map showing the farms I own in Cornwall.'

'I am entirely at your disposal,' Barton said. 'But first allow me to order a drink for you . . . tea?'

Tea was brought to them by a young woman who Roger Barton introduced as Amy.

'Amy is from the village,' he explained, when the girl had left the room. 'She has taken a course in secretarial work and typing. She has only been with me for a couple of months, but is already proving indispensable. I don't know how I managed before she came to work here – but, tell me, why are you so anxious to speak to me? I trust you are not unhappy with the manner in which I am managing the farms on your behalf?'

'You are doing a splendid job,' Perys assured him. 'My grandfather's solicitor is convinced they could not be in better hands. However, I have some ideas with which I fear you will not agree. They are philanthropic rather than businesslike.'

'I see,' Barton said, non-committally. 'Perhaps I may hear about them before I comment?'

'Of course,' Perys agreed. 'First of all, my grandfather's solicitor said that one of the farms is vacant at present. Is this still so?'

'Yes,' said the land agent. 'A farm not far from here, at Gorran. It was occupied by William Johns. He had two sons, both of whom were killed in France. William was a broken man. He lost heart in the farm, saying he had been keeping it on only in order to hand it over to them. I have rented out some of the fields – purely on a seasonal basis – to some of his neighbours, but have yet to find a new tenant.'

'This war has ruined so many lives,' Perys commented, sympathetically. 'How large is this farm?'

'Almost five hundred acres,' was the reply. 'It was in very good heart until the last year or so.'

'So it's more than twice the size of Peruppa?' Perys placed a finger on the map Roger Barton had produced and named the farm adjacent to that occupied by Walter Bray.

'Yes,' agreed the land agent. 'Does that have some significance?'

'Yes,' Perys said. 'I was talking to the Peruppa tenant yesterday. Without knowing I was his landlord, he told me he needed twice as much land if he is to continue in profit. Without telling him you have spoken to me, I would like you to offer him the larger farm. Tell him he can have it for two years at the rate he is currently paying for Peruppa, in order to cover the expenses of the move.'

Roger Barton opened his mouth to make a comment, but he closed it again without saying anything, aware that Perys had more to say.

Perys continued, 'When he has accepted – and I want you to ensure that he *does* – you will offer Peruppa to Martin Bray. Suggest that he and his father work their two farms as one, with a view to Martin taking over both in due course. If they agree, as I feel they will, you will tell them they may have both farms rent-free for two years, in order that Martin's capital can be put to use to stock the farms. If they query your generosity, tell them it is the Estate's way of saying thank you to Martin for his heroism and sacrifice during the late war.'

Roger Barton was silent for some time after Perys had outlined his plans for the various farms. When he eventually spoke, he said, 'You realise your proposals will have a considerable impact upon the profitability of the lands I administer for you?'

'Of course – and in your annual account you may explain the reason for any drop in profit.'

'Thank you.' The land agent was silent for a few moments, then he said, 'May I ask why you are making these extremely generous gestures?'

'Certainly. Martin Bray was my observer and gunner for a long time when I was flying in a reconnaissance squadron. His skill saved my life on more than one occasion, but his pride would not allow him to accept Peruppa Farm from me on such terms as I have suggested. I rely on you to persuade him to take the farm and so repay the debt I owe to him.'

Perys's reply seemed to satisfy the Heligan land agent. 'I understand and applaud such generosity, Mr Tremayne. I have no doubt that all the parties concerned will fall in with your wishes. Now, would you like me to tell you what is happening with your other properties?'

'I have not told anyone where I am,' Perys said. 'I should get back before they send out a search party for me. Perhaps you will write a report and send it to the big house with farm books and anything you feel I should see. I have time on my hands in which to study and get an idea of how things are with the lands here. I would be particularly interested with your views on the problems the farmers tell me they have been experiencing in recent years . . .'

72

Perys had been right to be concerned about his absence from Heligan House. He learned that the servants had been searching for him and the housekeeper was on the verge of reporting his disappearance to the sister-in-charge of the convalescent home – Morwenna.

Bewildered by the fuss, Perys asked the reason for such concern and why they were looking for him.

'You'll need to put that question to Polly,' said the housekeeper in a determined-not-to-be-offended tone. 'She was given the week off to be with her husband, but is in the house at the moment looking for you and will not tell me why. If you go to your room I will have her found and sent there.'

Perys had only just entered his room when Polly arrived in an agitated state. 'I'm sorry if I've caused you any trouble,' she said immediately, 'but Martin said I should come and find you right away. A policeman came to Annie's house early this morning to tell her that Jimmy is dead. He's committed suicide. The policeman took away the letters you wrote to her all those years ago.'

Perys was startled by both pieces of news. 'That's a dreadful thing to happen, Polly – but what has his death to do with my letters?'

'Winnie Rowe has told the police he killed himself because of them,' Polly declared.

Perys looked at her in disbelief. 'Jimmy's death is a dreadful tragedy, Polly, but to suggest my letters are to blame is quite ludicrous.'

'I know that,' Polly said, unhappily, 'and so does Annie, but it's what Winnie has told the police. They've taken your letters to give to the coroner. The policeman said there will need to be an inquest.'

The inquest on Jimmy Rowe was held in the town hall in Fowey, the town nearest to the Rowe farm. It generated considerable interest in the surrounding area because Winnie Rowe had let it be known that she was determined the coroner would not record a verdict of *Felo de se* – literally 'Felon of himself' – which would tell the world that Jimmy had deliberately and knowingly killed himself.

Such a verdict would preclude him from being given a Christian burial.

Winnie also let it be known that she intended to prove Jimmy had killed himself in a fit of temporary insanity, brought about by the discovery of his wife's infidelity with 'a gentleman of breeding'.

When the day of the hearing arrived, the public were forced to wait outside the town hall for a considerable time before the proceedings commenced.

The reason for the delay was that, in a surprise move, a solicitor attended the hearing and held a meeting with the coroner before it began.

When the public were admitted and the coroner appeared, he announced that because of the remarks made in public by a certain 'interested party', the solicitor had been engaged to protect the reputation of his unnamed client and ensure he was not slandered. After looking into the matter prior to the hearing, the solicitor, Mr Dean, had decided the best way this might be achieved was for him to represent Annie at the hearing.

The coroner then spoke to Winnie, warning her she was not to name the 'gentleman of breeding' she believed to have had an affair with her daughter-in-law.

When Winnie protested, the coroner informed her very firmly that if she did not heed his warning he would ensure she went to prison for a considerable period of time.

When he was satisfied Winnie fully understood, the coroner said, 'Good. Now, there is no dispute over the tragic fact that James Rowe, sorely wounded in the war, committed suicide. The sad task of this inquest is to ascertain the state of his mind when he committed this act. Was he aware of what he was doing, or was it carried out in a moment of temporary insanity? May we have the first witness, please?'

The first man to speak was the constable who had been called to the barn where Jimmy had been found hanging from a beam. He spoke of what he had found and said that in view of what Winnie Rowe had told him, he went to the house Jimmy had until recently occupied with Annie and took possession of a number of letters.

When the constable had completed his evidence, the coroner said, 'I have read the letters, which I believe you consider contributed to your son's actions, Mrs Rowe – Mrs *Winnie* Rowe. I would now like to hear what you have to say about them, if you please.'

Allowed to sit while she was addressing the coroner, Winnie looked defiantly across the room to where Annie sat beside Hubert Dean, her solicitor.

'When I found those letters I knew right away what had been going on – and was still going on, I've no doubt. So I took my Jimmy back home to where he belonged and away from *her*.' After identifying Annie with a jab of her finger, she remembered what it was that needed to be proved to the coroner. 'Our Jimmy was so upset he was out of his mind worrying about it, he was.'

'Was he upset because of what was in the letters, or because you were taking him away from his wife, Mrs Rowe?'

'It was them letters, sir. No doubt about it.'

'I see. You read the contents of the letters to the deceased, of course? I understand he was blind?'

'That's right, sir. He was in tears about it all. Sobbing his heart out.'

'I find that difficult to comprehend, Mrs Rowe. I have read the letters and find nothing in them to intimate any wrongdoing on the part of your son's wife. Indeed, I find them rather charming. The letters of an honourable young man to a young woman of whom he is quite obviously fond – and written when they were both very young, I understand?'

'That isn't the way I read them,' Winnie retorted. 'It wasn't what my Jimmy thought, neither. He was no fool. He realised, same as I did, that the only reason she married him was because she probably thought she was expecting by . . . by this man I can't name. She must have thought that with my Jimmy being so badly wounded in the war, he wouldn't know what had been going on – and is still going on, I dare say.'

There was a loud murmur of what might have been sympathy from the spectators in the court.

Solicitor Dean rose to his feet. Addressing the coroner he asked, 'Do I have your permission to put one or two questions to the witness, sir?'

'Please do, Mr Dean,' was the coroner's reply.

Turning to Winnie, the solicitor said, 'May I first of all sympathise with you on the loss of your son in this way, Mrs Rowe?'

She nodded an acknowledgement of his words, albeit warily, and he continued, 'However, it is my duty, indeed the duty of this court, to arrive at a true conclusion and not accept malicious tittle-tattle without question.'

There was an indignant gasp from the spectators and Winnie said, 'It's not tittle-tattle. I saw the letters to her with my own eyes.'

'So too have I – and the coroner. I will not go into the question of how *you* came to read them, but I am afraid that both the coroner and I disagree with your interpretation of them. However, we will move on to a rather more serious matter. Your suggestion that Annie married your son because she thought she might be pregnant. She was *not* pregnant, of course, but are you suggesting she was a young woman of loose morals before she married your son?'

'And afterwards too, if you ask me,' Winnie said, defiantly. 'Gentlemen of the likes of . . . him as I can't mention, don't go out with working-girls because they want to marry 'em. It's for what they take from 'em. She wouldn't be the first to be left in the lurch, and I doubt she'll be the last, either.'

There were sounds of agreement from the spectators and the coroner frowned in their direction.

'I see, Mrs Rowe,' the solicitor continued. 'What would you say if I could prove to you that your daughter-in-law *never* had an affair with this unnamed gentleman? Indeed, has never had an affair with anyone? Would you admit you drew the wrong conclusion from the letters you so disgracefully read? That you were wrong to take your son from the matrimonial home? Wrong to slur Annie in the manner you have? I will not go so far as to say it was your actions which resulted in the death of your son – but others may not be so kind.'

'What are you talking about?' Winnie demanded, angrily. 'Any fool can see what was going on behind Jimmy's back – and there's no way you can prove that it wasn't, neither.'

'That is where you are quite wrong, Mrs Rowe. You see, I *can* prove it.'

Addressing the coroner, the solicitor said, 'I have here a statement made by Doctor Fellowes – Doctor *Mary* Fellowes – a gynaecologist of national, indeed, *international* repute. The statement was witnessed by a Justice of the Peace in Plymouth three days ago, immediately after she examined Annie Rowe and certified that she is *virgo intacta*.' Turning back to Winnie, he said, 'Should you not be familiar with Latin, it means she has never been known by a man in the carnal sense.'

Returning his attention to the coroner once more, Solicitor Dean said, 'If you feel unable to accept the sworn statement of Doctor Fellowes, she is willing to give evidence to you in person, but it will mean adjourning this inquest for some weeks as she is a very busy doctor.'

'That will not be necessary,' the coroner replied, 'but are you saying the marriage of the deceased and his wife was never consummated?'

'It *could not* be consummated,' explained the solicitor. 'I have a copy of the medical discharge certificate issued to Private James Rowe. He had a number of serious wounds, one of which meant he could never be a husband in the full sense of the word.'

'That's a downright lie,' Winnie cried. 'Jimmy never said anything about that to me!'

'It is my understanding that he also failed to inform his bride before the wedding,' the solicitor said, 'but Annie kept his secret and remained with him through what must have been three very difficult years – even when faced with the scurrilous accusations of her mother-in-law.'

Somewhat apologetically, he added, 'I am aware that the purpose of this inquest is not to restore the good name of Annie Rowe, or absolve my client of any ungentlemanly conduct, but to ascertain, as far as is possible, the state of mind of the deceased at the time he took his own life. He was a weak-willed man and severely disabled. He was taken away from possibly the only person who really understood him by a strong-willed and domineering mother, and must have been a very unhappy man. I trust I have helped, in a small way, to show what might have driven him to such extreme action, sir.'

'Thank you, Mr Dean, you have carried out your duties admirably. You have made it unnecessary to call Annie Rowe. In view of her mother-in-law's actions she would have no knowledge of the events immediately before her husband's suicide. I suggest we now adjourn until after lunch. I would like time to consult my notes before a verdict is reached.'

When Annie left the town hall with Hubert Dean, she received a great many sympathetic glances from those who had listened to the evidence given to the coroner.

After spending the adjournment picking at her food in the dining-room of a nearby inn with the solicitor, Annie returned with him to the town hall.

When the coroner resumed his place, an expectant silence fell upon the courtroom. Eventually, looking up from the notes before him on the table, the coroner said, 'This has been a very sad and tragic case on which to reach a verdict. Sad, because of the bitterness and unhappiness which touched upon the life of James Rowe at a time when he needed kindness and understanding, although I am satisfied his wife did all – and more – that was expected of her. Tragic, because of a lack of willingness by others to understand his needs. Of that I will say no more. From the evidence presented to this court today it would not have surprised me had the deceased's reason suddenly snapped and in a moment of despair brought his life to an abrupt and uncalculated end. But that was not how he died. His suicide was carefully planned and executed. Choosing a time when everyone was absent from the farm, he carried a chair from the farmhouse to the barn, made his way to the stable and from there returned to the barn carrying a length of rope. Constructing a noose, he climbed upon the chair and secured the rope to a beam. Then, placing the noose about his neck, he kicked away the chair – and died. It was clearly a premeditated act. For this reason I have no alternative but to record a verdict of *Felo de se . . .'*

73

Perys was told the result of the inquest by Polly the next morning. It was in the study of Heligan House where he had maps of his Cornish properties and reports on the various farms spread out on the desk. They had been brought to the house by Amy, the land agent's clerk-typist.

Also mistakenly included among the papers were two Heligan employment books for the years 1914 to the present date.

When the knock came on the door and Perys called, 'Come in', the door opened and Polly entered carrying a coffee tray.

'I've brought your morning coffee, sir.'

Unused to such formality between them, Perys was taken by surprise, then he saw the housekeeper pass along the passageway beyond the maid.

Using her body to push the door closed behind her, Polly immediately dropped her servant-master pose.

'Perys! The solicitor who spoke for Annie at the inquest was marvellous! He was so good the coroner told Annie she didn't even need to give any evidence. Not only that, he cleared her name beyond all doubt; refused to let Winnie mention your name, and, although he wasn't so cruel as to blame Winnie for what Jimmy did to himself, Annie said he made it pretty clear that if she'd left him with Annie and not interfered in their lives, Jimmy might still be alive.'

'That's very sad for Winnie,' Perys said. 'It's something she'll have to live with all her life, but if I hadn't employed a solicitor Annie would have had to live with the stigma of Winnie's wicked tongue for the rest of *her* life. How is Annie taking it all?'

'She's still upset about Jimmy, of course. Although she never loved him, she did like him a lot. She's also embarrassed by what came out in court about her, but she realises it was the only way to put a stop to Winnie's lies, once and for all.'

'Tell Annie I'm very pleased that the solicitor was able to sort things out and make it easier for her at the inquest.'

'Why don't you tell her yourself? She's at the farm for most of the day but she'll be going back to the cottage tonight and every other night. At least, for the moment. She'll no doubt be moving back to Tregassick before too long.'

Perys smiled at the suggestion. 'You know how people gossip, Polly. Do you want them saying Winnie was right after all? Besides, although my leg is improving it's not yet up to walking as far as Annie's cottage. I've no doubt I'll see her, in the course of time.'

When Polly had gone from the study, Perys did not feel like looking over the various documents referring to the viability of his Cornish lands. Pouring himself a coffee, he picked up one of the Heligan employment registers and began looking through it.

Twenty minutes later, he rose to his feet and limped to the window, his mind filled with thoughts of the many – the very many – tragedies recorded within the pages of the small, marble-paper-covered note-books.

Against many of the names three words had been added: 'Killed in action'. Later, this was abbreviated to no more than three initials: KIA. Three initials to denote the end of a man's life.

He thought of the grief that was hidden behind the words. The late war had changed so many lives – not least his own.

When he had been with his squadron in France, death was commonplace, yet something that was rarely mentioned. Here, in this great old house, amidst such beautiful countryside, it seemed somehow grotesque.

Many of the names were of men he had once known, had spoken to and joked with as they went about their work as labourers, house-servants, woodsmen, gamekeepers and gardeners – and there had seemingly been more of the latter killed than from any other form of employment.

He thought of others, not on the list; men and women with whom he had been more closely associated. Flying friends – and Grace. Gentle, caring Grace. He thought too of Annie. She had also been a casualty of war, albeit in a different manner.

Lastly, he thought of himself. The war was over and he would recover from his wounds, but he had no idea what the future held for him.

One evening, towards the end of that week, Perys was sitting in his room writing a letter when there came a knock on the door. Before he could respond, the door opened to reveal Morwenna.

It was not unusual for her to come to his room in the evening to have a coffee with him, but tonight, instead of coming in, she smiled and said, 'You have a visitor, Perys.' Then she stood back to allow Annie to enter the room. She left, closing the door behind her, leaving the two of them alone.

'Annie! What are you doing here? Is everything all right at Tregassick?'

'Everything is very well at Tregassick, but may I take off my coat?'

'Of course – and your hat. I'll hang them up while you warm yourself at the fire.'

It was a winter's night outside, with a damp, cold mist hugging hills, filling valleys and causing moisture to drip from the branches of trees.

Annie perched herself on the edge of an armchair and held her hands out towards the fire.

'Can I get you something to drink? Coffee, tea . . . something stronger?'

'No, thank you.' Annie smiled up at him. 'Sit down, Perys, you should be resting that leg more than you do, according to Miss Morwenna.'

'I wasn't aware you and Morwenna knew each other,' Perys said.

'We often have a chat when I deliver things from

the farm kitchen,' Annie said. 'Most of our talk has been about you since you returned to Heligan. Morwenna is nice . . . but I have come here to thank you.'

'Thank me? For what?'

'For a number of things, Perys. First, for having Mr Dean see me and help me at the inquest.'

'I'm sorry it proved necessary,' said Perys. 'None of it can have been very pleasant for you.'

'It wasn't,' agreed Annie, 'but it would have been a whole lot worse without his help.'

There were a few moments of silence between them before Annie said, 'But that's not all the Bray family has to thank you for, is it?'

'Is it not?' Perys prevaricated.

'It most certainly isn't. The Heligan land agent came around today to see both Martin and Pa. It seems that Richard Keast, who farms at Peruppa, is giving up his tenancy and moving to a larger farm at Gorran. Peruppa has been offered to Martin – and the terms are unbelievable!'

She quoted the terms dictated by Perys to the land agent, adding, 'Then the agent said that Martin and Pa should work both their farms as one. If they agree they can have them rent-free for two years in order to put things on a secure footing. He says it's the Estate's way of saying thank you to Martin for his heroism and sacrifice during the war.'

'I can't see anything wrong with that,' Perys said cautiously, aware that Annie must know something about the arrangement he had made.

'There's nothing wrong with it at all,' Annie agreed, 'but why does there have to be such secrecy about it,

Perys? Why couldn't you tell us that ownership of the farms has passed to you? That it's you Martin has to thank for such an incredibly generous gesture?'

'You weren't supposed to know,' Perys replied. 'No one was. I told Roger Barton he was to tell no one.'

'You mustn't blame him,' Annie said. 'If you must know, it was Amy, the girl who works in the Estate office. I've known her for many years. I don't think she's aware it's supposed to be a secret. She prepared the tenancy agreements and when I met her late this afternoon she said how wonderful it was for everyone concerned. So it is, but . . . why have you done it, Perys?'

'As Roger Barton said, it's gratitude to Martin for his war service. Martin was my observer, remember? He was a first-class gunner, too. I'm not exaggerating when I say I probably wouldn't be here today if it were not for him.'

'Then why couldn't you have told him that?' Annie asked.

'Because by telling him I would have changed the relationship between us, Annie. Between all of us. We'd have gone back to the way things were when I first came to Heligan. When Martin was a servant here and I was one of the "master's family" – only I didn't really belong anywhere then. Thanks to Morwenna and her mother I *am* part of the family now, but in those days I was neither fish nor fowl. You, Martin and Polly were the first real friends I'd ever known – once we'd broken down the social barriers that stood between us. During the war Martin has been a flyer, like myself. He's proved himself the equal of any man – and better than most. He's also a friend. Martin told me that what he'd most like to do is have a farm of his own. I've been able to fulfil that wish, but I didn't want to do it at the expense of our friendship. For me to become his landlord and Martin and Polly my tenants. By having the Estate administer things I hoped it might remain a secret. It seems I was wrong.'

Annie remained silent for a while, before asking, 'Why should you want to help Pa, too? He has never been able to forget that you're one of the squire's family – and has certainly never done you any favours.'

'That isn't entirely so, Annie. True, I can never entirely forgive him for what he did with the letters, but I was always made to feel very welcome at Tregassick in those early days – those early, very *lonely* days. I couldn't see him and your mother thrown off the farm. Besides, Tregassick will be added to Martin's farm one day – that's if he hasn't earned enough money to buy a farm of his own by then.'

'I see, so you haven't done any of this out of a mistaken sense of pity for me?' she challenged him.

'Pity has never been included among the feelings I have for you, Annie,' Perys said. 'You've had a very difficult time during the past few years and I wish it might have been otherwise, but I knew the reason you took on such a commitment and have nothing but admiration for you.'

'I see.' Annie stood up. 'Thank you for being honest with me, Perys. I feel much better about everything now.'

'I've never been anything but honest with you, Annie,' he said. 'Do you intend telling Martin and your father that I am their new landlord?'

'Not if you don't want me to, but the truth is bound to come out sooner or later, you know.'

Relieved, Perys said, 'I hope that by then Martin will be so happy with his farm – and with a family – that he won't think of giving up and will be able to forgive me.'

'Forgive you? I doubt whether he will ever be able to *repay* you. None of us will . . . but I'd better go now, or we'll have people talking about us again.'

Fetching her coat and hat, Perys said, 'It's not a very nice night, Annie.' He added, jokingly, 'If I didn't have this gammy leg and if my motor-cycle was at Heligan, I would offer you a ride back to Tregassick.'

Annie smiled. 'You certainly couldn't try it the way you are. We'd both probably fall off again, and before we knew it we'd be right back where it all began.'

'Haven't you ever wished we *could* go back to those days, Annie? Start all over again, knowing what we do now? I have, often.'

Annie looked at him searchingly. 'Nothing has changed, Perys. In fact, there is even less chance that things could ever work out for us. I am still who I was then – and you are who you were, only now you have money.'

'You're wrong, Annie,' Perys replied. 'I am a very different man to the one I was then. After four years of war, watching men die long before they have had an opportunity to achieve any of the things life has to offer, I have learned to know what's important – and what's not. The barriers you are putting up between us are no longer important, Annie. They are artificial and not the really important things of life.'

She shook her head. 'You might think that at this

moment, when we're here together, talking—'

'No, Annie, I thought it then, when we first met. Now, all these years later, I am certain of what life is all about. A lot has happened since those days, to both of us. Only one thing hasn't changed for me. That's the way I feel whenever I see you. It's something I couldn't do anything about, even if I wanted to. It's there and it won't go away. I don't think it ever will. Does nothing like that happen to you when you see me, Annie?'

'That isn't a fair question, Perys . . .'

'Annie, if you *do* feel that way, can't we try again? Try to get to know each other all over again? It isn't often two people are given a second chance . . . don't let it slip away again, Annie. Please!'

She was silent for so long that Perys was convinced she was trying to think of another reason for rejecting his offer. Then she said, very quietly, 'Are you really sure that's what you want, Perys? Are you *absolutely* certain?'

'I've never been more certain of anything in my life,' he replied.

She nodded, gently at first, then with increased vigour. 'All right, if it's what you want.'

'That's not the right answer, Annie. It's not enough. It has to be what *you* want too.'

'I don't think I've ever wanted anything else, Perys. I've certainly never wanted anything quite as much. I know we haven't a motor-bike to fall from now . . . but do you think we might manage without one . . . ?'